THE
SHABTI

THE SHABTI

MEGAERA C. LORENZ

CamCat
Books

CamCat Publishing, LLC
Fort Collins, Colorado 80524
camcatpublishing.com

Hardcover ISBN 9780744310092
Paperback ISBN 9780744310108
Large-Print Paperback ISBN 9780744310139
eBook ISBN 9780744310122
Audiobook ISBN 9780744310146

Library of Congress Control Number: 2023948094

Cover and book design by Daniel Cantada

5   3   1   2   4

TO ROBERT RITNER
AN EXCELLENT AKH
TRUE OF VOICE

CHAPTER 1

DASHIEL QUICKE SAT AT the center of the stage, head bowed, a shimmering stream of ectoplasm flowing from his open mouth. Overhead, white-hot arc lamps illuminated the ethereal discharge as it cascaded over his lap. Perspiration prickled his scalp and soaked his shirt collar, but he welcomed the punishing heat of the lights. He'd spent enough time working under the cover of darkness. He was a man with precious little left to hide.

His audience's watchful eyes bored into him. The atmosphere was thick with their morbid curiosity. Even at a demonstration like this one, Dashiel didn't shy away from theatrics. If tonight's crowd of gawkers took nothing else from the experience, they would at least leave entertained. His shoulders heaved and he swayed in his seat as the ectoplasm continued to unfurl, pooling on the floor at his feet in a filmy heap. His hands, resting on his knees with the palms facing up, twitched spastically.

Someone in the audience let out a low whistle. Another onlooker, seated closer to the stage, groaned in disgust.

"Holy cats, mister," said a voice from somewhere in the middle seats. "How much of that stuff you got in there?" A handful of the heckler's neighbors broke out in raucous laughter.

Dashiel pulled the tail end of the ectoplasm out of his mouth, then rose to his feet and moved to the edge of the stage. He held it aloft in front of him, spreading it out wide between his hands. The ends trailed down on either side of him, sweeping up dust and grime from the battered floorboards as he walked.

"I hope you're all duly impressed by what you've seen here tonight, ladies and gentlemen," he said. "Your average Spiritualist would tell you that it's impossible to produce ectoplasm under these conditions. It's sensitive stuff. Disintegrates under full light, you see. The theory has it that light disrupts the ectenic force that the spirits use to manifest it out of the medium's body."

He paused, waiting for the crowd to settle. There was a smattering of whispers and laughter from the gaggle of hooligans in the middle seats. In the second row, a young woman snapped her gum with a sharp crack. Her neighbor swatted her arm and giggled.

"What they won't tell you," Dashiel went on, "is that it's made of common cheesecloth. Or muslin, if you're the type of medium who likes to live large and spring for the good stuff. It doesn't really matter which one you use, though. Either one looks mighty impressive if you've got a dark séance room and a strong will to believe. They're both just about infinitely compressible—perfect for hiding in tight spaces, away from the prying eyes and hands of doubters and debunkers. And to answer your question, young man," he added, smiling in the direction of his heckler in the middle seats, "unless the fellow at the general store shorted me, it's exactly three yards."

Satisfied that everyone had gotten a good look at the ectoplasm, Dashiel walked back to the center of the stage. Paint splatters, scuffs, and the faded remnants of spike marks from past theatrical productions marred the dark floorboards, which creaked beneath his feet with every step.

Like most campus theaters where he had performed, this one was a humble affair. It held enough seats for about two hundred spectators. Only a battered chalkboard sign outside the front entrance served to announce his performance that evening. *Tonight Only*, it proclaimed, *Renowned Ex-Spirit Medium Dashiel Quicke Unveils the Dark Secrets of the Psychic Flimflam Racket!*

"My spiritual instrument is speaking to me again," Dashiel said, nimbly winding up the trailing ribbon of muslin ectoplasm. The length of cloth vanished within seconds into a bundle small enough to fit between his cheek and his gums. "I'm receiving a very strong impression. The spirits have a gift for someone who is here in the theater tonight."

Someone in the audience snickered. Dashiel blithely ignored them. He tossed the roll of muslin onto the rickety table in the center of the stage, where it joined several other tools of his trade—a dented tin trumpet decorated with bands of phosphorescent paint, a stack of cards inscribed with forged spirit messages, and a fluffy drift of white chiffon veils. He turned his attention to the audience, squinting at them past the glare of the footlights and the bluish cigarette smoke hanging low and heavy in the air beyond the stage.

The spring of 1934 was proving to be a cold and dreary one, and that always meant good business. The house wasn't packed, but there was a decent crowd. Except for a lone middle-aged gentleman in brown tweeds seated in the front row, the audience was overwhelmingly youthful. Bored college boys and girls filled most of the seats, their dreams of necking with their sweethearts under the mellow April moon dashed by the chilly weather. So far, they had reacted to his routine with rowdy enthusiasm.

To these people, Dashiel was an amusing curiosity, a rainy-day diversion that they'd likely soon forget. He could only hope that he'd serve as an edifying cautionary tale for some of them as well.

A few short years ago, he'd drawn a different sort of crowd indeed. Throngs of affluent true believers once sat through his demonstrations in the chapel at Camp Walburton, eyes shining with devotion, entranced by his every word and gesture. When he closed his eyes, he could see himself there again, dressed in a pristine white suit and wreathed in the scents of fresh-cut chancel flowers and sandalwood instead of sawdust, cigarettes, and half-dried paint.

No point in dwelling. This was the path he'd chosen for himself.

"Is there," he asked, pressing his fingers to his temples, "a Professor Hermann Goschalk among us?"

It came as no surprise to Dashiel when the man in the tweed suit rose to his feet. He clutched his hat to his chest and cleared his throat, glancing around as if expecting some other fellow to step up and identify himself as the person in question.

"Um, I beg your pardon," he said at last. "That's my name. Do you mean . . . me?"

Dashiel smiled. "Unless there is more than one Hermann Goschalk in the audience, then I think I must. Join me on stage, if you please, sir."

Professor Goschalk made his way to the stage, accompanied by scattered applause, whoops, and whistles. In Dashiel's experience, there were few things that a collegiate audience liked better than the prospect of a faculty member making a spectacle of himself on stage, and this crowd proved to be no exception.

The professor didn't seem to mind. He trotted up the steps and stood smiling shyly at Dashiel like a starstruck kid meeting a matinée idol.

"Hello!" he said.

"Good evening, Professor," said Dashiel, with a brief bow. "Please, be seated." The professor nodded, blinking owlishly under the blazing lights, and took a seat in one of the two folding chairs beside the stage's central table.

Hermann Goschalk was a little gray mouse of a man, about fifty years old. Dashiel guessed that his well-worn suit was at least half as old as its wearer. His rumpled brown hair was generously streaked with silver, and he had large, uncommonly expressive hazel eyes—an excellent asset in a sitter. The more demonstrative the face, the greater the sympathetic response the unwitting shill would arouse in the audience.

"Thank you," said Dashiel. He sat down in the other chair and fixed the professor with a penetrating gaze. "Before we proceed, I hope you don't mind if I ask you a few questions, just to get my bearings. I want to be absolutely sure I do have the right Hermann Goschalk, after all."

"Of course!"

"Wonderful. Now, stop me if I'm mistaken in any detail. You are a member of the faculty here at Dupris University, a professor of Ancient Studies, specializing in the language and civilization of the ancient Egyptians. Is that right?"

"Yes, that's absolutely correct," said Goschalk, with an enthusiastic nod.

"Very good." Dashiel inclined his head and squeezed his eyes shut for a moment, as if drawing his next morsel of information from some deep, inscrutable well of hidden knowledge. "Is it true that you used to keep a black cat in your younger days, back when you worked as an assistant druggist at that pharmacy in—"

"Milwaukee, yes!" Professor Goschalk's astonished expression couldn't have been more perfect if he'd rehearsed it. "Good heavens, you even know about old Tybalt?"

"I do," said Dashiel, with a solemn nod. "He must have been quite the beloved companion."

The professor chuckled. "Oh, he was a terrible little yungatsh. He'd lie there in the windowsill soaking up the sun and hissing at anybody who dared to get too close. Did a fine job keeping the store free of mice, though." He smiled fondly. "Papa always said a pharmacy without a cat was a pharmacy without a soul."

"Ah yes, that's right. He was the drugstore cat. Your father owned the pharmacy, and he was hoping you'd carry on the family business. But you longed for greater things. You decided to pursue a degree in Egyptology. Once you completed your studies, you came to work here . . . about fifteen years ago."

"Gracious, yes! But how on earth did you know all these things?"

"Before a second ago, I knew hardly any of it," said Dashiel. "All I knew was that you once worked in a pharmacy and had a black cat. Just enough detail to impress you—and get you talking. It wasn't too hard to put the rest together from there." He winked and patted the professor on the shoulder. "I daresay you'd be a plum customer in the séance room, Professor Goschalk."

Goschalk gaped at him. "Well, I'll be a son of a gun," he said. Laughter rippled through the audience.

"Thank you, Professor, you've been very obliging," Dashiel went on. "But if you don't mind me taking just a little more of your time, there's one more thing I'd like to ask you before I let you go. At this moment, the spirits are telling me that you recently lost something of great sentimental value. Is that true?"

The professor nodded. "As a matter of fact, I have. Gosh, how uncanny! It was a cabinet card of my mother. I've kept it on my office desk for years, but I noticed it was gone not two weeks ago. I can't imagine what could have happened to it."

"That is too bad. But perhaps we can help you find it again." Dashiel rose and moved to stand behind Professor Goschalk, resting his hands lightly on the man's shoulders. He gazed out at the audience and spoke in a booming, authoritative tone. "Ladies and gentlemen, you are about to witness one of the most powerful forms of mediumistic manifestation. But I must ask for your help in amplifying our connection to the spirit realm. Please, raise your voices in a hymn of praise."

He nodded to the elderly organ player stationed at stage right. She curtly returned his nod, then began to grind out a shaky but serviceable rendition of "From the Other Shore." Three or four voices in the audience piped up with gusto, while a handful of others mumbled along uncertainly. It was hardly the sort of performance he would have gotten from his regular Sunday evening congregation back at the camp, but it would have to do. Dashiel let his eyes flutter closed, allowed his head to loll back as if he were falling into a trance.

"Dear ones who have passed beyond the veil," he intoned above the drone of the organ, "we beseech thee to reunite this gentleman with his lost portrait of his beloved mother. Keep singing, ladies and gentlemen! I am sensing a vibration from the other side. The spirits are with us!" He raised his arms in a dramatic, sweeping gesture, and as he did so, an object tumbled into Professor Goschalk's lap.

"Oh!" said the professor.

"Oooh!" echoed the audience.

Dashiel lowered his arms, letting his hands come to rest on the back of Goschalk's chair. He nodded again to the organist, who stopped playing. "Thank you, Mrs. Englebert. Please, Professor Goschalk—tell us what you have just received."

Goschalk pulled a pair of wire-rimmed glasses from the inner pocket of his jacket and slipped them on. Slowly, he picked up the item in his lap and squinted at it. He turned in his seat and blinked up at Dashiel in amazement. "Why . . . it's my photograph!"

"The same cabinet card of your mother that used to sit on your desk?"

"The very same, down to the faded spot in the corner. Oh, that is magnificent. Absolutely phenomenal!"

Dashiel bowed and smiled graciously as the audience burst into whistles and hearty applause. "Thank you, Professor. Ladies and gentlemen, what you have just seen is known in the spook business as an 'apport.' Impressive, yes? But of course, like everything else I have demonstrated this evening, a complete hoax. I hope you'll forgive me, Professor, when I explain that this photograph was stolen from your desk, in broad daylight, by one of my own personal agents—someone who is, what's more, entirely corporeal and very much alive."

"I'll be damned," said Goschalk, his eyes more saucer-like than ever.

"It was a simple matter for me to obtain a list of the names of people who bought advance tickets for tonight's demonstration. Having selected your name from the list, I sent my young assistant to gather some basic intelligence. Your students and colleagues were happy to share a few choice tidbits of information with someone who, they assumed, was a prospective pupil in the Ancient Studies program."

There was some crowing and hooting from the middle-seat gang. "Oooh, Professor," one of them called out, "he got you good!"

Dashiel raised his voice, speaking over the brief uproar of merriment that followed. "That, Professor Goschalk, is how I learned of your position in the department, your time as an assistant druggist, and yes—even old Tybalt. As for your photograph, all that my accomplice had to do was to pay a brief visit to your office, posing as a student with a rather vexing academic question. When you got up to consult one of your books, he quietly purloined the cabinet card from your desk. Thank you. You may return to your seat."

Professor Goschalk rose, clutching hat and photograph, and toddled off the stage, still looking delightfully befuddled. Dashiel was conscious of a pang of wistfulness. Had he still been in the business of fleecing the rich and bereaved, this was exactly the sap he would have wanted front and center at every service.

A STINGING WIND had picked up by the time Dashiel finished his act and wandered out of the theater. He turned up his collar and huddled against the wall by the side entrance, debating whether to hail a cab or brave the walk back to the modest room he had rented a few blocks away. Absently, he drew one of the last two cigarettes from the crumpled packet in his coat pocket and placed it between his lips.

"Those things are terrible for you, you know," said a soft, pleasant voice from the shadows.

Dashiel turned, slowly and deliberately, doing his best not to look alarmed. He'd managed to make himself a number of enemies over the past few years, with one thing or another, and he didn't relish being crept up on in dark alleys. When he saw that it was the little professor from his demonstration, his shoulders relaxed.

"So my doctor tells me," he answered with a wry smile. "But you can only ask a man to give up so many vices at once." He slipped the unlit cigarette back into the package and put it away.

Professor Goschalk chuckled. "I suppose that's true," he said, looking like a man who had little experience with vices, much less giving them up. "That was all very impressive, by the way, Mr. Quicke. Very impressive. If you hadn't explained how it was done, you might have made a believer out of me."

"Well, if I had, you would've been in good company, Professor," Dashiel assured him. "I've hoodwinked everyone from medical doctors to bishops."

"Please, call me Hermann." He extended a hand, and Dashiel gave it a firm shake.

"Dashiel. It's a pleasure."

Hermann's fingertips lingered on Dashiel's for a moment as the handshake ended, and his brow furrowed with sympathy. "Oh, gosh, your hands are like ice! It is awfully cold, isn't it? Well, this is what passes for spring here in Illinois, I'm afraid. Do you have far to go? I can give you a lift."

"That's very kind of you. I'm just over on 58th and Crestview."

Hermann beamed, and Dashiel realized that he was handsome, in his understated way. He wasn't sure how it had escaped his notice before. "Perfect!" Hermann said. "There's a nice little diner on Crestview. Please, let me treat you to dinner. Unless you have other plans, of course."

"No plans," Dashiel admitted with a hint of wariness. In his experience, this sort of amiable generosity tended to come with strings attached. However, the ex-medium business wasn't a lucrative one, and he was in no position to balk at the offer of a free meal. Besides, it had been a while since he'd dined with anyone socially, and the notion appealed to him. "Dinner sounds swell."

THEY WERE HAILED with a chorus of friendly greetings the moment they stepped into the Nite Owl Diner, one of those sleek little modern establishments that looked like a converted railcar. They sat across from each other in a cozy booth, lit by the yellowish glow of the lightbulb hanging overhead.

With Hermann's hearty encouragement, Dashiel ordered a dinner of roast lamb, buttered corn, and whipped potatoes that seemed extravagant by his recent standard of living. Coils of fragrant, shimmering steam wafted invitingly from the plate. He willed himself to take small bites, resisting the urge to scarf it all down.

"You must be quite the regular here," he said.

Hermann looked a little sheepish. "I suppose I do come here a lot. But their tongue sandwiches are truly the gnat's whiskers, especially after a late evening marking papers."

"This lamb goes down easy, too. Much obliged, by the way."

"Not at all!"

Dashiel took a sip of coffee before casually continuing. "So, the missus doesn't mind all those late evenings at the office, eh?" He was still casing the man, like one of his marks. In the old days, he would have gone home and written up a nice little file after a social tête-à-tête like this. Personal information, no matter how trivial, was a medium's true stock-in-trade, and old habits die hard.

"Oh, there's no missus," said Hermann, his cheeks pinkening. "I suppose I'm what you'd call a confirmed bachelor. No, it's just me and Horatio."

Dashiel raised his eyebrows questioningly. "Horatio?"

"My cat."

"Ah."

"Didn't the spirits tell you all this?" Hermann asked, blinking innocently. "Oh, don't mind me, I'm just making fun. What about you? Do you have any family?"

"Just my sister, back in Tampa. But I haven't heard from her in some time."

"Ah," said Hermann. "A Florida man."

"That I am. Born and raised in Tarpon Springs. My work took me all over, though. Before I left the business, I spent several years at one of the big Spiritualist camps in Indiana. But you heard about that at my demonstration."

Hermann nodded. He paused, as if weighing his words. Dashiel fancied that the flush in his cheeks grew a little deeper. "You mentioned an accomplice before. The person who purloined my photograph. Do you always work with a partner?"

"Oh, no. That was just a kid I hired for a couple of bucks to do the job for me, before the act. These days, I'm on my own." He hoped this answer would be enough to satisfy Hermann's curiosity.

The evening had been pleasant so far, and he had no desire to sour the mood by discussing the details of his former working arrangements. That way led to a morass of painful memories he'd rather not retread.

Lost in thought, Hermann scraped some horseradish sauce over a slice of bread. When he spoke again, Dashiel was relieved that he had moved on to a different subject. "What I can't understand," he said, "is why you decided to give it all up. As good as you are, you must have made a mint!"

"And how," Dashiel agreed, a little wistfully. "But I suppose even the most vestigial conscience starts to get a bit inflamed when you're bilking little old ladies out of their inheritance day in and day out. I just plain got sick of it."

"Hmm. And now you've made it your life's mission to expose all that fraud and humbuggery to the world. It's kind of poetical, don't you think?" Hermann leaned forward, his big hazel eyes shining. "I mean, who better to uncover a hoax than someone who knows exactly how it's done? All those parapsychologists and ghost-hunters and whatnot must have nothing on someone with your experience!"

"Oh, certainly."

"Which reminds me," he went on, a little more hesitantly. "If it's not too much of an imposition, I was wondering if you might help me with something."

Ah, there it is. As always, the ulterior motive.

Dashiel felt a sting of disappointment. He'd found himself enjoying Hermann's company for its own sake. Still, whatever he wanted, maybe it would pay something. "Oh? What did you have in mind?"

"It's—well, I feel a bit silly saying it," said Hermann, looking abashed. "But you see, in addition to being a professor here at Dupris, I'm also the curator of our modest collection of Egyptian antiquities. Sometimes I keep very late hours in the research archive upstairs from the museum, and lately, I've been noticing some, er, very strange activity in the building at night."

"Strange activity," repeated Dashiel, narrowing his eyes. "As in . . . ?"

Hermann fiddled with his fork. "Oh, you know. Weird noises. Things moving around when they ought not to. And, um, the bleeding walls. That sort of thing."

"The bleeding what?"

"I've tried to ignore it, but it's become more and more bothersome lately. I've had to stop bringing Horatio to work with me because it unsettles him, you see. The students have been asking after him, and I can't very well explain all this to them, can I? I mean, what would I say? And I know this is going to sound a bit peculiar, especially to you. But I just can't shake the feeling that it's, you know." He glanced around before continuing, dropping his voice to a conspiratorial whisper. "The real McCoy."

Dashiel set down his silverware and sat back, nonplussed. "Hermann, I must confess, I'm surprised. And a little disappointed. I thought you understood that the whole point of my demonstration this evening was to show that all that spirit stuff is bunkum."

"Of course, of course," said Hermann, now blushing a deep red. "But just because most mediumship is bunk doesn't necessarily mean that there's no such thing as spirits, does it? Anyway, whatever I'm experiencing, if it is a hoax—"

"I assure you, it is."

"Yes, well, if it is, why, I bet you'd sniff it out quicker than I could say Jack Robinson. You must know all the tricks."

"I suppose you do have a point there," Dashiel conceded.

"I'm sure you're right, of course. Only, if you'd just come and take a look, it would surely set my mind at ease. And, naturally, I'd compensate you for your time . . ."

He looked so comically earnest and plaintive that Dashiel had to fight back a chuckle. "All right, all right," he said, dabbing his mouth with his napkin to hide his amusement. "You've piqued my curiosity. I was planning to spend another day or two in town anyway. Shall I drop by tomorrow morning?"

"Oh, you're a mensch!" said Hermann, beaming with gratitude. "Tomorrow morning would be perfect."

CHAPTER 2

D URING HIS NEARLY TWENTY years in the medium business, Dashiel had met many people whom he would generously describe as "eccentric." Hermann Goschalk was certainly an odd one, but there was something different about him that Dashiel struggled to put his finger on.

It didn't surprise him to encounter a well-educated man who believed in spooks. Even the brightest were not immune to true-believer syndrome if believing in something—no matter how patently ridiculous—filled the right need in their souls. But Hermann's game seemed different.

For one thing, he wasn't in mourning for anyone, as far as Dashiel knew. Most believers were bereaved folks, groping for solace in the notion that their departed loved ones could still reach out to them from beyond the veil. Nor did he come across as especially spiritual. He seemed to regard his purported visitors from the other side as little more than an interesting nuisance.

Dashiel briefly entertained the idea that Hermann might be trying to pull a hoax on *him*, but that seemed unlikely. He had developed an excellent nose for fraud, and he detected none of the characteristic stink about Professor Goschalk.

Still, something about the situation made him uneasy. He passed a restless night in his drafty room in the boardinghouse on

Crestview, which was not helped by the fact that his bed felt like an unevenly laid pile of bricks.

The next morning, he rose early. He trimmed his already impeccable mustache, pomaded his dark hair, and donned an old but crisply pressed suit. He dithered for several minutes over whether to bring his cane before stubbornly deciding against it. It didn't take long for him to regret his choice. By the time he'd arrived at the Wexler Building, where Hermann's office was located, his leg was throbbing. Cursing his pride, he hobbled for the elevator.

Hermann's office was on the third floor. When Dashiel arrived and stepped out of the elevator, a secretary who looked like a rumpled and world-weary Janet Gaynor poked her head out of a door just down the hall.

"Are you Quicke?" she asked, squinting blearily at him.

He tipped his hat. "Guilty as charged, I'm afraid."

"Oh, thank God. Professor Goschalk's been asking about you every two minutes since he got in."

Dashiel glanced at his watch, perplexed. It was only just past eight o'clock; he was certain the building would have still been locked if he'd arrived any earlier. Aside from the somnolent secretary, the only other sign of life he'd seen there was an elderly janitor pushing a dust mop around in the lobby.

"Well! You can tell him that his lonesome hours are over." He smiled and spread his arms in a grand gesture. "I'm here."

The secretary rolled her eyes and disappeared back into the office. A moment later, she reemerged. "Okay, go on in. Room 302, around the corner and to your left."

Hermann was waiting outside his office door when Dashiel rounded the corner. "You're here!" he said, bouncing jovially on the balls of his feet. "Wonderful! Won't you come in? I'll have Agnes bring you coffee and a Danish."

"Good morning, Hermann. You're too kind."

As Dashiel approached, Hermann's grin faded. "Oh, gosh," he exclaimed, "you're limping!"

"Not to worry," said Dashiel smoothly. "It's an old injury. Flares up sometimes when the weather gets cold."

"Oh, I see. Did you serve in the war?"

"Lord, no. You flatter me. I was far too old for the draft. And even if they had called me up, I'm sure I would have found a way to slither out of it."

Hermann frowned and nodded sympathetically. "Well, I wouldn't blame you. Awful mess, that war."

"Why don't you tell me about your ghost?" Dashiel urged, eager to change the subject.

"Of course!" said Hermann, lighting up again. "But I really think it'd be better if I showed you. Take a load off for a moment, then we'll head downstairs."

Hermann's office was a cluttered affair, packed so densely with bookshelves, there was hardly any space to turn around. A sturdy wooden desk stood in the middle of it all, lit by a sunny window. Books, piles of papers, and framed pictures obscured most of the surface of the desk. Replicas of Egyptian objects crowded the windowsill, along with a potted geranium that boasted numerous clusters of bright red blossoms. Hermann moved a stack of papers off one of the two chairs by the desk and graciously invited Dashiel to sit.

"Where do you usually see these phenomena?" asked Dashiel, once Hermann had put in his request with Agnes. He leaned back in the chair, grateful for the chance to rest his leg for a moment.

"Mostly in the museum gallery," said Hermann, "down on the ground floor. But lately I've noticed some peculiar things in the research archive as well. The archive's right above the gallery, so I suppose that makes sense. It never wanders very far. Oh, that looks lovely, Agnes, thank you."

The secretary, who had just appeared in the doorway with the promised coffee and Danish, gave Dashiel a cool once-over before handing him the goods and striding out again without a word.

The breakfast did look lovely, but Dashiel had little time to savor it. He was still wolfing down the last few bites of his Danish when Hermann whisked him out the door, apologizing all the while. "It's just that I have class in a couple of hours, and this thing's been so distracting I haven't even had a moment to go over my notes," he said in a breathless rush as they stepped into the elevator.

The museum gallery lay behind a pair of ostentatious Gothic-style oak doors, currently closed to the public. Hermann produced a big brass key and unlocked them, ushering Dashiel inside. The Egyptian collection was confined to a single large room with a lofty ceiling and several bright, expansive windows.

When they entered, a tall, dark-skinned security guard of about seventy strolled over to greet them. Clearly at the end of his shift, he carried a tin lunch pail, and his coat was slung over his arm. "Morning, gentlemen," he said, touching the brim of his hat.

"Oh, Clarence!" Hermann beamed. "Just the man I wanted to see. Clarence, this is Mr. Dashiel Quicke. He's here to investigate our little . . . disturbances."

Clarence raised an eyebrow. "How do you do, Mr. Quicke? You a ratcatcher, by any chance?"

"Well, in a manner of speaking, I suppose."

"He's an expert in the realm of occult phenomena," said Hermann, dropping his voice to a stage whisper as he spoke the last two words. "Clarence is our night guard," he went on, turning back to Dashiel. "So far, he's the only person besides me who's witnessed any of the happenings around here. Other than Horatio, of course."

"Really!" said Dashiel, looking dutifully impressed.

"Come on, now, Professor," said Clarence, with the indulgent expression of a man who had had this conversation several times before. "Like I told you, I did hear—"

"And see!"

"—and see, yes—some sort of little critter skittering around in the gallery. But frankly, I think that kitty-cat of yours would be a better man for this job than any spirit hunter or what have you. No offense, Mr. Quicke."

Hermann's eyes widened in dismay. "Oh, no, I couldn't possibly bring Horatio back here! He was so frightened and disturbed last time that when I got him home, he hid behind the icebox for a week. Anyway, he wouldn't act that way if it was just mice or something like that. You might not think it to look at him, but Horatio is a very skilled mouser."

"Well, it may not be mice, Professor," said Clarence, "but squirrels do get in from time to time, especially when we leave that window open in the reading room."

Impossible as it seemed, Hermann's eyes opened even wider. "Oh, gracious," he said, clapping a hand to his mouth. "Did I do that again? If ever there was a sillier old goose . . ."

"Not to worry. Zoran spotted it and closed it last night when he was sweeping up. Good thing, too, because it looks like rain this morning. If you'll excuse me, gentlemen, I'd best be off home."

"Thank you, Clarence," said Hermann sheepishly. "Say hello to the wife for me."

"I certainly will, Professor. Good day, Mr. Quicke."

There was a moment of awkward silence as Clarence departed, leaving them alone in the hushed gallery. Hermann straightened his tie and chuckled nervously. "I'm sure you must think I'm absolutely cuckoo."

"Not at all," Dashiel said, not without sincerity. As one of his mediumistic mentors, Maude Pembleton Fink, had been fond of saying, *People don't believe in spirits because they're nuts, Quicke. They believe in them because they want to.* "You mentioned there were other manifestations?"

"Oh! Absolutely." Hermann gestured at the contents of the gallery. "As I was starting to explain to you upstairs, what you see before you is only a small part of our collection. The rest of it is in storage. This is where our star players get their moment in the spotlight."

As Hermann spoke, Dashiel moved to peer into a nearby case. Inside was a fragmentary statue of an Egyptian queen. Only her head, shoulders, and upper torso remained. She gazed serenely ahead, an enigmatic smile on her lips.

"Ah, yes," said Hermann, strolling over to join him. He regarded the queen with a hint of austerity. "She's on loan to us from Chicago. I was really after these inlays from the Tell el-Yahudiya palace, but Professor Breasted magnanimously decided to throw her in as well."

"She's lovely."

"I suppose so. But, between you and me, she's a fake."

Dashiel found himself intrigued. "What makes you think so?"

"Well, look at her!" said Hermann, as if he were genuinely surprised that it wasn't obvious to even the most casual of observers. "A *shebyu* collar, on a queen of the early Eighteenth Dynasty, no less? And the lappets on her headdress look exceedingly strange. I can't imagine how they didn't spot it."

"Why don't you set the record straight?"

For the first time that Dashiel could recall in their brief acquaintance, Hermann scowled. "As if those swellheads would ever take my word for it. Just because they've got John D. Rockefeller Jr. eating out of their hands and throwing checks like confetti, those Chicago boys think they're the be-all and end-all." He paused, looking contrite. "Gosh, I'm being uncharitable, aren't I? Don't mind me, it's just sour grapes."

"Ah, well, I know all about those," Dashiel assured him. "In the spirit business, we practically live on 'em."

"Really! Is it an awfully competitive profession?"

"Good lord, you have no idea. Anyway, you seem like a fellow who knows his onions. You ought to publish a paper on it or something. Make horses' asses out of the bunch of them."

Hermann flashed a bashful grin, then shook his head. "No, I couldn't. Well, maybe someday. Anyway, she's not the real troublemaker here. It's these little scoundrels."

He led Dashiel to a nearby case labeled *FUNERARY OBJECTS*. It was full of odd things—tiny figurines, ornate boxes, jars with lids shaped like human and animal heads, and jewels in the forms of beetles, eyes, and other objects that Dashiel couldn't begin to identify.

None of it meant much to him. He knew little about ancient Egypt beyond what he'd learned from idly perusing the news in the papers about Tutankhamun's tomb. That and a few tidbits of dubious veracity he'd picked up from his former partner, who had relished telling their clients that his Master Teacher from the spirit realm was an ancient Egyptian prince. Among the other illustrious spirit guides he had claimed over the years were a medieval Irish monk, a Roman centurion, and one of the original disciples of Confucius.

Hermann pointed out a little human figure, shaped like a miniature mummy with its legs bundled together and its arms folded over its chest. It was made of some coarse bluish-gray material, with traces of shiny glaze clinging to it here and there. A crude face was painted on it in black ink, and Dashiel could make out remnants of a faded hieroglyphic text running down the front of its legs.

"This shabti," Hermann said, "appears utterly unremarkable in every respect. The inscription is formulaic, and the style is typical of the early New Kingdom. But I'm always finding it in places where it ought not to be."

Dashiel frowned, puzzled. "You mean it leaves the case?"

"Ah! Well, no. Not of its own accord, anyway. But it's supposed to stay here, by its label, and it seems to just . . . wander. One morning I'll find it in the corner here, the next day over there, among the amulets."

"I see."

"But," Hermann went on quickly, "on occasions when I've had it out for study, that's when it ends up in all sorts of odd places. There was one evening when I'm quite certain I left it out on my desk, you know, in the tray with the cotton wool. When I came in the next morning, the tray was empty. I nearly had a coronary. I turned my whole office upside down looking for the little rascal, only to have it show up in my desk drawer."

"That is strange."

"Isn't it just!" He fixed Dashiel with huge, expectant eyes. "Well? What do you think?"

Dashiel rubbed his chin thoughtfully. "Does anyone else have a key to this case?" he asked.

"Oh no. Just little old me. I'm the sole curator."

Dashiel paced around the case, peering in at the objects. "These things aren't fastened down."

"I didn't really think it was necessary," said Hermann, frowning. "It's a flat case."

"Do you get a lot of traffic passing near this building? Streetcars going by, anything like that?"

"Not especially."

"Well, has there been any construction nearby? Something that would cause vibrations?"

"They have been doing some renovations in the Classics wing. It's extremely bothersome, actually. It seems like they always start jackhammering just when I begin a lecture. But do you really think . . ."

Dashiel moved close to the case and stomped his foot, hard. Hermann jumped, and so did the shabti. It now lay ever so slightly askew, its little feet turned accusingly in Dashiel's direction.

"Oh!" said Hermann.

"Now," said Dashiel, "imagine what could happen after a whole morning of jackhammering. Or even after a particularly enthusiastic crowd of museum visitors. Do you ever get schoolkids in here? They're like stampedes of tiny wildebeests."

"It must be because the back is a bit convex," said Hermann faintly. "It wobbles."

"I suggest you invest in a mount of some sort."

"Of course, yes, you're absolutely right. But what about when I had it in my office?"

Dashiel gave him an indulgent smile. "You probably got distracted and stuck it in the desk drawer by mistake. That sort of thing happens to the best of us. I'm embarrassed to admit how many times I've dropped the soap puck in my coffee and nearly taken a swig out of the shaving mug in the morning."

"I suppose." Hermann fiddled with his cuffs. "Yes, I suppose that does make sense."

"But you said there were other odd things . . .?"

"Yes!" said Hermann, brightening. "This mummified ichneumon, for example." He pointed to a pitiful little bundle of rags in the next case over, labeled *SACRED ANIMAL CULTS*.

"A mummified what, now?"

"It's a mongoose. One of the many animals revered by the ancient Egyptians. They were regarded as the enemies of inimical creatures, like snakes and crocodiles. They're also devious little sneak thieves, of course. And quite hard on the local bird life."

Dashiel squinted at it. "It doesn't look like much."

"It's missing its coffin," Hermann said with a rueful frown. "It would have been in the base of a lovely statuette, like that one." He pointed at an elegant bronze statue of a cat sitting proudly atop a sarcophagus-shaped base. "I had to inveigle an old doctor friend of mine into letting me take pictures of it with an X-ray machine to find out what it was. Anyway, I noticed the other day that there were some bits of loose wrappings scattered around in the display case. So, I opened it up and took the mongoose out to look at it. And I swear to you, Scout's honor—I felt it twist in my hand like it was alive."

"Curiouser and curiouser," said Dashiel, raising an eyebrow.

"You don't believe me."

"I didn't say that."

"Look, I know it sounds like a lot of meshugas, but I know what I felt. Here, let me show you." Hermann fumbled in his pocket and pulled out the ring of keys, then unlocked the case. He picked up the mongoose mummy and thrust it into Dashiel's hands before he could protest.

The mummy felt powdery and brittle, and it smelled both pungent and cloyingly sweet at the same time. Dashiel held it at arm's length, wrinkling his nose. "I'm sorry, Hermann. I'm afraid I didn't feel a thing."

Hermann sighed and retrieved the mongoose. Carefully, he laid it back in the case and shut the glass front.

"Do your hands often tremble like that?" Dashiel asked in a casual tone.

Hermann, who had just finished locking up the case, nearly dropped his ring of keys. "Beg pardon?"

"I couldn't help but notice it just now, when you handed me the mongoose." He reached out and rested his fingertips on the back of Hermann's left hand for a moment. "Yep. Shaking like a leaf. It's not uncommon among coffee drinkers." *Or drunks,* he charitably omitted to add, although Hermann didn't strike him as the dipsomaniac type.

"Oh no," said Hermann, rubbing the back of his hand where Dashiel had touched it. "No, not at all. I'm usually steady as a rock. Why do you ask?"

"Well, it would perhaps explain why you felt like the mummy was moving in your hand. A fellow can get all kinds of creepy-crawly sensations when he's had too much coffee."

Hermann shook his head. "I don't think that's it. It's just nerves, that's all. I've hardly spoken to anyone about this business before. Besides Clarence and Agnes, anyway, and I'm sure they both think the cheese has slipped completely off my biscuit."

"Trust me, people have believed stranger things," Dashiel said, with the reassuring tone he had often used with nervous first-time sitters at a séance. Hermann visibly relaxed under his gaze. "And I'm not here to judge. Only to help you discover the truth. Now, why don't you show me those bleeding walls you were talking about?"

There was, in fact, only one bleeding wall. It was located on the second floor, in the research archive. The archive was a cozy little library, mostly confined to a single reading room with a small annex attached. Floor-to-ceiling bookshelves lined the walls of the reading room. The back wall was dominated by a massive Gothic window, through which the pale morning light poured in. There were stacks of books and papers set out here and there on the heavy oak study tables in the middle of the room, some of them topped with hand-scrawled notes saying things like *George M's stack—ON NO ACCOUNT RESHELVE (that means you, Aloysius)!* A lone student sat slumped at the table closest to the window, his cheek resting on the pages of a massive, open tome, snoring loudly. The place was a little dusty, but it didn't feel the least bit sinister.

Hermann led Dashiel into a small back room packed with shelves and file cabinets. "The trouble is mostly back here, by the card catalog," he explained. "I first noticed it when I was working late a few weeks ago. I had come back here to get one of those big Epigraphic Survey folios, and I thought I heard something, like . . . like a person muttering or whispering or something. Then I looked up and I saw this reddish ooze trickling down the wall."

Dashiel peered up at where Hermann was pointing. There was a streaky reddish-brown stain on the wall and a dank, musty smell to go with it.

"It looks a lot more vivid at night," Hermann remarked. He frowned up at the stain critically, as if disappointed it didn't look more impressive.

Dashiel pulled a stepstool over and climbed onto it to get a closer look, grunting in pain as he hefted up his injured leg. He ran his fingertips over the stained area. It felt damp and clammy.

"Now, I'm not much of a betting man these days," he said, still squinting at the stain, "but I'd be willing to put down a hefty wager that there's a leaky pipe behind this wall. What you've got here is a rust stain. And I suggest you get a plumber in here before it invites its bosom chum, mildew, to the party."

"Oh, gee! D'you really think so?"

"I do. Bad news for the books, I'm afraid, but probably nothing supernatural."

"Well, I'll be damned." Hermann stared at the stained wall, shaking his head. "I mean, now that you say it, and I look at it again in the light, I can't imagine how I thought it was anything else. But I could have sworn—"

"A little daylight and a good night's sleep can make all the difference," said Dashiel, cumbrously stepping down from the stool. "And as for the whispering noises, I suspect our pal over there is to blame." He jerked his thumb at an unassuming cast iron radiator, wedged into the corner beside the cabinets that housed the card catalog. "Those things can make some mighty eerie noises, especially when you're alone in a spooky library in the dead of night."

Hermann seemed at a loss for words. He turned away for a long moment, gazing at the radiator in silence. "I suppose," he said at last. And then, with a little more conviction, "I guess they can, at that. The one in my apartment makes a hell of a racket at night. Banging in the walls and gurgling and everything. Yes, I'm sure you're right."

Dashiel gave him a reassuring pat on the shoulder. "It's all good news, Hermann. I'm positive you're not being haunted. And I don't think you're being bamboozled by anyone, either. If anything, you're the victim of a slightly overactive imagination."

Hermann turned back to look at him, his eyes filled with an odd mixture of relief, disappointment, and trepidation. "I guess that is good news," he said. "But—but I don't see how I could have gotten so carried away with it all. I've never had much of an imagination. I'm actually a very dull sort of fellow."

"You don't seem dull to me," Dashiel said frankly.

"Oh, go on," said Hermann, with a diffident grin. "You only say that because you've never had to sit through one of my lectures on Late Egyptian verb forms. But really, I'm not prone to imagining things. I just don't understand it. Everything you've said makes perfect sense, and yet . . ."

"Of course, if I were still in the spook business," said Dashiel with a wink, "I'd tell you that the spirits use exactly these kinds of mundane phenomena as a conduit for their messages from beyond the veil. But I'm afraid the fact is that sometimes a radiator is just a radiator."

Hermann chuckled a little but said nothing. His troubled gaze had drifted back to the rusty stain on the wall.

"I hope I haven't disappointed you too much," Dashiel went on. "The truth about these things is rarely very exciting."

That snapped Hermann out of his trance. "Oh, no, certainly not! I didn't mean to sound ungrateful. You've taken such a load off my mind, truly. Can't thank you enough. I'm just embarrassed to have put you to so much trouble over a whole lot of bupkis." He gave Dashiel a warm handshake. "How much do I owe you?"

Dashiel paused for a moment, nonplussed. He'd spent decades extracting money from naïve saps like Hermann, often in extravagant quantities. But that had always been in exchange for highly desirable, artistically crafted lies. Expecting someone to pay for a disappointing and lackluster truth almost felt like an even bigger swindle. At least the people who came to his debunking demonstrations got an entertaining show in exchange for the meager price of a ticket. Still, he could hardly afford to refuse the man's generosity.

"Whatever you feel is reasonable would be most appreciated," he said at last. Hermann fished a crisp five-dollar bill out of his wallet, which he accepted with a grateful tip of his hat.

"If you're ever in town again," Hermann said, darting a quick glance at Dashiel as he slid his billfold back into his pocket, "I hope you'll look me up. Just to have lunch, I mean. I promise I won't lead you on any more wild ghost chases."

Dashiel smiled. "I believe I might just take you up on that."

CHAPTER 3

A S IT TURNED OUT, Dashiel never left town, except for occasional forays into the surrounding suburbs. He had nowhere in particular to go. Few venues were looking for exposés by down-on-their-luck ex-mediums, especially in these lean times. His calls and letters to local theaters, schools, and social clubs yielded dismal results, and the inquiries he sent further abroad were less fruitful yet. His one promising lead, an engagement at the Egyptian Theatre in DeKalb, fell through. Business always slowed down when the weather warmed up, but this time he'd hit a spell as dry as the Great Plains.

He thought about moving on, but prospects looked equally disheartening everywhere. Besides, he didn't relish the notion of traveling through the choking dust storms now ravaging the greater part of the country.

So, he hunkered down in Willowvale, and for a few months, he managed to scrape by well enough on the money he'd saved from his last several engagements.

Spring hardened into a blistering summer, followed by the beginnings of a mercifully mellow autumn. Dashiel didn't visit Hermann, although he thought of him often. He certainly could have used the free lunch. And, as odd as their encounter had been, it was a notable bright spot in the dreary expanse of the past three years.

But he'd grown used to being alone, and he couldn't remember the last time he'd sought out somebody just for the sake of their company.

Anyway, he wouldn't be able to stay in Willowvale forever. The way he figured it, there was no point in forming any attachments there, no matter how charming and agreeable they might be. His meager savings were running out, and he'd already pawned most of his few remaining valuables. If he didn't get a break soon, he'd have no choice but to try his luck elsewhere.

On a gorgeous afternoon in late September, Dashiel strolled along the Main Street Bridge in St. Charles, swathed in a slightly outdated herringbone overcoat that he'd bought in more prosperous times. There was just enough nip in the air to justify wearing it. The coat looked respectable, but it didn't suggest a great deal of affluence, which could be a tricky balance to strike. The inner linings of the hip pockets had also been snipped out, but that defect would have escaped the notice of most casual observers. In one hand, he carried his cane; in the other, a large leather satchel.

He'd arrived early that morning by rail. Putting aside a depressingly unfruitful conversation with the manager of the swanky new Arcada Theatre, it had been a pleasant excursion so far. St. Charles was a pretty town, and the streets were still bustling with end-of-summer tourists.

A woman standing at the far end of the bridge caught his eye. She was red-haired and rosy-cheeked, wearing a gaudy but expensive-looking day dress. He guessed that she was in her middle thirties, but she was dressed and made up like a woman some ten years younger. She'd gone to stand by the railing of the bridge and ogle the river, leaving her purse and a couple of shopping bags on a nearby bench. A large dam churned the glassy water into dancing foam as it passed under the bridge, and the sight seemed to mesmerize her.

Dashiel sat down on the bench beside the parcels, setting his satchel at his feet. With seeming carelessness, he allowed the long skirt of his overcoat to drape over the woman's purse as he sat. She barely glanced at him. He sighed and leaned his head against the back of the bench, half-closing his eyes. Thrusting his hands into his coat pockets, he stretched out his aching leg.

Dashiel's right hand, in its unlined coat pocket, was free to roam the area beneath the coat at will. His deft fingers soon found their way inside the purse. Although he couldn't see the contents, he was familiar enough with the typical inventory of a woman's handbag to know when he'd latched on to something good. Within seconds, he'd withdrawn his quarry and slipped it into the fully functional pocket of his trousers.

After a minute or two, he opened his eyes and scooted to the other end of the bench, pretending to busy himself fiddling with the clasps on his satchel. The woman roused herself from her reverie a moment later and came to retrieve her bags, still all but oblivious to Dashiel's presence.

As she started to walk away, he rose to his feet. "I beg your pardon, ma'am," he called out, easing smoothly into the Floridian drawl of his youth. "Awfully sorry to bother you, but did you drop this?"

She turned back to look at him, and her eyes went round with surprise. Dashiel was holding up an elegant silver makeup compact, inlaid with enamel and mother of pearl. "Golly," she said. "How did I manage that? Thanks awfully! Oh, I would have just died if I'd lost that. It was an anniversary gift from the hubby."

"Was it, now! Lucky thing I happened to spot it," said Dashiel. "I think your bag must have tipped over and it spilled out. I found it lying under the bench." He turned the item over in his hands and gave a low whistle before handing it to her. "It's a beautiful piece. Looks like genuine mother of pearl."

"It sure is! That man just spoils me to pieces. Anyway, I'm much obliged," she said. "It's so nice to know there are still good, honest people in this world." She caught sight of his cane, on which he leaned heavily, and gave him a pitying look. "Are you a veteran?"

He took off his hat and clutched it to his chest, giving her a wistful smile. "Why, yes, ma'am. It was my privilege to serve. But nowadays, I'm just one of this great country's many forgotten men. Times are tough for us old doughboys, especially the crippled ones like me."

Her face melted with sympathy. "Aw, gee."

"The truth of the matter is," he said sadly, "I can't remember the last time I had three square meals."

She pressed a daintily manicured hand to her cheek. "Aw, gee! Listen, why don't you let me help you?" She started to rummage in her purse, no doubt looking for loose change.

"Well, now," said Dashiel, "I can see why that feller of yours spoils you so much. You're as pretty as a peach and twice as sweet. But listen, ma'am, my mama didn't raise any deadbeat sons. If you really want to help me out, at least let me give you something in return."

"Oh, there's really no need—"

But he was already opening his satchel. "My last occupation was as a traveling salesman," he said, "and I've been trying to get rid of what's left of my stock for weeks. It was great business until old Dr. Juniper closed up shop. But frankly, I think he was selling this stuff for about half of what it's worth." He pulled out a bottle, labeled *Dr. Juniper's Miracle Tonic*.

She backed up a step or two. "Well, I don't know . . ."

"Before you say no, just look at me and tell me one thing." He pinned her with an earnest look. "How old would you say I am? Be brutally honest, now."

"Gosh, I don't know," she said, with a nervous giggle. "Forty-five?"

He laughed heartily. "Bless your heart, dear, you're going to flatter an old man to death. I'm fifty-six."

"You're kidding! Are you really?"

"Yes, ma'am. Now, I won't swear I can credit it all to Dr. Juniper's tonic, but I will say that I take just a spoonful every night before bed, and it certainly hasn't done me any harm. You see this bum leg of mine?" He tapped the offending limb with his cane. "It doesn't trouble me half as much as it used to. Before I started taking Dr. Juniper's, I had to use a chair most days."

She looked dubious, but Dashiel pressed on. "I can see what you're thinking," he said, nodding sagely. "Why would a pretty young thing like yourself need this stuff? But here's the thing. It's not just a cure—it's a preventative. It's made with the extract of a rare flower that grows only in the mountains of Tibet. It's been a closely guarded secret among the natives for years. I don't know the science behind it, but the good doctor always told me it rejuvenates the cells and keeps you youthful from the inside out."

She gave him a wan smile and a shrug. "Well, I suppose it wouldn't hurt if I bought just one bottle. How much is it?"

He puffed out his cheeks thoughtfully. "When the business was going strong, twelve dollars a bottle was the going price."

"Twelve dollars!" she squeaked. "What's it made of, liquid platinum?"

"It might as well be. But I'm certainly not going to charge you all that. For eight dollars, I'll give you two of 'em."

She frowned and chewed on her thumbnail. She had the look of a woman who'd been ready and willing to fork over twenty-five cents, only to find her magnanimity being tested to its limits.

"That does sound like an awfully generous offer," she said at last. "Well . . . all right." She fished a ten-dollar bill out of her purse and started, with obvious reluctance, to hand it over. "Can you break a ten?"

Dashiel's face fell. "I'm afraid not," he said. Then he brightened. "But that's all right, honey. If you wait right here, I'll go to that shop over yonder and get change. If I can just trouble you to watch my bag for a moment . . ." He took the ten and started to hobble away, slowly and painfully.

"No, no! That's all right!" she called out. "Just—just keep it."

He turned around again, beaming with gratitude. "God bless you, ma'am, you're simply too kind. I'll just get those two bottles wrapped up for you."

He handed over the goods, and his mark hurried away. He was just closing his bag when he heard a roar of raucous laughter. The blood froze in Dashiel's veins—it was a laugh he knew well. Slowly, he straightened up and turned around.

A large woman sauntered toward him from across the street. She was wrapped in a mink coat, her marcel-waved hair peeking out from beneath a blue velvet turban. Her diamond necklace and matching earrings blazed with fire in the afternoon sunlight.

"Well, well, well," she said, still chortling, "that was quite the show. Boy, oh, boy! If that's not the richest thing I've seen all week."

"Maude Pembleton Fink, as I live and breathe," said Dashiel, greeting her with a grim smile. "What the hell are you doing here, Maude?"

"I might ask the same of you, Dashiel." She gave him a hard poke in the ribs with her handbag. "It is still Dashiel, isn't it? Or have you moved on to some shiny new soubriquet?"

"Still Dashiel. Not that it's any business of yours what I call myself."

"Out here making an honest living, are we, Mister Holier-Than-Thou?"

"I'm just doing what it takes to scrape by," said Dashiel, snatching up his satchel. "If you want to put selling glorified sugar water to pampered housewives on the same level as bilking widows and orphans out of thousands of dollars, be my guest. But I'm hardly enriching myself here."

Maude snorted. "Same old Quicke, I see. And I suppose next you're going to tell me your shit doesn't stink."

"Quite the contrary, Maude. My sense of smell works just fine, especially since I pulled all the ectoplasm out of my nose."

She smirked. "I don't seem to recall that's where you usually kept it."

"We won't even mention where you keep yours. There might be ladies present."

She tapped his cane with the toe of her shoe. "This was a nice touch, I must say. That gimp leg act was well worth the price of admission alone."

"Oh yes, it's been working out just great for me. I suppose I ought to thank you, or whichever one of your stooges is responsible for putting that slug in my thigh."

"What are you babbling about now, Quicke?"

"Come on, Maude, don't act like *you* don't know who shot me."

Her eyebrows shot up. "Shot you! Now, why on God's green earth do you think I'd waste my time and ammunition taking potshots at you? Even if I felt like it, I wouldn't have the time. Business at camp has been going like gangbusters since you left." She squinted at him critically. "Are you saying you don't know who shot you?"

"I'm afraid not. Whoever did it gallantly waited until my back was turned."

Maude gave another whoop of laughter and slapped her thigh. "Oh, is that rich! All right, who shot Quicke in the ass?" she demanded in a loud voice, spreading her arms and grinning around her as if she expected the culprit to run up and claim their prize at any moment. "I'd like to buy 'em a drink!"

"You always were such a delight, Maude."

"Be serious, though," she said. "Let's not pretend we don't both know who it was. What does that ridiculous partner of yours call himself again?"

Dashiel's heart sank. He hadn't expected a different answer, but he'd hoped for one. It wasn't outside the realm of possibility that another of his former colleagues had been responsible. Deep down, though, he felt certain Maude was right.

"*Ex*-partner," he said. "And it's Porphyrio." As if she could possibly forget.

"That's right! My goodness. The two of you were always like two oily little peas in a pod. Him swaggering around in those hideous yellow boots, with that pet alligator of his—"

"It is not," Dashiel cut in wearily, "an alligator. It's a goddamn Asian water monitor."

She waved her hand, jangling her bracelets. "Same thing."

"Not even remotely."

Maude lapsed into uncharacteristic silence for a moment, regarding him with a pensive expression. At last, she seemed to come to a decision. "Come on," she said, "why don't you let Auntie Maude buy you a drink? You certainly look like you could use one. Unless you've given up on those kinds of spirits too, of course."

Dashiel's sudden thirst for a Gin Rickey overpowered his better judgment. "Well . . . all right," he said grudgingly. "I don't see why not. Lead me, o my savior, to the fountain's crystal flow."

MAUDE TOOK DASHIEL to a bustling pub at the corner of Third and Main.

"Here's to the Twenty-first Amendment," she said, hoisting her glass.

"Long may it reign," said Dashiel, downing most of his drink in one grateful gulp. He sat back, savoring the pleasant warmth that flooded his veins as the alcohol entered his system. "You still haven't told me what you're doing here, Maude."

"Oh, haven't I?" she asked, taking a leisurely sip of her High-ball. "Well, I had a little business in the area and thought I'd take a gander at St. Charles while I was passing through. I've just had a very nice talk with Colonel Baker about holding a mediumship demonstration in that new hotel of his, the one down by the bridge. Have you seen the ballroom in that place?" She gave him a censorious once-over. "No, I suppose you probably haven't. They call it the Rainbow Room. The whole dance floor's made of glass tiles that light up in all different colors. They keep changing right under the dancers' feet. Can you beat that? Makes that ultra-modern cathedral you and what's-his-name were planning seem downright restrained."

"And? Did the colonel bite?"

"Oh, I think he did." Maude looked infuriatingly self-satisfied. "The guy wipes his ass with hundred-dollar bills, but he doesn't even have the sense God gave the paper they're printed on."

"Ah. The perfect man."

"You can say that again! He's addicted to spectacle. You can smell it the moment you walk into that damn-fool hotel. A man like that wouldn't dream of turning down the opportunity to host a good, old-fashioned Spiritualist revival."

"What's your main business, then?"

"Eh?"

"You said you were just passing through."

"So I did," said Maude, slugging down the rest of her drink and gesturing to the barkeep for another round. "I'm on my way to Dupris University, out in Willowvale. I got a letter from some kooky professor up there who thinks his museum is haunted."

Dashiel inhaled a generous mouthful of his Gin Rickey. When he finished coughing—and Maude finished laughing—he gasped, "You don't mean Hermann Goschalk?"

"Oooh!" said Maude, leaning back and regarding him with interest. "Do you know him?"

"I do, as a matter of fact." He was mortified to feel a flush creeping into his face.

"Well, if that don't beat all!" She leered at him. "Fond of him, are we?"

"What do you want with Hermann, anyway?" Dashiel entreated, ignoring the question. "The man would be chump change to you. He's just a harmless little bachelor who lives in an apartment with nobody to come home to but his cat."

"He's also a professor of Egyptology," said Maude, "with all sorts of letters after his name. He may not be big money, but the man's got credibility. And we both know you can't put a price on that. If I could bring a guy like that into the fold—"

Dashiel felt an odd surge of anger. "Stay away from him, Maude," he growled.

Maude's eyes widened in disbelief. "Come again, Quicke?" she said, theatrically wiggling her pinky finger in her ear. "I don't think I heard you right."

"I said, stay away from him." Dashiel was surprised at himself. Taking a hard line with Maude never went anywhere good, he knew that. But even though he barely knew the man, the thought of Maude wheedling her way into Hermann's life made him sick to his stomach.

His hand, which had been resting easily on the bar, balled itself up into a fist. "I'm warning you, Fink. If you get your greedy little talons anywhere near Hermann, I'll—"

"You'll what?" urged Maude, smiling sweetly. She scooted close to Dashiel and put an arm around him in an uncomfortably tight embrace. Her face was so close to his that he could smell the rose-scented powder on her cheeks.

"Listen, sweet pea," she said in a low voice, "before you met me, you were nothing. And now that you've left my flock, you've gone right back to being nothing. You just about broke my poor old heart, but it was your choice to make. It's not as if your silly antics have hurt me any. You know as well as I do that it only strengthens the faith of the rest of the flock when one of our little lambs goes astray."

Dashiel tried to pull away, but Maude's vicelike grip on his arm tightened, and she tugged him even closer. He stopped struggling and went still, breathing hard through his nose and staring down at the counter in front of him.

"But," she went on, "if you should ever try to interfere directly in my business, Quicke, I promise you, there will be hell to pay. And you can rest assured that whoever comes to deal with you will be a fair sight more competent than Porphyrio. Do I make myself clear?"

"Clear as crystal," grunted Dashiel. His pulse pounded in his temples. As furious as it made him, he didn't dare argue the point further. If nothing else, the Honorable Reverend Fink was a woman of her word.

The sweet smile returned, and Maude released him. "Good. I'm so glad we understand each other." She gave him a tender pat on the hand. "You know how I hate it when we quarrel. Now, it's been lovely catching up, but I really must run. And if I were you, honey, I'd give Willowvale a wide berth for the next twenty-four hours or so. Just to be safe. I've got friends in the area, and I wouldn't want there to be any misunderstandings."

Dashiel sat in silence while she settled the bill and rose to leave. Before she'd gone more than three or four paces, she turned back.

"Oh, by the way," she said, "I still see Porphyrio quite often. I'm sure he must be wondering how you're doing, Dashiel. I'll let him know I ran into you."

❧❀❧

It killed him to sit back and do nothing, but Dashiel didn't dare call Maude's bluff. He passed a miserable couple of days in St. Charles, half-heartedly peddling his Miracle Tonic and working himself into a glorious dudgeon. He hated Maude for inserting herself back into his life, and himself even more for lacking the spine to stand up to her. Even Hermann was not spared from his festering ire. The damn fool had written Maude, after all, so the blame for this mess ultimately fell on him.

What he really ought to do, he told himself, was to skip town altogether and wash his hands of the whole thing. He'd clearly overstayed his welcome in Illinois. He'd go back to Willowvale long enough to gather his things from the boardinghouse, then strike out for uncharted territory elsewhere. It was the only sensible course of action, especially if Maude had meant what she said about setting Porphyrio on his trail.

And yet, by the time he boarded the train back to Willowvale on a foggy morning two days later, his resolution had begun to falter. He tried to convince himself that his anger with Maude over the matter was just a flare-up of lingering professional jealousy. After all, Hermann had come to Dashiel first with his ghost problem, and however much his methods may have changed, a job was a job.

But the fact was, he liked Hermann. Hermann had been decent to him in a way most people weren't when they knew Dashiel for what he really was. He'd looked at him without scorn or pity or amusement—just good-natured curiosity and more than a hint of admiration. The more Dashiel thought of Maude taking advantage of his gentle nature, the more it nettled him.

It might already be too late, but he couldn't leave without at least checking in on the man. He'd give him a word of warning about having any sort of dealings with Maude and her ilk, then go on his way in good conscience.

Dashiel didn't dawdle after he disembarked. He hurried to the boardinghouse, washed up and changed, then made his way to campus. Finding Hermann's office closed, he poked his head in at the department secretary's door.

The secretary—Agnes, he remembered—looked even more harried than she had the last time he'd seen her. She sat hunched over her typewriter, pecking away at the keys with single-minded ferocity. He rapped the door frame lightly with the head of his cane to announce his presence. "Morning, Agnes," he said.

She started and looked up, wild-eyed. Then, her expression hardened. "Oh, God," she said.

Dashiel tipped his hat. "It's a pleasure to see you again, too, dear. Would you mind telling me where—"

"He's teaching right now," she cut in stonily. "Class ends in about ten minutes. Room 208, if you want to try and catch him."

"Thank you kindly." He withdrew and darted for the elevator. He wasn't sure what he'd done to earn such a frosty reception, but he was certain it didn't bode well.

Room 208 was a small classroom, located at the far end of the hall from the elevator. Dashiel positioned himself so he could see in through the narrow glass window in the door without being noticed by the occupants. About half a dozen drowsy, irritable-looking students sat at cramped little desks, each with an impressive pile of books and notes spread out before them. The professor wasn't visible from his vantage point, but there was no mistaking the voice of the unseen speaker at the front of the room.

"Now, would someone please tell me," Hermann was saying, "how we are to understand the verb at the beginning of line fifteen? I don't believe we've heard from you yet, Aloysius."

A greasy-haired beanpole of a kid in the second row, who had been slouching luxuriously in his chair, bolted to attention and shuffled his notes guiltily for a moment. "Gee, Professor, I guess I didn't get that far."

There was a collective groan from the rest of the class. The young man sitting closest to the door turned and fixed the unfortunate Aloysius with a haughty glare. "Anyone who's got eyes can see it's a hortative *sedjem-ef*," he spoke up in a cool tone. "Second-person singular, taking the dependent first-person pronoun as its object. 'May you place me upon the—'"

"Bananer oil!" scoffed the lone girl in the group, who was seated front and center. "That's an old perfective, first-person singular."

The other fellow turned to scowl at her. "Oh? And how do you figure that?"

"First of all, if it was a hortative, it would just be *di*, not *redi*. Second of all, if you'd been paying attention to the rest of the text, you'd know that nobody's *gonna* place him on the seat of his father because he's already *been* placed. It's *redi-kooie*, not *di-ek-wi*. Old perfective." She sat back, apparently satisfied that she'd made her case.

"That's the dumbest thing I ever heard," he snapped. The other students were beginning to perk up. Dashiel guessed that these conflicts were a regular highlight of the class. "How d'you know it's *redi* and not just *di*? There aren't any phonetic complements!"

"Oh, no?" demanded the girl, brandishing a book at him. Dashiel could just make out a photographic plate depicting some sort of tombstone-shaped monument. "What do you call that?" She angrily poked a spot on the page.

"I call it a flaw in the stone."

"Aw, what are you, blind and dumb? It's an 'r'!"

"Sure it is, and I'm the king of France. I'm telling you, a hortative fits the pattern. This whole text is full of hortatives!"

"So's your old man."

There was some scattered snickering from the rest of the class. Mr. Hortative turned back to Hermann, still out of sight at the front of the room. The young man looked incandescent with fury. "Do you even hear this, Professor? Say, where does she think she gets off? Who decided it was a good idea to let girls in these classes, anyway?"

Negotiations broke down altogether at this point. Miss Old Perfective rounded on Mr. Hortative, her face a mask of righteous indignation. Dashiel half expected one of them to start swinging. He'd never been to college himself. Was this the sort of excitement he'd missed out on?

The other students leaned forward in their seats, jostling each other, exchanging tense whispers. Aloysius sank down in his seat and chewed unhappily on his pencil. The young woman was just telling her colleague through gritted teeth where he could shove something she referred to simply as "your Gardiner" when Hermann's voice finally rose above the din.

"Now, now, settle down, gentlemen—and, er, lady," he said. "Sidney, Frances is quite correct. I've had the opportunity to examine the stela myself, and there is certainly an 'r' there. It just doesn't show up well on the plate."

Sidney groaned, and Frances stared him down with a look of steely-eyed triumph. A fellow in the back row elbowed his neighbor, who sighed and pressed a nickel into his waiting palm.

"As much as we all enjoy this sort of spirited scholarly discourse, I'm afraid we're out of time," Hermann went on. "Remember, your first examination is next week. Feel free to call on me in my office should you have any questions at all. You are dismissed."

Dashiel waited as the students packed up their books and filed out of the room, then moved to stand silently in the doorway. Hermann sat at a desk at the front of the room, head down, absorbed in the task of gathering up his papers.

"They're quite the lively bunch," said Dashiel. Hermann glanced up. "Do your classes always end in fisticuffs, or is that only on Tuesdays and Thursdays?"

Dashiel couldn't help but feel a little alarmed at how exhausted the man looked. There were dark circles under his eyes, his hair was more rumpled than ever, and it appeared as though he'd forgotten to shave for at least the past two mornings. But when his eyes met Dashiel's, his face lit up with a smile like the sun rising over a stormy sea.

"Why, Dashiel!" he cried, rising to his feet. "You came back!"

Dashiel did his best to ignore the odd little flutter in his chest. "Of course," he said, leaning casually against the doorframe. "I happened to be passing through town, so I thought I'd drop in."

"Oh," said Hermann, looking as though the weight of the world had been lifted from his shoulders. "I'm so glad."

Dashiel found himself unmanned. He'd arrived still feeling a bit uncharitable toward Hermann, but it was difficult to stay irked with someone who seemed so desperately happy to see him. Trying not to sound too eager, he asked, "Does that invitation to lunch still stand?"

"Of all the silly questions. Certainly, it does," said Hermann, shoving his books and papers into a briefcase and striding over to meet him. As he drew close, he stopped and peered at Dashiel keenly, his brow furrowing with concern. "Heavens, you do look like you could use a good lunch. You've grown so thin!"

"Have I?" said Dashiel, smoothing a hand over the front of his jacket. It had become a bit baggy around the middle. "Well, you look like you haven't slept in a month, so I suppose that makes us even."

"I really haven't been sleeping very well." Hermann fidgeted with the handle of his briefcase. "And it's not just me. Everyone's down to their last nerve around here. There's a very strange energy about the place these days. You saw what my students were like just then. Well, they've been carrying on that way for weeks now. I've never seen such bickering! My classes are usually pretty staid and civil sorts of affairs."

"You don't think it's just exam-time nerves?"

"Oh, no. It's not that at all." He leaned in conspiratorially, resting a warm hand on Dashiel's elbow. "The truth is, the disturbances have grown much worse since you left," he said in a low voice. "At first, I was sure you must be right, that I was letting my imagination run away with me. But I simply can't explain away some of the things that have been happening these past few weeks, no matter how hard I try. That's why I—oh, but I shouldn't be bothering you with all this. I promised you a ghost-free lunch last time we spoke."

"Actually, Hermann," said Dashiel, "I'm very interested in what's been happening here. I want you to tell me all about it."

"Really?"

"Oh, yes." He felt a bit of the old pique returning. "I'm especially interested to learn what on earth could have possessed you to write to Maude Pembleton Fink."

"You know her?" asked Hermann, wide-eyed.

"Quite well, I'm sorry to say."

Hermann frowned thoughtfully. "What an odd woman she is. I'm afraid she wasn't very helpful."

"Huh." Dashiel wasn't quite sure what this meant, but it was the first thing he'd heard in the past two days that he found the least bit reassuring.

CHAPTER 4

S ITTING IN A SUNNY café with a ham sandwich and a steaming bowl of clam chowder, Dashiel found his worries far less pressing. Hermann seemed more at ease, too. He still looked tired, but his eyes weren't quite so haunted as they had been, and that effulgent smile of his came more readily.

"Where have you been since we last met?" Hermann asked once they'd both had a moment to savor a few bites of food.

"Oh, here and there," said Dashiel. *Mostly here*, he declined to add. Guilt stirred in his belly. He'd learned in the medium business never to leave any encounter to chance. His preliminary research for the demonstration back in April had yielded a fair bit of information about Hermann's habits (he stayed on campus 'til well past eight most weeknights, except for Tuesdays, when he played bridge with a neighbor). He was not a hard man to avoid. The few times he'd happened to spot Hermann around town, Dashiel had melted into the shadows as if he were a ghost himself. He decided to steer the conversation in a new direction.

"Your secretary didn't seem very happy to see me today," he said.

"Oh, don't mind Agnes," said Hermann, with an apologetic wince. "As I said, everyone's been on edge. And she doesn't much care for mediums, I think."

"Smart girl. Neither do I."

"I've tried to explain to her that you're no longer in the business, but she still has this notion that your last visit put funny ideas in my head. Ridiculous, of course, since you did nothing but point out perfectly reasonable explanations for everything that was happening. It's a prejudice, I suppose. She may have some reservations against your former trade, you know, for religious reasons."

"Could be. We're not well-liked by the fire and brimstone types." He let out a huff of amusement. "She must have simply adored Maude."

Hermann nodded guiltily. "She gave me such a look when I told her she was coming. But I didn't know what else to do."

"What on earth happened with Maude, anyway?" Dashiel set down his spoon and leaned forward. "I want to hear the whole story."

"Oh," said Hermann, looking a little flustered under his attentive gaze. "I hardly know where to begin."

"You said things had gotten worse at the museum?"

"Ah, yes. It's become quite intolerable, actually. I did everything you suggested. I got a mount for the little shabti and the mongoose, and I brought in a man to patch up the wall in the archive. You were absolutely right about the leaky pipe, by the way. But it's almost as if all of that only made . . . whatever this is . . . even angrier."

"I see. And how does this anger manifest itself?"

"Well, the day after I put in the mounts, I found the shabti wedged up against the far corner of its case. The mount had been ripped out, and there was a crack in the glass, almost as if the shabti had been flung against it from the inside. What's more, on several occasions I am quite certain that I've seen things moving around in the gallery."

"More squirrels?"

"Clarence thinks so, but these things don't move like squirrels. I can never get a good look—I only catch them out of the corner of my eye. But some of them seem to skitter, and others slither, like snakes or centipedes. And, most disturbing of all, I've heard a voice. A definite voice. I'm sure it's not just a sputtering radiator this time."

Dashiel hated to admit it even to himself, but he was becoming concerned about the state of Hermann's sanity. This went beyond the sort of willful credulity that came from the typical believer. "What does this voice say?" he asked cautiously.

"It's hard to tell," said Hermann, taking a thoughtful bite of his cold pickle and potato salad. "I'm not actually used to hearing the language spoken, you see."

Dashiel lifted his eyebrows, surprised. "What language is that?"

"It seems to be Late Egyptian. I can read it with no trouble, of course, but we don't really know how most of the vowels were pronounced. Or several of the consonants, for that matter. Working backward from Coptic helps a bit with that, but it can only get you so far." He looked a little wistful. "It would be rather wonderful if it weren't all so disturbing."

"I see," said Dashiel, careful to keep his tone neutral.

"I think it may be saying something about a 'Great One,'" Hermann mused. "Or possibly an ass, but that hardly seems likely."

Dashiel leaned back and dabbed his mouth with his napkin, at a loss for words. "All right," he said at last. "I must confess, that all sounds extremely peculiar."

"Yes, and it makes it very difficult to concentrate on my work of an evening," said Hermann, frowning. "So, I wrote to Reverend Fink in the hopes that she might have some insight. She wrote back promptly and seemed quite eager to have a look."

"I'll bet," muttered Dashiel.

"She was very gracious when she arrived. She told me that she'd have no difficulty determining what sort of an entity I was dealing with, but that she needed time alone to commune with it."

Dashiel couldn't suppress a groan.

"I know, I know," said Hermann, sheepishly pushing a pickle around his plate with a toothpick. "Believe me, I was skeptical myself. But I thought if there was even the slightest chance she might know what she was doing—"

"She knows what she's doing, all right."

"Yes. Well, I didn't want to repeat the mistake I made with you." At Dashiel's questioning look, he explained, "You know, asking you to come by in the morning. It seems to go dormant during daylight hours. So I had her come in the evening, when most of the disturbances happen. She floated in right on time, serene as can be. I let her into the gallery to have a look around, as she'd requested. And then, not five minutes later, she ran out, looking white as a sheet."

Dashiel had just raised his sandwich to take a bite, but now he slowly lowered it again. "Hold on. Ran out? Like she was afraid of something?"

"The poor thing was petrified," said Hermann, nodding. "She wouldn't even tell me what she'd seen."

Now, that was odd. As Dashiel knew better than most, there were precious few things that could scare Maude Fink. "What did she charge you for her services, such as they were?"

"Nothing! She didn't stay long enough to even discuss it. She said she had to go, then she left. I haven't heard a peep from her since."

Dashiel stared at him, dumbfounded. "If that isn't the damnedest thing!"

It was simply not in Maude's nature to walk away from any sort of encounter without extracting her pound of flesh. Something must have truly frightened her. He took a bite of his sandwich and chewed it slowly, pondering.

"Let's say, just for the sake of argument," he said after a long silence, "that you do have a bona fide ghost raising Cain in your museum. Why call on someone like Maude? It seems to me that it would make more sense to bring in one of those serious psychical researchers, like Harry Price or Nandor Fodor."

"I suppose it would," admitted Hermann. "But those fellows live all the way across the Atlantic, and I didn't want to wait that long to bring someone in—assuming they'd come at all."

"Well, then, one of the American ones. Why not Walter Prince?"

Hermann chewed his lip. "I thought about that, too. But all these parapsychologist types like to publish the results of their investigations, don't they? As well they should, if they want to be properly scientific about it. And I really don't want to draw that sort of attention. At least, not until I know for sure what I'm dealing with." He gave Dashiel a shy glance. "Actually, I would have called you first, if I'd had the slightest idea of how to reach you."

"Fair enough. I don't know how to reach myself half the time." Dashiel sighed. He felt trapped in the tightening snare of his own curiosity. "Fine. I'll come back this evening and take another look."

Hermann melted with gratitude. "Would you really? Oh, bless you—"

"On one condition," he cut in sternly.

"Of course!"

"No more mediums from now on, Hermann. They'll bring you nothing but grief."

DASHIEL AGREED TO return to the museum at eight o'clock. In the meantime, there was little to do but go back to the boardinghouse and lay low. The landlady accosted him in the foyer the moment he walked in.

"Mr. Quicke, your rent for the week is three days past due," she informed him.

"I beg your pardon, Mrs. Kostakis," he said, doffing his hat. "I'm afraid I was detained on business out of town, and I—"

"I don't need reasons," she said curtly, "I need the rent. You understand I have a business to run here."

"Of course. I have it, Mrs. Kostakis, and I can give it to you right now." With a flourish, he produced the ten-dollar bill that he'd finagled from the woman on the bridge in St. Charles. "You can put the extra three dollars toward next week's rent."

"The extra will go to your last week's rent," she said, her mouth set in a grim line. "You were short, remember?"

"Ah. So I was. Sorry, must have slipped my mind."

She tucked the money into the pocket of her apron with a heavy sigh. "I don't like to do this, Mr. Quicke," she said. "I know times are tough, but I'm trying to make a living, same as you, and I've got a lot of mouths to feed. You've been late or short almost every week the past two months. If it goes on like this, I'll have to ask you to look for other arrangements."

"I understand, Mrs. Kostakis. I'll be on time next week, you can count on it."

"Good," she said, not unkindly. "There's fresh coffee in the kitchen."

Dashiel skipped the coffee, as inviting as it smelled, and retired straight to his room. His nerves were already buzzing like live wires, despite how tired he was. Hoping to get a bit of rest before his rendezvous with Hermann that evening, he curled up on his stony mattress and pulled the thin blanket up to his chin.

Strange and foreboding thoughts nagged at him, and the room seemed darker and colder than usual despite the mildness of the weather. The hearty meal he'd just eaten rested like a stone in the pit of his stomach. Still, some part of his soul that he'd thought was long buried tingled with an old, familiar excitement.

It didn't take long for fatigue to win the battle with his nerves. He drifted into a fitful sleep.

HERMANN WAS WAITING on the front steps of the Wexler Building when Dashiel arrived. He'd shaved since their last encounter, and when he doffed his hat, Dashiel saw that he'd also attempted to tame his unruly waves. As Dashiel approached, he beamed and extended a welcoming hand.

"So good of you to come again," he said, a little breathless, as he shook Dashiel's hand.

"Only too glad," said Dashiel, nodding, "although I'm not sure how much help I can be."

"Believe me, you're already helping more than you know. The building is usually locked at this hour, but—" he produced his enormous ring of keys and jangled it in triumph "—that will, of course, be no obstacle to us!"

The building was silent and empty when they walked in. The lights were dim, and the heavy oak doors to the gallery looked more imposing than Dashiel remembered. A handwritten sign that read *Closed for Renovations* hung on one of the doorknobs. Hermann unlocked the doors and pulled one of them open, revealing the unlit gallery beyond.

"Where's Clarence?" asked Dashiel, his skin tingling with unease. He was used to working in the dark, but he didn't care for the way the objects loomed in their shadowy cases, or for the oppressive silence that lay over the gallery now that night had fallen and the building was empty. It was a stillness just waiting to be disturbed.

"He doesn't work night duty anymore," said Hermann, kicking the doorstop into place. "And we haven't found anyone to replace him yet, I'm afraid."

"Oh?"

"He says he's getting too old to work the late hours, but I think he just didn't want to admit the place was starting to give him the heebie-jeebies after dark." He sidled into the room and flicked on a light switch, then turned to Dashiel with a nervous grin. "Well, it seems quiet for now, but I'm sure we'll get some action soon enough. Do come in!"

Dashiel took a cautious step across the threshold, then stopped short, coughing violently. A hideous smell of decay, pungent and cloying, had hit him like a punch to the nose. "Good God, what is that?"

"That's the smell of mummy," said Hermann, delicately covering his nose and mouth with a handkerchief. Dashiel hastened to follow his example. "It often becomes quite strong in the evenings, of late."

"How many mummies have you got in this place, anyway?" Dashiel demanded, blinking his watering eyes.

"Not so many as to make that sort of a smell. And they're all very well cared for, I can assure you. I have a conservator check them regularly for mold."

Hermann crept in a little further, and Dashiel reluctantly followed him. Mercifully, the smell was subsiding almost as fast as it had begun—either that or he was getting used to it, which wasn't the most comforting thought. The back of his neck prickled, and his heart began to beat faster. *This is absurd*, he told himself. *Pull yourself together, Quicke.*

"If you step this way, you'll see what I mean about the shabti case," Hermann was saying. "I haven't had time to replace the glass yet."

Dashiel warily approached the case. Cracks radiated out in a star-shaped pattern where something had struck the glass. He ran his fingers over the impact point at the center. It felt smooth; the damage did, in fact, seem to have originated from inside the case. The shabti was where it was supposed to be, more or less, but the fabric behind it was torn and frayed. He could see the drill holes where the mounting bracket must have been attached.

"I saw no point in reinstalling the mount," Hermann said. "Not if it's just going to rip it out again."

"Sensible," Dashiel murmured. There must be a mundane explanation for all this, but he couldn't guess what it might be. Seeing the damaged case in person was strangely unsettling. "Any more action from our mongoose friend?"

"Not since I restrained it," said Hermann. He drew a sharp little breath, as if struck by an epiphany. "Perhaps that's why it's so angry! The, er, entity responsible for all this, I mean. It thinks I'm trying to keep it from communicating with me. You told me before that spirits use mundane objects and phenomena as a sort of conduit for their activities—"

Dashiel straightened up and turned to fix him with a stern frown. "What I told you is that Spiritualists make up that sort of mumbo-jumbo to make their nonsense sound more plausible. That's how they get you, Hermann, they're sophists. They have an explanation for everything."

"I know that," said Hermann, all wide eyes and earnestness. "But have you ever considered that . . . well, there might be something to it? A kernel of truth buried somewhere in all the balderdash?"

Dashiel pushed down a flare of irritability. He was certain of very few things in life anymore, but his conviction that Spiritualism had no basis in reality was one of them. It was not a point he was in any mood to debate.

"No," he said flatly. "It's humbuggery, and it always has been. It was invented by a couple of bored little farm girls who got carried away with the thrill of playing people for suckers. They confessed to it all in the end, for all the good it did. I'm sorry, Hermann, but I'm not here to tell you what you want to hear. I don't play that game anymore."

"Yes, but—"

"I admit that this is strange," he said, indicating the broken case, "but one damaged display case and a nasty smell do not a haunting make."

"But those aren't the only things! As I said, I've also—"

"Heard voices, yes," said Dashiel. He took a deep breath, trying to calm his nerves. The atmosphere of the place was so discomfiting that he could hardly think straight. The hammering of his heart was becoming unbearable. He bristled all over, like a cornered cat. He'd only just arrived, but all he wanted to do was turn tail and leave. "Have you had anyone check the boiler for your steam heating system? If Clarence is right, and there are squirrels or rats or something in here, one of them could have chewed through a gas line. It could be poisoning the whole building, making you see and hear things that aren't there."

"No," Hermann said, a strained note entering his voice. "That can't be it. If it were something like that, why would I only notice these disturbances at night? And why just me? Surely everyone in the building would be hallucinating all day."

"I don't know what to tell you. I really don't." A deep shiver ran up his spine and he took a few steps back, toward the door. Hermann's ghost stories must have gotten under his skin more than he'd realized. "Whatever's happening here, I don't see what I could possibly do to help. I'm not a central heating engineer or a plumber or . . ." he waved his handkerchief vaguely ". . . whatever it is you need here. I'm sorry."

To his surprise, Hermann reached out and clutched at his sleeve. "Please, Dashiel. I know I promised I wouldn't drag you into all this again, and the last thing I want to do is waste your time. But you're here now. Won't you stay with me a little longer, just to see what happens?"

"Listen, Hermann . . ."

"We could make a nice little social evening of it," Hermann said, brightening. He seemed to realize he was still holding Dashiel's sleeve, and quickly let go. "I have a lovely bottle of brandy in my office that I've been saving for a special occasion. If you'll just wait here, I'll run and get it."

Dashiel squeezed his eyes shut and massaged his temple with his fingertips. "All right," he said, with a grudging nod. He couldn't deny that part of him still burned with curiosity. After all, something had scared away Maude, and he couldn't believe it was a mere case of the jimjams. Besides, he rather liked the idea of a drink of brandy in pleasant, if eccentric, company. "Fine, you're right. I'm here, I might as well give this ghost of yours a fair shake."

"Oh, wonderful," said Hermann. "I'll be back before you can say Nisubanebdjed!"

And he left, taking all the warmth from the room with him.

DASHIEL WASN'T SURE how long Hermann was gone, but it felt like decades. He paced the empty gallery, trying to ignore the crushing silence of the place. He stopped in front of the case with the fake bust of the queen in it, oddly comforted to see she was still there.

"Hello, queenie," he murmured, leaning in close to get a better look at her. "Nice to see another lonely old fraud again." A shadow flickered across her impassive stone face, and something rustled behind him. He flinched and pressed a hand to his galloping heart, annoyed with himself. When had he gotten so jumpy?

Slowly, he turned toward the source of the noise. His eye fell on the case with the animal mummies, but everything in it lay still. He crept closer, then reached out and tapped one of the legs of the case with his cane. There was no response from its silent occupants. The little mongoose rested in its new display bracket, looking as serene and emphatically dead as ever.

Still, that prickling feeling refused to subside. Something—a rivulet of perspiration, perhaps—tickled at the nape of his neck, just above the top of his collar. He swiped at the spot with his hand, shuddering.

He couldn't shake the sensation that someone—or something—was in the gallery with him. There were a lot of things looking at him, he realized. Perhaps that was what made the place feel so unnerving. From one case, an uncannily realistic portrait of a young man, painted on a plank of wood, fixed him with a penetrating gaze. A mummy mask, gleaming here and there with bits of gold leaf, stared at him from another display. He almost fancied that its eyes followed him as he moved.

The tickling on his neck intensified. He felt certain now that something was crawling on him. Uttering a startled curse, he dropped his cane and scrabbled at the back of his neck with both hands. Whatever it was worked its way under his collar and began skittering down his spine.

With a yelp of dismay, he tore off his jacket and flung it to the floor. He had shrugged off his suspenders and was halfway out of his shirt when he heard footsteps behind him. Wheeling around, he found Hermann standing in the doorway, clutching a bottle and a pair of snifters and staring at him in round-eyed wonderment.

"Um," Hermann said, swallowing visibly, "you all right there, Dashiel? Do you need a moment? Or a hand?"

Dashiel straightened and hastily pulled his shirt back up over his shoulders. "No, no, I'm fine," he huffed, fumbling with the buttons and avoiding Hermann's gaze. "I just—it felt like there was a spider on me or something."

"Gracious! Did you get it?"

"I think so. I don't feel it anymore, anyhow." He brushed himself off and bent to retrieve his jacket and cane. "How about some of that brandy?"

"Ah!" said Hermann. "An excellent notion. Follow me." He led the way to a bench near the back of the gallery. Dashiel sat, and Hermann set about pouring their drinks.

The bench stood in front of a piece that must have been one of the stars of the collection. It was a large, flat slab of stone mounted on the wall, carved to resemble a door or gateway. The doorframe, surrounding a narrow central indentation, was ornamented with columns of hieroglyphic script.

A carved scene at the top of the doorway depicted a broad-shouldered man in a white kilt, seated on an elegant, lion-footed chair and facing a table laden with food.

Just beneath that, a pair of eyes, dramatically lined with kohl, stared out at Dashiel. The whole thing was painted in jewel-like shades of blue, red, and gold.

Hermann handed him a glass brimming with brandy, his eyes sparkling. "Isn't it beautiful?"

"It certainly is," Dashiel replied, eagerly eyeing the glass. He was beginning to feel more at ease.

"It's a false door," Hermann went on, settling down beside him on the bench. He held his own glass under his nose and inhaled the brandy's spicy aroma before taking a sip. "A magical portal between the realms of the living and the dead. They were built into the walls of tomb chapels so that visitors could commune with their departed loved ones."

Dashiel smiled and nursed his brandy. It was smooth and warm and comforting. "Sounds like something that would've come in handy in my old line of work."

"Why, I suppose it would, at that!" said Hermann. "We were very fortunate to get such a fine example for our little museum," he went on, warming to the topic. "This one dates to the First Intermediate Period, but the style is quite refined for the . . ."

He trailed off, apparently realizing that Dashiel's attention was elsewhere. Dashiel stared at the false door, his glass of brandy raised halfway to his lips.

"Are you all right?" asked Hermann. He spoke softly, but Dashiel still flinched, splashing a little bit of the brandy over his trembling hand.

"I'm not sure," he said. "Hermann, you didn't put anything in this drink besides brandy, did you?" The inside of his mouth felt like cotton wool.

"Certainly not!" said Hermann, sounding both surprised and mildly affronted. "Why would you . . ."

"Shhh," said Dashiel, setting down his glass. "Look. Are you seeing what I'm seeing?"

Hermann stared in silence for a moment. "Yes," he said at length, his voice low and steady. "I believe I am. Goodness, this is a new one."

Dashiel rubbed his stinging eyes and blinked hard, but there was no mistaking what he was seeing. Several of the signs inscribed around the doorway writhed and twisted, like worms squirming in shallow mud.

Something that looked like a snake with horns wriggled across the top of the stone doorframe. The pair of eyes below the offering scene rolled and blinked. Among the items piled on the table of offerings to the dead, the disembodied head of a bird twisted and thrashed on its long neck.

Dashiel felt the bile rising in his throat. An intense cold crept over him; his pulse roared in his ears. Instinctively, he took hold of Hermann's wrist. "Sweet Jesus," he whispered.

Hermann put his glass down and laid his free hand on top of Dashiel's. His palm felt clammy, and his hand shook, but his voice was strangely calm when he spoke. "Did you ever read the novel *Tabubu*?"

"What?" Dashiel croaked. He became aware of a soft rustling noise, something between a whisper and a heartbeat. It was so faint that he thought it must be the sound of blood rushing through his veins.

"Or see that picture with Karloff that came out a couple years back—what was it called, *The Mummy*? Either way, they're both based on the same source," Hermann said. "The story of Setna and the mummies. It's a fascinating little masterpiece of Ptolemaic literature, chock full of uncanny imagery. Do you know it?"

Dashiel glanced at him sideways, incredulous. He wanted to shake him, to demand to know how the hell he could babble on about movies and ancient literature at a time like this. But his voice dried up in his throat, so he just silently shook his head.

"All this brought it to mind, and I wondered if you might be familiar—" Hermann stopped, drawing in a shuddering gasp. "Oh, dear," he whispered.

Dashiel forced himself to follow Hermann's gaze back to the false door. Something was coming through the indentation at the center of the doorway, like inky tendrils of obsidian-black smoke. They wrapped around the edges of the stone portal, coalescing into finger-like forms too long and sinuous to belong to anything human.

Dashiel's glass fell to the floor and shattered as he leaped to his feet, nearly tumbling backward over the bench. "All right," he gasped, "I've seen enough." He ran for the exit as fast as his injured leg would allow.

Hermann caught up with him as he reached the lobby. Once they were both safely across the threshold, he swung the heavy door shut and locked it behind them. Dashiel slumped against the wall beside the doorway, panting and gasping.

"There, now, it's all right, we're all right," Hermann said, sounding winded. He took Dashiel's elbow and pulled him over to a nearby bench, then gently pushed him down to sit. "Just rest a moment."

Dashiel complied without a word, waiting for his heart to stop hammering against his ribs. Once he'd had a moment to collect his wits, he realized that Hermann looked almost as terrified as he felt. A sheen of perspiration glistened on his pale forehead, and his eyes were bright with fear. Somehow, he'd had the presence of mind to gather up Dashiel's jacket and cane before they fled, and he was still clutching them tightly.

"You saw it," said Hermann. Despite his obvious fright, there was an unmistakable note of excitement in his voice. He sank down onto the bench next to Dashiel. "By God, someone else finally saw it! Oh, I've felt so alone in all this, Dashiel, you have no idea."

"I sure as hell saw something," said Dashiel. His voice came out hoarse and tremulous. He clenched his hands into fists, trying in vain to control their violent shaking. "I can't do this. I have to go."

"Go?" cried Hermann, dismayed. "No, please, you've only just—"

"Listen to me, Hermann. I'm sorry I ever doubted you. You got me, I'm convinced, there's something in there. Either that or I've completely lost whatever was left of my marbles. But I can't help you. I'm not the man you want for this job."

"But you are!"

He shook his head helplessly. "I'm a fake, don't you understand? Always have been. I don't have the slightest notion of what to do with a genuine ghost, or demon, or whatever that thing is. Hell, I doubt you could find someone less qualified to deal with this mess if you tried!"

"I don't believe that for a moment," said Hermann, giving his wrist an ardent squeeze. "Maybe you don't know the first thing about real spirits, but you're clever and observant and resourceful. If we just work together—"

Dashiel pulled away from him and rose on unsteady legs, raising his hands in a gesture of rebuff. "No, no, no. You don't need some washed-up old phony medium, you need . . . Christ, I don't know, an exorcist or something!"

"An exorcist?" said Hermann, incredulous. He pondered the idea for a moment. "Well, I don't know any priests, if that's what you have in mind. And I very much doubt that anyone at my synagogue would even know where to begin with such a thing. They don't deal with dybbukim. This isn't eighteenth-century Poland."

"Well, I don't think that . . . that . . . thing cares what century it is," said Dashiel, waving a hand at the closed gallery doors. As he did so, it occurred to him that he had no reason to think that a locked door was enough to stop the whatever-it-was from coming out after them, and a fresh wave of horror washed over him. He couldn't seem to gulp enough air into his lungs, and his hands tingled as though he'd taken hold of a live wire. "Call your rabbi, Hermann," he panted. "Or don't. It's all the same to me. I'm leaving."

Hermann looked crushed. "But . . . will you be back?"

"I very much doubt it."

"Where will you go?" he entreated, trotting after Dashiel as he groped his way toward the door.

"For now, back to my boardinghouse. Then—I don't know. California, maybe. And at some point, into the bottom of a nice deep bottle, where I can hopefully forget any of this ever happened."

"Dashiel, wait, please! Can't we go somewhere else, somewhere safe, and just talk things over?"

He didn't answer. He turned his back on Hermann and stumbled out the door and down the front steps, feeling as if all the muscle and sinew in his legs had been replaced with jelly. Hermann called after him, but he kept going, determined to put as much distance as possible between himself and whatever he had just seen.

It wasn't until he was about five blocks away—and right around the corner from his boardinghouse—that he noticed the searing pain in his bad leg and realized that he'd left both his cane and his jacket behind.

The full impact of what had happened hit him all at once, like a steel mallet to the solar plexus. He bent over at the waist and gripped his thighs with his hands, gasping for air. Those shadowy fingers from the gallery insinuated themselves into his mind's eye, and an icy flood of nausea surged through him. He retched and spat onto the grassy verge beside the sidewalk.

"What seems to be the trouble, mister?" someone called out.

He forced himself to stand up straight and turn toward the source of the voice. His stomach, which already felt as though it was resting somewhere in his lower pelvic region, managed to sink even deeper.

A policeman was strolling toward him, his thumbs thrust through his belt loops.

"I'm fine, officer," Dashiel lied, his voice little more than a husky whisper.

"Now, I'm as happy as the next guy that Prohibition's over," the cop said as he drew near, "but just so you know, folks in this neighborhood don't look too kindly on drunks staggering around on their public walkways and puking into their chrysanthemums."

"I promise you, officer, I'm not drunk," said Dashiel miserably. "I wish I was. I'm only trying to get back home."

The policeman gave him a dubious look. "Need me to point you in the right direction?"

He shook his head and forced himself to breathe evenly. "No, sir. I know where I'm going."

"Then I suggest you head straight there, buddy. Don't dawdle, now."

Dashiel responded with a curt nod and limped away as fast as he could. He could hear the policeman chuckling unpleasantly as he rounded the corner, but he didn't have it in him to care.

He hurried into the boardinghouse and closed the front door behind him, leaning against it for a few moments as he inhaled the comforting, mundane scents of cigar smoke and beef stew. The raucous snores of one of the other boarders—an elderly fellow named Agoston who boasted an impressive set of whiskers—issued from an armchair in the sitting room.

Under normal circumstances, it was Dashiel's custom to avoid his fellow lodgers. These days he preferred to spend most of his time in solitude. Now, though, there were few things he liked less than the idea of curling up in his dark, drafty room with nothing to keep him company but his own thoughts. Even the society of a sleeping octogenarian would have to be better than that. He crept into the sitting room and sat on the faded velvet settee across from Agoston.

Part of him wanted to wake the old fellow up, just to have someone to talk to. But they'd never exchanged words beyond the occasional perfunctory greeting over breakfast, and he couldn't imagine what he might say to him now. He couldn't remember a time when he'd felt so frightened, or so utterly alone.

Spiritualism was a lie, he had always known that. For almost two decades, he'd devoted himself to propagating that lie. Nurturing it and perfecting it. Keeping it alive and growing. He'd since renounced it, but he had never walked away completely. Instead, he'd turned his attention to tearing the lie down and exposing it to the rest of humanity for what it was. As much as he despised it, it remained the axis around which his world revolved.

It was a lie, but it was his lie. His one constant. The old reliable. And now, he had lost even that.

He tried clinging to some comforting shred of doubt. Could the things he'd seen and felt in the gallery have been tricks of the light? The power of suggestion? A hoax perpetrated by Maude or even Porphyrio?

That struck him as unlikely. He was all too familiar with the techniques his former colleagues used to create their séance room razzle-dazzle, and none of it had looked anything like what he'd seen in the museum that evening. The unsophisticated nature of their craft was almost a point of pride. Who needed elaborate trickery when it was just as easy to dupe a willing audience with the crudest of ruses? And if one of his old associates was trying to trick him . . . to what end?

"Mr. Quicke," said a voice from the doorway. He bolted up in his seat with a gasp. It was Mrs. Kostakis. "Are you well?" she asked, squinting at him with concern.

"Not feeling my best, I'm afraid."

"You're white as a sheet. Go lie down!" She bustled over and started to take hold of his arm, intending to help him to his feet.

"No, no," he said, waving her off. "I just need to sit for a while, that's all."

"Suit yourself. But if you're sick, you ought to rest. You'll be in no shape for company in the morning if you don't get some sleep."

Dashiel turned, slowly, and stared up at her. "What company?"

"Your visitor," she said, frowning at him in puzzlement. "While you were out, a very well-dressed gentleman stopped by looking for you. He said he was an old friend, and that you'd be expecting him."

In an instant, the floor seemed to drop out from under him. He dug his fingers into the cushions of the settee so hard that his knuckles stood out white. "Did—did he say anything else?"

Mrs. Kostakis shrugged. "Just that he was sorry he missed you, and he'd be back tomorrow morning. Oh, he was very charming! Like a movie star or something."

Dashiel stood. "Mrs. Kostakis, you can put your 'Vacancy' sign back in the window," he said. The words sounded strange to him, as if he were listening to someone else speak with his own voice. "I'm leaving tonight."

"Tonight? But this is very sudden, Mr. Quicke!"

"Yes."

"What should I tell your visitor?"

"Tell him I've taken the train down to Cairo, on urgent business. And tell him . . . tell him I won't be coming back."

CHAPTER 5

I T DIDN'T TAKE DASHIEL much time to pack his belongings. Everything he owned in the world, aside from his satchel of Dr. Juniper's Miracle Tonic, fit inside his handsome Goyard wardrobe trunk. Ignoring the protestations of his leg, he dragged the heavy trunk out of his room, down the front steps of the boardinghouse, and through the sleepy streets of Willowvale.

The trunk had been outrageously expensive. It was one of the last luxuries he still retained from his former life. At the moment, he wanted nothing more than to hurl the beastly thing into a deep ravine, preferably with lots of craggy rocks at the bottom. Sadly, those were in short supply in northern Illinois, but a fellow could dream.

He didn't stop until he reached the train depot, where he threw down the trunk and sat on it. His eyes watered with pain and exertion, and he angrily swiped at them with the sleeve of his overcoat.

It was late, and the depot was empty except for one or two shadowy figures lingering by the tracks. A warm, yellow light illuminated the inside of the ticket office, and the ticket agent lounged in his chair, reading the evening paper. Dashiel forced himself to stand and hobbled up to the counter, wincing with every step.

"Evening," he said with a tight-lipped smile and a quick tip of the hat. "How far west of here will two dollars and fifty cents get me?"

The ticket agent lowered his paper and peered at Dashiel over the tops of his spectacles. "That'll take you as far as Woodbine," he said, "assuming you're not talking about a round trip."

Not far enough, Dashiel thought grimly, but at least it was a start. "That'll suit me just fine. A one-way ticket to Woodbine, if you please." He reached into the pocket of his overcoat to find his billfold, but his fingers met only empty air.

Despair weighed on Dashiel. In his rush to leave the boardinghouse, he'd put on the coat with the snipped-out pockets. His billfold, he now remembered, was in the pocket of the jacket he'd worn to meet with Hermann. The one he'd left behind when he fled the museum.

"Aw, hell," Dashiel groaned.

The ticket agent cocked an inquiring eyebrow at him. "Something the matter?"

"Oh, nothing. I just forgot something," he said, with a wan smile. He groped in the pockets of his trousers and came up with a nickel and a penny. "I don't suppose this'll get me anywhere?" He laid the coins on the counter.

"It'll get you a nice cup of coffee at the delicatessen on Fifth and Maywood." The agent picked up his newspaper again and settled back in his chair.

Dashiel sighed and pocketed the coins. "That's what I thought. Thanks anyway."

The ticket agent, already absorbed in the sports pages, did not respond.

Dashiel returned to his trunk and sat down on it again, dropping his head into his hands. A damp chill had crept into the air, and the occasional cold droplet of rain tickled at the back of his neck.

He considered skipping town by hopping the next freight train. As down-and-out as he'd been for the last two years, he'd never had to resort to riding the rails. Just the thought made him queasy with anxiety. He was in no condition to hop onto anything, let alone drag his monstrous trunk onto a moving boxcar. Another part of him couldn't help but imagine Porphyrio's smug satisfaction if he ever found out. He decided he'd just as soon lay his head down on the track and let the train hasten his departure that way.

Perhaps he could find a sucker to buy some of his dwindling supply of Miracle Tonic and make himself enough money to get a few miles out of town. But selling the stuff took time and finesse, and time, at least, was something he did not have in great abundance. Porphyrio was not the sort of man to lie low and bide his time. He was probably out prowling the streets of town at that very moment. Any place where Dashiel was likely to find potential customers at this hour, he was also likely to find Porphyrio.

What he needed was a place to hide, just for the night. And, if he could retrieve his jacket from Hermann, he'd have enough money to put some distance between himself and Willowvale.

Cursing himself, Porphyrio, Maude, and every decision he'd made in his life leading up to this moment, he heaved himself up off the trunk and opened it. It didn't take him more than a minute or two of rummaging to find what he was looking for—a brown envelope containing the dossier he'd put together on Hermann a few months before, in preparation for his demonstration.

❧❀❧

MERCIFULLY, HERMANN'S APARTMENT was only two blocks from the train depot. In the condition Dashiel was in, though, it might as well have been twenty miles. At some point during the interminable journey, the rain started in earnest. By the time he'd dragged himself and his belongings onto the front stoop of Hermann's charming brownstone, he was soaking wet. Despite the meager protection of his hat, his hair clung damply to his forehead, and icy rivulets trickled down his face and dripped from the end of his nose.

His leg silently screamed in agony, but he didn't dare sit down to rest it, even for a moment. He wasn't sure he'd be able to get up again, and he didn't intend to spend the night curled up on a doorstep. With a final burst of effort, he wrenched open the door, flung his trunk and satchel into the vestibule, and staggered inside.

He located the call box and picked up the receiver with a shaky hand, then took a slow, deep breath before pushing the button labeled "3S – H. Goschalk."

For a long and agonizing moment, there was no answer. It occurred to Dashiel that, even as late as it was, Hermann might still be on campus. The thought was almost a relief. He didn't look forward to facing Hermann again after his frankly craven display at the museum.

He was just trying to decide between buzzing again and slipping out into the night to take his chances with Porphyrio when a pleasant, familiar voice crackled over the speaker.

"Hello?"

Dashiel swallowed a few times, trying to moisten his parched throat. "Hello, Hermann," he said.

There was another long silence, and for a second, he wondered if Hermann had disconnected the line. And then the voice came again, high and soft with astonishment. "Dashiel?"

He leaned forward and let his damp forehead rest against the top of the call box, bracing himself against the wall with his elbow. The words tumbled out of him in a rush.

"Yes, it's me. Look, Hermann, I'm awfully sorry to call on you unexpectedly like this. I know it's late, and after the way I ran out on you earlier, I wouldn't blame you if you told me to go straight to—"

"Don't move," Hermann's voice cut in. "I'm coming down."

Hurried footsteps creaked somewhere above him. Then a door softly opened and closed. A second later, Hermann came trotting down the stairs in slippers and a dark blue dressing gown.

"I hope I didn't get you out of bed," said Dashiel, making a dubiously successful attempt to sound nonchalant.

"No, no, certainly not. Don't give it another thought," said Hermann. His brow creased with concern as he drew near. "Goodness, look at the state of you! What in the world happened?"

"Let's just say I've had an unwelcome visitor," said Dashiel.

"What! The ghost didn't follow you home?"

"No, just a bit of my past catching up with me." He took a few shuffling steps away from the wall, and his knee nearly buckled.

"Oh, no," said Hermann, wincing. "Don't tell me you've been out there schlepping all this heavy luggage around on foot, and without your cane!"

"I'm afraid so." He took another deep breath, steeling himself. "Listen, I hate to ask you for anything after what happened today . . ."

"Dashiel, say no more. Whatever it is you need, if I can provide it, it's yours. But first, let's get you upstairs and out of that wet coat. And then, what do you say we talk about whatever it is over a drink of brandy? We never got to finish the one we started at the museum."

"That sounds—" Dashiel began, but he couldn't seem to get the rest of the words out, so he just swallowed and nodded. He hobbled over to his luggage and started to reach for the handle of his trunk, but Hermann waved him off.

"Leave it, leave it! I'll come back for your things," he said. "Come here."

Before he knew what was happening, Hermann had taken Dashiel's left arm and draped it over his shoulders, then wrapped his own right arm firmly around Dashiel's waist. "All right, up we go," he urged. "Take your time."

At a loss for words, Dashiel allowed Hermann to help him up the stairs. Despite the awkwardness of it all and the excruciating pain he was in, he realized with growing dismay that he was enjoying the experience. Hermann was very warm and smelled of olive soap and some sort of pleasantly spicy aftershave. It took every ounce of Dashiel's willpower to resist the urge to lay a cheek on his dark, tousled hair.

This, he decided, would not do at all. The last thing he needed, the very last thing, was to get attached to this silly little man with his ghost-infested museum in this Porphyrio-ridden town. He had to get out of Willowvale, and the sooner, the better. As soon as they reached the top of the stairs, he gently disentangled himself from Hermann's embrace and took a couple of steps back.

"Thanks," he said, with a stiff nod. "I'm all right from here."

"Of course," said Hermann, his ears and neck flushing bright crimson. He opened the door and gestured Dashiel inside. "Come in, make yourself at home."

Dashiel's first impression of Hermann's apartment, as he stepped into the living room, was that it looked like the sort of place a kindly grandmother would inhabit. There was a fire on in the gas fireplace, and the flames bathed the room in a flickering, golden light. A couple of overstuffed velvet armchairs and a small love seat with embroidered upholstery, all draped with antimacassars, stood clustered around the fireplace. The floor was covered in ornate rugs, which vied for the eye's attention with the pink and cream floral wallpaper.

He also noted several bookshelves and an inordinate number of small, decorative tables. Knickknacks and framed photographs crowded every available surface. He was still taking all this in when a light touch on his arm startled him out of his reverie.

"Here, let me take your coat," Hermann was saying. He clicked his tongue as he eased the sopping overcoat off Dashiel's stooped shoulders. "Look at that, it's nearly soaked through! You must be chilled to the bone."

Within minutes, Dashiel found himself ensconced in one of the armchairs, a warm blanket draped over his knees, a towel around his shoulders, and a glass of brandy in his hand. Hermann bustled out to retrieve the luggage, and he was left alone with his troubled thoughts. Not entirely alone, as it turned out. No sooner had Hermann left the room than a rotund gray tabby cat strolled in on incongruously dainty paws, its long, skinny tail held aloft like a flagpole. The cat regarded Dashiel with curiosity, but it didn't seem alarmed to find a stranger in its midst.

"You must be Horatio," said Dashiel, taking a slow sip of his brandy. He hadn't had anything to eat since lunch, and the alcohol went straight to his head, making him feel pleasantly detached and woozy. "I've heard so much about you."

The cat chirruped at him and trotted over, then jumped into his lap. Dashiel let out an "Oof!" of surprise. Horatio was a dense little animal, and those tiny paws hit home with unexpected force. But then he turned around a few times in Dashiel's lap and lay down, purring like a tiny diesel engine. Once he settled in, his weight and warmth felt soothing on Dashiel's aching thigh.

Dashiel let his head loll back against the cushions and closed his eyes. He stroked Horatio's sleek fur with one hand and brought the brandy glass to his lips with the other. It was the most comfortable he'd felt in years. He would absolutely have to leave first thing in the morning, there was no question about that. But perhaps there wasn't any harm in allowing himself to relish the moment while it lasted.

Hermann reappeared a moment later, huffing and puffing, with the luggage in tow. He deposited the bag and trunk in a corner of the room and came to sit down in the other armchair. "Ah," he said, once he'd caught his breath, "I see you've met Horatio."

"Yes." Dashiel shifted in his seat as he turned toward Hermann. "He came right over and—ow!" Horatio, still purring, had grabbed his hand in both paws, claws extended, and given it a playful but not insubstantial nip.

"Horatio, gai shoyn!" Hermann scolded. "You little noodge."

The cat jumped off Dashiel's lap and wandered over to rub himself on Hermann's ankles, unperturbed. Hermann tutted at him, but scratched his ears for a moment before turning back to Dashiel with an apologetic look. "Sorry about that. He's a dear, but he likes to cut up rough sometimes when he plays."

"Cats is cats," Dashiel remarked with a shrug and a clement wave of his hand.

Hermann chuckled. "Isn't that the truth." He picked up his glass from the little table by his chair, then leaned forward with his elbows on his knees. He fixed Dashiel with an earnest, questioning gaze. "Now—why don't you tell me everything?"

Dashiel took a generous gulp of brandy and shook his head. "There's not much to tell. Someone's come looking for me, a former . . . business partner. I'm not sure what he'll do if he finds me, but he already shot me once, so I'm not too eager to stick around and find out."

Hermann sat back again, his mouth agape. "Shot you! Is that what happened to your leg?"

Dashiel nodded.

"But why on earth would he do such a thing?"

"It's complicated," said Dashiel, giving him a pained look. "Anyway, I need to leave. First thing tomorrow, if not sooner. I already tried to skip town, only I wasn't able to get very far. All my money is in that jacket I left behind at the museum."

"Oh, gracious, of course," said Hermann. "Well, not to worry. I have it here, and your cane. But I hope you're not planning to go right away. Not in the condition you're in! Besides, it's still raining cats and dogs out there."

Dashiel shook his head, staring into his glass. "No, you're right, I don't think I could," he said. "That's why I wanted to ask if I could stay here, just for the night. I know it's an imposition, but I'll be out of your hair first thing in the morning, I promise."

"Don't be silly!" said Hermann, affronted. "It's no imposition at all. Stay as long as you like. And frankly, I don't think you'll be in any fit state to go anywhere tomorrow, either. If that leg of yours is sore now, it'll be practically immobile by then. Listen, why don't you stay a day or two, give yourself a chance to recover?"

Dashiel looked up and met Hermann's eyes. "That's about the kindest offer I've ever heard," he said quietly, "but I don't think I could risk it."

"Why not? What makes you think this fellow will come looking for you here? Does he even know you're still in town?"

Dashiel rubbed his jaw thoughtfully. "I don't know. I told my landlady I was leaving for Cairo tonight, so I can only hope that'll be enough to throw him off the trail."

"Perfect!" said Hermann, beaming. "All you have to do is lie low for a couple days, then. Give him time to get bored and move on, if he hasn't already."

"Hermann, I can't."

"Well, say you do try to leave in the morning, and this bounder is lurking around by the depot or something. You aren't very well going to be able to run away from him if you can barely even walk."

He sighed. "I suppose that's true."

"So, stay a while. Rest."

"Maybe." Dashiel slugged down the rest of his brandy. He was so bone-tired, and the thought of holing up in this cozy little home for another day or two was irresistibly appealing. "Maybe you're right. I'll think about it."

Hermann smiled so hard that Dashiel thought his face would split. "I'm so glad," he said. He picked up the bottle of brandy and gestured for Dashiel to hold out his glass.

"I probably shouldn't," said Dashiel, but he passed the snifter over anyway. He felt blissfully warm and drowsy.

Hermann refilled his glass and handed it back. "However did you find me, anyway?"

"Oh." Dashiel raised an eyebrow and took another swig. "If you want to find out everything there is to know about someone, forget hiring a private dick. Get yourself a medium. We have our ways. It's all part of the racket."

Hermann shook his head in wonderment. "Incredible!"

They both gazed at the fire for a moment in silent contemplation. Even though he'd only had one and a half glasses of brandy, Dashiel was beginning to feel decidedly cockeyed. Not that he minded. The throbbing in his leg and his recent emotional turmoil began fading into the background of his awareness, like quiet radio static.

"May I ask you something, Hermann?" he said.

"Of course. Anything you like."

"Not that I'm complaining," he continued, savoring another sip of the ambrosial drink, "but why are you being so kind to me?"

Hermann looked taken aback by the question. "Why shouldn't I be? It's the right thing to do. And besides, I like you, Dashiel. I have from the moment I met you."

"I can see that! I just dunno why. I've been less than helpful to you." He waved his glass in a sweeping gesture as if to indicate the broad expanse of his failings. "The first time we met, I gave you the brusheroo, wrote your ghost off as a pile of applesauce. Then I let months go by without so much as dropping a line to say hello. And today, I left you alone with that . . . thing at the museum. Put my tail between my legs and ran away."

"Now, now, I don't blame you for that," said Hermann gently. "Honestly, after the way you left today, I felt awful. I was worried sick about you. And you were never under any obligation to help me with my haunting in the first place, you know. I certainly didn't expect you to come back for a second look. But you did. And for that, I'm more grateful than I can say."

"Well, I'm only sorry I couldn't do more."

"Oh, you've done plenty, Dashiel, believe me. Just knowing that someone else knows, and that I'm not just an old kook with an overactive imagination—why, it makes all the difference in the world."

None of this did much to ease the guilt that kept tugging at Dashiel's conscience. He wished he could say something, anything, that might be of actual help. An idea slowly permeated into his foggy brain, and he sat up a little straighter.

"Say, Hermann—am I right in thinking the ancient Egyptians believed it was possible for the living to communicate with the dead?"

Hermann brightened, pleased to be asked something about his area of expertise. "Yes, naturally! I should say it was one of the central tenets of their belief system."

"How did they do it?"

"There were a variety of methods," he said, with a thoughtful frown. "I know several accounts of people communing with spirits and other supernatural beings in dreams. It was a way of meeting in the middle, I suppose, in the liminal realm between the worlds of the living and the dead."

Dashiel cocked his head, intrigued. "Sounds a bit like trance mediumship."

"Really?" Hermann's eyes were aglow with curiosity. "How so?"

"Well," said Dashiel, "the idea is that the medium opens himself up and lets go of his worldly surroundings. He goes into a dreamlike state, if you will. Once you're there, it's easier to pierce the veil and contact those who've crossed over. And of course, that opens the door for the spirit to convey messages to the living through the medium's body, or voice, or what have you." He shrugged. "That's the theory, anyhow."

"Do you . . ." Hermann hesitated, as if debating whether he should ask the question that was on his mind. "Do you know how to do that? Theoretically, I mean."

Dashiel snorted. "Theoretically? Sure. Tried it a million times when I was training with my first mentor, before I met Maude and learned the real tricks of the trade. She was one of the shut-eye types, the ones that believe in their own claptrap. She taught me all these fancy Yogic meditation techniques, samatha and vipassana and all that. I practiced my little heart out, but never once met a ghost. Got mighty good at faking it, though."

"Gosh," said Hermann, enthralled. "Maybe you just weren't close enough to any spirits for it to work."

"Close enough?"

"Well, there is an element of proximity in some of these stories. In the account of Thutmose IV and Harmachis, the future king fell asleep in the shadow of the Sphinx, and it spoke to him in a dream. Of course, that was a god, not a ghost. Still . . ."

Dashiel laughed and shook his head. "Forget it, Hermann, it's moot. As an actual medium, I'm about as useful as a wet sack of flour. Anyway, you couldn't pay me to take a nap next to that thing, let alone try to channel it."

"Oh, heavens no, of course not," said Hermann, reaching out to give him a reassuring pat on the arm. "I wouldn't dream of asking you to. I was just curious."

"You said there were other methods, though."

He nodded. "They would also write letters to their departed loved ones. We have a lovely example in the museum from a widower to his wife, written on an old cooking pot."

"Letters, eh? You don't say." Dashiel fell quiet for a moment. He felt foolish attempting to offer any sort of advice on the matter. After all, until earlier that evening, he'd never had the slightest inkling there even was such a thing as a genuine spirit. But it seemed only right to at least try and say something constructive.

"Well," he said, "here's what I think you ought to do. Write your ghost a letter. You can write its language, yes? Ask it what the hell it wants. You said it got mad when you tried to stop it from communicating, so . . . why not let it know you're listening?"

Hermann's hazel eyes sparkled. "Why, Dashiel! There, you see, now we're cooking with gas! Goodness, why didn't I think of that? I suppose I've been too busy worrying that I was losing my mind to give it a passing thought. I'll start writing something up first thing tomorrow, before classes." He regarded Dashiel thoughtfully. "In the meantime, I think you'd better get some sleep. You look like you're about to topple over. Come on, you can have the spare room."

Dashiel didn't argue. He set down his glass and let Hermann help him to his feet. They staggered together into the spare room, where he sank down onto the small feather bed in the corner. After months of dossing on the lumpy cot in the boardinghouse, it felt almost indecently soft. Gratitude welled up inside him like a warm spring.

He sat watching Hermann as he fluffed the pillows and tidied the nightstand. Maybe it was just the influence of the alcohol on his exhausted brain, but it seemed to Dashiel that he was easier on the eye than ever. The deep blue of the dressing gown brought out the color of those splendid eyes of his, and the warmth of the brandy and the fire had given his complexion a comely glow.

"There you are, make yourself comfortable," he was saying. "I'll bring you your things. And if you should need anything at all—"

"Why aren't you married, Hermann?" Dashiel blurted out.

Hermann's eyebrows lifted in surprise. "Goodness! You sound like you've been talking to my mother."

"Come on, I'm being serious. A bright, good-hearted, attractive fella like you . . . why hasn't some nice woman come along and—" he made a vague grabbing motion, as if he were trying to capture a moonbeam in his hand "—snatched you up?"

"Attractive?" said Hermann, with an incredulous laugh. "Go on with you, you're pixilated. Anyway, I should ask the same of you."

"Mmm," murmured Dashiel, lowering his head to the pillow and closing his eyes. "Mysterious."

"Pleasant dreams, Dashiel," he heard Hermann say, and after that, he wasn't aware of much else. Within minutes, he was dead to the world.

CHAPTER 6

I T TOOK DASHIEL A few moments to remember where he was when he woke up. His mouth tasted sour, his head felt like it was stuffed with rocks and cotton batting, and his leg was alarmingly stiff. But he still felt immeasurably better than he had the night before. Pale morning light filled the little spare room, and all was quiet except for the sounds of birds outside his window.

A pitcher of water, a glass, and a bottle of aspirin stood on the nightstand by the bed. Dashiel sat up and poured himself a glass of water, then noticed a handwritten note tucked under the aspirin.

Fresh towels in the hall cupboard, it read. *Help yourself to anything in the icebox. Be back this evening. —Hermann*

A further survey of the room revealed his cane leaning against the nightstand and the missing jacket hanging from a hook on the door. His satchel and trunk were tucked against the foot of the bed.

Dashiel grabbed his cane and hauled himself upright, trying very hard to ignore the inconvenient glow of fondness in his breast. He'd have to leave soon, certainly by tomorrow, and it would be nice if he could do it with his heart more or less intact. He changed into clean clothes, made a desultory attempt at tidying himself up at the washbasin, and slipped out to explore the rest of the apartment.

It had been a while since he'd had free rein to poke around in someone else's home, but his old snooping instincts kicked in at once. There was a time when he would have gone straight for the master bedroom. But, curious as he was about what he might find there, he resisted the urge. Instead, he limped back to the living room for a closer inspection.

Seeing the place in daylight didn't alter his original impression that it appeared to have been decorated by somebody's grandmother. Among the pictures on the wall were several dusty old needlework samplers, a series of prints of cats dressed like Victorian ladies and gentlemen, and a large photographic portrait of a handsome couple holding a wide-eyed baby dressed in white lace. He recognized the woman in the portrait as Hermann's mother, looking much the same as she had in the cabinet card that he'd filched from his office months before.

A black Bakelite telephone sat on a little table by the love seat, with a small pile of books and papers beside it. A quick perusal of the stack revealed a recent volume of the *Journal of the Society for Psychical Research*, a telephone directory, and a leather-bound address book.

A loose sheet of paper fluttered out of the address book when he lifted the cover. Maude's name and address were scrawled on it in Hermann's distinctive, flowing hand. He snorted and tucked it back into the book, ignoring the temptation to crumple it and toss it into the fireplace.

He opened a small drawer under the telephone table and found it stuffed with loose papers. *Support your A. F. T. Local*, entreated a leaflet on top, *Education is the Foundation of Our Democracy!* Under that was a letter about an upcoming academic conference in November, where Hermann was slated to deliver a lecture about pseudo-verbal constructions in narrative texts of the New Kingdom. Further rummaging produced a pamphlet published by the NAACP and a receipt for the purchase of several books from a shop with a Chicago address.

Dashiel slid the drawer shut, feeling a bit guilty. All this would have been immensely useful to him in his ghostmongering days, when every tidbit of personal information could be crafted into an impressive evidential message from the spirit world. But there was little point in thinking along those lines now. The only purpose this kind of nosing around could serve was to satisfy his own curiosity.

Something bumped against his ankle, and he looked down to see Horatio staring up at him with lambent green eyes. "Don't give me that look," he said. "It's just force of habit. Once a snoop, always a snoop, eh?"

He left the telephone table and went to examine the fireplace. The mantelpiece was covered in a variety of quaint knickknacks and figurines—mostly cats, although there was among them a little porcelain boy that Dashiel recognized as a statuette of the Infant Samuel at Prayer. He picked it up and stared at it, perplexed.

"You know, Horatio," he said, setting down the figurine, "you need to sit your old man down and have a serious talk with him about his interior decorating. No self-respecting bachelor's abode ought to look like this."

Horatio yawned, licked his chops, and began washing his face with a delicate paw. He had the look of a cat who had just eaten a hearty meal, and it made Dashiel keenly aware of the cavernous state of his own stomach. He abandoned his reconnaissance mission and made his way to the kitchen.

Taking Hermann's note to heart, he prepared himself a sumptuous breakfast of eggs, toast with marmalade, and coffee. He'd just cleaned his plate and was contemplating a second helping when a sharp knock sounded at the door. An ice-cold current shot through his veins and his appetite vanished. He rose and padded to the door as silently as he could, pulse increasing with every creak of the floorboards. Resting a trembling hand on the doorframe, he leaned forward and peered through the peephole. The figure standing outside the door was not Porphyrio, as he had feared, but a tiny Black woman of late middle age, smartly dressed in a peacock blue woolen day suit and cradling an empty baking dish in her hands. Dashiel exhaled, then unlocked the door and opened it.

"Morning, ma'am," he said.

"Oh!" she said, blinking up at him in surprise. "You're not Hermann."

"No, ma'am, I'm afraid not. I'm . . . an old friend, visiting from out of town. He should be back this evening, though. Shall I tell him you called?"

"Thank you, that would be wonderful. Tell him Mrs. Luckett came by. And give him this for me." She handed him the dish. "I meant to give it back yesterday, but he never turned up."

"I'll certainly let him know, ma'am."

"I do appreciate it, Mr.—"

"Quicke."

She gave him a thoughtful once-over, then smiled. "I'm glad to see that Hermann has some company, Mr. Quicke. I think it'll do him good." She leaned in closer, lowering her voice. "To tell you the truth, I've been worried about him. He just hasn't been himself the past few weeks. It's not like our Hermann to miss a bridge game, let alone two in a row."

"Oh, I'm sure he's just been busy," said Dashiel. "But I'll ask him to ring you up if you'd like."

"I'd like that very much," she said, with a polite nod. "Have a lovely morning, Mr. Quicke."

❧

THE REST OF the day dragged on uneventfully. Dashiel dozed, ate lunch, dozed some more, and tried not to think about things. He perused Hermann's bookshelves and picked out a promising-looking Agatha Christie novel, but he couldn't concentrate on reading. He sat in the armchair by the unlit fireplace and stared blankly at the pages. The image of the apparition in the museum kept creeping back into his brain, and with it came a horror that numbed his fingers and toes and stole his breath away.

There were few things that terrified a phony medium more than the thought of an actual spirit. That was a well-known axiom in the ghost business. In the past, Dashiel had poked his share of fun at his more credulous colleagues, the ones who jumped at shadows and sprinkled salt in the doorways before every séance. But it wasn't a feeling he'd ever experienced himself. Before now. His world was suddenly much bigger and stranger. It was as if a door had been wrenched open in his mind, but he could see only a vast, shadowy expanse beyond it, with baleful, indistinct forms gliding through the darkness.

A little after seven o'clock, he heard the tread of feet and the jingling of keys in the hall. Relieved at the prospect of human companionship, he heaved himself out of his chair. Horatio chirped happily and trotted to the door. A moment later, Hermann stumbled in, looking pale, wild-eyed, and unkempt. He was holding his handkerchief to his cheek. Dashiel's relief instantly turned to dismay.

"What happened?" he demanded.

"Dashiel, you're still here. Thank heaven!"

"Of course I am! What's going on? Are you hurt?"

"Nothing serious," said Hermann, with a dismissive little wave. "Just a minor contusion. I took your advice and wrote that letter. Left it in front of the shabti case in the morning with a little food offering. Just a bit of cheese Danish. Not traditional, of course, but it was what I had on hand. And, oh, my, it certainly seems to have gotten our ghost's attention!"

Dashiel snatched up his cane and stumped over to Hermann with as much speed as he could muster. "Christ almighty! What did it do to you?"

"It threw the book at me," said Hermann. "Quite literally, I might add." He grinned, clearly amused with himself despite how shaken he was.

Dashiel gaped at him in horror. "What are you talking about? What book?"

"A very dry volume on animal husbandry in the Eighteenth Dynasty. I wouldn't recommend it. I was in the archive, pulling texts for the Middle Egyptian exam next week, when all of a sudden—"

"Hush, let me see." Hermann was still pressing the handkerchief to his cheek. Dashiel grabbed his hand and gently pulled it away, revealing a scrape over his cheekbone with an angry purple bruise blooming beneath it. He sucked in his breath through his teeth. "Hermann, for God's sake!"

"Oh, I'm all right, I'm all right," Hermann assured him, but he made no attempt to move away. "It's nothing. I'll put an ice bag on it. How's your leg?"

"What? Fine. Stiff as a board, but it'll limber up again. Hermann . . ."

"Good." Hermann flashed him a shy smile, then took a step back. Dashiel let go of his hand. "I'll get supper on."

He walked into the kitchen, and Dashiel limped after him, dismayed. "But . . . this is crazy, Hermann! That thing could have really hurt you. Hell, it did really hurt you. You didn't tell me it could throw things."

"I didn't know!"

"What did you say in that letter, anyway?"

"Why, just what you suggested. I asked it what it wanted. Kept it short and to the point. I was very polite about it, though. I certainly don't see any reason why it would take offense."

Dashiel took hold of his elbow. "Listen, you can't go back there. You just can't. It's too dangerous."

Hermann turned back to him, surprised. "I work there, Dashiel. I have to go back! I've got research to do, coursework to prepare. And someone has to care for the collection. My colleagues certainly wouldn't know what to do with it, they're all classicists and biblical scholars. Half of them wouldn't know a *was*-scepter from a *djed*-pillar. What's this?" He held up the baking dish, which Dashiel had left sitting on the dining table.

Dashiel blinked, disoriented by the sudden turn in the conversation. In the excitement, he'd completely forgotten about the morning's visitor. "What? Oh, yes. A woman came by and left that for you. Mrs. Larkin or Limpet or something." The strain of the past few days was taking its toll. That wasn't the kind of detail that would usually have escaped his memory.

Hermann clapped a hand to his brow. "Oh, no, Mrs. Luckett! I completely forgot. She must be worried half to death. Excuse me a moment, Dashiel, I have to give her a ring."

He darted into the living room, and Dashiel sank down onto a kitchen chair, deeply disquieted. He half-listened to Hermann's conversation in the next room, which drifted into the kitchen in quiet bits and pieces.

"I'm sorry, Lucille, dear . . . I know, I know, I should have called. I was so tired yesterday, I plum forgot. Yes, my students are running me ragged. Pardon? Oh, but last week was Yom Kippur, I thought you knew . . ."

Dashiel ground his teeth. He wanted to kick something. Once again, his ill-informed advice had only made things worse, and now he'd put Hermann in danger.

He couldn't leave, he realized.

Not now. But damned if he had the slightest idea of how to make things right.

Hermann's voice filtered into his awareness again. "He's doing a fantastic job, isn't he? No, never in a million years did I think I'd vote for a Democrat, and now I've done it twice in a row. I can just imagine what Papa would say. Gosh, if only Al Smith had gotten in back in twenty-eight, the country might not be such a mess right now . . ."

If Porphyrio were going to come looking for him here, he decided, he probably would have done so by now. Anyway, he had bigger fish to fry. He'd just stay a few more days, that's all. Long enough to do something, even if it was only to talk Hermann out of this cockamamie notion that he could keep carrying on with his regular routine of hanging around that house of horrors every night after classes.

He got up and moved to the doorway, sensing that the telephone call was winding down. "Of course I'll sign it," Hermann said. He was sitting on the love seat, gingerly holding the receiver to his ear. Dashiel tried not to wince at the sight of his bruised and puffy cheek. "Bring it by any time. If I'm not around, slip it under the door, or knock—if my friend's still here, I'm sure he'll be happy to let you in. Same to you, dear . . . and I'll be there next week, I promise. Goodbye."

He hung up and met Dashiel's gaze with a weary smile. He looked utterly exhausted.

With a sigh, he said, "Bless my soul, I just don't know if I'm coming or going these days."

"Hermann," said Dashiel, "I'm not letting you face that thing alone again."

"But—"

"Now, listen. If I had my way, you wouldn't set foot in that godforsaken museum at all. Whatever's in there, it's worse than creepy. It's dangerous, and God only knows what it's capable of. But if you insist on going back, well . . . I'm going with you."

Hermann stared at him for a long moment, speechless. "I couldn't possibly ask you to do that," he said at last.

"That's all right." He gave Hermann a reassuring half-smile. "You aren't asking me, I'm volunteering."

CHAPTER 7

ASHIEL ARRIVED AT THE Wexler Building a little after
five-thirty the next evening. He didn't see the point in
hanging around the place all day while Hermann taught his classes. Besides, he figured that the less time he spent out and about,
the better—at least until he was quite sure that Porphyrio was no
longer a threat.

His leg was still stiff and sore, but it had recovered enough that
the short walk to campus was not inordinately difficult. He kept his
hat pulled low over his eyes and his collar turned up until he was
safe inside the building.

He headed straight for the third floor, giving the museum gallery a wide berth. As soon as he stepped out of the elevator, he
was greeted by the sounds of boisterous conversation coming from
Agnes's office. He recognized one of the voices as that of Frances,
the girl from Hermann's class.

"All I can say is, if the Sox aren't in the World Series next year,
someone's gonna be hearing from me."

"How long has it been, anyway?" came Agnes's reply.

"Hell if I know. Too long. I must have been in nursery school."

"Don't say that! You'll make me feel like an old lady."

Dashiel slid by as quietly as he could, intending to head straight
to Hermann's office. But despite his efforts, his arrival didn't go

undetected. "Give me a minute, Frances," Agnes said in a steely voice. Seconds later, the sharp click of her heels echoed in the hall behind him.

"Excuse me, mister," she said, drawing up alongside him. "Just a minute, please."

"Evening, Agnes," said Dashiel, tipping his hat.

Agnes frowned at him. "The building's about to close for the night, you know. We're locking up in about twenty minutes. And visitors are supposed to check in at the office."

"I know. Hermann asked me to meet him here."

She put a hand on his elbow, drawing him up short. "What's going on with Professor Goschalk?" she asked in a low voice.

"I'm not sure what you mean."

Agnes took a deep breath, visibly biting back her frustration. "Look," she said, "things have been getting weirder and weirder around here for months, and frankly, I'm worried about him. He was already acting a little flaky before you showed up, but ever since then he's been completely obsessed with this ghost business. Then he shows up this morning looking like he's had a run-in with Primo Carnera. Gets real cagey any time someone tries to ask him about it, too. And I'm sorry, but I can't believe it's a coincidence you turned up again right before it happened. Something's up, and if you know what it is, I'd sure like to know."

"Agnes, I can assure you that I had nothing to do with it, if that's what you're implying." *Not entirely true*, a nasty little inner voice piped up. "But frankly, I'm not sure you'd like the truth any better. I certainly don't."

She narrowed her eyes. "I hope you're not trying to tell me it was a ghost that slugged him," she began, "because I don't believe for a minute—"

"Ah, Agnes," someone called out from behind them. Dashiel turned and saw a bald-headed gentleman striding toward them, looking red-faced and irritable. "Sorry to butt in, but I need you for a moment. Will you ring the custodian's office again? That buzzing noise in my office walls is driving me out of my head. There must be a hornet's nest in there. Either that, or something's gone wrong with the electrical wiring. In any case, it should have been looked at by now."

Agnes sighed. "Right away, Professor Birchwood." She stared daggers at Dashiel for a second before turning on her heel and marching back down the hall.

Dashiel found Hermann's office door open when he rounded the corner.

Hermann sat at his desk, his wire-rimmed spectacles perched on the end of his nose, examining an object in a small box. The bruise on his cheek had darkened to a deep purple hue.

Noticing Dashiel's presence in the doorway, he looked up. "Oh, hello, Dashiel." He broke into a warm smile. "I just need to gather my things, and we can head down to the research archive. That is, if you still want to go."

"I wouldn't have come if I didn't," said Dashiel, although "want" was too strong a word. "Are you sure you can't just wait and do this work during daylight hours, though?"

Hermann shook his head. "I really can't put it off any longer. As it is, I spent every spare moment I had today researching ancient Egyptian methods for dealing with malignant spirits when I should have been pulling texts for my Demotic class."

Dashiel found himself intrigued. "Oh? Did you find anything useful?"

"It's hard to say. I turned up a warding spell from one of the medical papyri, but I'm not sure I'd be able to pull it off. For one thing, I don't know how to tie the required amuletic knots. And it involves ingredients I don't have access to."

"Such as?"

"Let's see," said Hermann, picking up a sheet of paper on which he'd scribbled some notes. "The hair of a dun-colored donkey, for one. And the liver of a turtle."

"Hmm." Dashiel pondered for a moment. "Well, I can't help you with the donkey hair, but I remember seeing a lily pond over by the dining hall last time I was on campus. I imagine there'd be plenty of turtles there this time of year."

Hermann gaped at him, appalled. "Dashiel! I hope you're not seriously suggesting I go out and murder one of those sweet little turtles."

"Wouldn't be my first choice, either," Dashiel admitted, "but I thought I'd mention it."

"I know those turtles. I eat my lunch by that pond almost every day when the weather's nice. They're very fond of turnip and carrot salad. No, I'm afraid that's where I draw the line. I don't care if they are the earthly representatives of Set."

Dashiel raised his hands in surrender. "Understood. Ixnay to the turtle plan."

"Anyway, I may have found something better. A good temporary measure, at least."

"Really? What's that?"

Hermann scooped up the little object from the box in front of him and displayed it to Dashiel. It was a clay figurine of a rearing cobra.

"It's a uraeus amulet. A protective talisman. I'm sure you've seen this little snake on the brow of Pharaoh in statuary and reliefs and so on, but ordinary people also used them around the home to ward off unwanted visitors from the realm of the dead. I thought I'd take it along to the archive this evening while I finish preparing my exams."

"You really think that'll help?" Dashiel asked, giving the object a dubious look. It was a crude and lopsided little thing, with a vacant, dopey look in its eye. It didn't exactly radiate power and majesty.

Hermann shrugged and set the snake back in its box. "Well, it's worth a shot. Maybe our friend will be less likely to chuck books at my head if little Wadjet is there to keep an eye on things. Besides, given its penchant for reanimating mummified mongooses, I suspect it doesn't like snakes very much." He began shoving books and papers into his briefcase.

"I'm not sure I follow."

"Venomous snakes were considered a formidable danger both in this world and the next," said Hermann. "The mongoose is one of their few natural predators."

Dashiel nodded. It made about as much sense as anything else he'd heard in the past few days. The whole situation felt downright farcical, yet his flesh was creeping with dread at the thought of what might be in store for them in the archive. He wasn't about to turn up his nose at any possible measure of protection, no matter how far-fetched.

Hermann rose, gathering up his briefcase and the box with the snake amulet. "All right," he said, squaring his shoulders like a soldier preparing to march into battle, "shall we go?"

⁂

THEY STEPPED INTO the reading room, and Hermann pulled the door shut behind them. "I'm not used to having company while I do this," he said cheerfully, setting his briefcase and the clay snake down on one of the reading tables. "Not of the living kind, anyway. Make yourself at home. I'll try not to be long."

The student that Dashiel had seen last time they were in the archive was in the same spot he had occupied before, at the far end of the room. He sat slumped over the table with his head resting on the pages of an open book, snoring sonorously. Hermann bustled over and gave his shoulder a gentle nudge. The young man sat up with a snort.

"Time to go home, Aloysius," said Hermann. "It's after hours, and you're drooling on the Medinet Habu plates again."

"Sorry, Professor," mumbled Aloysius. He blinked the sleep from his eyes, then gave a little shudder before rising to his feet. "Gee, every time I fall asleep in here lately, I have the weirdest dreams!"

With Aloysius dispatched, Hermann came back to the spot where he'd laid his things and busied himself pulling books off a nearby shelf. Dashiel sat down across from his place at the table, feeling ill at ease and prickly all over. The sun inched its way down toward the horizon, painting the bookshelves that lined the walls with burnished gold.

The next twenty minutes or so passed in companionable silence. Hermann settled in with several books spread out in front of him. He opened one of them and flipped through it until he found a plate depicting a hieroglyphic text carved on a round-topped slab of stone.

Dashiel watched as Hermann copied lines of hieroglyphs in a flowing and elegant hand, then scrawled his exam questions beneath them. His feeling of disquietude began to ease as the minutes crawled by without incident. He sighed softly through his nose and rested his chin on his hand, enjoying the tranquility of the moment.

"I hope you're not too bored," said Hermann, glancing up at him over the tops of his spectacles. "I'm afraid it's pretty dull around here before sunset."

Dashiel smiled, settling back in his seat. "Dull is fine by me. I've had about all the excitement I can stand these past few days."

The sun sank out of view, and the shadows crowded in around them. Hermann leaned over and switched on the reading lamp in the middle of the table. Dashiel felt so pleasantly at ease in his quiet company that he almost wondered if he'd been working himself up into a lather over nothing. His eyelids grew heavy.

A hush fell over the room that amplified the smallest noises— the scratching of Hermann's pencil on his pad of paper, the soft sounds of both men breathing, the distant rumble and wail of a passing train. Night creatures began to stir and chirp outside.

And then, underneath it all, another sound, something dry and rustling and almost inaudible, like onionskin being rubbed between calloused fingers. It seemed like a noise cobbled together from the natural ambiance of the room rather than a sound with a distinct source of its own.

Dashiel felt the hairs on his arms and neck rise, and he slowly straightened in his chair. The rustling coalesced into a whisper, so low and indistinct at first that he thought he must be imagining it. But then he glanced at Hermann and saw that he, too, was listening, tense and still, his writing hand frozen with the tip of the pencil hovering over the paper.

Dashiel could make out the merest suggestion of words now, in a language that sounded utterly alien to him. The voice was feeble and faint, like a distorted radio transmission obscured under swirling drifts of static. He caught a whiff of a foul, cloying odor.

Out of the corner of his eye, he saw something moving among the deepening shadows by the front door of the reading room. A bit of shadow detached itself from the rest and drifted toward them.

Heart in his throat, Dashiel laid a trembling hand atop Hermann's. Hermann drew in a breath to say something, but Dashiel shook his head. He gestured toward the shadow thing with a subtle tilt of his chin.

Slowly, Hermann turned his head to glance over his shoulder. The color drained from his face, putting his dark bruise in stark relief. He picked up the snake amulet with his free hand and cleared his throat.

"Hello," he said. The sound of his voice was so jarring in the crowded near-silence of the room that Dashiel flinched in his seat. "Er, *nedj her-ek*. Oh, dear, I doubt I'm pronouncing that correctly."

The thing grew still and blended back into the shadows around it, becoming nearly invisible. The whispering quieted.

"Listen," Hermann went on, "I haven't the slightest idea if you can understand me right now, but I want you to know that we mean you no harm. However, you should also know that we are here under the protection of the goddess. She has fire in her jaws, and I'm afraid she will most definitely burn you to a crisp if you try to attack us." He raised the little snake amulet in his quivering hand.

Even in his panicked state, the notion of this eldritch horror being cowed by a goggle-eyed clay snake filled Dashiel with a sort of grotesque amusement. He bit his knuckle to stifle a burst of mirthless, hysterical laughter. But, to his astonishment, the shadow thing shrank back.

"It's all right. We just want to know what it is you want," Hermann said, lowering the snake. "That's all."

For an endless moment, the room was silent. Then the entity gathered the surrounding darkness into itself, congealing into something suggestive of a human form. It glided smoothly and silently closer to them, like the shadow of a tree outside the window being propelled across the room by the headlamps of a passing car.

"Don't," Dashiel tried to whisper, but only a breathless croak came out. He tightened his grip on Hermann's hand and felt a reassuring stroke of Hermann's thumb over his knuckles in response.

The thing was upon them now, hovering soundlessly at the end of the table, just a few scant feet away from where they sat. The beams in the walls around them groaned and creaked, and a subtle tremor passed beneath their feet that Dashiel could feel all the way into the marrow of his bones. The reading lamp on the table hummed and flickered.

Hermann's briefcase lay on the table to his left, near his pile of books and papers. Something rustled inside of it. An ink pen wiggled its way out of the open top of the bag, moving seemingly of its own volition. It clattered onto the table and rolled toward them in a series of short, jerky movements.

Then, under some kind of immense but invisible pressure, the barrel of the pen imploded in a spray of red ink and a shower of stinging celluloid shrapnel. Hermann gave a shuddering gasp and squeezed his eyes shut for a second, staying resolutely in his seat.

The two men watched in silent horror as the ink smeared across Hermann's notes as if dragged by invisible fingers. It formed a few crude shapes, then trailed off in a wobbly line that slipped off the edge of the paper and ended in an incoherent smudge on the table. Whatever was producing the marks seemed to lack the strength or the dexterity to keep going. The humming of the reading lamp grew louder, then the bulb blew out with a quiet pop.

The whispering returned, almost unbearably loud, sounding this time like a rustling thunder within Dashiel's skull. He clutched at his brow with his free hand, his breath coming in short, panicked gasps. The edge of his vision began to blur.

Just when he was certain he was going to faint, the sound went quiet, and there was a subtle brightening of the atmosphere in the room.

The thing was gone.

Hermann leaped to his feet, and his chair toppled to the floor behind him. His face and collar were spattered with droplets of red ink. "Dashiel, are you all right?" he quavered.

"I think so," Dashiel managed to whisper. "You?"

"Fine, fine. Just a bit rattled. Goodness, wasn't that a hell of a thing!"

"You have a gift for understatement, Hermann," said Dashiel. His teeth were chattering.

He let go of Hermann's hand and fumbled for his handkerchief, then wiped his face with it. The handkerchief came away streaked with red.

Hermann's eyes glittered with fear and excitement. "It was trying to write something, I'm sure of it. Did you see that?" He pulled the ink-smudged paper close to himself, his glance flicking rapidly back and forth across the page. "I just can't make it out, it's such a mess."

A peculiar thought wormed its way into Dashiel's fear-numbed brain. "It's a spirit," he murmured, twisting the handkerchief absently in his hands. "It can only do so much on its own. If it's going to communicate with us . . . it's going to need help."

Hermann slowly lifted his gaze to Dashiel's face. "You mean—"

Dashiel stared back at him, dazed. The words seemed to tumble from his mouth of their own accord. "It needs a medium."

Before Hermann could answer, the building groaned again, and they heard a distant, low keening from somewhere below them.

"Time to go," Hermann said in a small voice.

Dashiel assented with a quick nod. Without another word, Hermann gathered up his ink-smeared papers and shoved them haphazardly into his bag. Dashiel grabbed the snake amulet and its box and fumbled them into the pocket of his jacket. Leaving the pile of books and the ruined pen on the table, they dashed for the exit.

They stumbled to a stop in front of the elevator door. Hermann reached for the button, but Dashiel laid an arresting hand on his arm. He could all too easily imagine that shadow monster oozing in under the door the moment it slid closed, cornering them in the claustrophobic confines of the elevator.

It was clear from the look on Hermann's face that the same thought had occurred to him. "We'll take the stairs," he said.

As they began their descent to the ground floor, Dashiel felt slower and clumsier than ever.

For a dizzying moment, he was convinced that he would lose his footing and tumble down the stairs, leaving them at the mercy of the ghost. But then a sense of numb serenity settled over him. One step at a time, with Hermann's hand on his elbow, he made the endless journey to the lobby. Before he knew it, they were both stumbling out the front door of the building and into the cool night air.

Hermann's little blue Model A coupe was parked on the street not far from the building. In a daze, Dashiel followed him to it. They clambered in and pulled the doors shut, then sat there in stunned silence.

Hermann gripped the steering wheel with trembling hands and stared straight ahead, struggling to catch his breath. Dashiel turned to look back at the building behind them, afraid he would see a shadowy form drifting toward them through the night, but saw nothing out of the ordinary.

"You don't think it could follow us, do you?" he asked once he'd found his voice.

"Oh, no, I don't think so," Hermann panted. "I'm quite sure it's tied to the shabti. It won't wander far from the museum."

Dashiel leaned against the backrest of the passenger seat and closed his eyes, waiting for his heartbeat to slow down and his legs to stop shaking. His pulse pounded in his ears.

"Dashiel," said Hermann, "when you said it needed a medium, did you mean . . ."

He shook his head, his eyes still shut tight. "Not me, if that's what you're thinking. I'm not a real medium, it wouldn't do any good. Forget it, it was just the first dumb thought that popped into my head while I was sitting there, scared out of my wits."

He heard a quiet movement beside him and opened his eyes. Hermann had turned toward him and was regarding him with a strange intensity he'd never seen before.

"Good," Hermann said. "I wouldn't want you to try it, even if it could work. Especially if it could. I can't stand to think of what that thing might do to you if you just . . . invited it in like that." He laid his hand on the seat between them, close to Dashiel's knee. "God forbid anything should happen to you, Dashiel."

A torrent of emotion swept over him.

Fear and loneliness had been Dashiel's constant companions for so long that he'd grown used to them, but the events of the last few days had turned them into a pair of crushing behemoths that were impossible to ignore.

He hadn't realized, until that moment, how desperately he needed a friendly shoulder to lean on.

Before he could stop to think about what he was doing, he flung his arms around Hermann and pulled him into a tight embrace.

For a brief instant, he held him close, savoring his warmth, the softness of his hair against his cheek, and the gentle thrum of his heart against his own chest.

Hermann drew in his breath in a startled gasp, and reason abruptly returned. Chagrined, Dashiel let go and retreated to his side of the seat. Hermann stared at him, wide-eyed, with an expression on his face that he couldn't quite read.

"I'm sorry," Dashiel mumbled, rubbing his aching eyes with the heels of his hands. "Don't know what came over me. This thing's got me so shaken up I can't think straight."

"Don't be silly, Dashiel!" said Hermann. "Come here." He opened his arms, and Dashiel gratefully sank into them. "No more ghosts tonight," he went on, muffled by Dashiel's collar. "Let's not say another word about it. We'll go home and have dinner and sit by the fire with something warm to drink, and we won't worry about any of this again until tomorrow."

Dashiel was too overcome to answer right away. He clung to Hermann for a lingering moment, bunching the fabric of his jacket in his clenched hands.

Then, with a monumental effort of will, he pulled away. "That sounds just fine to me."

NEITHER OF THEM spoke again until after they'd stepped into the apartment and hung up their ink-spattered jackets.

"Shall I make us something to eat?" Hermann asked.

"I don't have much of an appetite."

"To tell you the truth, neither do I. But we need a distraction. How are you at gin rummy?"

For the first time that evening, Dashiel laughed. "You don't want to play cards with me, Hermann. I don't think I could remember how to play without cheating if I tried."

"Checkers, then. And at least have a hot toddy with me."

Dashiel nodded. He had little interest in playing checkers, or anything else, for that matter, but Hermann was right. He sorely needed a distraction. Going to sleep was out of the question, and the last thing he wanted was to be by himself.

What he really wanted to do was to crawl back into Hermann's comforting arms and stay there, but that shot was off the board. He had no desire to toy with Hermann's feelings, and he couldn't afford to be reckless with his own. He forced himself to stop thinking about how good it had felt to hold him and how much he longed to do it again.

A short while later, they sat huddled over the checkerboard together at the little dining table, a steaming mug beside each of them. The muted sounds of a dance music orchestra floated in from the radio in the next room, softening the tense silence. It all should have been perfectly cozy, but Dashiel was still on edge, his nerves humming.

Every passing shadow cast by the world outside the kitchen window set his heart racing again.

"Your turn, Dashiel," said Hermann.

"So it is." He stared blankly at the board, not really seeing the pieces in front of him. "Where'd you get that shabti thing, anyway? What do you know about it?"

Hermann clicked his tongue. "No ghost talk, remember?" he chided.

"I'm not talking about the ghost, just the shabti."

"Same thing," said Hermann, "and I don't know much about it, really. It was a gift, like most of the collection. Very little of it is provenanced, I'm sorry to say. Almost everything we have came from a wealthy benefactor who donated his private collection to the university about fifteen years ago. They didn't have anyone who specialized in Egypt at the time, but they couldn't very well turn it down, so they had to hire someone to manage it all." He smiled. "That's where I came in."

"So, why is this thing causing trouble all of a sudden?"

"The shabti is relatively new. An anonymous donation from another private collector. Those still come in from time to time. All I know about it is that it was purchased in Cairo sometime before the war, back before the Antiquities Service started really cracking down on that sort of thing."

"Could you send it back?"

"To Egypt, you mean?" Hermann shook his head. "Oh, they wouldn't want it. Little faience shabtis like that are a dime a dozen. Besides, I wouldn't wish that thing on anyone else."

"Maybe you could destroy it. Bury it somewhere or throw it into Lake Michigan or something."

Hermann looked scandalized. "That's like asking a doctor to poison one of his patients! My job is to preserve the past, not to destroy it."

"Seems to me that these are exceptional circumstances. It's not like that thing has any interest in your well-being."

"No, no," Hermann said, waving the notion away. "That would be an absolute last resort." He looked thoughtful. "I did consider trying an execration ritual on it, but I think I'd need to know the owner's name for that. And besides, I'd much rather help whomever it is if I can."

"Help it?" said Dashiel, frowning. "What makes you think this thing needs help?"

"You saw what happened tonight," Hermann said earnestly. "It was trying to tell us something. Why go to the trouble, if all it wants is to cause chaos? The ancient Egyptians believed that ghosts could be reasoned with. When they started hassling living people, it was because they wanted or needed something. Usually, they were looking for help rectifying some injustice that had happened to them when they were alive. If we could only figure out a way to help it communicate—a safe way, I mean—"

"Hold on," Dashiel cut in. "You said you needed its name to do that ritual you were talking about. Doesn't the shabti have writing on it? Have you tried to decipher it?"

"Oh, naturally. That was one of the first things I did. But it's just a standard formula, nothing special as far as I can tell. The usual boilerplate stuff about how the shabti will stand in for its owner if he's called upon to do labor for the gods in the afterlife."

"Labor? What kind of labor?"

"The same sorts of things one might have to do in life. You know, corvée work. Quarrying stone or ferrying sand around. Whatever kind of work happens to be needed."

This struck Dashiel as an odd way for people to be spending their afterlives, but he wasn't in the mood to question it. "So, no name, then? No hint of who this person might have been?"

"There is a name, but it's mostly worn off, I'm afraid. All I could make out was Amun-something."

"Well, that's a lead, isn't it?" said Dashiel. "How many Amun-somethings could there be?"

To his surprise, Hermann burst out laughing. "Oy vey, Dashiel," he said. "This is the Eighteenth Dynasty we're talking about. Probably Thebes, at that. Everyone was an Amun-something. You might as well try to track someone down when your only lead is that their given name is Bill."

Dashiel shrugged and swallowed his frustration. He felt like he was groping his way through a maze, taking one promising turn after another, only to find himself back in the same place where he'd started. "Well, it was a thought."

"And a good one, too," said Hermann, growing solemn again. "I'm sorry, I shouldn't have laughed. I'm just—I'm just so very tired." He folded his hands in front of him on the table and rested his forehead on them.

Dashiel was overcome by the urge to reach out and stroke Hermann's hair, to tell him everything would be all right. Instead, he watched him in silence from across the neglected checkerboard, at a loss for what to say or do. He'd spent half a lifetime giving people false comfort. Now he wanted more than anything to offer the real thing, and there wasn't a shred of it to be found.

Hermann raised his head after a moment and took a deep breath, collecting himself. "Anyway," he said, "I've decided to consult my friend, Louis Speleers, in Belgium. He's more of a shabti man than I am. I took a picture of it, and as soon as the prints come in, I'm going to send it off to him. Maybe he can tell me if there's anything out of the ordinary about it."

"And, in the meantime?" asked Dashiel.

Hermann sighed and gave him a quick pat on the wrist. "That's enough worry for now. Go ahead, Dashiel. Make your move."

"Things can't go on like this. We have to do something, and soon. I don't think we can wait for a letter from Belgium." He picked up one of his pieces and plunked it down on a new square, too distracted to give strategy a passing thought.

"I know that," said Hermann, staring down at the board. "But let's say we do find a solution to all this, and somehow lay the spirit to rest. What will you do then? Are you still planning to go to California?"

"Well—I mean, yes, of course," said Dashiel. The notion of staying on longer hadn't even occurred to him. He was unsettled by how much it appealed to him. "I've already been here far too long."

"You're absolutely set on leaving, then."

"I really don't have a choice. Even if this person who's been looking for me has already moved on, it's only a matter of time before he catches up. If not him, somebody else. I made a lot of enemies when I renounced Spiritualism, and these people are completely without scruples. I ought to know. I was one of the worst of them. No, I'm afraid I must keep moving. Just as soon as I'm back on my feet and you're out of the woods, anyway."

Hermann turned his face away for a moment. "And . . . would I ever see you again?"

"I don't know." His heart sank as he said it, but he owed Hermann an honest answer. "I'm sorry, Hermann, I just can't say."

"Well, then," Hermann said haltingly, as he skipped one of his pieces over Dashiel's and plucked the captured token off the board, "if—if that's how it has to be, it seems to me that we ought to enjoy each other's company as much as we can in the time we have."

Dashiel sat back and stared at him. "What do you mean?"

Hermann turned scarlet, but he lifted his chin and boldly met Dashiel's eye. "Why, I mean just what I said. Right now, we need each other, Dashiel. Whatever else happens after it's all done, I believe we're meant to get through this business together. So, let's make the best of it."

Dashiel's face felt as hot as Hermann's looked. He leaned forward in his seat and slid his hand across the table toward Hermann's until their fingertips nearly touched, then stopped short. His heart beat erratically, suspended in a strange limbo between elation and despair. "Goddamnit, Hermann," he said desperately, "no, listen. I promised myself I wouldn't—"

"You wouldn't what?" Hermann urged. His fingers closed around Dashiel's. "Tell me."

"Oh, hell, it's too late anyway." Dashiel pushed back his chair and swiftly stepped around the table to the other side, where Hermann was already rising to meet him. He slipped one hand around the back of Hermann's neck and let the other one come to rest on the small of his back, then pulled him close and kissed him. Hermann wrapped his arms around Dashiel and held on to him, like a shipwrecked passenger clinging to a life preserver.

CHAPTER 8

I T HAD BEEN A FEW years since Dashiel had awoken in another man's bed, and even longer since he'd last felt so good about it. Even before he opened his eyes, he felt Hermann's peaceful presence beside him, and an unfamiliar glow of well-being flooded through him. It was almost comical, he reflected, how fast his resolve had crumbled. The rational part of his brain knew this had all been a terrible idea, but he couldn't bring himself to care.

He rolled over and sat up gingerly. The clock on the nightstand informed him that it was just past nine, and the room was bright with mid-morning sunbeams. Hermann was still sleeping. He looked serene and lovely, and somehow younger, without his usual stuffy brown tweeds and starched collar. Unable to help himself, Dashiel leaned down and lightly kissed his bare collarbone.

Hermann stirred, opened his eyes, and beamed up at him. "Good morning, Dashiel," he murmured. His voice was husky with sleep.

"You're still here," Dashiel said, reaching out to smooth back his tousled hair. "Not that I'm complaining. I just thought you'd be up with the dawn and off to campus by now."

"Oh, no. Today is Friday. I only have two classes, and the first one doesn't start 'til eleven. I don't intend to arrive any earlier or stay any later than I must."

"No late hours in the archive or the gallery, then?" asked Dashiel, with more than a little trepidation.

"Absolutely not. I have everything I need to finish preparing my exams at home. Once I'm done with classes, I see no reason to go anywhere near that godforsaken place again until Monday. I'm not letting any spectral third wheels spoil our weekend." He laid a soft hand on Dashiel's face and brushed his thumb across his cheek. "I'm so glad you're here, Dashiel."

Dashiel smiled. "So am I." He leaned in and pressed a tender kiss to Hermann's lips, then his cheek, then the curve of his jaw.

Hermann closed his eyes and tilted his head back, letting out a blissful sigh. "Listen, I've been thinking . . ."

Dashiel continued kissing him, working his way down his neck. "Mmm. I've been trying not to."

"Believe me," said Hermann, winding his arms around Dashiel's neck, "I'd stop if I could. But I just can't shake off what you said last night. About the ghost needing a medium, I mean. I know you don't want to channel it, and heaven knows I don't want you to try. But aren't there other methods? Ones that don't involve letting the spirit steer the ship, so to speak? Some of the things you did during that demonstration of yours—"

"Hermann." Dashiel pulled back to gaze at him with a mixture of amusement and exasperation. "You know I can't really do any of those things. That trance stuff I told you about the other day is the realest thing I ever learned, and that's not saying much."

"Of course, I understand that. But let's just assume, hypothetically speaking, that some of those methods might be possible under the right conditions. How would you go about giving our ghost a voice?"

Dashiel frowned thoughtfully. "Well, if you're talking about a literal voice, there's what we call 'direct-voice mediumship.' The idea is that you use a trumpet to amplify spirit sounds, instead of having the ghost speak through the medium. But even if we could get it to talk through one of my old spirit trumpets, it wouldn't do us much good if you can't understand what it's saying, would it?"

"True enough," sighed Hermann. "What we really need is to give it a way to communicate in writing. If we could do that, we'd be on velvet."

"Or silk."

"Pardon?"

"Precipitations on silk," said Dashiel. "When I was a working medium, it was one of my favorite gimmicks. You have the sitter lay out a piece of silk in the middle of the séance circle, and everyone prays and sings over it. All in total darkness, of course. When the lights finally come up, there's a message from a spirit written on it, or sometimes a picture. That one was a real showstopper. Always brought the house down."

Hermann's face lit up. "Yes, now I remember you mentioning that! You'd swap out the blank silks for ones you'd marked up in advance. But if you were going to attempt it, you know, for real—"

"I suppose we could put out a piece of silk for it and see what happens," Dashiel said with a shrug. "Problem is, even if it could work, it would be up to the ghost to figure out what to do with it, not me. And after seeing what it did with a pen and paper, I don't have a great deal of confidence."

"Then there's nothing you could do, theoretically, to help it along?"

Dashiel shook his head. "The medium's role in that sort of physical manifestation is supposed to be passive. I read a whole treatise about it back in the day. Don't know if I've ever seen so much nonsensical bloviating shoved into a single pamphlet." He spread his hands and spoke in a low, mysterious tone. "The spirit manipulates the magnetic vibrations that emanate from the medium's body in order to move ponderable objects and effect changes in the physical realm."

Hermann shivered and touched his bruised cheek. "Well, it doesn't need anyone's help moving ponderable objects."

"It certainly doesn't. Anyway, even if we assume it's not all hooey, manifestation mediumship isn't really a skill you can cultivate. Either you vibrate at the right frequency, or you don't. And I have no reason to think my vibrations are any more special than anyone else's."

"Oh, now, I wouldn't say that," said Hermann, the corners of his eyes crinkling with an affectionate smile. "I think your vibrations are glorious."

Dashiel laughed. "Shucks, Hermann, I'll bet you say that to all the mediums." He pulled Hermann in for a slow, luxurious kiss. Hermann caressed his shoulders and chest, sending pleasurable shivers down his spine. His hands were just making their way further south when a vigorous knock sounded on the front door. Both men flinched and bolted apart as if someone had dashed a bucket of cold water over their heads.

"Oy, gevalt!" said Hermann, pressing a hand to his chest. "That nearly gave me a coronary. Wait here, I'll go see who it is."

He started to get up, but Dashiel grabbed his hand. "Be careful."

"I'm sure it's just Mrs. Luckett," said Hermann. He smiled and gave Dashiel's hand a reassuring squeeze. "She said she'd be coming by." He began pulling on his pajamas and dressing gown. "Be with you in a moment!"

Horatio, who had been curled up in a square of sunlight by the end of the bed, jumped up and trotted to the bedroom door, meowing hopefully.

Dashiel sat on the edge of the bed, his heart racing and his hands clammy with anxiety, and listened as Hermann padded across the apartment. There was a brief pause, then the sound of the bolt sliding in the lock and the door opening.

"Ms. Lucille, good morning! Do come in," Hermann said a moment later. Dashiel slumped with relief, then got up and began dressing quietly.

"Why, Hermann! What in the world happened to your face?" Mrs. Luckett's voice piped up. "Who did this to you?"

"Oh, this? It was more of a 'what' than a 'who.' Just a silly accident. I'm embarrassed to say . . ."

"My word, you do worry me, Mr. Hermann. I wish you'd tell me what's been going on."

"Really, dear, it's nothing at all. Just a lot of late nights doing research and marking papers. I always become a bit of a klutz when I don't get enough sleep. It'll all be better once exams are over. Can I get you something? Coffee? Tea?"

"Thank you, honey, but I can't stay. I just wanted to bring this by before my shift."

Dashiel slipped out of Hermann's bedroom and across the hall to the spare room, where he hastily combed his hair and changed out of his ink-stained shirt. When he emerged a few minutes later, Hermann and Mrs. Luckett were still in the living room. Mrs. Luckett wore a crisp, impeccable nurse's uniform. Hermann stood leaning over the side table by his armchair, scribbling his signature on a piece of paper.

Mrs. Luckett greeted Dashiel with a polite nod. Her expression was pleasant but carefully composed. He had the distinct impression that she was on the qui vive. It occurred to him that she, like Agnes, might be pondering his role in the unfortunate condition of Hermann's face. He prickled with chagrin.

"Good morning, Mr. Quicke," she said. "How nice to see you again."

"Morning, Mrs. Luckett," Dashiel replied. "Likewise."

Hermann glanced up in surprise, then smiled broadly. "Goodness, I must be in a state," he said. "I completely forgot you two had met." He followed Dashiel's curious gaze to the paper he'd just signed. "Lucille is putting together a local NAACP unit. Why don't you leave the charter application with me, Lucille? I'm sure I could get at least fifteen more signatures if I bring it by the YMHA this afternoon after classes. You could come back and pick it up tomorrow."

She gave his arm a squeeze. "Oh, bless you, honey. Only if it's not too much trouble. It seems to me you've got more than enough on your plate as it is."

"It's the least I can do, dear. I must be the world's poorest excuse for a committee member. It's about time I started holding my end up." He turned to Dashiel. "Say, Dashiel, why don't you sign up too? We can use all the signatures we can get."

Dashiel raised his eyebrows, nonplussed. He'd made a lifelong habit of remaining staunchly apolitical.

The ghosts he'd manifested in his Spiritualist days tended to vaguely align themselves with whatever he'd managed to glean about the ideological leanings of his current sitter, but that was about the extent of it.

"Oh," he said. "I mean, I suppose I could. But I don't live around here, if that matters."

"You do for now," said Hermann, with a wink. He handed Dashiel the pen.

"All right. I don't see why not."

Mrs. Luckett smiled. "That's very good of you, Mr. Quicke. We just need your name and a local address. I won't collect any membership fees until I have enough signatures."

Dashiel scrawled his name on the list, just below Hermann's. Moving on to the adjacent blank, marked "Home Address," he hesitated for a moment. Then, feeling a spark of some emotion he couldn't quite define, he scratched in a ditto mark beneath Hermann's address.

※☆※

THE DAY DRAGGED on interminably after Hermann left for campus. Dashiel was used to being lonely, but this loneliness was a completely different sort of animal—a persistent, dull ache in his heart somehow distressing and pleasurable in equal measure. It was a sensation he hadn't experienced in so many years that he'd nearly forgotten what it felt like.

He considered going out for a walk to get his mind off things, but decided against it. He was fairly confident that Porphyrio must have moved on by now, but he saw no point in taking unnecessary risks.

He would hunker down at least for the remainder of the weekend, just to be safe.

Hermann arrived home around five that evening, looking chipper and rosy-cheeked, with a pile of envelopes tucked under his arm. Dashiel, who had been sprawled on the love seat reading while Horatio napped on his legs, eagerly rose to greet him.

"Good news and more good news," said Hermann. "I got twenty-two signatures for Lucille, and the prints of the shabti arrived today." He flourished a beige Kodak photo print envelope before tossing it onto the telephone table with the rest of the mail. "I'll get a letter off to Louis with a photograph of the little mamzer first thing Monday morning."

He hugged Dashiel close, then pulled back and regarded him with a sympathetic frown. "You must be going out of your mind, staying cooped up here all day."

"I suppose I have a mild case of cabin fever," Dashiel admitted, smiling. "But I don't mind. It's a small price to pay for keeping

Porphyrio off my tail. And I've got your company to look forward to at the end of the day."

Hermann gave a surprised chuckle. "Porphyrio! Is that his name? The one who's looking for you? Gosh, what a moniker."

"I thought I'd told you that," said Dashiel, feeling himself flush. He slid his arms around Hermann's waist. "Never mind, let's not talk about Porphyrio. He doesn't matter, anyway."

Hermann didn't answer, having turned his attention to a minor commotion that was playing out behind them. Horatio had jumped up onto the arm of the love seat and was sniffing intently at the pile of mail on the telephone table. He reached out a tiny paw to swat at the envelope on top. When the whole stack cascaded to the floor, Horatio shot straight up into the air before dashing from the room at a speed that Dashiel would not have thought possible for a cat of his build.

"Horatio, for heaven's sake," sighed Hermann. "I'm all for empirical research, but must you test the law of gravitation every day?"

"Any action on the ghost front?" Dashiel asked as they gathered up the scattered mail.

"No, but it never does much during daylight hours," said Hermann. "I did leave a silk hanky in the shabti case, though, along with a note asking the ghost to leave a message on it if possible. As powerful as it is, maybe it can do a precipitation under its own steam. I'm all agog to see what it'll throw at me next."

DASHIEL HAD NEVER been much of a home cook, but there was something undeniably appealing about the cozy domesticity of preparing a meal with Hermann. They stood elbow-to-elbow at the kitchen counter, and Dashiel chopped celery and peeled carrots while Hermann diced potatoes and groused fondly about his students.

Before long, the apartment was filled with the savory aroma of chicken soup simmering away on the stove. The sun crept down in the sky, and Hermann set a pair of white candles on the table and lit them. The pale yellow flames bobbed and swayed as the two of them bustled around the table, laying out the place settings.

"Listen, Dashiel," said Hermann. "As soon as you feel it's safe, I want to take you out somewhere."

"Oh? What did you have in mind?"

"I don't know. Whatever you'd like. Maybe we could go to the pictures or the theater. Have a nice dinner somewhere. Go out dancing. Anything, so long as it lets us forget about our troubles for a little while."

"Dancing, eh?" mused Dashiel. He smiled wryly. "Well, there was a time I was a regular Fred Astaire, but I'm afraid those days are behind me."

"Surely you can still slow dance, at least!"

"I suppose I probably could. But frankly, Willowvale doesn't strike me as the sort of town where a couple of fellas can go out dancing together anyway."

"It's not," Hermann said with a rueful smile. "I just like the idea of it, that's all."

Dashiel reached out and clasped his shoulders. "Listen, Hermann. Someday, when all this is over, we'll head down to Chicago together and visit Towertown. I'll take you to the Ballyhoo Café and show you a night of dancing and debauchery the likes of which the local yokels around here couldn't even begin to imagine. How does that sound?"

Hermann laughed softly. "I think I'd like that. I don't get nearly enough debauchery in my life."

"Well, we'll certainly have to do something about that. In the meantime, if you want to dance, I don't see why we can't do it right here. We have some time before dinner is ready, don't we?"

"Oh, yes. That soup ought to simmer for at least another half hour."

"Good. Go ahead and crank up the old Victrola, then. I'll try not to trample your toes too much."

Dashiel had not attempted to dance since before he was shot, but he was pleasantly surprised at how fast it came back to him. Hermann moved with a confident grace that somehow compensated perfectly for his own hobbled steps. They swayed along to a record of "What Is This Thing Called Love" that was, judging by the velvety patina of static that overlaid the music, quite well-loved.

"You're a good dancer, Hermann," Dashiel said, tucking his chin into the crook of Hermann's neck.

"Well! There's no need to sound so surprised about it," said Hermann, feigning indignation. "I'll have you know I was the toast of the social dance scene back in Milwaukee. The girls were practically falling over each other for the chance to cut a rug with old Hermann. Although looking back, I'm sure that was mostly because I always kept my hands strictly where they belonged."

"Quite the eligible bachelor, were you?"

He felt Hermann's smile against his cheek. "Oh yes. Perpetually. The whole thing drove my poor mother right around the bend. I'm sure she would have been thrilled if I'd ever gotten into the slightest bit of trouble with a girl, let alone gone steady with one."

"And the boys? Were they lining up to pencil their names in your dance card, too?"

"There was very little dancing with boys, I'm afraid," Hermann said. "Or much of anything else, for that matter. I didn't know where to go for that sort of thing back then, either. I've never been very good at . . . finding other people like me."

"That doesn't surprise me," said Dashiel. "I don't think there are many people like you. You're in a class by yourself."

"Hush, you. You know what I mean."

"Yes. I know."

"Well, what about you, Dashiel? You must have had all sorts of fascinating dance partners over the years."

Dashiel shook his head. "Nobody worth mentioning," he said firmly. "Certainly no one as interesting as you."

He stopped dancing and took Hermann's face in his hands. He leaned in and kissed him, lightly at first, then more deeply. Hermann's breath quickened against his cheek and his pulse throbbed under Dashiel's fingertips where they rested on the side of his throat. He slid his hands down to Dashiel's hips and gripped them tightly. The record came to an end and faded into a soft, rhythmic crackle of static, but they both ignored it, too absorbed in each other to notice.

Dashiel fumbled for the knot in Hermann's tie and had just managed to get it undone when Hermann abruptly broke the kiss and clutched his hands. Dashiel took a step back, surprised.

"Sorry," he said. "Was that too—"

"Shh," whispered Hermann. "No, it's not you. Look."

Slowly, Dashiel turned to look over his shoulder, following Hermann's gaze. Horatio sat hunkered in the doorway, ears flattened almost invisibly against his head, tail bristling like a bottle brush. Dashiel became aware of a low, guttural noise and realized the cat was growling.

"Something's not right," Hermann said. "This isn't like him."

He let go of Dashiel's hands and went to kneel in front of Horatio. He reached out to stroke the cat's head, but Horatio ducked away from his hand and continued growling, staring at a point somewhere behind Hermann, at the far end of the room.

Hermann's shoulders stiffened, and Dashiel knew instantly what he must be thinking.

"Hermann," he said, hesitant to even give voice to the thought, "you don't suppose—"

Hermann turned to meet his gaze, looking pale and tense. "I don't see how it could be possible. But the last time I saw him like this . . ." He trailed off.

The last sliver of sunlight slipped away, deep shadows taking its place. Dashiel darted to the doorway and flicked on the overhead light switch. They both waited, in silence, for something to happen.

The only sounds Dashiel could hear were the crackling hiss of the gramophone, the ticking of the clock on the mantel, and Horatio's quiet growling. Slowly, his taut muscles relaxed, and his breathing slowed. But, to his surprise, a sting of anger followed swiftly on the heels of his sense of relief. Hermann's home was the one place in the world where he felt safe. The thought that this undead nightmare could take even that away from him was maddening.

"This is ridiculous," he said. His voice sounded gruffer than he had intended. "Look at us, a couple of grown men, jumping at shadows. We can't let that thing bully us in our—your own home, especially when it's not even here!"

Hermann rose shakily to his feet. "You're probably right. I'm sorry, Dashiel, I wasn't trying to put a damper on our fun."

"That's all right," said Dashiel, softening his tone. "I didn't mean to snap like that, I'm not sore at you. This whole situation has me on edge, that's all. Listen, Horatio's probably just getting sick of me taking all your time and attention. Why don't I go get him a little cream or something, as a peace offering?"

Dashiel gently shooed Horatio toward the kitchen. The cat bolted away from him and he followed, leaving Hermann hovering by the doorway. Before he could grab the cream, Horatio somehow squeezed his rotund little body behind the icebox.

"Come on, now, kitty, what's wrong?" he asked. He took the cream out of the icebox and poured a dollop into Horatio's bowl. "Come out and get some cream."

He crouched down and waved the bowl in front of the space beneath the icebox, clicking his tongue coaxingly. Horatio made a little disconcerted humming noise, but he made no move to emerge.

"All right, suit yourself," said Dashiel, frowning. "But I wish you'd cut it out. You're scaring your pop. Not to mention me."

He straightened up, sniffing the air. The atmosphere in the kitchen was still heavy with the scents of chicken, garlic, and simmering vegetables, but there was an underlying odor—something pungent, sweet, and sickly, lingering just on the edges of his perception. Out of the corner of his eye, he saw the candles on the table guttering. His heart sank.

Warily, his skin crawling, he began backing out of the kitchen. Just as he bumped up against the edge of the doorway, Hermann's hand closed around his upper arm.

"Dashiel," Hermann hissed, "come here. Listen."

Hermann led him to the gramophone, where the record still spun away on the turntable. Dashiel leaned in close, listening. Mingled with the hiss of the needle, sliding over the empty final groove, there was a softer noise—a whispered phrase in a language he couldn't understand, repeated again and again in a muffled, rhythmic chant. His arms and neck burst out in gooseflesh.

"I don't understand," said Hermann. They stood clinging to each other, staring in horror at the record. "My God, I didn't think it could find us here, Dashiel, I really didn't."

"What's it saying?"

"It's too distorted, I can't—"

There was a soft sound from the other side of the room, and they both snapped their heads around to look. The pile of mail had fallen from the telephone table and scattered on the floor. The Kodak envelope lay closest to them, and the top flap had come undone. The corners of the photographs inside poked out of the opening.

"Oh," said Hermann, a look of horrified realization dawning on his face. "No."

"What is it?" Dashiel started to say, but the words died on his lips. A thick, dark vapor was seeping out of the envelope, pooling and eddying on the floor like black ink poured into a glass of water.

Before he could object, Hermann pushed away from him and darted for the envelope. Snatching it up, he swiftly hurled it into the lit fireplace. As he did so, something small and white fluttered to the floor at his feet. The corners of the envelope curled and twisted, and it was soon engulfed in strangely colored flames. Briefly, the inky tendrils still oozing from the envelope writhed wildly around it before sinking down into the glowing embers and vanishing. The distorted hissing of the record rose to a high-pitched, piercing keen, then abruptly stopped.

Hermann sank into the closest chair, then dropped his head into his hands. "Oh, Dashiel," he groaned. "A broch tzu mir! How could I have been such an idiot?"

Dashiel moved to his side as fast as he could. "I don't understand. How did it get in here? That was just a photograph, how could it possibly—"

"A shabti is a stand-in for the dead," said Hermann, scrubbing his hands over his face in frustration before lifting his eyes to meet Dashiel's questioning gaze. "An image that could act on its owner's behalf or be a vessel for the soul itself if need be. And I don't see why a photograph of a shabti shouldn't work just as well. I should have known better than to bring a picture of that thing home with me."

"Jesus!" Dashiel breathed. "What are we going to do now?"

Hermann put his head back in his hands. Dashiel could not recall ever having seen him so distraught. "I don't know. I think it's gone for now, but the photos are gone, too. And I couldn't possibly send them to Louis after this, even if I did still have them. Not that he'd probably be able to do anything anyway. We're back to square one."

Dashiel's eyes fell on the white object that had tumbled from the envelope when Hermann threw it into the fire. He walked over on shaky legs and knelt to pick it up. It was a silk handkerchief—slightly crumpled, but unmarked.

"Well, Hermann," he said, holding up the handkerchief, "the silk experiment was a bust. But for whatever it's worth, our ghost seems to be a crackerjack with apports."

Hermann gazed up at him with a look of profound weariness. "Oh," he said flatly. "Splendid."

Dashiel wanted to say something helpful, or at least comforting, but words failed him. Instead, he sat down on the ottoman beside Hermann's chair and silently reached up to rest a hand on his knee. They sat staring into the fire, watching the remains of the envelope burn away until there was nothing left but a drift of pale gray ashes.

CHAPTER 9

THE NIGHT WAS A long and restless one for Dashiel, and the little sleep he got was disturbed by unsettling dreams. If it hadn't been for Hermann's soothing presence beside him, he doubted that he would have slept at all. At around six in the morning, he gave up and got out of bed.

He climbed wretchedly into his pajamas and slunk out into the living room. The sky was already brightening, which was some comfort. He was also relieved to see Horatio napping peacefully on Hermann's armchair, curled up like a soft, striped croissant.

The threat of the ghost seemed to have passed for now, but the fact that it had been there at all, even if only for a few moments, was enough to turn his stomach. It made him feel helpless, and there were few feelings he despised more than that. Something had to be done, but what? Everything they'd tried so far had been a washout. Holding a séance was out of the question. At best, it wouldn't work, and he didn't care to contemplate the worst.

Coffee, he decided, would have to help. He soon had a pot percolating merrily away, and the warm, earthy smell did lift his spirits a little. Still, he couldn't banish the mental image of that envelope and the swirling inky tendrils. He hadn't touched a drop of liquor the night before, but he felt foggy, hungover, and shaky with fatigue.

He poured himself a cup of coffee and made to set it down on the counter, but it slipped out of his hand and crashed to the floor. The mug shattered, splashing hot coffee across the cuffs of his pajama trousers.

Dashiel seldom resorted to vulgarity, but the moment seemed right. "Son of a bitch," he cried, grabbing the dish towel that hung on the handle of the oven and flinging it to the floor in disgust. "If that don't put the pickle on the shit sandwich!"

He was just picking up the fragments of the mug when a loud knock sounded on the front door. He suppressed a second round of swearing. "Be with you in a minute, Mrs. Luckett," he called out.

Having thrown out the shards and sopped up the mess as well as he could, he hobbled out into the living room, casting about for the list of signatures. He didn't see it with the other papers on the telephone table. Presumably, it was still somewhere in the depths of Hermann's briefcase. There was another knock at the door.

"All right, all right," he muttered, giving up on finding the document for the time being. He went to the door, unlocked it, and flung it open.

The person standing on the other side of the door was not Mrs. Luckett. Dashiel caught a glimpse of ash-blond hair, stormy gray eyes, and a gleaming smile that turned his blood to ice.

He flung himself against the door, trying to slam it shut again, but the toe of an elegant yellow muleskin boot had already wedged itself between the door and its frame. The visitor pushed the door back open with ease, and Dashiel stumbled backward, powerless to stop him as he strode in.

"Now, hold on just a minute there, high pockets," said the guest, chuckling warmly. "You're not gettin' away from Porphyrio that easy."

Porphyrio had always been an imposing specimen, and their time apart had done nothing to diminish the unnerving effect he had on Dashiel. He was tall and broad, and his bright blond curls, as always, were brilliantined to a rippling, mirror-like shine. He wore a double-breasted coat with a broad sable collar that made him look even larger than usual.

Despite his size, there was a boyish roundness to his face that made him look younger than his forty-odd years. The youthful effect was enhanced by the pair of dimples that appeared in his cheeks whenever he smiled, as he was doing now. He beamed at Dashiel like a lighthouse beacon, stepping toward him with open arms.

"Dashiel, darlin'," he said, "it's been a dog's age. My, my, aren't you a sight for sore eyes! You're looking a little more moth-eaten than you were last time I saw you, but still just as handsome as can be."

"What are you doing here?" Dashiel demanded, deftly side-stepping his embrace.

Porphyrio looked genuinely hurt. "Now, really, Dash, what sort of a way is that to greet an old friend? I'm here looking for you, of course. I've missed you something awful, you know."

"You're no friend of mine," Dashiel snapped. "Come to admire your handiwork, have you? Or are you here to finish the job?"

"What in the blazes are you talking about?"

Dashiel ground his teeth. "You know damn well what I'm talking about."

"No, I can't say as I do."

"You shot me, damn it!"

"Well, now," said Porphyrio, his eyebrows lifting in surprise. "So that's what all this fuss is about. Who's been telling you tall tales, Dash? Was it Maude? You and I both know you can't trust that woman farther than you can throw her. Anyway, whoever did it, I'm sure it was a crime of passion. You hurt a lot of people when you left like you did, darlin'. Including me."

"I'm not your darling," said Dashiel, struggling to keep his voice steady.

"Oh, pshaw. You know you are."

"And you're not welcome here. You need to leave."

Porphyrio hung up his hat and coat on the cast iron rack by the door, pointedly ignoring him. He strolled past Dashiel into the living room and glanced around, taking in his surroundings with an amused quirk of the lips.

Then he flung himself down on the love seat and swung his ankles up over the armrest. He produced a monogrammed gold cigarette case from the inner pocket of his jacket, pulled out a cigarette, and gave it a couple of languid taps against the lid of the case.

"Is that coffee I smell?" he asked, sticking the cigarette in a long tortoiseshell holder and lighting it. "Why don't you go get me some, sugar-pie?"

Dashiel didn't move.

"Oh, come on, now, Dash," said Porphyrio in a cajoling tone. "Don't be like that. Even after everything you put me through, you know I'd still take you back in a heartbeat. It's all water under the bridge, far as I'm concerned. Why don't you stop this nonsense and come on home with ol' Porphyrio?"

"I already am home." It wasn't what he'd meant to say, but the words came out before he could stop them.

Porphyrio sat up a bit, raising an eyebrow. "Are you, now?" He made a production of looking around again, then broke out in a slow grin. "Well, I must say, this is a mighty cozy place you got yourself here. Where's the sweet little maiden aunt who decorated it?" He looked up, his attention arrested by something at the far side of the room. "Oh. There she is."

Dashiel followed his gaze. Hermann stood in the entrance to the living room in his shirtsleeves, his hair damp and freshly combed. He glanced back and forth between Dashiel and Porphyrio with an expression of quiet alarm on his face.

"What's going on here?" he asked.

"Well, well, well," said Porphyrio, easing into the creamy, cultured accent that he always employed in the séance room, "aren't you precious. Not Dashiel's usual type, but my goodness, how charming! Why don't you introduce me to your little friend, Dashiel?"

"I'm sure he already knows who you are," said Dashiel, tight-lipped with anger.

"Well, sure, but it's only polite to make a formal acquaintance." He turned to Hermann again, grinning wolfishly. "Since Dashiel's decided to be an old stick-in-the-mud, allow me. Hermann Goschalk, I presume? You can call me Porphyrio. Dashiel and I go way back. I'm sure he must have told you all sorts of stories about what a dreadful cad I am."

"Actually," said Hermann, "he's spoken very little about you."

Porphyrio turned to Dashiel, looking wounded. "Is that true, dearheart? Well, I suppose I can't blame you. Wouldn't want to make the new squeeze too jealous, now, would we?"

More than anything, Dashiel wanted to pick up the nearest heavy object and hurl it at Porphyrio's head. Instead, he clenched his fists and met his gaze with stony silence. He couldn't bear to even glance at Hermann.

"I think he's told me enough," Hermann said, his voice calm and level. "Now, would you mind telling me what your business is here? I certainly hope there isn't going to be any trouble."

"Trouble!" Porphyrio chuckled. "Why are you both so determined that I'm here to make trouble? Land sakes, I never saw such a pair of nervous old nellies." He took a long drag on his cigarette and squinted at Hermann. "Speaking of trouble, what happened to your face? Dashiel didn't do that to you, did he?"

"Of course not!" said Hermann, aghast.

"Now you listen here—" Dashiel began, almost simultaneously.

"All right, all right, calm down. I didn't really think it looked like your style, Dash. You've always had other methods of inflicting your wounds, and they sting a lot worse than fists do. Still, it's a shame someone had to chip that pretty mug."

"You should see the other fellow," Hermann said dryly.

Porphyrio chuckled again. "I can see why you like this one, Dash. He's just as cute as a button."

"Enough," growled Dashiel. "How the hell did you find me here, anyway?" No sooner had he said it than he realized, with a sickening lurch of the gut, that Maude must have gotten Hermann's address off the letter he'd sent her. No doubt the old pot of poison had been only too happy to point Porphyrio in the right direction.

"Oh, you didn't really think I'd believe that cock-and-bull story you fed your landlady about going down to Cairo, did you?" said Porphyrio. "Have you forgotten who you're talking to, Dashiel? You know I've always had an excellent nose for fish." He tapped his nose with an elegant finger. "Especially red herring. Now, why don't you go gather your things, darlin', and we'll go home."

"I'm not going anywhere with you."

Porphyrio let out a long-suffering sigh and turned to Hermann, addressing him like an old confidant. "That's what he says now, but he'll change his mind. He gets like this from time to time, you know. Works himself up into a snit and goes off to have his little fling. You mark my words, though, he always comes creeping back to Porphyrio in the end. Isn't that right, Ralphie?"

Hermann glanced at Dashiel in confusion, and Porphyrio grinned. "Don't tell me he hasn't even told you his real name," he said. "My goodness, Ralph, how many other things are you keeping from this poor, sweet little fella? Have you told him about the revenue men, at least?"

"You know I settled with them a long time ago, *Gomer*."

"Did you? I lose track of all the messes you get yourself into." Porphyrio swung his legs back over the arm of the couch and rose gracefully to his feet. "Well, if neither one of you gents is going to bring me any of that coffee, I suppose I'll have to go get some myself."

He started to move toward the kitchen, but Hermann took a quick sideways step into the doorway, blocking his path.

"My goodness, look at you," said Porphyrio. "Is this the kind of hospitality you show all your guests?"

"Only the ill-mannered ones," Hermann replied.

At that moment, Horatio, noticing action happening in the vicinity of the kitchen, jumped down from his perch in the armchair with a quiet trill. He trotted over and wound his way around Hermann's ankles, then moved through the kitchen doorway and out of Dashiel's line of sight.

Porphyrio let out a loud snort of amusement. "What in the world was that?"

Hermann glanced after Horatio, then turned back to Porphyrio, frowning. "Are you talking about my cat?"

"If you can call that a cat! Good lord, that's just a sausage with stripes," Porphyrio said, throwing his head back and laughing heartily. "Look at it, it doesn't even have a neck. You know, I don't see the point of a cat like that, I really don't. You couldn't even make a decent stole out of that sad little butterball. My ocelot Dierdre, now—may the light perpetual shine on her sweet soul—she was a cat."

Hermann drew himself up with quiet dignity and pointed to the front door. "It's time for you to leave, sir. I suggest you go at once. Unless you'd like me to summon the law, that is."

Porphyrio held up his hands in a placating gesture. "All right, don't get excited. There's no need for any of that. Old Porphyrio can see when he's not wanted." He stuck his cigarette holder between his teeth and sauntered back to the front door, where he picked up his coat and hat and made a show of slowly putting them on. He gave Dashiel an entreating look. "I don't suppose you're going to do the manly thing and stand up for me here, eh, Dash?"

"Go to hell," said Dashiel.

"Fine, I see how it is. But when you change your mind, you know where to find me." He pulled an object out of his pocket and tossed it to Dashiel, who instinctively caught it. It was a hotel room key.

Porphyrio turned back to Hermann, shaking his head. "I'm disappointed in you, you know. You didn't strike me as the sort of man who would just toss a fella out on the street like this. Especially an old friend of your houseguest."

"Oh, I'm sure you can find someplace else to go," Hermann said, moving to open the front door for him. "In fact, if you're open to recommendations, I'd be happy to provide one."

"Is that so?" said Porphyrio, looming unnecessarily close to Hermann as he pushed past him through the door and out into the hallway. "I'd love to hear it."

"Gai kaken ahfen yam," said Hermann politely. Before Porphyrio could respond, he slammed the door shut and bolted it.

The silence in Porphyrio's wake was thunderous. Hermann stood facing the door for a long moment, hand resting on the bolt, before visibly pulling himself together. He squared his shoulders, lifted his chin, and stalked back into the living room.

Dashiel couldn't remember the last time he'd felt so mortified. With difficulty, he forced himself to meet Hermann's eyes. "My God, Hermann," he said, "I am so sorry."

Hermann blinked at him as if the sound of his voice had snapped him out of a trance. "What a singularly unpleasant man!"

"He's a goddamn prick."

"Did you hear what he said about Horatio?"

"No, I take that back. Pricks are useful. I never meant to let him in here, I just couldn't stop him. I heard the knock and I thought it was Mrs. Luckett, and he pushed right past me the moment I opened the door. Damn it all, if I hadn't been so tired and distracted . . ."

"Horatio has a perfectly good neck," Hermann said heatedly. "It's always served him just fine. Keeps his dear little head attached to his body."

"After the way I broke things off with him, if he wants to have his beef with me, I suppose I can't blame him. I'm sure he sees it as a betrayal, and in a way, I guess he's right." Dashiel dug his fingers into the back of one of the armchairs, trying to quash his urge to punch something. "But for him to come barging in here and hassle you like that? Why, it makes me want to spit!"

"I think he's a very handsome cat. Imagine, talking about making him into a stole."

"But damn it, he's right about one thing. I should have told you about him."

Dashiel's side of the conversation seemed to register on Hermann for the first time. "But you did tell me about him."

Dashiel shook his head and squeezed his eyes shut, struggling to dam up the deluge of unwanted memories. For twenty years, for all their many bitter quarrels, he and Porphyrio had been everything to each other—business partners, lovers, the closest thing either one of them had to family.

In the end, it had been Dashiel's choice not just to throw it all away, but to burn it down and stomp on the ashes. He'd raked Porphyrio across the coals in front of colleagues and clients, then stormed off without looking back, leaving him humiliated and alone.

It had been the right choice, he was certain of it. Why, then, could he not silence the small but persistent voice of doubt that kept crying out from the shadowy depths of his mind?

"No," he said. "I mean—about us. You deserved to know, I just couldn't bring myself to say it. For God's sake, I've been sharing your home, your bed, and now I've brought that lunatic right to your doorstep. This was the last way I would have wanted you to find out what he really was to me."

"Oh, gracious, Dashiel," said Hermann, blushing, "now's hardly the time to be worrying about things like that! I was never under any illusion that I was the first man to go to bed with you, anyway. I'm just glad he didn't try to start anything."

"I'd say he started plenty."

"Well, yes. But I don't know what I would have done if he'd tried to take a swing at you, or God forbid, pulled a gun." He paused for a moment. "I must admit, it's hard for me to imagine you with someone like that."

Dashiel winced. "Please, don't try."

"I mean, he's certainly handsome enough . . ."

"He's a bloated, delusional old fraud," said Dashiel, glaring at the door through which Porphyrio had recently departed. "I have no interest in going back to him, Hermann, none. I hope you know that. Why, if I never see him again in my life, it'll be much too soon."

"I know," said Hermann gently. "Do you think he'll be back?"

Dashiel swallowed and gave a quick nod. "Yes, he'll be back. We won't be safe here as long as he's around. He doesn't give up until he gets what he wants, and he's dangerous—a real loose cannon. God knows what he'll do."

"What *does* he want?" asked Hermann.

"Me." Dashiel spread his arms in a helpless gesture. "As far as he's concerned, when I walked away, I took something that belonged to him."

Hermann looked dismayed. "And what does he think he's going to do with you, once he has you?"

"Win me back. Wear me down. Punish me until I beg forgiveness. It's all the same to him. And he probably wants to bring me back into the old Spiritualist con game. He always did his best work when we were together." He looked away again, avoiding Hermann's gaze. "In the meantime, he'll do whatever he can to drive a wedge between me and anyone else he thinks might get in his way."

They lapsed into strained silence. When Hermann spoke up again, his voice was troubled. "We should call the police."

"And tell them what?" asked Dashiel. "He didn't make any threats, and you saw how quick he left when you asked him to go. I've already tried to set the law on him once for fraud and swindling, and he slipped out of their clutches like a buttered eel. They couldn't make a damn thing stick."

"But he shot you!"

"I can't prove that. I just know he did it. And that's not enough to hold up in a court of law." Even as he said it, a spark of uncertainty flared in Dashiel's gut. Porphyrio was unscrupulous and quick to anger. When aggrieved, he could be breathtakingly cruel. But was he really capable of that sort of wanton violence?

He went and sat in the love seat. The odor of cigarette smoke, mingled with Porphyrio's heavy cologne, still lingered in the air around it. Dashiel felt an unsettling upwelling of emotion the moment he smelled it, a combination of disgust and something much older and deeper. A sort of twisted, nostalgic yearning. He shoved the feeling down as far as he could, angry at himself for even acknowledging it.

"The way I see it," he said, "we've got two choices. Either I leave, or . . . or I deal with him myself. And I'm tired of running."

"Well, I certainly don't want you to leave! But what do you mean when you say you'll deal with him yourself? Just what do you intend to do?"

"I don't know. I think I need to go talk to him. Somehow, I've got to get it through his thick skull that it's not worth his while to keep chasing after me like this."

Hermann's eyes widened in horrified surprise. "You're going to go to him? Dashiel, I really don't think that's wise. What if he hurts you? My God, he could shoot you again!"

"Not unless I turn my back. He wouldn't have the guts," said Dashiel, with more bravura than he felt.

"I don't like it."

"Neither do I. But I don't want him bothering me anymore, and I'm sure as hell not going to have him coming around here again and bothering you. Or Horatio, for that matter."

Hermann did not look reassured.

"You know him better than I do, of course," he said, "but from what I've seen of him, he doesn't seem like the sort of man who can be reasoned with."

"No, he's not. But I must at least try."

"When are you going?"

"As soon as I can. This afternoon. I don't see any point in waiting."

"I could go with you."

The mere thought of Hermann and Porphyrio being in the same room again was enough to make Dashiel's stomach start cramping. He put a firm hand on Hermann's shoulder and shook his head. "Absolutely not, Hermann. I don't want him anywhere near you ever again, not if I can help it. I have to deal with him alone."

❦

PORPHYRIO'S KEY LED Dashiel to the Grande Hotel on Baneberry Avenue, just north of campus. He rode the elevator to the top floor and made his way to the suite at the end of the hall, where he stood outside the door, the key clenched in his fist for what felt like an eternity. He'd considered bringing the revolver that was buried deep in his trunk but decided against it. Now, standing outside Porphyrio's door, he began to have second thoughts. Part of him wished he could kick the door in, shoot the bastard, and be done with it. But that line of thinking couldn't lead anywhere good. He gritted his teeth and shoved the key into the lock.

Porphyrio had, naturally, reserved the most luxurious suite the Grande had to offer. Compared to some of the accommodations they had shared in the past, it was a humble affair. Still, it didn't lack for either space or ostentation.

The bedroom featured an ornate four-poster bed, a pair of Morris chairs upholstered in red velvet, and a bearskin rug spread out in front of the fireplace. From where he stood, Dashiel could make out the entrance to a spacious kitchenette and dining area in the rooms beyond.

There was no sign of Porphyrio, which he did not find comforting in the least. The best he could hope for was that he was still out. Otherwise, he was left with the unnerving possibility that Porphyrio lurked in the room somewhere out of sight, able to see Dashiel while remaining unseen himself.

He hugged the wall by the front door, listening. After a moment, he became aware of the soft hiss of running water and realized that the shower must be on. He fancied he could also make out the muffled sounds of unmelodious humming.

He relaxed a little. A freshly showered Porphyrio would be vulnerable and, more importantly, unarmed. He made his way to one of the Morris chairs and sat down to wait in silence, clenching and unclenching his hands. Within a few minutes, the whisper of the water grew quiet, and he heard footsteps. Porphyrio emerged from the bathroom a moment later with a towel around his waist, looking massive and pink from the heat of the shower.

"Hello, Gomer," said Dashiel.

Porphyrio gasped and rounded on him, clutching the towel tightly. Then he relaxed and broke out in a slow grin. "Well, bless my soul, look what the cat dragged in! I knew you wouldn't be able to stay away for long, darlin', but I didn't expect to see you quite so soon."

"We need to talk."

"Yes, I should say so! We have a lot of catching up to do," said Porphyrio. He whipped off the towel and flung it onto the bed before reaching for his red silk jacquard robe. When Dashiel averted his eyes, he laughed. "Aww, now what's wrong, Dash? Getting shy in your old age? You never used to mind admiring the merchandise."

"I'm not going back to you, Porphyrio," said Dashiel, keeping his gaze fixed on the far wall. "Not now, not ever. That's why I'm here—to make that perfectly clear to you."

Porphyrio sighed and pulled on his robe. "I was afraid you might be like this," he said, his voice surprisingly gentle. "Come on, let's not quarrel. Let me fix you a drink, and we can have a proper talk."

"I'm not having a drink with you."

"Fine, suit yourself. But I'm having one, just the same." He moved to the bar trolley by the fireplace, uncorked a crystal decanter of scotch, then poured himself a generous helping and downed it in a single gulp. He turned back to Dashiel and regarded him with solemn gray eyes. "Every time I look at you, Dash, I keep thinking of that song, 'Too Many Tears.' You know it?"

"No."

"Well, you ought to give it a listen. I think it was written about me and you."

"Oh, spare me the dramatics," snapped Dashiel. "Listen, if you ever turn up at my doorstep uninvited again—"

"All right, all right. I'm sorry, Dash," said Porphyrio, raising his hands in surrender. "I didn't mean to embarrass you in front of your friend. But you know how jealous I get, seeing you with another man like that. You'd think I'd be used to it by now, but my poor heart still goes to pieces every time. It just brings out the devil in me."

"Your devil doesn't need much bringing out," said Dashiel, eying him coldly. "What are you doing here, anyway? Did you come all the way out to Willowvale just to harass me? Because it seems to me there are better uses for your time."

"Well, of course I wanted to come see you, Dash," said Porphyrio. "But no, you're not the only reason I'm in town. I'm also here because of dear old Fink." He took a pair of cigarettes out of a box on the mantel and held one of them out to Dashiel.

Dashiel started to shake his head, then reconsidered. It had been months since he'd indulged in a smoke, and God knows he could use one now. He extended his hand. Porphyrio's cheeks dimpled with a warm smile as he handed the cigarette over.

"Maude, eh?" said Dashiel, placing the cigarette between his lips. "What'd she tell you about her business out here?"

"Oh, not much," said Porphyrio. He took an ornate lighter from the mantel and knelt in front of Dashiel's chair, beckoning him to lean forward. Dashiel complied, taking a long drag as the lighter bathed the end of the cigarette in a tiny jet of golden flame. A warm tingle ran up his arm and into his chest as Porphyrio's fingers brushed his hand. The harsh burn of the smoke flooded his nose and throat, and his face and scalp prickled. He leaned his head back and closed his eyes, savoring the exquisite wave of lightheadedness that passed over him.

Porphyrio whistled. "Good night a' livin,' baby doll, just look at you," he said. "Don't tell me that sugar daddy of yours ain't even keeping you in smokes. Anyway, Maude told me she had some job out here with your sweet Hermann, but she wouldn't say a whole lot about it. Just that you seemed real keen on him when she brought him up." He rose to light his own cigarette and set the lighter back on the mantel. "I must admit, he is a pretty one, with those big ol' soulful eyes of his . . ."

"Stay away from Hermann from now on, you hear me?" said Dashiel, his hand tensing on the arm of the chair. "I don't want you ever setting foot in his presence again. Don't even talk about him. And you can tell Maude that she'd better not so much as breathe in his direction again, either."

"Okay, don't cast a kitten," said Porphyrio, his eyebrows rising. "Boy, you've really got it bad this time, don't you?" He dragged on his cigarette and exhaled slowly, obscuring his features in blue-white smoke. "Hermann wasn't the headline news, anyway. Maude's organizing a big revival at a swank hotel over in Saint Chuck, owned by some kind of loony old Kentucky colonel with an oil fortune. It's gonna be a real high-class do, Dash. And I want you there with me, as my partner."

Dashiel stared at him. "You can't be serious."

It was so like Porphyrio to casually drop such a proposition, as if nothing out of the ordinary had happened. As if Dashiel hadn't spent the past three years doing everything in his power to maintain the gaping chasm he'd rent between them when he left. And yet, the audacity of it still set him back on his heels.

"Do I look like I'm pulling your leg?" asked Porphyrio, looking at him with wide, earnest eyes. "Listen, dearheart, I know we've had our differences—"

"Differences! You tried to murder me!"

Porphyrio looked hurt. "I don't know why you're so set on the idea that I shot you, Dashiel. Lord knows you made enough enemies when you left, draggin' the whole camp's name through the mud in front of our parishioners like that."

"We both know what you did."

"Well, even if I did do it, could you really blame me?" His brow darkened, and a muscle twitched in his jaw. "Hell, Dash, it's one thing to throw a man's heart away, but to try and destroy his livelihood along with it? That was low, even for a sneaky little snake like you."

Dashiel waved his cigarette, indicating their surroundings. "You seem to be doing all right for yourself."

Porphyrio scoffed. "Well, sure I am. But it ain't the same, doin' it all without you by my side. No matter how bad you hurt me, Dash, I can't forget how good things used to be between us. I've never stopped loving you, not for a moment. And seeing you like this, all skin and bone, practically dressed in rags? It tears me up inside, darlin', it really does." He walked over and perched on the arm of Dashiel's chair, then reached down to take his hand, twining fingers through Dashiel's. "Let me help you, Dashiel. It doesn't have to be like this. You could have your old life back again. All of it."

Dashiel yanked his hand away. "I don't need your help."

"Don't you?" Porphyrio dragged an appraising gaze over Dashiel, from his drawn, tired face to his scuffed shoes. "Maybe not right now, but you will. We've been through this a million times before, and it always ends the same way—with someone's heart gettin' broke. Usually yours. And who's always there to pick up the pieces? That's right. Ol' Porphyrio."

"Not this time," said Dashiel, taking an angry drag on his cigarette. "It's over. Let it go."

Porphyrio gave him a long, pitying look. "Oh, really? And what makes you think it'll be any different this time? It may be all sunshine and roses now, but I guarantee you things'll go sideways faster than a crab on greased roller skates once that sweet little slice of pumpkin pie finally realizes what kind of a man you really are."

Dashiel groped for a sharp retort, but nothing presented itself. All he could do was sit there in silence, fuming with anger and embarrassment. Porphyrio stood and mashed out his cigarette in the ashtray on the mantel. He then strolled over to the chifforobe, yanked open the doors, and started laying out clothes on the bed.

"Listen, darlin'," he said, without turning to look at Dashiel, "all I'm asking is for you to do one more job with me, for old time's sake. Even if it really is over between us, you at least owe me that much."

"One more job," Dashiel echoed, staring down at the cigarette in his hand. Excitement crackled over long unused pathways in his mind at the thought of it, like the cool buzz of the nicotine. It would be so easy to fall back into his old routines, so refreshing to hold an audience of believers enrapt again. And how much more convincing could his act become, now that he'd experienced the real thing?

He rose and flicked the cigarette into the fireplace, furious with himself. "And then just one more after that, and one more after that—is that it? Well, you can forget about it. I'm not getting anywhere near this chiselers' convention of yours. And frankly, if you and Maude and all the rest were smart, you'd get out, too. You have no idea what you're messing around with."

Porphyrio, who had disrobed again and was stepping into a pair of chalk-stripe trousers with a pleat so sharp it could cut glass, regarded him with amusement. "If you're talkin' about yourself, I'd say I know exactly what I'm messing around with."

"I'm talking about spirits, Porphyrio."

Porphyrio looked at him in genuine surprise. "Why, Dash," he said, "don't tell me you've suddenly become a true believer after all these years."

"I don't know what I am anymore. But real or no, ghosts are bad news. I do know that much."

"I do believe you've finally gone around the bend," snorted Porphyrio, pulling on a shirt and deftly shoving a set of mother-of-pearl studs into the buttonholes. "Come to think of it, you and Maude have both been acting a little tetched in the head since meeting that Hermann character of yours. What's he got up his sleeve, I wonder?"

"I told you to leave Hermann out of it. This is between you and me, Gomer." He squinted at the belt that Porphyrio was fastening around his waist. It was made from some sort of scaly skin, mostly black, interspersed with rosettes and speckles of pale yellow. "Is that . . . Hershel?"

Porphyrio looked down at the belt and shook his head sadly. "It certainly is. May the unseen Force of Creation guide him eternally toward the light. You were a good lizard, Hersh."

"Got tired of him, did you?"

"Of course not! What do you take me for? He started doing very poorly after you left. Passed beyond the veil of his own accord a few months ago. I just couldn't bear to part with him, so now I carry him with me always." He gave Dashiel a smile that turned his stomach. "I hope someday my loved ones will do the same for me. Wouldn't I look lovely, darlin', wrapped around your waist for eternity?"

"You're a sick man, Porphyrio," said Dashiel. "And if you think you're getting anywhere near my waist again in this life or the next—"

"Come on, don't be like that," said Porphyrio, moving toward him with open arms. "I know you miss me, deep down. And God knows you must miss the life. You were the best in the business.

The very best. I know—I've had other partners since, but none of 'em came close. We had it all, you and me."

"You wanna know something?" said Dashiel, taking a few steps back. "I liked you better when we first met, back when you were just plain old Gomer Buttz from Nowheresville, Alabama. Back when you had no money and no ambition. You were a pretty sweet kid back then. What happened to you, anyway?"

Porphyrio's gray eyes grew hard and steely, and his smile faded. "Hell, Ralph, you know what happened," he said softly, still advancing. He closed in on Dashiel with dangerous, predatorial grace. "You happened. You come in here acting all high and mighty, but we both know you're the one who opened my eyes to this path. Any time I had doubts, you were right there, egging me on. Then one day you decided to—what, grow a conscience all of a sudden? And now it's your mission in life to make me and all the rest of us pay for it. You're the one who's sick, Dash, not me. I never pretended to be anything I'm not. I'm just out here making a living, the way you taught me."

"There were things we both agreed we'd never do," said Dashiel, bumping up against the edge of the mantel as he continued backing away.

"Oh, don't I know it," said Porphyrio, almost nose to nose with him now. His breath smelled of scotch and cigarette smoke. "We drew so many lines in the sand, and you were right there with me up to the very end, trampling over all of 'em. You know what the big difference is between you and me, though?"

Dashiel didn't answer. He turned his face away, unable to keep meeting Porphyrio's burning gaze.

"Look at me, Ralphie," said Porphyrio, taking hold of his chin and turning his face back toward him. His grip was gentle, but it tightened painfully as Dashiel tried to struggle away. "You lost your nerve, that's what."

"It was more than that," gasped Dashiel, "and you know it."

"No." Porphyrio laughed bitterly and shook his head. "Don't try to tell me it was scruples. You always loved the work at least as much as I did. I'll tell you exactly what it was. You got it into your pretty head that after all your years of grifting and stealing and playin' the duck on the income tax man, the law was finally closing in on you. So you decided to just give up and take the rest of us down with you instead of standing up and fighting for yourself like a man. If you want, you can go on pretending to me and yourself and the rest of the world that you're the noble one here, but we both know the truth."

He pushed in close, crowding Dashiel up against the hearth, and braced his hands against the mantel on either side of Dashiel's shoulders. "Sometimes I think you never did truly care for anyone but yourself, darlin'," he said, his expression softening. "But bless me, I guess that means I have to do enough caring for the both of us."

Dashiel froze, certain for a moment that Porphyrio was about to kiss him. His heart throbbed in his throat, and his whole body burned with anticipation. But instead, Porphyrio reached past him and took another cigarette from the box, then tucked it gently behind Dashiel's ear.

"Go on home to your playmate for now, Dash." He brushed back a lock of hair that had tumbled over Dashiel's forehead, then allowed his hand to linger for a moment on his cheek before taking a step back. "But just you think about what I said, you hear? Maude's revival is comin' up in about a week and a half, and I need to start planning. I'll be waiting for your answer."

CHAPTER 10

D ASHIEL HAD ENTERED THE Grande despising Porphyrio, and he left despising himself, consumed by an inferno of shame and confusion. It should have been the easiest thing in the world to stand up to Porphyrio. He knew the man's bag of tricks better than anyone, could recite all his little methods for wriggling through the chinks in his armor. But the moment he was alone with him again, none of that mattered. All his old weaknesses had come rushing up to engulf him.

Part of him was desperate to say yes to Porphyrio's offer. Just one word, and everything would be fixed. The crushing poverty of the past three years would be just another distasteful memory. He could walk away from Willowvale, with its supernatural horrors and its shadowy specters of future heartbreak, and never look back.

Camp Walburton would welcome him back if he was properly penitent, of that he was certain. Even with all the bad blood he'd left in his wake, his colleagues understood all too well the way true believers thought. The return of a disgraced medium, his pride humbled and his faith restored, would only serve to galvanize the flock.

He knew Hermann would be waiting anxiously for him, but he didn't return to the apartment. Instead, he dragged himself to the nearest bar and bought as many highballs as he could with what little money he had left. By the time he made his way back, it was after five o'clock. He stumbled up the stairs, flung himself against the apartment door, and pounded on it with a heavy fist.

It wasn't long before the bolt slid back in the lock, and Hermann's pale, distraught face appeared in the doorway. "Dashiel!" he cried. "Thank God, I was worried sick. Are you all right?"

"No," said Dashiel.

Hermann grabbed his arm and pulled him inside, then hastily shut and bolted the door behind them. "What's happened?" he demanded, holding Dashiel out at arm's length and looking him over. "Are you hurt?"

"No, I'm not hurt." Dashiel turned away and staggered into the kitchen, Hermann close on his heels. He yanked one of the chairs away from the dining table and collapsed into it, letting his cane clatter to the floor. "I'm just a goddamn fool. Do you have any of that brandy left?"

"I think you've had enough to drink," Hermann said. "Why don't I make you some coffee?"

"Coffee's not going to cut it. I'll settle for cooking sherry if that's all you've got. Or Sterno."

"Dashiel! What on earth's the matter?"

The solicitous expression on Hermann's face didn't improve Dashiel's dark temper. He was in no mood to receive sympathy or comfort, and he wanted even less to feel scrutinized. He folded his arms on the table and laid his head down on them. "Leave me alone, Hermann," he mumbled.

"Dashiel . . ."

"I mean it," he snapped, lifting his head to glare at him. "Leave me be. What the hell are we playing at here, anyway? I can't even help myself, let alone you. We both ought to cut our losses before I bring even more trouble down on your head. Trust me, I'd be doing you a favor if I left."

Hermann drew himself up, bristling with indignation. He took a sharp breath through his nose before speaking again. "Now, look here," he said. "It would break my heart if you left now, but I wouldn't try to stop you. Only, please, do it because you want to, not out of some sort of misguided notion that you'd be protecting me. I don't know what that putz said to you, but—"

"Do you want to know what it took to finally make me walk away from it all?" Dashiel cut in. His voice cracked and his face went cold as he said it. But he needed to hear it as much as Hermann did.

Hermann looked bewildered by the sudden turn in the conversation. "Dashiel, I hardly think now is the time to get into all that. Right now, we need to focus on—"

"Please." Dashiel reached out and clutched at his sleeve. "I need you to hear it. Sit down and just—just listen."

Hermann still looked doubtful, but he nodded. He pulled the other chair around next to Dashiel's and sat.

Dashiel stared down at the table, unable to meet Hermann's eye. "There was this elderly widow," he said. "Mrs. Monseruud. She was one of the true faithful. Every Sunday at the little chapel down at Camp Walburton, she'd be right there in the front row. If Porphyrio and I had let her, I think she'd have been in the séance room with us every day. Wouldn't make a move without our advice."

Hermann had grown still and quiet, as if he was afraid that any sound or move would cause the door that had swung open between them to slam shut again. He listened intently, his hands folded on the table in front of him.

"She was a sweet woman, Hermann," Dashiel went on. "So determined to see the best in everyone, she was downright pigheaded about it. I remember she'd bring me fresh-baked crullers every time she came in for a séance. Always telling me I was too thin." He let out a soft huff of amusement. "If only she could see me now. One day, she came to us all distraught. Told us her doctor had found a tumor in her belly, and she was terrified to get the operation she needed to take it out." He looked up and forced himself to lock eyes with Hermann. "Well, do you know what we did?"

Hermann shook his head.

"We told her we could use the power of the spirits to heal her," said Dashiel. The words tasted bitter on his tongue. "I don't suppose you've ever heard of psychic surgery. Not many people practice it here, but there are rumors among those in the know that they've been doing it in Brazil for years. The medium lays his hands over the afflicted part of the body and draws out the sickness. No knives, no pain. You get a nice bloody chunk of liver or something from the butcher, and it's easy enough to convince some poor credulous sap that you've magically pulled a tumor out of 'em with a little sleight of hand. Porphyrio'd learned of it recently, and he was just itching to give it a try. We'd be among the first mediums in this country to do it."

"Oh, no," breathed Hermann, his eyes widening in dismay. "Dashiel, that's . . ."

"I know. We both agreed from the start that we'd never practice any kind of faith healing. But we'd already broken so many of our promises by that point, I suppose it was only the natural next step. Just an interesting challenge, a new bit to add to our repertoire. At first, I was fascinated with the idea. We'd lie awake long into the night talking about how we were gonna pull it off. But as the day got closer, I realized that—well, damn it, I just couldn't do it. Not to her. I told Porphyrio I'd changed my mind, but he laughed me off. Said I must be going soft, that we'd done worse things a million times before."

He shrugged. "Maybe he was right. We'd done so many awful things, and God knows I'd gotten attacks of conscience before.

Like the time we stole a pair of bronzed baby shoes from a grieving parishioner's parlor to use as an apport at our next séance with him. Or when we—" He stopped and rubbed his throbbing brow with both hands, as if he could scrub the memories away. "Never mind, you get the idea. I tried to leave, oh, I don't know how many times. But I was always back a few weeks later, like a goddamn boomerang."

Hermann was still listening, enrapt. He looked deeply troubled, but beyond that, Dashiel couldn't read his expression. A powerful wave of exhaustion hit him. He wanted to tell Hermann he was too tired to go on with the story, but he gritted his teeth and forced himself to continue.

"This felt different, though. I took her aside. 'You need to see a real doctor,' I said to her. 'Not a couple of slippery old frauds like us.' She just smiled and told me she had faith, and that I should, too. I guess she thought I was getting cold feet since we'd never tried a spirit healing before." He took a long, shuddering breath. "I didn't want any part of it anymore, and I told Porphyrio as much. So, he did it on his own. A few months later, she was dead."

Hermann drew in a breath through his teeth. "May her memory be a blessing."

"He had an explanation for why the healing didn't work, of course," Dashiel said. "He always has an explanation for everything. When she started getting sicker, he told her it was just her time, that she had some great destiny in the next realm and that they needed her there." He buried his face in his hands and kept speaking, his voice muffled through his fingers. "I went to visit her in the hospital, right at the end. She held my hand and told me I was like a son to her. And when she passed . . . even after all that, even after everything we'd taken from her, we learned she'd willed most of what she had left to our church.

"The day after I found out, I stood up in front of the congregation and let it all out. I told them everything we'd been doing. Not just me and Porphyrio, but everyone at the camp. I explained about the fake billet readings, the chiffon ectoplasm, the phony apports, everything. Then, I gathered all my things and left. Not that it did any good. People will believe what they want, no matter how much evidence you throw at them. A few people left, but most of them rallied around Porphyrio, like he was the one who was wronged. My God, Hermann. I might as well be an accomplice to murder. That's what it amounts to."

He fell silent and waited for some kind of response, but for an agonizing eternity, there was nothing. Then he heard the scrape of Hermann's chair over the tiles as he pushed it back and rose from the table, followed by the sound of footsteps. His heart plummeted like a stone, but he couldn't bring himself to lift his head from his hands and look to see where he was going.

A moment later, there was a hiss of water from the tap, followed by the soft thunk of a glass hitting the table beside him.

"Here," Hermann said. "If you won't have any coffee, at least drink this. You've got enough to worry about without making yourself sick."

Dashiel lowered his hands and stared up at him. He hadn't expected an outpouring of comfort and absolution. But he'd half hoped that Hermann would excoriate him, or even ask him to leave. Either one would have been better than no reaction at all.

"Is that it?" he demanded. "Don't you have anything else to say to me?"

Hermann shook his head. "Not now, Dashiel." His expression was stern, but his tone was gentle. "Not while you're drunk. Go on. Drink the water."

Dashiel picked up the glass and took a listless sip, feeling wretchedly sorry for himself.

"Nu, shoyn! All of it!" Hermann said with an impatient gesture.

He obediently gulped down the rest of the water. It didn't do much to ease his misery, but his stomach felt a little less sour, and the room stopped spinning with quite so much vigor.

"Now," said Hermann, sitting down beside him again and leaning in close, "tell me what happened today."

Dashiel stared into his empty glass. "It's like I said. He wants me back. As his partner, and more. Maude Fink is planning some grand Spiritualist jamboree in St. Charles in a couple weeks, and he wants me there with him."

"And?" Hermann put his hand on Dashiel's shoulder. He leaned into the comforting touch.

"You were right, Hermann. I can't get near him again. We're like poison to each other, Porphyrio and me. Or opium. We make each other sick, but we just can't quit, not as long as we're around each other." He reached over to cover Hermann's hand with his own. "I told him I wouldn't do it, but he won't take no for an answer. He's going to pull me back into the game. Or kill me trying."

DASHIEL SLEPT FOR hours. When he woke up, it was night, although he couldn't have guessed the time. The room was lit with soft, golden lamplight. He rolled over in bed and found Hermann seated at his desk by the window, writing, books and papers spread out in front of him.

"Hermann, are you working?" Dashiel croaked. "It must be late." His throat was parched, and his head pounded, but the world didn't seem quite as bleak as it had before he went to sleep. He squinted at the clock on the nightstand. It read twelve thirty-five.

Hermann turned around. "Oh, you're awake! Yes. I couldn't sleep, so I thought I'd rewrite my notes for the exam. How are you feeling?"

"Got a hell of a bottle-ache, but I'm all right." The light from the lamp made his eyes throb, so he closed them again. "I'm sorry. About before. I shouldn't have unloaded all that on you."

"It's all right," Hermann said quietly. "I'm glad you told me."

A lump rose in Dashiel's throat. He swallowed it down and nodded.

"Are you hungry?" asked Hermann. "You slept right through supper."

Dashiel didn't open his eyes. "It would break my heart, too, you know," he mumbled.

"Pardon?"

"If I left. It seems ridiculous, seeing as I haven't known you very long at all, but . . . it's getting harder all the time to imagine any kind of a future without you in it."

There was no immediate reply, but a moment later the mattress shifted slightly as Hermann sat down on the bed beside him. Gentle fingers caressed his cheek.

"We'll figure this out, Dashiel," said Hermann. "I'm sure of it. We'll find a way to lick both of them. My ghost and yours."

Dashiel half smiled and opened his eyes a crack. "Gee, I wish I had your optimism."

"Well, I don't have any ideas yet," Hermann admitted. "But believe me, I've been thinking about it. Until we come up with something, though, we both need to be a lot more careful. No more opening the door without looking through the peephole. And please, Dashiel, no more visits with Porphyrio. Not on your own, anyway."

"Agreed. And you," he said, fumbling for Hermann's hand and giving it a listless pat, "no more photographs. Or late nights at the museum."

Hermann nodded. "From now on, I'll bring my work home with me. I can borrow books from the archive if need be. But I think you ought to come with me when I go to work. It's not safe to be here alone anymore."

※☀※

THE REST OF the weekend was blessedly uneventful, but a sense of grim inevitability hung over them. It was hard to enjoy anything with the looming specter of Porphyrio. And, when he was not thinking about Porphyrio, Dashiel worried about the ghost. Sunset, which had once been one of his favorite parts of the day, filled him with a creeping unease. He stuck close to Hermann's side throughout the evening and clung to him in bed all night.

When Monday morning rolled around, they got up, dressed, and ate breakfast in near silence. The atmosphere was thick with their shared anxiety. It wasn't until they were almost to campus that Hermann began to talk.

"You can make yourself at home in my office, or wherever you like," he said, pulling his car up to the curb. "But I don't think it's wise to wander around outside too much on your own. I'll be done by five, then I'll gather a few things and we can beat it out of here before sundown."

"That's fine," said Dashiel, who was barely listening. It was a sunny morning and the building looked normal, even cheerful, in the golden autumn light. Still, his heart pounded just looking at it.

Hermann must have noticed how apprehensive he looked. "I'm sure it'll be all right," he said, patting Dashiel's knee. "It's never bothered me much during the daytime."

There were already a few students milling around in the lobby when they walked in. They looked tense and moody. An elderly custodian shuffled along behind a dust mop, shaking his head and muttering to himself. A sense of foreboding hung in the air like a static charge. The moment they stepped out of the elevator on the third floor, Agnes emerged from her office and pounced on them. She looked as if she was down to her last frazzled nerve.

"Morning, Agnes," said Hermann.

"Oh, it's been a morning, all right," she said. "Professor, whatever's going on around here, it's getting out of hand. There are weird messes all over the building. Some joker broke into the graduate student lounge over the weekend and wrecked it. I found that brand new Toastmaster on the floor, in pieces!"

Hermann looked aghast. "No. The lounge, you say? But it never wanders that far from the gallery."

"That was a good toaster," Agnes went on ruefully. "It had an automatic timer and everything. I can take a joke as well as the next gal, but there are limits, and this has gone on more than long enough. One of these days I'm going to stay late and catch whoever's been causing all this trouble."

"No, Agnes, you mustn't!" said Hermann. "It wouldn't be safe."

"Whoever it is, I'm sure I can handle 'em." She cast a meaningful glance at Dashiel.

Hermann put a hand on her arm. "Please, I assure you, you can't. It's not safe to come anywhere near this place after sunset. Even I won't do it anymore. Whatever this thing is—"

"Professor, please don't try to tell me it's spooks, not today. I'm not in the mood."

"Believe what you like, but promise me you'll stay away at night," he implored. "I couldn't have it on my conscience if anything should happen to you."

Agnes drew in a deep breath as if she were preparing to argue, then let it out in a huff. "Fine," she said. "But things can't go on like this, they just can't. I swear, the whole place has gone cuckoo." She strode back into her office.

Hermann turned to Dashiel, frowning. "Oh, I didn't much like the sound of that."

"Me neither," said Dashiel. "It sounds like our ghostly friend may have gone on a bit of a bender over the weekend."

They crept down the hall to Hermann's office under a growing cloud of apprehension. Hermann opened the door and started to go in, then stopped so abruptly that Dashiel bumped into him. He gave a little gasp of dismay.

"What . . .?" Dashiel started to ask, peering over his shoulder. But he trailed off without finishing the question.

The office was a wreck. Books and papers were scattered everywhere. The drawers of the desk had been wrenched out and overturned, their contents piled on the floor. The potted geranium that had sat in the window lay in a heap of soil and shattered crockery. An inkpot on the top of the desk was upset, and black ink ran off the edge and pooled on the floor below. Someone—or something—had used the ink to smear wobbly shapes on the wall behind the desk.

"Oh, Hermann," said Dashiel. "I'm sorry. This is just awful."

"Heaven knows, it's not your fault," said Hermann, staring at the wreckage. "Good lord, look at this balagan! It must be getting more powerful. It couldn't have done something like this just a few weeks ago, I'm sure of it."

"I'm not so sure it isn't my fault," said Dashiel, edging into the room and poking at some of the debris with the end of his cane. "At least partly. It seems like the more we interact with it, the stronger it gets. I should never have told you to write that letter."

Hermann waved off the idea. "It was already getting worse before you came back. Anyway, it's at least as likely that my offerings gave it the shot of pep it needed to do all this mischief."

"Offerings?"

"You know, the cheese Danish. Not to mention the silk. Fine textiles are part of the standard offering formulae for the dead. Offerings like that nourish and strengthen the souls of the deceased.

But they're supposed to placate a spirit, not make it mad. Why, even the word for 'offering' is the same as the one that means 'to pacify.'"

"So, you're telling me," said Dashiel, giving him an incredulous look, "that a piece of pastry and a hanky were enough to give this thing psychokinetic abilities beyond your average Spiritualist's wildest nightmares?"

"Oh, not on their own," said Hermann. He walked over and began to assess the damage to his desk. "This entity must have been extraordinarily powerful already. No doubt it's an *akh*, presumably of someone who was a great mage in life. Or at the very least, someone who managed to gain access to some potent magical texts, licitly or otherwise." He sighed. "It wants something, I just don't know how to provide it."

Dashiel bent to pick up a pile of ink-spattered papers. The cabinet card of Hermann's mother was among them, and he was relieved to see that it had mostly escaped damage. He handed it to Hermann, who slid it into an inside pocket of his jacket. "What if it's already getting what it wants?" he asked.

"Oh? What would that be?" said Hermann, puzzled.

"I don't know," he said grimly. "To make your life miserable, I suppose. What if it's just a big old spectral bully?"

"Seems like an awful lot of trouble to go through just to pester me," Hermann muttered, dabbing at the spill on his desk with an ink blotter that was woefully inadequate for the task. "Surely it could find someone more entertaining to pick on."

"You said it was a—what did you call it, an *akh*?" said Dashiel. "What does that mean?"

"A transfigured spirit." Hermann plied the ink blotter with an increasingly aggressive hand, irritability creeping into his voice. "A ghost with the ability to influence the realm of the living."

"Well, what sort of a person would become a spirit like that after they died? If you could narrow it down—"

"In theory, any old shmuck could become an *akh*," said Hermann. "Although you had to be at least privileged enough for a proper burial. All it means is that this person underwent the appropriate funerary rites to reunite and empower the separate aspects of his soul after he died."

"But you said he was probably some great mage," Dashiel insisted.

"I know I did, but that doesn't mean I have the foggiest inkling of who we're dealing with. It can't be Setna Khaemwaset, because we know from the inscription on the shabti that he's an Amun-something. Besides, if this shabti belonged to a Nineteenth Dynasty prince, I'll eat my hat. The style's all wrong. And I doubt very much that it's Amunhotep Son of Hapu. A man that influential would have sprung for something a fair sight finer than that crude little faience thing, especially at the height of the Eighteenth Dynasty's glory. I'd expect cedarwood and gold leaf at the very least." The words all rushed out of him in a single breath. He paused to fill his lungs, then flung the soaked blotter down on the desk and rounded on Dashiel, his face flushed with vexation. "Hang it all, Dashiel! If there were simple answers to any of these questions, don't you think I would have figured them out already?"

Dashiel blinked at him in surprise. He felt his own hackles beginning to rise and deliberately tamped down his temper. "Okay, simmer down," he said. "I was just asking."

Hermann looked chastened. "I'm sorry, Dashiel. I know you're trying to help." He shuddered and passed a hand over his brow. "I feel so strange. Something about being near that thing, even when it's dormant. It's as if it radiates pure anger."

"That's all right," said Dashiel. He brushed his thumb over a smudge of ink on Hermann's forehead, wiping it away. "I'm sure we'll both feel better after we get this stuff picked up."

They tidied up the worst of the mess together, then Hermann went off to class, leaving Dashiel alone and ill at ease. For a while, he sat and stared at the ink blotches on the wall, but he couldn't make anything of them. He turned his attention to the novel he'd brought from Hermann's bookshelf back at the apartment, but the words blended into a meaningless jumble, and he found himself reading the same line over and over without comprehending it. The longer he sat there, the worse he felt. Hoping to distract himself, he went back to cleaning up.

It didn't help much. His leg hurt, and the work was tedious. He grabbed handfuls of junk and flung them haphazardly into drawers. After about ten minutes of this, his blood was boiling.

How had it come to this? This time three years ago, he would have been stretched out on a beach in Florida, letting the sun warm his skin. He'd had two perfectly functional legs and the muscular physique of a man who was both well-fed and had the luxury of time for self-cultivation. He'd been beautiful then, always impeccably dressed. The kind of elegant figure who turned heads wherever he went. Today, he was a shabby, broken-down shadow of his former self. Hermann, he reflected, was a fool to want this version of him. Not that he'd ever know what he was missing.

A small but persistent part of him began wondering why he'd ever left it all behind. Sure, it had been wrong, but most of the rich idiots he'd swindled were convinced he'd been doing them a favor. He'd never forced anyone to hand over their money; it was hardly his fault that they kept coming back for more. He certainly didn't belong here, hiding in a dull, cluttered little office, picking up another man's mess. It made him feel like a child again.

He was reminded of a time when he was eleven, when he'd huddled in a shed full of dust and cobwebs with his head on his knees and blood dripping from his nose, waiting for the neighbor boy, Tommy Goeppert, to grow tired of hunting for him and go home. He burned with anger and humiliation at the thought, as if it had happened only yesterday.

Where was Tommy now, he wondered? He sincerely hoped that he was dead. It wasn't unlikely, he thought, slamming a drawer shut with grim satisfaction. He was just the sort of bastard who was bound to end up getting himself shot. After all, it took one to know one. He snatched up a piece of the broken plant pot from the floor under the window, and the sharp edge bit into his finger and drew blood. Uttering a loud curse, he hurled the shard across the room. It bounced off the wall, leaving a smudge of potting soil behind.

Dashiel straightened up, shocked by the potency of the rage brewing inside him. He forced himself to draw slower breaths, focused on the way the floor felt through the soles of his shoes. Blood dripped onto the floor from his finger. He wrapped it in his handkerchief and squeezed it tight.

"All right, Quicke," he murmured to himself, "pull yourself together. This isn't you, it's that thing downstairs."

Staying in Hermann's office was not an option. Dashiel's mind was a dark and treacherous place under the best of circumstances, and he was horrified to think what it might be capable of if he went on stewing under the influence of this hostile spirit. A peek under the handkerchief revealed that his finger was still bleeding, which did nothing to diminish his growing agitation. Having wrapped it up again, he tucked his book under his arm, grabbed his cane, and made a hasty exit.

HERMANN WAS IN the middle of a polite but terse exchange about passive participles with one of his students when Dashiel arrived at the classroom door. Dashiel rapped on the doorlite and frantically beckoned him over.

"What's all this about?" Hermann whispered, opening the door a crack and peeking out. He looked pale and haggard. "Did something happen?"

The students grumbled moodily in the classroom behind him, craning their necks to see what was happening.

"We need to get out of here," said Dashiel. "Right now."

"But I can't leave now! There's still twenty minutes left of Middle Egyptian, and then I've got Demotic. Dashiel, for heaven's sake—"

Dashiel grabbed his elbow and tugged him out into the hall. "Please, Hermann, I can't stay here another minute, and I don't think you should, either. Tell Agnes you're sick or something, I don't care what. That thing is getting inside my head, and I don't know what'll happen if I keep hanging around it."

Hermann hesitated for a moment, then nodded. "All right, Dashiel, all right." His shoulders slumped in defeat. He looked close to tears. "It wouldn't be stretching the truth much to say I'm sick, anyway. I feel awful. Just give me a few minutes to gather my things."

CHAPTER 11

WHEN HERMANN EMERGED FROM the building several minutes later, he carried his overstuffed briefcase in one hand and a metal lockbox in the other. A small stack of books was tucked under his arm. Dashiel, who had gone to wait in the car, leaned over to open the driver's side door for him. He tossed his burden onto the seat between them and clambered in.

The instant the box hit the seat beside him, Dashiel's chest tightened. His vision clouded for a moment, as if he'd stood up too quickly after a long nap. He gasped at the sudden shock of it.

"Hermann," he said, staring at the lockbox with a growing sense of dread, "what's in that box?"

Hermann locked eyes with him and swallowed. He looked as though he could scarcely believe what he was about to say. "The shabti."

Dashiel scooted as far over as he could, crowding himself up against the passenger-side door. His flesh crawled with horror. "Why in the hell would you put that thing in the car with us? Are you out of your mind?"

"That's certainly up for debate," Hermann said. His tone was calm and measured, but his eyes were dark with distress. "But really, I should have done this ages ago. I'd just hoped there was another way."

"Should have done what, exactly?"

There was a determined set to Hermann's jaw. "I'm going to get rid of it."

"Oh." A tiny spark of surprised relief flared up amid Dashiel's dismay. "But I thought you were dead set against destroying it."

"I am not destroying it." Hermann's hands tightened on the steering wheel. "Just relocating it."

"To where?"

"The bottom of the Kishwaukee." He let out a shaky sigh and gave the box a pat. "I'm sorry, khaverl. I wish it didn't have to come to this, but you don't leave me much choice."

HERMANN DROVE THEM to a quiet, empty park on the banks of the Kishwaukee, and they walked down a sun-dappled path that ran alongside the river. Lazy geese scuttled out of their way, grumbling and hissing softly as they passed. The tips of some of the trees were edged with crimson and gold, and frogs hummed and trilled in the shallows. Under any other circumstances, it would have been a lovely stroll. But Dashiel's heart raced and his head throbbed to a pulse that was not his own, as if someone was pounding a slow rhythm on a bass drum deep in his brainstem.

They soon arrived at an old wooden footbridge and turned onto it, making their solemn way to the center. Hermann rested the metal box on the handrail and gazed down into the churning, muddy waters.

The throbbing in Dashiel's skull grew more intense by the minute. He almost fancied he could hear a low, rhythmic thrum emanating from the box. "What are you waiting for?" he hissed.

Hermann jumped at the sound of his voice, but he didn't look up. "I don't know if I can do this."

"You know it's the only way. Go on, just do it. Get it over with."

"The paperwork is going to be a real veytik. I'll have to fill out a deaccession and destruction form."

"Hermann, for crying out loud—"

Hermann hung his head and closed his eyes. "I know, I'm sorry. It just feels wrong."

Dashiel wanted to snatch the box away from him and hurl it into the river. Instead, he gulped in a few deep, calming breaths and laid a gentle hand on the small of Hermann's back. "Listen, Hermann. You're the one with the principles. Why don't you let me do it? You can put it down on the forms and everything. 'Artifact destroyed by cad.'"

Hermann laughed, but there was little joy in it. "Don't say that, dear. You're not a cad."

"Says who?"

"No, the shabti is my responsibility. If anyone's going to do it, it has to be me." He hefted the box and held it out over the edge of the railing. "All right. Here goes nothing."

After a moment of agonized hesitation, he let go of the handle. The box plunged into the river, the water closed over it, and it sank out of sight into the murky depths. Hermann winced and looked away.

The pounding in Dashiel's head stopped, and the crushing sense of foreboding that had hung over him since they'd arrived on campus that morning evaporated in an instant. He sagged at the knees, giddy with relief. Hermann took off his hat and clutched it to his chest as if paying respects to a fallen comrade.

"Is it over?" asked Dashiel. "Do you think it'll leave you alone now?"

Hermann nodded. "I think so," he said. "In the museum, it was surrounded by the artifacts of its civilization, objects whose magical potency it could draw on and use to its advantage."

"Not to mention throw."

"Exactly. But I can't imagine there's much it can do from inside a box at the bottom of a river five miles away." He stared fretfully into the water. "Three boxes, actually. It's nested inside an archival storage box and an old lunch tin. I took a cue from the story of Setna, where the gods put the Scroll of Thoth in a series of chests and dropped it into the Nile for safekeeping. Of course, those chests were made of precious materials, and the whole thing was guarded by an army of venomous creatures and an ouroboros, but I did the best I could with the materials at hand."

Dashiel felt lightheaded, wrung out, and in desperate need of a diversion. He wanted to forget about everything, even if just for an hour or two. "Come on," he said, gathering Hermann into his arms and kissing the top of his head. "We both need to get our minds off things for a while. Let's go to the movies. How about *The Case of the Howling Dog*? You can't go wrong with a Warren William picture."

Despite his obvious weariness, Hermann managed one of his glorious smiles. "Oh, I do like that idea, Dashiel. Yes, I think that's just the ticket," he said. "And after that, dinner. We'll eat out."

THE MOVIE TURNED out to be just the sort of distraction they needed. Willowvale boasted a lavish picture palace with seats covered in red velvet plush and gilt columns flanking the screen. It was the middle of the afternoon, and there were few other moviegoers in the audience with them. They sat with their hands clasped between them under the cover of the flickering darkness, half watching the film and enjoying each other's silent companionship.

By the time they returned to the apartment, it was almost sundown, and Dashiel's uneasy mood had nearly evaporated. He was still exhausted, but there was a warm glow of contentment about him. It had felt wonderful, going out into the world with Hermann and doing ordinary things. He wanted more than anything to do it again, and to keep on doing it as often as possible for the foreseeable future.

"What an awful picture that was," Hermann said as they walked in through the front door. He turned to beam at Dashiel. "I enjoyed every minute of it."

Dashiel grinned back at him. "If you followed enough of the plot to know it was a stinker, you've already got me licked."

"Gee, but I'm bushed." Hermann dropped his books on the telephone table and yawned. "I think I'd like to go straight to bed."

Dashiel stepped up behind him and slid his arms around his waist. "So would I."

"I meant to sleep, you masher," said Hermann, but he didn't try to pull away. Dashiel could hear the smile in his voice.

"Did you really just call me a masher?"

"Absolutely. And I stand by it."

He untucked the front of Hermann's shirt and slid his hands underneath it, enjoying the warmth of his skin beneath his fingers. "I'll have you know I've been a perfect gentleman all afternoon. Do you have any idea how many improprieties I could have committed in that dark theater?"

Hermann turned around in his embrace so that they were facing one another and wrapped his arms around Dashiel's neck. "Well, why don't you show me a few of them now?"

"I'd be only too happy to."

Still locked in each other's arms, they sat down together on the love seat. Hermann lay back against the cushions and pulled Dashiel down on top of him, wrapping a leg around his hip and pulling him as close as possible.

But as the sun dipped below the horizon, they both grew silent and sober. They lay still together on the love seat, clinging to one another and listening hard as the shadows crowded in around them. The only sounds they heard were the trilling of night creatures outside and Horatio's quiet snoring from his spot in Hermann's armchair.

Hermann slowly relaxed again in Dashiel's arms, his eyes drifting closed. "I'm sorry, Dashiel," he mumbled, "but I really am beat. I need to sleep."

Dashiel sat up, suppressing a sigh of frustration. Part of him wanted to argue. Despite the horrors of the morning, it had been a glorious afternoon, and he wasn't ready for it to end. Still, he couldn't deny that sleep sounded appealing.

"All right," he agreed grudgingly. "I suppose the mashing can wait until tomorrow. Let's go to bed."

⁂

WHEN DASHIEL AWAKENED, it was still dark. It took a moment for him to get his bearings. He'd been having a dream. A strange one. He recalled standing in a dark marsh, surrounded by shadowy, swaying shapes.

And someone was with him—a vague silhouette on the horizon, drifting ever closer. But as he woke, the images faded like mist in the morning sunlight.

Something had startled him awake, but he wasn't sure what. Had it been a scream?

He realized, abruptly, that Hermann was sitting bolt upright beside him, breathing in ragged gasps. He'd kicked the blankets off, and they lay in a crumpled heap at the end of the bed.

"Hermann," he croaked, "are you all right? What's going on?"

"Something grabbed me," Hermann said in a strangled voice, squeezing Dashiel's wrist so hard that it hurt. "Something grabbed my ankle."

Dashiel's face grew cold. He flung his arm across Hermann's chest and fumbled for the lamp on the bedside table. He finally managed to switch it on, and they sat blinking in the sudden flood of light that filled the room.

"I don't see anything," said Dashiel. "Are you sure you weren't having a nightmare?"

"Maybe, maybe, I don't know," whispered Hermann. "It felt so real." He pulled his knees up to his chest and lifted the cuff of his pajama trousers. They both gasped. Dark bruises bloomed on his ankle, in the shape of a handprint.

"Jesus!" hissed Dashiel, horrified. "But how—"

Hermann grabbed his arm, and he fell silent. It was a warm night for early autumn, and Hermann had switched on the electric fan in the corner of the room when they retired to bed. As they listened, the fan's thrum grew louder and more rhythmic. It came in pulses, like a heartbeat.

And underneath that, a whisper—barely audible, but unmistakably there. At the same time, a familiar, foul odor filtered into the edges of Dashiel's awareness.

"Oh, hell," he cried, scrambling to his feet. "Hermann, it's here again!"

"I know that," said Hermann, anguished. "But I don't understand how. I threw it into the river, you saw me do it."

"Another picture?" Dashiel said, groping desperately for an answer.

"No! I don't have any more photographs, and even if I did, I certainly wouldn't have brought them here. I destroyed all of them, even the negatives."

Dashiel crept up to the door. It was ajar. Only the sliver of lamplight escaping from the bedroom illuminated the hallway beyond. He forced himself to reach out and push the door open further, then recoiled at the putrid blast of air. He pulled the lapel of his pajamas across his nose, coughing and gagging. Something touched his shoulder, and he started violently, stifling a cry of fear.

"Sha," whispered Hermann, giving his shoulder a squeeze. "It's just me." He brushed past Dashiel and began inching down the hallway, hugging the wall. Dashiel moved to follow him. The whispering grew louder, angrier, and more distinct as they went.

When they reached the end of the hall, Hermann peeked around the corner into the living room, then recoiled with a gasp. "Oy, Gotenyu," he groaned. He let his head fall back against the wall and squeezed his eyes shut.

"What? What is it?" hissed Dashiel.

"Things are—are moving in there," said Hermann. He shuddered. "It turns my stomach just to look at it."

Dashiel leaned past him to look and immediately regretted it. The curtains were open, allowing pale moonbeams to filter in through the windows. Dozens of eyes rolled and blinked at him from the pictures on the wall. Shapeless forms undulated among the shadows that had pooled in the corners of the room untouched by moonlight. On the mantel, all the little figurines writhed and squirmed and shoved themselves back into the shadows as far as they could go, as if burned by the soft illumination from the windows.

And in the middle of them all, propped up among the other knickknacks as if it had always been there, was the shabti.

Dashiel retreated around the corner, clamping a hand over his mouth in a vain effort to quiet his own panicked breathing.

"Dashiel—" Hermann began, but Dashiel held up a hand, stilling him.

"The shabti, Hermann," he said in a hoarse whisper, once he trusted himself to speak. "It's here! That little son of a bitch is sitting right there on your mantelpiece. The goddamn thing aported itself."

"What?"

"Quiet, quiet, for Christ's sake—"

"But how in God's name—Dashiel, wait!"

Dashiel darted into the living room. Every impulse in his body screamed at him to turn around and run in the opposite direction, but he forced himself to stride, on wobbly legs, to the fireplace.

"Dashiel!" Hermann cried out. "Dashiel, come back! What are you doing?"

"Looking f-for your fireplace matches," Dashiel stammered through chattering teeth, rummaging frantically on the mantel.

Something skittered over his fingers. It was the ceramic figurine of the Infant Samuel at Prayer, scrabbling on its hands and feet like a little animal. Dashiel yelped and yanked his hand away. Knocked off balance by his sudden movement, the figure teetered and fell to the floor. The shattered pieces continued writhing and twisting at his feet, making a strange, high keening noise. A wave of nausea crashed over him. He kicked the debris out of the way as best he could and kept searching.

"They're in the box by the end of the—no, to your right," said Hermann, still hovering at the entrance to the living room. "What on earth are you trying to do?"

"I'm trying to light the fire, damn it, what's it look like?" He finally spotted the box of matches and grabbed it. "Come on, give me a hand!"

Hermann hurried to the light switch and flipped it on, causing a frantic stir of activity among the little figurines. With a cry of horror and disgust, Dashiel swept his arm across the top of the mantel, sending them all crashing to the floor. The shabti spun and bounced over the tiles in front of the fireplace, coming to rest, unharmed, a few feet away from him.

With numb, trembling fingers, he fumbled a match out of the box. He dropped to his knees, wincing at the shock of pain that lanced through his injured leg, and wrenched open the gas knob in the fireplace. His hands shook so hard that it took him five tries to light the match. The incessant whispering noise intensified, drawing strength from the hissing of the gas line. Dashiel thrust the match up to the pilot and held it there for what felt like an eternity before the fire blazed into life with a quiet, velvety whoomph.

A deep rumble passed through the floor beneath his knees, and the wooden beams in the walls shifted and groaned. Out of the corner of his eye, he saw something moving in the shadows to his right—a spot of unnatural darkness at the edge of the room, as if a bit of the light there had been burned away. It was drifting closer to him. His skin crawled.

He crept on his hands and knees toward the shabti. It lay serene and still amid the squirming wreckage of the ornaments from the mantel. The whispering grew almost unbearably loud when his fingers closed around it, as if someone were blowing compressed air directly into his ears. A heavy object flew past his head, grazing his ear and crashing against the wall behind him. Hermann cried out in alarm.

Dashiel turned and hurled the shabti into the fireplace as hard as he could. It bounced off the back of the firebox and tumbled behind the ceramic logs, disappearing among the leaping flames. The whispering turned into a high-pitched howl, and the shattered figurines on the floor twitched and convulsed sickeningly. Filaments of shadow swirled and slithered around his knees as they rushed into the fireplace and vanished. The incandescent bulb on the ceiling blazed impossibly bright, then blew out, plunging the room into flickering shadow. Dashiel's ears rang in the sudden silence that followed.

Hermann rushed over and dropped to his knees beside him, then hurriedly examined his face and ear. Apparently satisfied that his injuries were minor, he turned his attention to the fireplace.

"Do you see it?" whispered Dashiel.

"There," said Hermann. He pointed. Dashiel craned his neck to look. The shabti was wedged up against the back of the fireplace, its little feet poking up over one of the ceramic logs. They watched as it cracked and crumbled into a pile of powdery fragments at the bottom of the hearth.

"Come on," gasped Dashiel. "We have to get out of here."

Hermann looked stunned. "But it's destroyed."

"Maybe. But I don't feel safe here, just the same."

He struggled vainly to get to his feet. Hermann stood, took hold of his arms, and hauled him upright.

"We could go stay in a hotel for the night," Hermann said.

"Good idea. As long as it's not the Grande."

Hermann nodded and swallowed hard, still gripping Dashiel's arms. "Horatio," he said, "I can't leave him here. But I don't think they'll let me bring him into a hotel. We'll have to leave him with Lucille."

"Whatever you need to do, Hermann, but for God's sake, do it fast."

✦

THEY SCRAMBLED TO change out of their pajamas, then went in search of Horatio. He was wedged as far beneath the icebox as he could get. Dashiel managed to drag him out, growling and spitting, and Hermann wrapped him in a towel. They hurried out, not bothering to gather any of their belongings aside from their jackets, Hermann's keys and billfold, and Dashiel's cane. Horatio yowled piteously all the way down the stairs to Mrs. Luckett's apartment.

Since Hermann's arms were full, Dashiel pounded on her door. After two or three bursts of frantic knocking, he heard the quiet creak of footsteps from inside.

There was a pause, and then Mrs. Luckett opened the door. She was wrapped in a flowery bathrobe, her hair tucked under a pink silk scarf.

"Why, Mr. Quicke!" she said, staring up at them in alarm. "Hermann! What's all this about?"

"Sorry to trouble you at this hour, ma'am—" said Dashiel.

"I'm so sorry, Lucille," Hermann cut in. He spoke haltingly, as if in a daze. "I know it's late, but something's happened, and we need to leave. Just for the night, I think, but I don't feel safe leaving Horatio in my apartment. Can you take him?"

"Of course I can!" She opened the door wide, gesturing for them to enter. "Come inside. Tell me what's going on."

Hermann shook his head. "Thank you, dear, but we can't stay," he said. He held out Horatio, who gave a mournful little mew. Mrs. Luckett gave Hermann a long, searching look, then reached out and scooped the frightened cat into her arms.

"If you boys are in some kind of trouble, I might know people who can help," she said.

"I don't think so, Lucille," said Hermann, looking at the floor. "Not with this kind of trouble."

"You don't have to hide things from me, Hermann, you know that. You and me, we've always looked out for each other. Whatever it is, you can . . ." She trailed off. Hermann's face had crumpled. "Oh, honey! Are you all right?"

"I'm—I'm not sure." A tear rolled down his cheek, and he hastily wiped it away. Dashiel put a hand on his elbow.

"We're okay," said Dashiel. "Just a little shaken, that's all. Can't thank you enough, Mrs. Luckett, but we really do have to go. Come on, Hermann."

His heart ached for Hermann, but his nerves were still crackling with horror after their ordeal. He hated the idea of lingering in the building an instant longer than necessary.

Mrs. Luckett bristled. "None of this looks okay to me, Mr. Quicke."

"No, he's right," Hermann assured her, pulling himself together. "I'll be fine. I've just had a good scare."

"If you say so," she said, frowning. "But I don't like this one bit. Hermann, you promise to call me when you get wherever you're going, you hear me? I don't care how late it is."

Hermann nodded, sniffing and dabbing at his eyes with his handkerchief. "Of course I will, dear. I'll call you and—and I'll explain everything. Or at least, I'll try." He leaned in and gave her a quick kiss on the cheek, then scratched Horatio behind the ears. "Be good for Aunt Lucille, ketzeleh. I'll be back before you know it."

⁂

THEY CLIMBED INTO the car in silence. Hermann turned on the ignition and sped away, seemingly with a destination already in mind.

"Where are we going?" asked Dashiel.

"DeKalb," said Hermann, keeping his gaze locked on the road ahead of him. "We'll stay at the Rice Hotel."

Dashiel's eyebrows lifted. "That's a ways off."

"I know. That's why I chose it. I want to put some distance between us and . . . all of this."

"What are you going to tell Lucille?"

Hermann let go of the steering wheel for a second to spread his hands in a helpless gesture. "The truth, I suppose. I certainly owe her an explanation after what happened tonight. I should have told her ages ago. She's my oldest and dearest friend here in Willowvale. We've been there for each other through thick and thin. She already knows I'm a bit peculiar, and she's always accepted that without judgment, bless her. But I don't want her thinking I'm a complete meshugeneh."

"I don't think friends put quotas on their pals' idiosyncrasies," Dashiel said, frowning sympathetically. "Not good ones, anyway."

"I know, there's no logic in it. I guess I just wanted one thing in my life to still feel normal." He looked like he was trying hard not to start crying again. "This thing's taken so much from me, Dashiel. It's interrupted my work. The few friends I've told think I'm absolutely crackers, and I'm afraid to tell the rest. Now I can't even feel safe in my own home. You've been the one bright spot in all this, do you know that? I don't know what might have become of me by now if you hadn't turned up when you did."

Dashiel managed a wan smile but said nothing. A half-formed idea had wormed its way into his weary brain that he was loath to put into words. He did his best to push it away.

"Do you think there's a chance it might be gone now?" he asked after a moment. "Really gone, I mean."

"I don't know," said Hermann. "We seem to be dealing with an incredibly powerful spirit. Even if the shabti itself really is destroyed, I don't trust it not to find some other way in."

<hr />

HERMANN WAS AS good as his word. As soon as they had checked into the hotel, he called Lucille. Dashiel lay back on one of the little twin beds and closed his eyes, half-listening to his conversation.

"Yes, I'm all right, I'm safe," Hermann was saying. "We're in DeKalb. No, nobody's hurt. I'm so sorry to drag you into all this. I feel just sick about it . . . What? Why, of course not! He's a good man, Lucille. Yes, I trust him. I would trust him with my life."

Dashiel winced and rolled over to face the wall. He was sure Hermann was talking about him. He'd heard himself described in similar terms before, usually by doddering old widows trying to explain to their dismayed loved ones why they were signing their pensions over to him. He knew that Hermann meant it kindly, but it made him burn with chagrin to hear it from his lips.

"What?" said Hermann. "Oh, good lord!"

The note of alarm in his voice was enough to distract Dashiel from his momentary embarrassment. He turned back toward Hermann and gave him a questioning look.

Hermann looked distraught. He put his hand over the phone's mouthpiece and said to Dashiel in a low voice, "She says she can hear noises upstairs, in my apartment. Like someone's throwing things." He removed his hand and spoke into the phone again. "No, please don't call the police. It wouldn't do any good. Whatever's up there isn't human . . . not anymore, at least."

Dashiel's heart sank. He'd known that it was optimistic to hope they'd gotten rid of it, but this was worse than he'd imagined. He sat up and felt reflexively for the long-absent packet of cigarettes in his front coat pocket. He was all out of ideas save for one, and his confidence in it was close to nil. Still, it was something.

He got up and went into the bathroom. In a stumbling, hesitant way, Hermann had begun explaining the situation to Lucille. Dashiel felt bad leaving him alone, but he needed to clear his head, and he thought a hot shower might help.

He stood under the steaming water for some ten minutes, just staring at the blue ceramic tiles on the wall before he even bothered to pick up the soap. He was lathering himself up in a half-hearted way when a quiet knock sounded on the door.

"Come on in," he said, peering around the edge of the shower curtain. The door opened, and Hermann entered. "How'd it go?"

"For better or worse, I told her everything," Hermann said, closing the door behind him and leaning against it.

"Did she believe you?"

"I don't know. If she does think I'm cuckoo, at least she was kind about it." He rubbed his hands over his face and yawned. "I don't think I've ever been so tired. I'd better lie down before I fall down."

"Hold on," said Dashiel. "There's something I need to talk to you about."

Hermann paused with his hand on the doorknob, his brow creased with concern. "What is it?"

"If what Lucille said is true, that damned spirit must have come right back after we left. We didn't get rid of it at all."

"I know. But there's not a thing we can do about it right now. It should go back to rest by sunup. We'll go back tomorrow, and I'll . . . I don't know what I'll do. We can figure it out in the morning."

"Hermann, this can't go on. Destroying it is obviously a bust. It's time to go back to Plan A. We need to communicate with it."

Hermann dismissed the idea with a weary wave of his hand. "We tried that already."

"No. You wrote it a letter. It still hasn't been able to answer. We need to give it a way to talk back. If we can find out what it wants—if there's even the slightest chance we can do something to help lay it to rest—then I think that's our best hope."

"What are you suggesting?" asked Hermann, but the tension in his shoulders told Dashiel that he already knew the answer.

"I want to try a séance."

"No."

"Hermann, it's the only idea I've got. I have to try it. I have to. We're out of options."

"No," Hermann said again, taking a step closer. "Absolutely not. I won't allow it."

"It's not a question of you allowing anything," said Dashiel, frowning at him. "I've already made up my mind. I'm going to do it, with or without your blessing."

"You said yourself that it wouldn't work!" Hermann said desperately. "What's the point? You'd just be needlessly endangering yourself."

Dashiel scrubbed at his shoulder with stubborn determination, avoiding Hermann's imploring gaze. "I don't know if it would work. Probably not. I've never channeled a real ghost, far as I know. Until recently I didn't know there was any such thing. But I studied trance mediumship. I know the techniques, and I know the theory behind them, such as it is."

It felt bizarre to say it out loud. The whole notion was ridiculous.

At the same time, it both thrilled and frightened him.

"And what if it did work?" Hermann said. "What then? You've seen what that thing is capable of. You'd have to be crazy to invite it inside your head like that. You can't do it, Dashiel, it's too dangerous."

"Well, we have to do something, for Christ's sake! This is no way to live."

"Better this than the alternative!"

"I thought you wanted my help," Dashiel snapped. "That's the whole reason you dragged me into this ghost mess of yours, isn't it? Well, this is the only help I know how to offer."

"Of course I want your help," said Hermann, his voice thick with emotion. "But not as much as I want you. Don't you understand? I can't lose you to this thing on top of everything else. I need you. I love you."

Dashiel froze. He was still searching for a fitting answer when Hermann spoke again.

"I guess I can't stop you if you're determined to do this thing," he said. "But I hope it's an unqualified failure. May you find out that you're just as much of a humbug as you always thought you were. I'm going to bed, Dashiel. Goodnight."

Dashiel finished his shower and crept out of the bathroom. Hermann had already curled up on one of the beds and switched off the light. Without bothering to get dressed again, Dashiel squeezed himself in behind him on the narrow mattress and wrapped an arm around him, pulling him close. He felt Hermann's hand close around his, but neither of them spoke. They lay together in silence until sleep finally overcame them.

CHAPTER 12

A FTER A QUIET, UNHAPPY breakfast in the hotel's dining room the next morning, they headed back to Willowvale. Before they left, Hermann had reluctantly rung up Agnes to let her know that he would be out sick again. They didn't talk about the séance again, or much of anything else, until after they got back to Hermann's building.

Before they went up to the apartment, Hermann knocked on Lucille's door. She opened it almost immediately, this time dressed in her nurse's uniform.

"Oh, it's good to see you safe and sound," she said, wrapping Hermann in a tight hug. "Come on inside. I have to leave in half an hour, but there's time for coffee before I go."

Lucille's apartment was bright and tidy, and far less cluttered than Hermann's. Her tastes ran more to fresh-cut flowers and bowls of wax fruit than old knick-knacks and dusty books. Dashiel noticed that there was only one place setting at her little dining table.

He guessed that Mr. Luckett must have passed on or was otherwise no longer in the picture.

Horatio trotted up to greet them after they sat down. Hermann scooped the cat into his lap, and he tucked his little striped head into the crook of Hermann's elbow and purred.

"You boys gave me a hell of a scare last night," said Lucille, setting a cup of coffee down in front of each of them and taking a seat.

Hermann took her hand. "Oh, Lucille, I feel like such an awful
putz," he said. "If I'd been thinking half-straight, I would have told
you to clear out of here, too. What happened after we spoke on the
phone? Did the noise keep you up all night?"

"No," she said. "It went on for about twenty or thirty minutes,
then things got quiet. What are you going to do now? Is it safe to
go back to your place with . . . whatever it is in there?"

Hermann nodded. "It goes dormant during the day. We should
be fine until sunset. After that—God knows."

"After that, we're going to have a talk with it," said Dashiel
with grim determination.

Hermann groaned and rubbed his temples. "Please," he said,
putting a hand on Dashiel's wrist. "Not this foilishtik again. There
must be another way."

"If there is, I'd sure like to hear it."

"I think the first thing we ought to do is figure out how it got
back into my apartment. I hate to think what we're going to find
up there—"

"Hold on," Lucille cut in. She narrowed her eyes at Dashiel.
"What do you mean, 'have a talk with it?'"

"Dashiel's got it into his head that we need to have a séance,"
said Hermann. "He thinks we might be able to find out what it
wants and put it to rest."

"I'm a medium. Or at least, I used to be," Dashiel explained.
Lucille continued to regard him dubiously, but she nodded. Hermann must have filled her in. "I'm thinking automatic writing
would be just the ticket. If it could use my hand to write a message . . ."

Hermann was shaking his head with increasing vehemence,
but Lucille seemed intrigued. She gave Dashiel a long, penetrating

look. "That doesn't sound like a half-bad idea to me, Mr. Quicke," she said slowly. "You think there's any chance it could work?"

"Very little, I imagine," he said. He'd been trying not to think too hard about that. If it didn't work, which seemed the most likely outcome, then he would have upset Hermann and wasted everyone's time for nothing. But if it did . . . He took a deep breath and met Lucille's gaze. "Look, my mediumship was always phony. I don't deny that, and I leveled with Hermann about it right from the start."

She took a sip of her coffee, her expression cool and carefully neutral. "I never said otherwise, Mr. Quicke."

"But I did study some trance techniques back in the day, for what that's worth," he went on. "Anyway, this spirit seems real enough, and it certainly has the will to communicate. So, I figure there's a slim chance, at least."

"And more than a slim chance that you could end up hurt, or worse," said Hermann.

"When are you planning to do this?" asked Lucille.

"Never, if I have anything to say about it," Hermann said, pinning Dashiel with a reproachful glare.

"Tonight," said Dashiel. He gazed ahead stonily. "As soon as possible."

Lucille considered for a moment. "Well, whenever you decide to do it, you let me know," she said. "I want to be there."

Hermann's eyes went round with dismay. "Lucille, no!"

"Hermann, listen," said Lucille. She put a steady hand on his shoulder. "We've been friends for almost fifteen years. I know you're not lying to me or making up tall tales. If you tell me there's an ancient Egyptian ghost in your apartment, I figure you've got a darn good reason for believing it. But I want to see for myself whatever or whoever it is that's been causing you so much grief."

"It's Tuesday," said Hermann, dropping his head into his hands. "We're supposed to be playing bridge tonight, not practicing necromancy. And I'm not interested in any solution that involves people I care about getting hurt!"

"Hermann," said Dashiel, "it's too late for that. It's hurting people already, and that's not going to change if we just sit back and do nothing. Just look what it's done to you." He gestured to Hermann's face. The bruise was still there, but it had begun to fade to a mottled greenish color. Hermann touched his cheek self-consciously and looked away.

"Something certainly needs to change," said Lucille. "If Mr. Quicke here is determined to try this séance business, I say we let him. And if you're that worried about someone getting hurt, don't you think it would make sense to have a nurse there?"

Dashiel was certain that her keen interest had at least as much to do with her suspicions about his motives as her desire to see the alleged ghost in action. He didn't hold it against her. He could only imagine how alarming the events of the past several days must have looked from her perspective. Besides, he was grateful to have her on his side in the debate, whatever her reasons might be.

"She's got an excellent point," he said. He brushed his foot gently against Hermann's ankle under the table. "Come on. At least let me try to help you. I can't stand watching you suffer like this."

Hermann drummed his fingers on the table in agitation. "All right, all right, I'll think about it. But let's not talk about it anymore right now. My head is killing me."

Lucille suggested they leave Horatio in her care a little while longer, at least until they'd had a chance to assess the state of the apartment. They finished their coffee, thanked her profusely for her help, and made their way upstairs with pounding hearts and clammy palms.

They exchanged a wordless look of trepidation before Hermann put his key in the lock and opened the door. He poked his head in, heaved a deep sigh, and beckoned Dashiel inside.

The place was, as expected, a wreck. In the living room, one of the chairs had been overturned, and the telephone table was knocked over. Books and papers littered the floor. A quiet electric hum led Dashiel to the phone, which lay by the wall near the kitchen entrance. He wondered if that was the object that had grazed his ear the night before. He knelt to pick it up and put the receiver back on the hook.

"My God," said Hermann, who had wended his way through the piles of debris to the mantel. "Dashiel, come look at this."

Dashiel rose and moved to his side, murmuring, "What in the hell . . .?"

The ceramic figurines that he'd knocked off the mantel the night before had all been restored and set back in place, as if they had never been broken at all. And there, in the middle of all of them, was the shabti. It was impossibly intact, without so much as a scorch mark to show for its adventure in the fireplace. Hermann reached out and picked it up with a trembling hand. He turned it over and over, shaking his head in disbelief.

"How did it do this?" asked Dashiel. He could sense the sinister energy radiating from the little figure like heat off a warm griddle. And there it was again, that same low thrumming he'd felt in his skull when they carried it to the river. He shuddered.

"I don't know," Hermann said. His lips were pale, and the skin around his eyes was tight with anxiety. "I'm reminded of the sorcerer Djedi, from the Westcar Papyrus tales. He was said to have magically reattached the heads of decapitated animals and brought them back to life."

Dashiel peered at the reassembled figurines on the mantel. "Why would it bother fixing these?" he asked, poking at a ceramic cat with the tip of his finger. Parts of it looked mismatched, as if it had been put together from pieces of several different figures.

"It wants its little army of *djed-fet*, I suppose."

"*Djed-fet*?"

"Creepy crawlies," said Hermann. "It's a Demotic Egyptian expression. It usually refers to snakes and centipedes and scorpions, that sort of thing. It means 'Things that say *fffft*.'"

Dashiel snorted, amused despite his unease. "When you put it that way, it sounds downright adorable."

"The ancient Egyptians took the power of graven images very seriously," said Hermann, who scarcely seemed to have heard him. "In some tomb chapels, they neutralized hieroglyphs of dangerous animals by drawing them cut up into separate segments or run through with knives, in case some unfriendly force animated them and sent them after the soul of the dead. The literary texts are full of references to magicians bringing wax figures to life and making them do their bidding."

"Speaking of creepy crawlies," said Dashiel, picking up one of the figurines and showing it to Hermann. It had the body of a cat, but the head of the Infant Samuel had been attached to its neck with the face turned backward. There was no obvious joint between the two pieces—it looked as if it had been designed that way.

Hermann recoiled. "This is all so ghastly." He set down the shabti and turned away from the mantel, wringing his hands. "What an awful mess. I don't even know where to begin."

"Why don't you go rest?" Dashiel suggested. "Let me work on it for a while."

"I couldn't possibly rest while that miserable shabti is here. I should take it back to campus until we can figure out what to do with it. Only I told them I was out sick, so I don't know how I'd explain . . ." He spoke absently, still scanning the wreckage of the living room. "That's it." He pointed at a pile of books by the overturned telephone table. "Right there. That's how the little monster got in."

Dashiel followed his gaze to a book that lay slightly apart from the rest. The pages were open to a large, glossy plate of a false door.

"Shit!" said Dashiel. He waded through the debris and snatched the book up off the floor, then roughly took hold of the offending page. He was about to start ripping when Hermann rushed over and grabbed his arm.

"Hold on, what are you doing?"

"I'm going to rip this page out and destroy it. And if there are any more pictures of one of these things in here, I'm taking them out, too. Hell, we ought to burn the whole damn book."

Hermann took the book out of his hands, looking pained. "Don't do that, Dashiel. It's not my book, I borrowed it from the archive."

"It's not the only copy in the world, is it?"

"Dashiel, please. I'll go put it in my car. And the shabti. I'll drop them off on campus this evening after the building closes, before sundown."

"Not the shabti. I'm going to need it for the séance."

Hermann snapped the book shut and glowered at him. "And where are you planning to hold this séance of yours? Not in my apartment, I hope. We've had enough trouble with the ghost here already without you laying out a welcome mat for it."

"Well, where would you propose we do it, then?" said Dashiel, fighting to keep his tone level. He could feel the shabti's baleful influence seeping into him, darkening his mood and making his temper rise. "I'm open to suggestions."

"I would propose we don't do it at all," said Hermann, who was losing the battle to keep his own dander down. "But if you insist on being a stubborn ass about it, then I'd say we should do it someplace very plain and austere and empty, where it won't have any tchotchkes or sculptures or pictures or any nonsense of that sort to send after us. And, preferably, nothing it can throw. Excuse me, Dashiel. I'm getting these accursed things out of here."

He tucked the book under his arm, grabbed the shabti from the mantel and stalked out, slamming the apartment door behind him.

Dashiel sensed the shabti's influence diminishing as Hermann moved away with it. A feeling of relative tranquility settled over him. He set about righting the toppled furniture and shoving books back onto shelves, all the while pondering what Hermann had said about the location of the séance.

He couldn't deny that he'd made a good point. The more he thought about it, the less he liked the idea of holding the séance in the apartment. The museum gallery was out of the question, and he didn't much care for the idea of doing it in the archive or in Hermann's office, either. Too many books, which were both highly throwable and full of pictures.

An empty classroom, he decided, might be just what the doctor ordered. He'd seen a small one down the hall from the room where he'd observed Hermann's class. It contained a heavy table with chairs around it, instead of a row of desks and a lectern. They could carry out most of the chairs and put them in the hallway. They'd just have to hope the ghost wasn't powerful enough to throw the table.

Hermann returned a moment later, just as Dashiel was dumping a pile of papers back into the little drawer of the telephone table. He closed the door softly and hovered in the entrance of the living room, looking abashed. "I put the book and shabti in the car," he said. "We can decide what to do with them later. Dashiel, I'm sorry. I shouldn't have snapped at you like that."

"You don't have a thing to apologize for," said Dashiel, straightening up and brushing the dust from his hands. "Forget about it, kid. I already have." He went to Hermann and put his arms around him. Hermann melted into his embrace.

"All right." He sighed, leaning his head against Dashiel's shoulder. "Tell me about this séance plan of yours."

❦

THEY ARRIVED AT campus shortly after five o'clock. Hermann made the drive in white-knuckled silence. Lucille sat beside him up front, while Dashiel took the rumble seat. He didn't mind sitting by himself for the brief ride. It gave him time to meditate on his upcoming task. He wouldn't have admitted it to Hermann, but the closer they got to their destination, the more frightened and uncertain he felt.

Hermann parked the car in front of the Wexler Building and twisted around in his seat to rap on the rear window. "Are you sure about this, Dashiel?" he said, raising his voice to be heard through the glass. It must have been the hundredth time he'd asked that evening. "It's not too late to change your mind."

"I'm sure," Dashiel called back, with far more confidence than he felt.

With a resigned nod, Hermann hopped out of the car and walked around to the passenger side to open the door for Lucille. "What about you, Lucille?" he asked, offering her his hand. "This could be dangerous for you, too, you know. If you want to go home, I could—"

"You know I wouldn't miss this for the world, Mr. Hermann," she cut in calmly. She paused to pin a stray curl back into place beneath her hat, then took his hand and stepped out of the car. "Come on, let's get going. It's almost sunset."

They both helped Dashiel clamber out of the rumble seat, then made a solemn procession up the sidewalk to the building.

Dashiel hadn't bothered to bring all his usual mediumistic accouterments. He didn't need the trumpets, the gauze ectoplasm, or the flowing chiffon robes. For his purposes, a paper and pencil would suffice. He decided to bring a candle as well. He had little faith in the notion that darkness was necessary for an effective séance, but doing it by full incandescent light went against all his instincts.

As they gathered their things, Dashiel realized he still had the box with the little clay snake amulet in one of the side pockets of his jacket—something he and Hermann had both forgotten about in the excitement that followed their fateful evening in the archive. They'd added it to the collection of necessities, and Hermann had tucked all of them—along with the shabti—into his briefcase, which he now carried under his arm.

It was after hours when they arrived, but the building was still unlocked. Hermann led them up the front steps and ushered them through the doors. After some brief vacillation over whether it was safe to take the elevator, they decided to use the stairs to the second floor instead.

"Here it is," said Hermann, stopping in front of the classroom that Dashiel had marked out for their grim venture. "Room 210. After you." He opened the door and gestured Dashiel and Lucille inside.

Having stepped into the room, Dashiel gave it an appraising once-over. "This should do nicely," he said. "No pictures, no clutter. The blackboard looks secure." He walked up to it and gave it an experimental rattle, just to be sure. "What's that door in the back?"

"Just a supply closet," Hermann said. "I think there's a slide projector in there, but it's usually locked up unless someone needs it." He went and shook the doorknob, confirming that it was locked.

"All right," said Dashiel. "Let's get these chairs out of here. We only need enough for the three of us to sit in."

"This should go, too," said Lucille, bending to pick up a brick that someone must have brought in to use as a doorstop.

"Good spotting, Mrs. Luckett," Dashiel said with an approving nod. "The last thing we need is to have that sailing through the air at someone's head."

A quick sweep for other odd objects about the room turned up a metal wastebasket and an abandoned coffee cup. Lucille put the brick and the cup inside the wastebasket and carried the entire caboodle away down the hall, while Hermann and Dashiel set about moving the chairs. They lined them up neatly in the hallway, leaving only three of them clustered around one end of the table.

Once they were satisfied that the room was empty of most of its moveable contents, Hermann opened his briefcase and brought out the candle and candlestick. Then he handed over the pencil and paper, the snake amulet, and, finally, with great reluctance, the shabti. Dashiel took a seat at the head of the table and laid the objects out in front of him in a row.

"Here, you take the snake," said Dashiel, pushing the little box toward Hermann. "Maybe you can use it to scare it off, just in case things go—"

"Yes," Hermann interrupted, pulling the box close to himself.

Dashiel patted his hand and smiled. "Listen, it'll all turn out just fine. I promise."

Hermann eyed him anxiously but said nothing.

"What happens now?" asked Lucille, taking the seat to Dashiel's right. Hermann sat down across from her, at his left.

"Well," said Dashiel, rising to light the candle with his sterling silver lighter, "I'm not entirely sure. But if we're going to follow the traditional procedure, we'll have to switch off the lights. Then, I suppose, we wait. Once the sun goes down, that thing will wake up, and I'm sure it'll give us quite a show. Meanwhile," he added with a wry smile, "I'm going to try to open myself to it. Just like they taught me in medium school."

"I'll get the lights," said Hermann, who looked utterly miserable. "But let's at least leave the blinds open."

"That's fine with me," agreed Dashiel.

Hermann was making his way to the light switch at the far end of the room when one of the doors banged open. He gave a yelp of alarm and stumbled backward, bumping up against a corner of the table.

Lucille cried out and pressed a hand to her chest. Dashiel rocketed to his feet, almost upsetting his chair. When the room finally stopped spinning, he realized that Agnes was standing in the doorway, glaring at them.

"What's going on here?" she demanded.

"Agnes," said Hermann, nearly bent over double trying to catch his breath. "For God's sake, you almost frightened me to death. Why are you here? You should go, it isn't safe!"

"I'm sorry, Professor," she said, "but I need answers. Yesterday was the last straw. Whatever's been happening, I'm getting to the bottom of it, tonight." She rounded on Dashiel. "You! I knew you had something to do with all this monkey business, mister. Just what the hell are you people up to, anyway?"

"Looking for answers, same as you," said Dashiel, with all the patience he could muster. "If you must know, we're holding a séance."

"We'd better get started, too," said Lucille, glancing at her wristwatch. "The sun's going down any minute."

Agnes raised an eyebrow, unimpressed. "A séance, huh? Oh, this I have to see."

"Agnes, I must insist that you leave," said Hermann, reaching out to take her arm.

She took a step back. "I'm not going anywhere," she said, crossing her arms over her chest and staring him down. "Not until I find out what this is all about."

"Agnes, please," said Hermann, but his appeal fell on deaf ears. She ducked out of the doorway and returned carrying one of the banished chairs. She dragged it around the table and shoved it into place next to Hermann's seat with a loud clatter, then plopped herself down in it.

"What now?" she asked, fixing Dashiel with a hard stare. "Are we all supposed to hold hands or something?"

He shook his head. "Not necessary."

"Good. Let's get on with it."

With a weary sigh, Hermann went and switched off the lights, then settled into his chair between Dashiel and Agnes. Dashiel could feel Hermann's leg bouncing beneath the table. The sun sank lower in the sky, and the candle's tiny glow became grander, filling the room with dancing light and flickering shadows.

Dashiel judged that it was time to begin. He raised his hands in a grand, sweeping gesture, instantly capturing the attention of his small group of sitters. There was no need for this sort of pomp and ceremony, but the well-worn familiarity of it put him at ease.

"Ladies and gentlemen, I will need complete silence," he said, speaking in the lilting cadence of the séance room. "I'm going to attempt to attune myself to the vibrations of the spirit realm. You may see me enter a trancelike state. Try not to be alarmed. If all goes well, the spirit will be able to use me as a conduit to write a message for us."

Agnes snorted. Hermann put a hand on her arm and whispered something to her before turning his attention back to Dashiel. He took the little snake out of its box and fidgeted with it. On Dashiel's other side, Lucille remained silent and watchful, her gloved hands folded elegantly before her.

Once everyone was settled, Dashiel picked up the pencil and held it loosely, with his hand resting atop the sheet of paper. Then he leaned back in the chair and closed his eyes.

The act of going into a mediumistic trance was a routine he'd performed more times than he could count. Under normal circumstances, it was a theatrical affair, with lots of eye-rolling and swooning and wild, convulsive movements. The latter could be used to cover up all sorts of sleight of hand devilment. This time, he focused on simply relaxing instead.

It was no easy feat. The nervous breathing and fidgeting of the sitters distracted him, and the thudding of his own heart was so loud he was sure it must be audible to the rest of them. But he gently guided his attention to the sensation of the cool tabletop beneath his hands, the solidity of the floor under his feet, and the firm support of the chair behind his back.

In the darkness behind his eyelids, he let his inner walls fall away. He could feel the presence of the dormant shabti in front of him, a seething little ball of ancient malice and rage. Instead of obeying his impulse to withdraw from it, to try to shut it out, he reached out to it with his mind. He imagined opening a door and beckoning it in, like an old friend.

Come on, you miserable little bastard, he silently urged. *Come to me. Show me what you want. I'm all yours.*

Still, aside from the fact that he was now fuming with unfocused anger, he didn't seem to be accomplishing much. The minutes dragged by in uncomfortable silence. A clock ticked loudly on the wall, which only added to his growing frustration. He realized that his fist had clenched around the pencil and forced his hand to relax again. The pencil dropped from his fingers and clattered onto the table.

"Is something supposed to be happening?" grumbled Agnes. "Because I don't—"

Hermann and Lucille both shushed her, and Dashiel suppressed a surge of irritation. In his days as an active medium, he'd never had much patience for hecklers or doubters. He'd escorted more than one of them out of his séance room back at the camp with a rough hand and a harshly whispered threat. The recollection gave him a little spark of vicious joy.

"Silence, please," he said, between clenched teeth.

Even with his eyes closed, he could sense the room growing darker. The ticking of the clock continued its relentless assault on his ears and nerves. But the sound seemed distorted, as if it had developed an echo. It was an odd, susurrating noise, a vibration that was almost a whisper . . .

And then came the smell—that familiar, cloying mixture of decay and sweet spices. Dashiel breathed it in, defiantly welcoming. Lucille made a soft sound of displeasure. Agnes began to cough.

"Jesus, Mary, and Joseph," she said in a hushed voice. "What the hell is that?"

Dashiel sensed Hermann growing still beside him and heard his breath quickening. On his other side, Lucille shifted in her seat. "Oh, my lord," she whispered.

"Oh God, do you see that?" said Agnes. "How is he doing this?"

"He's not," said Hermann. His hand tightened around Dashiel's wrist. "Dashiel, it's here."

A thrill of fear ran through Dashiel, and he fought the overpowering urge to open his eyes. That infernal whispering grew louder and closer. The table vibrated beneath his hands; he could hear the chalkboard rattling on the wall. He leaned his head back, relaxed his muscles as well as he could, and let his breath come in a slow, easy rhythm. *Just like preparing for the dentist's drill*, he told himself. *Let it happen, get it over with.*

In an awful, sinister way, it felt good to open himself to it. The rest of the world began to fade from his awareness as he allowed the angry presence to flood over him, filling his veins with a cold, righteous fury. He inhaled deeply through his nose, willing it to take him completely.

His nostrils and lungs stung with a sudden, icy chill, as if he'd just taken a deep whiff of midnight air in the dead of February. His whole body spasmed with the shock of it, and he flung himself back, hard, in the chair. Warm human hands grabbed at him, preventing him from toppling over backward and crashing to the floor.

The others were shouting and screaming, but he could hardly hear them. They sounded distant and muffled, like they were yelling underwater. He tried to turn his head, to open his eyes and look at what was happening, but he couldn't. His body simply wouldn't respond to his brain's commands.

He felt like someone had replaced his blood with ice water. Something cold and thick and viscous oozed from his ears, his nose, even his eyes. It filled his mouth, escaping through his parted lips, and trickled over his chin. Someone was retching, coughing, gasping for air. He realized, with detached dismay, that it was him.

He lurched forward in his seat and began to spit and paw at his mouth and eyes. No, that wasn't quite accurate. Someone else was doing it for him, like an amateurish puppeteer operating a ghastly marionette. His hand flopped and swiped at his face like a limp, meaty paddle before falling back to the table with a thud. Then whoever or whatever it was forced his mouth open, and a voice not his own came out, rasping and guttural and gurgling.

It was agony. His throat burned as if it had been rubbed raw with sandpaper. Even if he knew the language that his tongue was being used to utter, he wasn't sure he could have understood it. His jaws and tongue flapped clumsily in a crude parody of speech. His mouth and throat were gummed up with slime.

Dashiel was fading into the background of his own mind, sinking into a vast ocean of rage and frustration. Reality slipped away from him, and for a time that could have been anywhere between a split second or an eternity, he couldn't remember where he was, who was with him, or what he was supposed to be doing.

"I can't understand you," he heard someone say. It was a man's voice, distant and nearly inaudible through the muck in his ears, but familiar. The small part of him that was still himself clung to that voice like a buoy. It was the voice of a friend. Someone who loved him. Hermann. His head turned toward the voice, but through no volition of his own.

"You have to write," Hermann said. He sounded terrified. "Don't hurt him. He's trying to help you. Pick up the pencil, go on. Go on, you can do it. Oh God, Dashiel, are you in there somewhere? Please, you must tell it to write."

The thing inside Dashiel seemed to recognize Hermann's voice as well. It responded with a renewed burst of outrage, as if Hermann were somehow at the center of its frustrations. It raised Dashiel's hands like useless, floppy claws and struck out at him with them. Someone's arms encircled his body from behind, pulling him back. Another pair of hands took hold of his wrists and held them tightly.

Stop that! He's a friend, you damn fool, Dashiel tried to scream at his unseen operator. *Tell him what you want. Pick up the pencil and write it down.*

He focused every remaining ounce of energy that he had on visualizing the pencil, imagining the feel of it in his hand, picturing the act of writing. His rigid body began to relax, and a wisp of understanding floated up and mingled with the anger roiling in his breast.

The fingers of his right hand slowly opened, and his head nodded. Or at least, it wobbled in a grotesque approximation of a nod. Someone put an object in his hand and closed his fingers around it, then guided his hand to the paper.

His grip tightened on the pencil. There was a pause, then his hand jerked into action. Its movements were clumsy and spastic at first, but his puppeteer seemed to gain confidence quickly. His hand kept writing, scribbling away at a frantic pace, while the rest of his body slumped ever lower in the chair, apparently forgotten in the spirit's single-minded quest to get its message out and onto the paper. He realized, with a distant spike of alarm, that he was no longer breathing.

There was a sudden commotion around him. Someone reached into his breast pocket and pulled something out of it, while another of his companions pounded on his back with a firm hand. He thought he heard someone shouting. All at once, his ghostly visitor slithered wetly out of him like a bucket of eels being poured through a grate, departing as abruptly as it had entered.

Dashiel slid out of his chair and tumbled to the floor, too weak to hold himself up. The tiny flame of his consciousness guttered and went out like a snuffed candle.

CHAPTER 13

D ASHIEL WOKE UP TO the sight of an unfamiliar ceiling
above his head. The sun was out, but he had no idea what
time of day it was. Gauzy curtains filtered out much of the light,
but not enough to keep it from hurting his eyes.

At first, he was only aware of sleepiness and confusion, but
soon other sensations came into focus. His head hurt, and so did
his muscles and bones. His throat was on fire. His chest crackled
with every breath, and his nose was so stopped up that breathing
through it was a hopeless endeavor. A terrible taste lingered on his
tongue.

Gradually, he began to recall what had happened. Parts of it,
at least. The séance, he remembered—more or less. After that, it
was just bits and pieces. He remembered someone—a woman, he
thought—tipping him over her knee like a newborn and pounding
on his back until he started coughing and gasping for air.

Then, somehow, he had ended up in a bed. A small group of
people stood over him and spoke in hushed, worried voices. For a
time after that, someone had lain alongside him, hugging him close
and stroking his hair.

He struggled to sit up, feeling shaky and feeble, and blinked his
gummy eyes. He wasn't in a hospital room, which was a relief. He
decided he must be in a spare bedroom, but it wasn't Hermann's.

A glass of water stood on a low table by the bed, and he realized as he looked at it that he was desperately thirsty. Ignoring the searing pain in his throat, he gulped it down.

"Hermann?" he tried to call out, but only a faint croak emerged from his lips. He tried again, but his voice was gone. He could barely whisper.

His cane lay propped up against the bedside table. He picked it up and rapped it against the wall with as much strength as he could manage.

He heard the padding of footsteps outside the door a few minutes later, and Lucille's face appeared in the doorway. She lit up with relief and rushed to his side. "Why, Mr. Quicke! It's so good to see you awake. How do you feel?"

"Terrible," he whispered. He realized that he was shivering. "I'm so cold. Cold and hot at the same time."

Lucille frowned and put her hand on his forehead. "You still have a high fever. I'm going to bring you some aspirin and a cool cloth."

"Where's Hermann?"

"He's upstairs, honey. I told him to go get some sleep before he made himself sick, too. You're in my apartment. We thought it would be safer for you to stay here for now, so I can keep an eye on you. You've been in a very bad way."

The longer Dashiel sat up, the dizzier he felt. He lay back down, pulling the covers up to his chin. "You saved my life," he murmured.

"Yes, I did. But it was a close call. Far too close for comfort." Lucille pressed her cool fingertips against his wrist, feeling for his pulse. She looked deeply troubled, and despite her calm demeanor, there was the slightest tremor in her touch. "You're not what I thought you were, Mr. Quicke, and I'm glad about that. Especially for poor Hermann's sake. But at least I know how to handle ordinary flesh and blood crooks. Whatever I saw last night, on the other hand . . ."

Dashiel felt he should say something to her, but he was too exhausted and sick to form a coherent thought. Instead, he clasped her hand and squeezed it, unsure if he was offering reassurance or seeking it.

"All right," she said gently. "You just sit tight for a moment. I'm going to ring Hermann up and let him know you're awake."

❦

DASHIEL DRIFTED OFF again after she left. When he woke up, there was a damp cloth draped across his forehead, and Hermann sat in a chair at his bedside, holding his hand. His eyes were downcast, and his brow was furrowed with worry.

"Hello, handsome," said Dashiel, resting his other hand on top of Hermann's. "How's tricks?"

Hermann's head snapped up, his eyes wide. "Dashiel!" He got out of the chair and sat on the edge of the bed, then pulled Dashiel into his arms and held him tight. "Dashiel, thank God you're awake. You gave us all such a scare. Oh, I've been so worried, you have no idea." He lifted the cloth so he could kiss Dashiel's forehead and temple. "Poor thing, you're burning up. Here, Lucille asked me to give you these."

He handed Dashiel a couple of aspirin tablets and a fresh glass of water. Dashiel swallowed them down, then settled back onto the pillows. "Do I look as awful as I feel?"

"Not to me," said Hermann, brushing Dashiel's hair out of his face and repositioning the cloth on his brow. "You're the most beautiful sight in the world. I really thought we were going to lose you."

"I thought I was going to lose me, too."

"I've never seen anything so frightful. All that—that schmutz coming out of you. What was that stuff?"

"Ectoplasm," whispered Dashiel. "The real thing. Gee, if the other mediums could see me now." He chuckled a little and immediately regretted it.

"Good lord. I can't imagine what that must have felt like."

"A head cold from Hell." He was racked with a sudden, hard cough. His ribs and throat protested angrily. "My throat hurts like a son of a bitch."

"Oh, my dear, I'm so sorry. Hold on, I'll get you some hot tea."

Dashiel forced himself to stay awake until Hermann returned. The tea was soothing, as was the company. Once he'd swallowed most of the warm brew, he spoke again.

"What happened after I passed out?" he asked.

"It's all a bit of a blur," said Hermann. "After you'd been writing for a minute, I realized you weren't breathing. So, I took the snake amulet and grabbed the lighter out of your pocket, and I tried to make it look as if the flame was coming from the snake's mouth. I told the spirit that I was banishing it with the flame of Wadjet. I know it sounds awfully dumb, but it was the only thing I could think of at the time."

Dashiel blinked at him. "And . . . it fell for that?"

"So it would seem. I was surprised, too. But I suppose it's probably never seen an automatic lighter before. It must have been impressive enough to convince it. Anyway, you fell to the floor, and Lucille got you breathing again, thank God. After that, we didn't wait around to see what the ghost would do next. The ladies helped me carry you to the car and we got you home as quick as we could."

"Good thing they were there." Dashiel nestled back into the pillows, too tired to keep holding his head up.

Hermann sighed. "I can't bear to contemplate what would have happened if they hadn't been."

"And the ghost?"

"I haven't heard a peep from it since the séance. But I went back early this morning, just after sunrise, and did an execration ritual on the shabti—a proper one this time, although I'm afraid it might be only a temporary measure. I bound it with seven knots of red thread, to represent the hair ribbons of the Seven Hathors. And now that I know the spirit's name, I was able to invoke—"

Dashiel pushed himself up on his elbows, infused with a burst of renewed wakefulness. "You know its name?"

"Oh, heavens, that's right, you don't know." Hermann clapped a hand to his forehead. "Why, that's the first thing I ought to have told you. You did it, dearest—it worked!"

He pulled a piece of paper out of the inside pocket of his jacket, unfolded it, and held it out for Dashiel to see. The paper was crumpled, stained, and torn at one corner. It was also covered nearly top to bottom with pencil markings. Dashiel squinted at the scribbles for a moment, uncomprehending.

"Looks like chicken scratch."

"No," said Hermann. His eyes shone. "No, not at all! It's hieratic. The paleography is atrocious, but it's hieratic, just the same."

Dashiel was too dazed and exhausted to absorb the full impact of this remarkable news, but a tepid sense of relief washed over him. "Well, well. How about that. What's it say?"

A peculiar expression crossed Hermann's face. "I'm still working it out," he said, "but it's . . . well, it's a bit difficult to explain. Just give me a chance to go over it one more time and make sure I'm really reading it correctly."

After Dashiel finished his tea, Hermann helped him walk to the bathroom. Having answered nature's call, he stood in front of the washbasin and stared at himself in the mirror.

As he'd suspected, Hermann's assessment of his appearance had been extremely kind. He looked terrible. His hair was disheveled and matted with dried ectoplasm. There were purplish circles under his eyes and a dark five o'clock shadow on his cheeks and jaw. His eyes were bloodshot and gooey.

It was clear that someone had made an effort to clean him up, but he could still see crusted remnants of ectoplasm around his nose, his eyes, and the corners of his mouth. He wondered what color the stuff had been when it was fresh. The traces had an iridescent sheen, like tiny oil slicks.

He did his best to wash his face and tidy his hair, but he felt too weak to stand for long. After a minute or two, he staggered out and let Hermann half drag him back to the bed.

***

Night was falling by the time Dashiel went up to Hermann's apartment a few hours later. Thanks to the aspirin and a lengthy nap, he felt almost human. He curled up on the love seat with Horatio snuggled in the space behind his knees, enjoying the warmth of the fire crackling away in the hearth. Hermann sat across from him in one of the armchairs, a pile of books on the ornamental table beside him and a sheaf of papers in his lap.

"All right," said Dashiel. "Tell me about that text."

Hermann frowned down at his notes. "Oh, it's strange, Dashiel. Exceedingly strange."

"In what way?"

"Well, I've had a hell of a time making anything of it. Hieratic is always a bit tricky, but when the handwriting is this bad, it's a real struggle."

"Sorry about that. Never tried my hand at it before."

"It's not your fault, you silly thing. It's the ghost. Of course, perhaps it wouldn't have been so bad if he were writing with his own hand."

Dashiel nodded. "I can't imagine being dead would do a body's penmanship any favors either way."

"True. Still, somehow I doubt this person was any great shakes at writing even when he was alive." Hermann pulled his spectacles out of his breast pocket and put them on, then flipped through his notes until he found the page he was looking for. "This is what I've got so far, although I still wonder if I'm really understanding it correctly."

He cleared his throat and began to read aloud:

"'O you living ones who are upon the earth, I am a beatified spirit, Amunnakht by name. What is the matter with you, that I keep speaking to you, but you do not hear me? Are your ears stopped up with mud like a . . . ?' And here there's a word that I simply can't work out. Then it goes on:

"'I have been exceedingly wronged by a man of my town. His wrongdoing against me is great, indeed greater than any evil that has occurred since the primordial time. Truly, he is a wicked one who slinks upon the earth like a serpent. May his head be turned around backward and his buttocks be reversed with his mouth, so that anything that he eats may come forth from his face as excrement, and may his descendants be cursed likewise.'"

"Sounds like fighting words if I ever heard them," said Dashiel, raising his eyebrows.

Hermann gave a delicate cough. "Curses involving the reversal of various body parts and, er, processes are fairly common in the magical literature."

"I see. So, what did this fellow do to him?"

"Well, it goes on: 'Pay attention, pay attention. I am speaking of my neighbor, Ramose. I lent him my donkey, and he did not return it to me. For ten years I sought it from him. I was vigilant; I did not cease in my demands, and still, he did not bring it back. For ten more years, I went on asking him, *Where is it? Where is it? Give it back!* But he did not answer. It was an excellent *donkey*, finer than any other in the town. I shall not be pacified until I have gotten back that which belongs to me.'

"And so it continues, in much the same vein. I haven't quite finished, but from what I've seen, it's clear he's out for revenge. It seems he wants help getting it from anyone who'll listen. And after I wrote him that letter, he realized he had a willing audience. Only he couldn't figure out how to answer, and that made him madder than ever."

Dashiel gaped at him in disbelief. "Hermann," he said, "do you mean to tell me this monstrosity that's been haunting you relentlessly for months, this vicious spirit that nearly killed me out of its desperation to communicate with us, is blathering on about a *donkey*?"

"So it would appear," said Hermann. He found the page with Dashiel's automatic writing on it and peered at it, at first up close through his spectacles, then at arm's length over the top of them. "I thought I must be mistaken at first, but the animal tail determinative is quite clear."

"Well, I'll be damned. It must have been quite the fine ass!"

"If my translation is correct," said Hermann, tapping the paper, "we're dealing with someone holding on to an extraordinarily ancient and powerful grudge. I was convinced all this time that he must be some great magician—an Imhotep, or a Djedi, or a Setna Khaemwaset. But it turns out he's just some ordinary, petty shmuck with a bone to pick who could never let it go, not even in death."

Dashiel raised his hands in exasperation. "But this is absurd, Hermann! This spirit is obviously an immensely powerful being. This is what he's chosen to squander his immortality on? A squabble over a donkey?"

"Living men have fought and died over sillier things," said Hermann with a shrug. "Did you ever hear of the War of the Bucket?"

"Can't say that I have," sighed Dashiel. Before Hermann could begin to explain, he charged ahead. "But now we know his name, at least. Does it mean anything to you? Or the name of his rival—what was it again?"

"Nothing at all. I don't suppose you could throw a brick in Eighteenth Dynasty Egypt without hitting a fellow named Amunnakht or Ramose. I really don't think this is anyone particularly distinguished, Dashiel. Just someone very, very angry. I guess after all this time, the anger is just about all that's left of him. But underneath all that sinister energy and malice, this thing really is human, after all. Perhaps that's not such a bad thing."

Dashiel closed his eyes tight, trying to wrap his exhausted brain around what he'd just heard. "But . . . if he's really just some ordinary slob, how did he get so powerful?"

"The Egyptians believed that there were ways to obtain and use magical knowledge even if you weren't particularly well-educated—or literate at all," said Hermann. "There are tales of people absorbing the power of magical scrolls by writing out a copy, then dissolving the ink in a cup of wine and drinking it. Who knows how he did it, but he must have gotten his hands on a very special document or object of some sort."

"Well, that's something, isn't it? Whatever it is, we could . . . I don't know, find it and destroy it."

"I don't think that would do any good, even if we could find it," said Hermann. "He has the knowledge already. Wherever he got it is irrelevant. It's part of him now."

"Fine. That's all well and good for him, I guess," said Dashiel. "But where does that leave us? Surely that neighbor of his has been dead for at least, what, three thousand years? Not to mention the donkey. How the hell are we supposed to give the guy what he wants? Is there some way we could find a descendent of this Ramose person?"

"Find the descendent of a man who lived and died thousands of years ago, in another country, about whom we know nothing but his name—an incredibly common name, at that?" Hermann threw up his hands in frustration. "I wouldn't know where to begin, and frankly, I'm not sure we have that kind of time. Who knows how long the binding spell will last, assuming it works at all. That's why I hate these antiquities market acquisitions. There's not a lick of helpful context. If I had some prosopographical data to work from—"

"What do we do, then?" Dashiel cut in, anxious to head off the brewing academic rant.

"I don't know," said Hermann. A deep crease appeared between his eyebrows, and he took off his glasses and put them back into his pocket. "Maybe . . . maybe all we need to do is make him think we're giving him what he wants."

Dashiel gave him a long, hard look. "Hermann," he said at last, "are you actually suggesting that we try to flimflam a ghost?"

Hermann's hazel eyes sparkled with excitement. He leaned forward in his chair. "Well, why not? We've already seen that he can be tricked. He's just a person, Dashiel, a person who wants something very badly and is willing to go to ridiculous lengths to get it. And you know better than most that people who want the impossible badly enough will listen to anyone who's willing to tell them what they want to hear."

"What exactly are you proposing?"

"Well, I . . . I didn't really have a specific idea in mind," Hermann admitted. "This is more your area of expertise. But you made a career of convincing living people that they were communicating with their dead relations. What if you could do the same thing, but in reverse?"

Dashiel was still groping for a reply to this bizarre proposition when a knock sounded on the door. His hands went cold and clammy, and he saw his own apprehension mirrored in Hermann's face.

Hermann rose and crept to the front entrance. He peered through the peephole, then turned to Dashiel with a reassuring nod before sliding back the bolt and opening the door. "Why, hello, Agnes," he said. "Please, do come in."

Agnes stepped in and hovered in the entryway, an uncharacteristically subdued expression on her face. She carried an ornate bouquet of roses, dahlias, and lilies tucked loosely beneath her arm, as though it were an afterthought.

"Professor," she said in a hushed voice as Hermann reached past her to shut and bolt the door, "I hate to be the bearer of bad news after everything that happened last night, but there's something I've gotta tell you."

"What is it?" asked Hermann, eyebrows rising in alarm.

"You know how you said the ghost has been making everyone in the building feel hacked off for months?"

He nodded.

"Well, I noticed today that the place felt different," she said. "Everyone seemed calmer, including me. I mean, I was still pretty rattled by what happened at the séance, but not as touchy as I have been, you know? It was like there'd been a pebble in my shoe for ages, and I didn't notice it until it finally fell out. But when I was closing up this evening, I got the funniest feeling all of a sudden. Like I wanted to go out and punch the first mug who happened to cross my path."

Hermann's face fell. "Oh, no."

Dashiel knew he ought to be upset, but all he could manage was a sense of numb resignation as he waited for the inevitable punchline.

"It was over in a few seconds," Agnes went on. "I felt like I'd been hit by a train. I had a suspicion it had something to do with that shabti thing, so I asked Zoran to let me into storage so I could check on it. And you know those knots you tied around it?

Well, one of 'em's busted, and the one next to it is looking pretty frayed."

Hermann rubbed his hands over his face and sighed. "I was afraid of this. By the time he gets done breaking all those knots, that spirit's going to be madder than a wet hornet. I only hope he holds off long enough for us to come up with some kind of solution."

Agnes clutched at his sleeve. "Speaking of solutions, how's Mr. Quicke?"

"He's—"

"Better," said Dashiel, who had managed to prop himself upright on the love seat.

She jumped and pressed a hand to her chest, whirling to face him. "Jeekus crow!" she gasped. "I didn't even notice you over there, Mr. Quicke. Gee, it's good to see you up and breathing. After what happened last night, I was sure we were gonna have to call the meat wagon."

Dashiel smiled. "I'm afraid you're not getting rid of me that easily."

"Listen, I'm awfully sorry for the times I gave you the third degree," she said. "You too, Professor. I should have taken you seriously back when you first started telling me about this ghost business. I was just sure it was pure bunkalorum."

"Oh, Agnes, don't give it another thought, really," said Hermann. He patted her shoulder. "My only concern right now is that everyone stays safe until we can fix this mess. Why don't you let me put those flowers in a vase? Sit down and rest for a minute."

She mumbled a vague assent and handed them over, looking harried and distracted.

"It was very sweet of you to bring these," Hermann remarked. "They're lovely."

Agnes blinked at him. "What? Oh, they're not from me," she said. "Some guy brought them by my office about an hour before closing time and asked me to give them to you. He said it was an old joke between friends and that you'd understand the message."

Dashiel stiffened in his seat and his heart palpitated painfully, setting off a brief coughing fit. Hermann and Agnes both looked at him with concern. "What sort of guy?" he rasped, once he was able to speak. "What'd he look like?"

"Big fella, blond, real fancy dresser. He looked kinda like a circus ringmaster. Why, do you know him?"

"Hermann, let me see those," said Dashiel, beckoning him over. Hermann handed him the flowers.

A tiny envelope was tucked in among the blossoms. Dashiel removed it and opened it with a flick of the finger. A familiar scent of cologne mingled with the aroma of the bouquet. He instantly recognized the bold, extravagant scrawl of the note inside.

To newfound friends, it said.

"What does it say?" Hermann asked, his voice faint with trepidation.

Without looking up to see his reaction, Dashiel passed him the note. His fingers had encountered a small, solid object tucked into the paper wrapping around the flower stems. He ripped the paper away with shaking hands, and whatever it was tumbled to the floor. It bounced off the carpet at his feet and came to rest with a series of quiet, metallic tings on the tiles in front of the fireplace.

"What the hell was that?" Agnes asked. "A ring or something?"

Hermann bent and picked the object up. He peered at it through his spectacles, his brows knitted with bewilderment. "No," he said. "It's an empty revolver shell."

CHAPTER 14

D ASHIEL DRAGGED HIMSELF TO his feet and fumbled for his cane. "Excuse me," he said. "I have to go lie down."

"Dashiel . . ." Hermann began, but trailed off. Dashiel didn't look at him or at Agnes, but he felt their worried eyes following him as he limped out of the room and groped his way down the hall.

He turned into the spare room and switched on the light. His satchel of Dr. Juniper's Miracle Tonic still sat where Hermann had left it when he first arrived. He picked it up and set it on the bed, then sank down beside it. He wanted to scream with rage, to smash something, to weep or throw up. Anything to exorcise the knot of despair that had settled in his gut like a pernicious black bezoar. But he was too feeble and tired to do more than sit and stare numbly at the floor.

His thoughts simultaneously crawled and galloped. The injury in his leg throbbed as if freshly inflicted. Deep down, he'd known all along that it was Porphyrio who'd shot him. But he hadn't been able to fully admit it to himself before now.

He wasn't certain that the shell in the bouquet had come from the same bullet lodged in his thigh, but he'd be willing to wager so. It would be just like Porphyrio to hold on to a grisly trophy like that.

Porphyrio had always said that Dashiel was his one-and-only, the love of his life. If he was capable of coolly inflicting that sort of injury on the man he claimed to adore, then he wouldn't hesitate to do the same, or worse, to anyone who stood in his way. The thought of him shooting Hermann was too much to bear. It paralyzed him with fear and fury.

Only one solution presented itself to his feverish brain. He'd go back to Porphyrio. He'd go back to him, and he'd kill him.

After that, he'd have to skip town. That would leave Hermann to deal with the ghost on his own, but the more immediate threat to his life would be gone. Perhaps it would buy him enough time to find the solution he needed.

Feeling profoundly weary, Dashiel opened the clasps on his satchel and peered inside. There were four bottles of Dr. Juniper's left. They might be enough to get him across state lines if he played his cards right, but not much farther than that. He pulled one of the bottles out of the bag and turned it over listlessly in his hands.

"Dashiel? Are you all right?"

He looked up. Hermann hovered in the doorway with a look of gentle solicitude on his face. Dashiel forcibly composed himself. He had to act normal. Hermann couldn't know what he was planning. He took a few slow, measured breaths, and a detached sense of calm flowed through him.

"Fine," he said. "Just thinking things over."

Hermann came and sat down beside him on the bed. "I'm not going to let Porphyrio intimidate me," he said, "and I don't think you should, either."

"Intimidation isn't what I'm worried about."

"I walked Agnes out to her car, just in case he was lurking around. I told her to call the police if she catches a whiff of him around campus again—"

"Hermann."

"—and we'll do the same the instant he comes nosing around here. In fact, I have more than half a mind to ring them up right now."

"Hermann, please. It's no good. Even if the cops did take an interest in something as vague as an old shell in a bunch of flowers, he'd sweet-talk his way out of it. He always does."

"Well, in the meantime, the door's bolted. If he really wants to come in here and shoot someone, he'll have to force his way in." He huffed out a soft sigh and fell silent for a moment, then craned his neck to peer at the bottle in Dashiel's hands. "What's this?"

"My bread and butter for the last few months," said Dashiel, handing the bottle over. "Hawking this stuff is what kept me going any time the speaking engagements dried up."

"'Dr. Juniper's Miracle Tonic,'" Hermann read, holding the bottle out at arm's length and squinting down the end of his nose at the label. "'Restores youthful vigor and cures most common ailments.' I can't say I remember this one from my pharmacy days."

"You mean your pa missed his chance to stock his shelves with this marvelous panacea?" said Dashiel, forcing a smile. "What a shame."

Hermann's eyes twinkled. "I'm sure he'd at least have bought a bottle off you. We had quite the collection of patent medicine samples and advertising tokens and whatnot. Gosh, some of them were a riot. I still have a few of those Cascarets Candy Cathartic tokens around here somewhere." To Dashiel's surprise, he unscrewed the cap of the bottle and took a sip. "Why, Dashiel! This is nothing but sugar water."

"Well, sure it is. It's just snake oil, you know that."

Hermann tutted in disapproval and handed it back to him. "You ought to at least put a little cocaine in it," he said. "You'd get a lot more repeat customers that way. Oh, well. At least it tastes better than Colden's Liquid Beef."

Dashiel started to laugh, then felt a surge of undefinable emotion welling up inside him. He threw an arm around Hermann's shoulder and buried his face against his neck to hide the looming threat of tears.

"Hermann, you're a mighty odd duck, do you know that?" he said.

"Am I? Well, I suppose you'd have to be, to go into my line of work." Hermann wrapped his arm around Dashiel's waist. "You never have to sell that stuff again, you know. Not unless you really want to."

"I know."

They held each other in silence for a long moment. Hermann finally pulled back and tilted Dashiel's chin up to kiss him, then looked at him searchingly.

"You look absolutely exhausted, Dashiel," he said. "You'd better get some more sleep."

Dashiel nodded, then stretched out on the bed and closed his eyes, far too tired to get up and walk across the hall to Hermann's room. He felt Hermann pulling off his shoes, then heard the quiet clink of the bottles in the satchel as he set it back down at the foot of the bed. The world beyond Dashiel's heavy eyelids darkened as the light switch flicked off.

He lay there alone with his eyes shut for an agonizing eternity, but he didn't sleep. Come morning, he told himself again and again, he'd be gone.

SOMETIME NOT LONG before dawn, Dashiel rose and padded into the bathroom. His face was shiny and flushed with fever. He found a tin of aspirin in the medicine cabinet and swallowed two of the pills with a mouthful of water from the tap, then tucked the tin into his pocket. He took a moment to tidy himself, then made his way to Hermann's room, treading as quietly as he could manage.

Hermann was sound asleep. Dashiel bent down and brushed his cheek with a featherlight kiss.

"Goodbye, Hermann," he whispered.

Moving to the nightstand, he was relieved to find his silver lighter tucked in among Hermann's things. It was one of his few remaining valuables. If need be, he could sell it, hopefully for enough money to get him well on his way across the country. He nestled it into his pocket alongside the aspirin tin, then slipped out of the room.

He returned to his room and dug through his trunk until he found his revolver. He slid the gun into the waistband of his trousers, behind his back. The trunk itself would stay behind. It was simply too much to manage. Besides, there was no reason to keep dragging his old mediumistic equipment around with him. He couldn't see his way to continuing the demonstrations after everything that had happened. The thought left him feeling disingenuous and hollow. He would leave with the clothes on his back, his cane, and his gun. And, of course, the satchel of Dr. Juniper's Miracle Tonic.

Satisfied he had everything he needed, he limped into the living room, picked up the phone, and asked the operator to put him through to the Grande Hotel. "Suite 502, please," he said to the sleepy front desk clerk.

A moment later, Porphyrio's voice crackled over the line. "Hello?" he said. He sounded wide awake. Dashiel suspected he'd been waiting up for a call.

"Hello, Porphyrio."

"Dash, is that you? Speak up, dearheart, I can hardly hear you."

Dashiel hesitated. Once he stepped off this precipice, there was no turning back.

He closed his eyes and took the plunge.

"You were right about everything," he said. "It's all over between me and Hermann. He wants nothing more to do with me. I can't keep running from my destiny like this forever."

"I knew you'd come around, darlin'," said Porphyrio. His voice was gentle, even tender. "You know where to find me. Come right on over. I'll be waitin' up for you."

Dashiel swallowed hard. "I'm on my way." He hung up the receiver.

He had every intention of marching straight out the front door without stopping to look back.

But the moment he touched the doorknob, he froze up, and a painful lump formed in his throat. *Just go*, he told himself. *You sentimental old idiot.*

Ignoring his own eminently sensible advice, he set his satchel down by the door and wandered back into the living room.

While almost every flat surface in the room was crowded with framed photographs, very few of them were of Hermann by himself. Among the various family portraits and class pictures, he spotted a snapshot of a young Hermann with his father behind the counter in the pharmacy, their arms around each other's shoulders. He picked it up and started to take it, then thought better of it and set it back down.

With a little more searching, he found what he was looking for—a small studio portrait of Hermann dressed in graduation regalia, looking about twenty years younger and strikingly handsome. He'd have preferred something more recent, but he'd lingered long enough already.

Silently cursing himself, and trying to ignore the persistent prickling in his eyelids, he shoved the photo into the inside pocket of his overcoat, took one last look around the room, and left.

As HE DREW closer to his destination, the steely determination he'd felt when setting out gave way to icy dread. It wasn't until he had turned onto Baneberry Avenue that the full impact of what he was doing sank in.

He stood rooted to the spot, staring up at the silhouette of the Grande Hotel, its imposing shape limned by the red-gold light of the rising sun.

Back in the apartment, when he was delirious with fever and boiling over with rage at Porphyrio's threat, he'd been dead certain of what he needed to do. Now, he wondered what had ever possessed him to believe he could go through with it. For all his many faults, Dashiel had never been a violent man. The thought of spilling anyone's blood, even Porphyrio's, made his stomach churn.

Maybe he didn't have to kill him right away. Or at all. Perhaps it would be enough just to draw him off. He could appease him for now, do Maude's revival with him, then leave. He'd head out west, like he'd planned from the beginning. He could learn a new trade, start fresh. Or just fall apart and disappear, like one of his flimsy chiffon phantasms.

But he knew himself well enough to see how that would go. If he went back now and he didn't kill Porphyrio, it would all be over. He felt weaker and sicker by the minute. He didn't have the strength to resist Porphyrio in his current state. Truthfully, he'd never had the strength for any of this. How had he allowed himself to get in so far over his head? Right now, he couldn't even remember what the surface looked like.

He had to walk away from all of it, once and for all. Porphyrio, the shabti, Willowvale.

. . . Hermann.

Dashiel sat on a bench at the depot and stared, unseeing, at the train tracks. Someone was speaking to him. He had to repeat himself twice before Dashiel realized he was being addressed.

"Mister! Excuse me, mister!"

He slowly lifted his head. A young man hovered nearby, holding an unlit cigarette in his hand. He was auburn-haired and olive-skinned, with earnest, dark brown eyes. Dashiel guessed he was no older than sixteen or seventeen.

"You talking to me?" asked Dashiel.

The kid grinned at him. "Yeah. You got a light, mister?"

"Too bad you didn't ask me that a few hours ago. I just pawned my lighter for train fare." He looked down at the ticket in his hand. The lighter had sold for less than half of what he'd paid for it. It wouldn't take him quite as far as he'd hoped, but it was enough to get him to Cheyenne.

He'd slept for hours on a secluded park bench before heading to the depot. Thanks to the rest and another dose of aspirin, he wasn't quite as close to death's door as he had been. But that was cold comfort. He still felt sick through and through, body and soul.

The young man chuckled. "Just my rotten luck. Pawned it, huh? I guess you must want to get out of here pretty bad."

"'Want' isn't really the word."

"Me, I'm just trying to get as far away from my folks and this one-horse town as possible." He gave Dashiel a challenging look. "Actually, I think I might make my way out to Los Angeles. Try to make it in the pictures."

Dashiel gave him a tired nod. "Well, best of luck to you, kid. You've got a good face for it."

"Wow, thanks!" he said, beaming. Then his eyes narrowed with suspicion. "Wait, you're not going to try and talk me out of it?"

"Do you want me to?"

"No, not really. I just thought you might. That's what people usually do." He paused for a moment. When Dashiel didn't say anything, he piped up again. "I mean, I have it pretty good here, I know that. I'm doing okay in school, I have a roof over my head, get my three squares a day and all. I just feel like I'm meant for greater things than taking over the old man's flower shop, you know? I don't even like flowers." He trailed off, clearly hoping Dashiel would put in his two cents.

Dashiel sighed. As much as he needed a distraction from his misery, he was in no mood to make chitchat. He turned and looked the young man dead in the eye. "Are you looking for my advice?" he asked.

"I dunno." He shrugged. "Maybe."

"Okay, listen, Mac. I don't know if I've ever made a single right decision in my life. I used to think I knew what I was about, but the older I get, the less goddamn sense it all makes. I haven't a clue what the hell I'm supposed to be doing right now, let alone you. So, what I think you ought to do is go ahead and get your advice from absolutely anybody in the world but me." He yanked his handkerchief out of his pocket and shook it out with an angry snap of the wrist, then mopped his eyes with it. "All I know is that none of this feels right."

The kid stared at him for a second, nonplussed.

His brow creased with sympathy. "Gee," he said. "Rough day, huh?"

"Rough week. Rough couple of years. Rough life." He folded the handkerchief and tucked it away again. "Sorry, kid. I'm afraid you're not catching me at my best. What's your name?"

"Nikolaos Sotiropoulos."

"Well, Nikolaos—"

"Just Nick is fine."

"All right, Nick. It sounds like we're headed in the same direction. I'm California bound, too."

Nick brightened. "Really? Hey, that's swell!" His face fell. "I only have fare to Omaha, though. Don't know how I'm going to scrape together the rest. How about you?"

"Wyoming," said Dashiel. "Seems like we're in the same boat, more or less."

"Hey, Wyoming's pretty close!" said Nick, a little wistfully. He gave Dashiel a keen look. "It kind of seems like you don't really want to go, though."

Dashiel had a sharp retort about the kid's stunning powers of observation ready on the tip of his tongue, but he didn't have the heart to fire it off. Instead, he just shook his head. "I don't."

"Why're you going, then? You on the lam or something?"

"I suppose you could say that."

Nick gazed at him in awe. "From what? The law? The Mob?"

"Nope. Ghosts."

"Now, wait." Nick scratched his head. "When you say 'ghosts,' are we talking literal, or—" he snapped his fingers, trying to conjure up the word he wanted "—figurative?"

"Yes," said Dashiel.

"Oh." He settled in on the bench next to Dashiel, twiddling the unlit cigarette between his fingers. "So, how come you're so broken up about leaving? Do you really like Willowvale that much? 'Cause it seems to me the only thing this dump's got that Los Angeles doesn't is a hell of a lot more snow."

"Willowvale's nice enough. But it's not the town," said Dashiel. He poked at a stray bit of gravel with the end of his cane. "It's . . . a friend. I have a good friend here, probably the best I've ever had. Certainly better than I deserve. That's why I'm leaving. To protect him."

"I thought you were leaving because of the ghosts."

"Look, kid, it's complicated. All I know is, whether I stay or go, a good man is going to get hurt. It's just a matter of how much. I figure me leaving will give him the best possible shot at coming out of all this okay."

"What does your friend think? Does he want you to go?"

Dashiel scoffed. "Of course he doesn't. He seems to think I hung the moon, for some godforsaken reason. But as long as I stay here, he's between the devil and the deep blue sea. And I'm the one who brought the devil around."

"Wait, you're losing me again," said Nick, squinting in confusion. "Is it ghosts, or devils?"

"Six of one, half-dozen of the other. Point is, if I go, I'll take half of his troubles with me. And leave half of mine behind, I suppose."

"Makes sense, I guess," Nick said, but he looked unconvinced. "Sounds to me like you'd both be losing a lot more than your troubles, though. Say, you got the time? My watch is busted."

"Ten after four," said Dashiel, glancing listlessly at his wrist. "Train's due any minute now."

"Holy smokes, already?" The kid's knees started bouncing with nervous excitement. "Hey, do me a favor, mister. Don't let me chicken out. I've been trying to work up the guts to do this for months."

A low whistle wailed in the distance. The Overland Limited was roaring down the track toward them. All the warmth bled out of Dashiel's veins at the sound. He gripped his ticket so hard it crumpled in his hand. He had to do this. Had to. He was desperate not to.

"Sure thing, Nick," he said. "But you've got to do something for me in return."

"What's that?"

"Give me one good reason to stay."

Nick blinked at him. "Gee, um—okay. Because your friend wants you to?"

"Not good enough." He swallowed hard and closed his eyes. The clatter of the wheels over the railroad ties grew steadily louder. "Come on, give me something I can work with. It's now or never."

"I don't know," said Nick helplessly. "Maybe you're not doing your pal such a favor by leaving. I mean, if it was me, I'd rather face a whole gang of ghosts with a friend than deal with just one of them by myself."

"It's a stretch, kid," said Dashiel, shaking his head. "I don't know if I buy it. You're going to have to be a little more resourceful if you want to make it in show business, you know."

"I'm sorry, mister. The train's almost here, and I'm running out of ideas."

"Okay, I've got one for you." Dashiel let his ticket slip from his fingers and fall to the ground at their feet. "How about if I stay, because some punk kid saw the chance of a lifetime and swiped my ticket to sunny Cheyenne while I wasn't looking?"

A breeze snatched at a corner of the ticket, threatening to rip it away. Nick gasped and reflexively stuck out his foot, trapping it under the toe of his shoe. "Are—are you serious?" he stammered.

"You'd better make it snappy," Dashiel said, his voice gruff. "Before I notice what you're up to."

Nick reached down and grabbed the ticket, looking like a skittish alley cat stealing a sardine from a stall in the fish market. His face flushed scarlet. "I don't know what to say," he said.

"Don't say anything," said Dashiel. "Just take it and get on that damn train before I come to my senses and change my mind."

The train lumbered into the depot and squealed to a slow stop, smelling of heat and iron and dust. The doors swung open, and the conductor stepped out with his brass buttons gleaming in the late afternoon light. "Overland Limited," he bellowed. "Westbound for Los Angeles."

The boy started for the door, then hesitated. He turned to stare at Dashiel with wide, questioning eyes.

"Don't just stand there, go on!" urged Dashiel, waving him away impatiently. "Just be careful out there. Don't take any wooden nickels."

Nick swallowed and gave him a quick nod, then turned and darted onto the train with the ticket clutched close to his chest.

Dashiel didn't wait for the train to depart. In a daze, he rose to his feet and hefted his satchel. Then, after a moment of consideration, he opened his hand and let the bag drop to the hard cement pavement of the platform. The bottles inside shattered with a muffled crunch. He turned and walked away from the tracks without pausing to look back.

CHAPTER 15

T HE MOMENT DASHIEL TURNED onto the block where Hermann's building stood, a shiver of horror passed through him. A red Rolls-Royce Phantom with gleaming whitewall tires was parked haphazardly on the street, just a short distance from Hermann's Ford. Dashiel didn't recognize the car, but he knew it could only belong to one person. He stopped for a moment, heart hammering in his throat, before breaking into an awkward, hobbling run.

When he reached the building, he flung open the door to the vestibule and paused for a second to listen. A loud, irate voice drifted down from somewhere above him, and although he couldn't distinguish any of the words, the timbre was unmistakable. He gritted his teeth and bounded up the stairs, ignoring the pain in his leg.

He could see from the landing that the door to the apartment was ajar. He inched closer, struggling to catch his breath. His lungs burned and crackled with the effort, and his vision pulsated with each throb of his heart.

"Don't you try to tell me you don't know where he's at," Porphyrio snarled. "Spit it out, now."

Hermann's reply was just loud enough to be audible. "He's gone," he said. Dashiel's chest tightened at the anguish in his voice.

"That's all I know. He didn't say where, and even if he had, I certainly wouldn't tell you."

"What a load of heifer dust. His trunk's still here, and Dash never goes anywhere without that thing. If you know where he is, you'd better start singin' before I give you a busted lamp to match that dent in your fender."

"Threaten me all you like, but it's not going to change the truth. He left sometime during the night, before I woke up. He must be miles away by now."

Porphyrio laughed nastily. "I'll tell you one thing, little fella, you must value his sorry skin a lot more than he does yours. You'd better just hope and pray he shows up soon, 'cause you're not going to like what happens if he doesn't."

Dashiel rallied his flagging energy, pushed the door open, and strode in. Porphyrio's back was turned to him when he stepped into the living room. He held Hermann by the lapels of his jacket, nearly lifting him off the floor. Aside from the dark circles under his eyes and the faded bruise on his cheek, Hermann's face was the color of sheetrock. His hands were clenched around Porphyrio's wrists.

The sight struck Dashiel dumb with fury. It had been his intention to say something when he walked in, but for a few seconds he could do nothing but stand there, clenching his fists so hard his hands shook.

When Hermann's eyes met his, his knees nearly buckled with relief. "Dashiel!" he gasped. "Oh, Dashiel, I thought you'd gone—"

Porphyrio turned his head in Dashiel's direction. His gray eyes widened in surprise, but Dashiel didn't wait for him to react further. He dropped his cane and flung himself at Porphyrio, shoving him away from Hermann with all the force he could muster. Porphyrio released his grip on Hermann's jacket and staggered back, bumping against one of the bookcases that lined the wall beside the fireplace. Hermann stumbled away in the opposite direction.

Dashiel charged again, drew back his fist, and swung it at Porphyrio's jaw. But despite the burst of energy from his anger, his reflexes were sluggish, and he could feel his strength rapidly ebbing away. Porphyrio caught Dashiel's wrist in a crushing grip before the punch could hit home, then swung him around and slammed his back against the bookcase. He pinned Dashiel in place with one powerful forearm across his neck. Dashiel clawed at his sleeve with both hands and twisted his head to one side, trying not to panic as he fought to draw air into his weakened lungs.

"Just what the hell do you think you're playin' at, Dashiel?" Porphyrio growled. His face was red and sheened with sweat, and his breath reeked of tobacco and stale booze. "What exactly did you think was gonna happen when you stood me up like that?"

"You stay away from Hermann," Dashiel choked out. "He didn't do a goddamn thing to you. This is between you and me, you got that?" He jabbed a knee at Porphyrio's groin. Porphyrio grunted and jumped back a little, easing the pressure on Dashiel's throat, but he didn't let go.

"Wipe your chin, sweetheart," he said, grabbing Dashiel by the arms and giving him a rough shake. The back of Dashiel's head thumped painfully against the hard wooden shelf behind him. "If you think you can get away with jerkin' my chain like that, you've got another thing comin'."

With Porphyrio distracted, Hermann moved to the fireplace in a few quick, quiet steps. Dashiel watched over Porphyrio's shoulder as he snatched up a poker from the wrought iron rack by the hearth and hefted it in his hands. But as he advanced, poised to swing the vicious-looking hooked end of the poker at Porphyrio's broad back, Porphyrio wheeled on him. His hand darted into his jacket and emerged holding a pistol.

Dashiel had seen this gun before. It was a ridiculous-looking little thing with mother-of-pearl inlay on the grip, but he had no doubt that it worked just fine. Porphyrio leveled the barrel at Hermann's head, keeping his other hand clamped around Dashiel's upper arm.

"You just put that thing right back on the rack where it belongs, Mary," he said, "and let Uncle Porphyrio and his old friend Ralph finish their little talk."

Hermann didn't move. The poker trembled in his white-knuckled fists, but his eyes were flinty with defiance. Porphyrio raised his thumb and pulled back the hammer of the pistol, and the cylinder rolled into position with a sickening click.

Dashiel tried to swallow, but his throat was dry as paper. "Better do what he says, Hermann."

Without a word, Hermann lowered the poker. Porphyrio kept the gun trained on him. "Drop it," he said, a menacing growl in his voice.

Hermann still hesitated, but Dashiel shook his head, meeting his gaze with a silent plea in his eyes. At last, Hermann's hands opened, and the poker fell to the carpet at his feet with a quiet thud.

"Good," Porphyrio said. He didn't take his eyes, or his gun, off Hermann. "Now that we've got that settled, it's time to quit messin' around. Come on, Dash, we're leavin'. Right now."

Panic clawed at the inside of Dashiel's chest. He fell still, trying to force his brain to form a coherent thought. The cold grip of his own revolver pressed into the small of his back, hidden beneath his jacket. If he was quick enough, he could grab it and shoot Porphyrio now. It would all be over in an instant. But then there would be so much blood—all over the soft rugs and the pretty floral wallpaper, on Hermann's neat white collar and pale, terrified face.

No, he would go with his original plan: leave with Porphyrio, follow him back to his hotel, then shoot him. That way, Hermann would never have to see the mess. Porphyrio gave his arm a hard yank, and Dashiel started to stumble after him.

Or—

He stopped. His eyes swept over Porphyrio from head to foot, taking in every detail. It was an old séance room habit that Maude had instilled in him from his earliest days at the camp. *If you're stuck for ideas, scan the sitter. Look for anything you can use.* Porphyrio was as smartly dressed as ever, but disheveled. His patterned silk ascot was askew, the top button of his coat undone. A splatter of mud marred the otherwise pristine yellow leather of his left muleskin boot.

"Well?" said Porphyrio. "You gonna just stand there gapin' like a stuck pig? I said let's go! I'll carry you outta here if I have to."

Dashiel stared at the boot for another second or two before dragging his gaze back to Porphyrio's face. An idea had begun to take root in his mind, something vague, half-formed, and utterly preposterous.

He fought back a hysterical and wildly inappropriate urge to laugh. It was ridiculous, but it was a start, and that was more than he'd had a few seconds ago.

He just needed to buy a little time.

"Hold on," he said. His voice was thick and raspy with phlegm. A hard, racking cough gripped him for a moment before he could continue. "Hold on, calm down. Just put the gun down for a minute and let's talk."

"There's nothing to talk about."

"Yes, there is, for God's sake," said Dashiel. "There's no need for any of this. I was on my way over to meet you." Hermann gasped, and Dashiel silently willed him to understand. "But I'm sick as a dog. You must be able to see that. When I stumbled out of here this morning, I was delirious. About halfway to your hotel, I had to stop and lie down to rest. I realized when I came to that I'd slept half the day away and left all my things behind. My trumpets, my clothes, everything. So, I came back here to get my trunk and call you."

Porphyrio bared his teeth in a cold sneer. "Fine. So, go get your precious trunk and let's go. I ain't got all day."

"And just how the hell do you expect me to do that," Dashiel demanded, "when you're standing there with a goddamn gun pointed at my friend's head? I am trying to give you what you want, Porphyrio, but you're not making it easy. Exercise an ounce of temperance for once in your life, if you have it in you. Put the gun away."

Porphyrio gave him a long, hard stare, his nostrils flaring with each angry breath. But he eased his thumb off the hammer of the pistol and lowered it. At the same time, he relaxed his grip on Dashiel's arm.

"All right," said Dashiel, taking a step back. "Now, are you going to be a man and step outside so I can gather my belongings and say my goodbyes properly, or are we really just a bunch of boorish, uncivilized children here?"

"Step outside?" said Porphyrio, his eyes widening with incredulity. "So that, what, your little pal over there can call the constabulary the moment I'm out of sight? You must think my knife's so dull it wouldn't cut hot butter."

Dashiel strode over to the telephone table and yanked the cord out of the wall, then picked up the phone and shoved it against Porphyrio's chest. "Go ahead, take it outside with you, if you're going to be that much of a possum about it. You can leave it on the front stoop when we go."

Porphyrio snatched the phone from his hands and hurled it into the nearest armchair, his lip curled in disgust. "Fine. I'll be outside. But whatever it is you think you need to do, make it quick. Don't keep me waitin'."

He stalked past Dashiel, bumping him hard with his shoulder, and slammed the door behind him with such force that the windowpanes rattled. The moment he was out the door, Dashiel hobbled over and bolted it. He waited, slumped against the doorframe, and listened to the creak of Porphyrio's footsteps on the stairs, followed by the bang of the foyer door closing.

When he turned back, Hermann was still standing in the middle of the living room, silent and white with shock. Dashiel limped toward him.

"Are you all right?" he asked. "Did he hurt you? How did he get in here?"

Hermann straightened his tie and brushed off his jacket with trembling hands. "No, he didn't hurt me," he said. "Just . . . pushed me around a little. And I don't know how he got in. After I woke up and found you gone, I went to campus. When I came home, he was here. He must have picked the lock."

Dashiel reached out for him, but he flinched away. The pain in his eyes hit Dashiel like a knife to the gut. "Hermann, listen to me," he implored. "I know what this must look like—"

"For the life of me, I can't make sense of what just happened," said Hermann. "If you needed to leave, to get away from him, I'd understand. I know it was selfish of me, trying to keep you here. I should have helped you get out of town back when you first turned up on my doorstep."

"No, Hermann, please—"

"But why go to him? Why now?" Dashiel moved closer to him, and Hermann took another step back. "There are five knots left on that shabti. Five. My time is running out."

"I know," said Dashiel. His whole body felt leaden with remorse. "Believe me, this is the last way I wanted things to happen.

You can hate me if you want, I wouldn't blame you. But I'm begging you to trust me."

Hermann dropped his gaze to the floor. "I don't hate you, Dashiel," he said quietly. "I don't think I could, even if I wanted to."

"Then hear me out. I have a plan. The start of one, at least."

"I've already asked too much of you."

"No. If I can help you, it'll be the one worthwhile thing I've ever done in my life. Even if this turns out to be my last rodeo, at least I'll have that. But if I don't try—" His throat tightened, and he had to clear it before speaking again. "I can't make any guarantees, but this is the best idea I've got. And if I'm going to pull it off, I'll need your help. Lots of it. We need to talk about it quick, before that madman comes back up here and kicks the door in."

Hermann didn't answer. Dashiel extended both his hands. "So?" he said, his voice soft with supplication. "How about it, kid?"

Slowly, Hermann reached out and took Dashiel's hands in his.

"All right, Dashiel," he said. "Tell me what you need."

CHAPTER 16

THE NEXT EVENING, DASHIEL sat across the table from Porphyrio in the Grande's Blue Pearl Tea Room. Between the two of them, they'd ordered a feast of lavish proportions. Dashiel's mouth began to water the moment the waitress approached them with a steaming dish of roast ducklings bigarade on one hand and a platter of filet mignon on the other.

Porphyrio leaned forward as she walked away and laid his hand on the table, uncomfortably close to Dashiel's. "Don't try to tell me you didn't miss this, darlin'," he said. The candleflame in the middle of the table accented his smiling gray eyes with a glimmer of gold.

Dashiel pulled his hand away. "The food? Certainly. The company, I could do without."

Porphyrio waved him off with an amiable chuckle. Yesterday's dangerous mood had given way to warm congeniality, as if he thought he could batter down the barriers that had grown up between them with the sheer force of his charm. His moods had always been as capricious as summer weather—sunny skies one minute, pewter-colored thunderclouds and stinging hail the next. In the early days, that was something about him that had thrilled Dashiel. He despised the brutal, bitter spats, but the inevitable aftermath, once they'd both cooled off, was always exquisite.

"Don't pout, Dash," said Porphyrio. "You know it don't suit you. Besides, you'll have forgotten all about that fella in a couple weeks. He'll be just another notch on your belt, like all the others." He sighed and sat back, then shook out his napkin and laid it on his lap. "You sure you won't order a drink?"

It was more tempting than he cared to admit. Porphyrio's glass brimmed with gleaming champagne the color of pale straw in the late afternoon sun, shot through with rising threads of tiny bubbles. Dashiel could almost feel the bright, cool prickle of it on his tongue.

"Coffee is just fine," he said. He busied himself cutting a tender slice of duckling. The tart and savory scent of it was enough to make him lightheaded. "We have a lot to talk about, and I intend to be wide awake and sober for it."

Porphyrio shrugged and sipped his champagne. "Suit yourself. But I wish you'd let your hair down a little bit. We oughta be celebrating. That's what I intend to do."

Dashiel didn't dignify him with a reply. He took a bite of duckling and chewed it in moody silence. The bitterness of the bigarade mingled exquisitely with the natural sweetness of the meat. He couldn't help but close his eyes for a moment and draw in a deep, appreciative breath through his nose as he savored the taste of it. When he opened his eyes again, Porphyrio was beaming at him.

"Now, that's more like it," he said. "You enjoy that, dearheart. We'll put a little meat back on those old bones yet."

"Your filet mignon's getting cold."

"Don't rush me, honey," said Porphyrio, settling back in his chair. "Let me enjoy the view. Why, you look good enough to eat yourself, in those fine new threads of yours. I just can't wait to get you out of 'em."

Dashiel had collapsed on the couch the moment they arrived at the suite the previous evening, then passed the night and the first half of the following day in a fitful stupor. By the time he dragged himself out of bed in the early afternoon, he felt more himself, although he still had a mild fever and a lingering cough. At Porphyrio's insistence, they drove into town to get Dashiel a haircut and a new department store suit. The suit was a far cry from the bespoke finery he'd been accustomed to in his glory days, but he looked better than he had in months.

"We don't have time to waste on distractions and tomfoolery," Dashiel said coldly. "That revival is coming up in four days, and I intend to give it my best."

"Come on, don't be like that. All I want is for things to go back to normal between us. Just you and me, like it used to be."

"Things were never normal between us, Porphyrio," said Dashiel, shaking his head. "And they can never go back to how they used to be. We burned that bridge to the ground a long time ago."

Porphyrio grew solemn. "Confound it, Dash, I still can't understand where things went so wrong. Lord knows we've had our tiffs over the years, but we were always able to patch things up in the end, far back as I can remember."

"You know what happened."

"If this is about old Mrs. Monseruud, I was just sick as mud about what happened to her, too. I was only trying to give her a little hope, that's all, give her a chance to go out peaceful. You saw how scared she was of letting those butchers cut her up. And you know they couldn't have given her much more time, anyway. Maybe another year of suffering, that's all."

"No, I don't know that," said Dashiel, his face cold with anger. "Neither do you, and neither did she or anyone else. And now, we'll never have a chance to find out, will we?"

An unfamiliar expression flickered across Porphyrio's face. Was it remorse? He turned his gaze downward as if noticing his meal for the first time. "My, oh, my, this does look good," he muttered, grabbing his knife and fork and attacking his filet mignon.

Dashiel was caught off guard by a sting of pity. He cleared his throat. "Listen, Porphyrio," he began, then stopped, unsure if he should say what was on his mind.

Porphyrio's eyes flicked up to meet his. "Hmm?"

"Things can't go back to how they were," said Dashiel. "But they don't have to go on like this, either. You could get out. Tell Maude where she can stow her revival and just walk away from it all. Go lead an honest life somewhere."

Porphyrio blinked at him in surprise, then snorted incredulously. "Doin' what? You want me to go back to totin' hay bales? Or run off and join the circus?"

"I don't know. You're a talented man. Clever, even, when you choose to be. You'd figure something out. Maybe I could even . . . help you."

"You?" said Porphyrio, his eyes widening. "Help me? Why, bless your little heart, Dash, you can't even help yourself. What're you gonna do, precious? Take me on as an apprentice snake oil salesman? Oh, I know! You could help me find a sugar daddy. Unless you want to share the one you got, that is. I'll tell you one thing, though—he's gonna need a bigger bed!"

He slapped his hand down on the tabletop and roared with laughter. A silver-haired woman seated at a nearby table flinched and turned to glare at them.

"Get ahold of yourself," hissed Dashiel. "We're in public."

"Oh, cool off, darlin'. Anyway, why would I want to do anything else?" Porphyrio went on, wiping tears of mirth from his eyes with the corner of his napkin. "This life's been pretty sweet to me, up until about three years ago. But I reckon my fortune's about to change again, now that we're back together."

"It is," said Dashiel, "but not the way you want it to. Trust me, Porphyrio, staying on this path—it's not going to end well for you."

Porphyrio's grin faded, and he narrowed his eyes. "What is this, Dash? Did you get religion or something? You worried about the fate of my immortal soul all of a sudden? Because yours ain't exactly untarnished, either."

"Nope. Not what I meant."

"Well, you'd better not be threatening me." His eyes went steely, and Dashiel could see the muscles in his jaw tightening. "Because if you are, remember that it's not just your sorry hide that's on the line here."

The last vestiges of Dashiel's goodwill trickled away in an instant. "It's not a threat," he said stonily, "it's a warning. And believe me, I won't forget. Not for one second."

"A *warning*," scoffed Porphyrio, rolling his eyes. "Goodness gracious, Dash, you've got me trembling in my boots." The amiable grin returned as abruptly as it had vanished, but there was a tension in his shoulders and a cold gleam in his eyes that hadn't been there before. "All right, sweetheart, let's quit messing around. We've got a demonstration to plan."

"So we do," said Dashiel. He took a sip of his coffee, then set down the mug and fixed Porphyrio with a hard gaze. "First off, there's something I'd like to clear up before we go any further."

"Oh? What's that?"

"I'm not going to appear as your partner at this revival."

Porphyrio stiffened and sat up, his genial expression transforming back into a dangerous scowl. "Now, hold on just a minute—"

"I wasn't finished," said Dashiel, holding up a hand. "I'm not going to be your partner. You're going to be mine. Just like how it used to be. I run the show, you follow my lead."

Porphyrio relaxed a little, but he continued to eye Dashiel doubtfully. "I don't know about all that, Dash," he said. "You've been out of the game a long time. Besides, you're not really in a position to make demands here, are you, darlin'?"

← 234 →

"We're doing this on my terms," said Dashiel, "or not at all."

"Is that so?"

"It is." He smiled. "I don't think you quite realize what you're dealing with, Porphyrio."

"Don't be ridiculous," said Porphyrio, downing the rest of his champagne. He yanked the bottle out of its ice bath and refilled his glass. "I know you better than anyone, Dash. You really think you can put on airs with me?"

"If you think I've been idle during our time apart, you're very much mistaken," said Dashiel. "I'm not the same penny-ante huckster you used to know. I've been developing my mediumship in ways you can't even begin to imagine. I'm the real thing now."

Porphyrio laughed heartily. "Aww, now don't sell yourself short, dearheart. You were always the real thing, far as I'm concerned. One of the best."

"No." Dashiel shook his head. "Not even close."

"Well, I must say, you do know how to pique a man's curiosity," Porphyrio said, raising an eyebrow. "Still can't say as I like it much, though."

"You'll still get your glory, if that's what you're worried about," said Dashiel. "I know how to give credit where credit is due. Just imagine. You'd be the shepherd who brought this poor little lost lamb back into the fold."

Porphyrio swirled his champagne in his glass and frowned thoughtfully. "Let's say I let you do this, Dash, just for the sake of argument. I'd need your word that you wouldn't try to pull any funny business. You know there'd have to be consequences, and I truly don't want any more unpleasantness between us, darlin'."

"I know what's at stake. Believe me, I don't intend to disappoint anyone."

"All right, then, I'll bite. What do you have in mind? You always were mighty handy with those spirit trumpets . . ."

Dashiel waved his hand. "I have no interest in using trumpets. I'm focusing on trance work and physical manifestations these days, not voice mediumship. I'd like to use apports, of course. And impressions on silk."

"Silk!" Porphyrio curled his lip. "Don't tell me you've gone back to that tired old gag."

"We'll use silks," said Dashiel, his voice low and dangerous, "because I like them. And because it's critical to the program I have in mind."

Porphyrio scowled. "You sure are acting awfully bold for a man in your position, Dash."

"And what position is that?" Dashiel demanded. "From where I'm sitting, it looks like you're the one who needs something from me—pretty badly, I might add. Otherwise, you wouldn't have put yourself to all the trouble of hounding me for so long. Now, I've got better things to do with my time, so don't waste it, or I'll be out the door and gone before you can blink."

"You were singing a pretty different tune yesterday."

"I was at death's door yesterday," Dashiel said smoothly. "And, frankly, I didn't want to upset Hermann any more than you already had, barging in like that and waving your silly little gun around. You've made things very difficult for me with him, you know. I've had a hell of a time talking him around to all this."

"What the blazes are you on about?" said Porphyrio. He was beginning to look increasingly agitated and red in the face. "Talking him around to what? I don't see why he needs to be involved in our business at all."

"He's going to help us, Porphyrio. And if there are any brains left in that swollen head of yours, you won't turn your nose up at that. He's got something that we need, something that's rarer than hen's teeth and more valuable than gold in our business."

"And just what the hell is that?"

"To quote a dear old mutual friend of ours, the man's got credibility. And if you don't keep making an ass of yourself around him, he might just be willing to lend us some of it. You always claimed that your Master Teacher was an ancient Egyptian spirit, didn't you? Well, who better to give him an air of legitimacy than an honest-to-God Egyptologist?"

"An Egyptologist who just so happens to be canoodling with my man," said Porphyrio, lowering his voice to a harsh whisper. "Awful convenient."

"I'm not your man," Dashiel muttered. "Anyway, do you know any other Egyptologists? I didn't think so. It's kismet, Porphyrio. He's meant to be there."

Porphyrio shook his head. "No. We did just fine without him for twenty years, and I don't see a single goddamn reason why that should change now. He's out of the picture, sweetheart, and if you knew what was good for the both of you, you'd stop trying to drag him back into it."

"All right," said Dashiel. He pushed away his plate and started to rise from the table. "In that case, you can count me out."

"Siddown," growled Porphyrio. He banged his fist on the table, eliciting another round of glares and murmurs from their neighboring diners. "We're not done here."

"We are done, unless you're willing to talk turkey."

There followed a tense stare-down that felt as though it lasted for at least a full minute. At last, Porphyrio heaved an irritable sigh and gestured for Dashiel to sit. "Fine, let's talk. Tell me why on God's green earth I should agree to this, and maybe I'll consider it. And I'm sorry, but that 'credibility' claptrap ain't gonna cut it."

"All right," said Dashiel, sinking back into his seat. "I'll try to put this in terms you can understand. I already told you I've been developing my mediumship."

"Yes, you did. Whatever the hell that means."

"Well, Hermann's been the key to all that. With his help, I've elevated my craft from crude parlor tricks to something truly phenomenal. You let me work with him, and we'll give the crowd at that revival a show that they'll never stop talking about for the rest of their natural lives. But I can't do it without him. He's my lucky charm, Porphyrio. The source of my mojo. I can't explain it any better than that."

Porphyrio stared at him in bafflement. "I don't get it, Dash. What is this guy, The Shadow or something? The second coming of Harry Houdini? 'Cause I sure as hell haven't noticed anything particularly special about him."

"Of course you haven't," said Dashiel. "You've always had a talent for underestimating people. But believe me, he's got something. Maude saw it too, even if she won't admit to it. Frankly, I think it scared her."

"Well . . . I'll think about it." Porphyrio looked intrigued despite himself. "But even if I do agree to this scheme of yours, I sure don't want him hangin' around you in the meantime. Whatever mumbo jumbo he's going to do, he can come in and do it on the day."

"Good," said Dashiel. "And in the meantime, you're to leave him alone. No threats, no harassment. If I get the slightest hint that you've been sniffing around him, it's all off."

Porphyrio scoffed. "You got nothing to worry about on that score. I'd just as soon forget he even existed."

"I'm glad we got that settled." Dashiel gave him a cold smile. "Now, eat up, we've got a lot of work ahead of us. And take it easy on that champagne. Wouldn't want you to get so goosed you can't think straight."

Dashiel's trunk was still sitting in the entryway where the bell-hop had left it the night before, and Porphyrio nearly tripped over it when they walked into the suite. He swore and kicked at it with the toe of his gleaming red and black spectator shoe. His earlier conviviality was gone, replaced by a foul, perilous mood.

"I need to speak to Hermann," said Dashiel.

"What for?" snapped Porphyrio, turning to glare at him.

"To let him know I'm still alive, for one thing. And, for another, to talk to him about his role in our demonstration."

"I don't recall actually agreeing that he'd have a role."

"He will," said Dashiel, "or I walk. Does this suite have a telephone?"

Porphyrio glowered and pointed at the gossip bench standing near the mantel. Dashiel went to the bench and started to pick up the receiver. Porphyrio followed him and stood leaning against the mantel, staring, his arms crossed over his chest.

"A little privacy, if you don't mind," said Dashiel as he slowly lowered the receiver again.

"I do mind," said Porphyrio. "Anything you want to say to him, you can say in front of me."

"Fine." He raised the receiver to his ear, pointedly ignoring Porphyrio's icy gaze. To the operator, he said, "Yes, WIL-1450, please."

Hermann picked up almost instantly. "Hello." The tension in his voice was audible, even over the hum of the line. "This is Hermann Goschalk. To whom am I speaking?"

"Hermann, it's me."

"Dashiel! What's been happening? Are you all right?"

"I'm just fine. Listen, I've been talking with Porphyrio, and he agrees that your help at this revival would be a great benefit to both of us. I know you're reluctant to do it, and I don't blame you one bit. But he's already promised me he'll be on his best behavior."

"I see," said Hermann. His tone was clipped and quiet. Dashiel wondered if he realized their conversation was being observed.

"We'd only need a few minutes of your time. And you know how much it would mean to me. Will you do it?"

"Of course."

"Good. Now, we'll need some time to work out all the details, but I'll be in touch as soon as I can. We're going to be awfully busy between now and the revival, so I'm afraid you and I won't see one another before then. How are those threads holding up?"

"There are four knots left, and one of them'll go any time now. I've tried adding new ones, but . . . it won't let me."

Dashiel's neck and arms prickled with alarm. "I don't understand."

"I can't explain it any better than that. I walk into the room with the thread, and the next thing I know I'm back in my office, or giving a lecture, or chatting with Agnes in the hall, and I can't remember how I got there. Like Setna after the sorceress Tabubu sent him off in a trance."

"It's just a few days, that's all," Dashiel said, as much to reassure himself as Hermann. "Don't you worry, everything's going to be just fine. I'll talk to you soon, Hermann. In the meantime . . . shrayb dem briv."

"Understood," said Hermann. "Goodbye, Dashiel. And for God's sake, be careful."

"What was that?" Porphyrio demanded the moment he'd hung up the receiver.

Dashiel looked up at him. "What was what?"

"Don't play dumb, Dash. What'd you say to him just now?"

"Well, that's a silly question. You were standing right there the whole time, I'm sure you heard all of it."

"What did you have to say to him that you couldn't say in English?"

"Oh, that. Porphyrio, you know as well as I do that there are some things a man can't say to another man over the telephone. You never know when there might be some shady operator listening in."

Porphyrio sneered at him. "Real cute, Dash. Just you remember what I said. No funny business. I'm gonna be keeping a real close eye on you."

"Oh, I'm sure you are." Dashiel stood and poured himself a glass of water from the bar trolley. "Why don't we get to work? We can start hashing out our program right now."

"I'm too bushed for that," said Porphyrio. His surly expression softened, and he moved close to Dashiel and laid a hand on his shoulder. "You probably are, too, sick as you've been. Let's go to bed, darlin'. We'll talk things over in the morning."

"Fine." Dashiel pushed his hand away. "I'll take the couch."

From behind, a pair of arms encircled him like steel bands as he turned to walk away. The front of Porphyrio's body was pressed so close against his back that Dashiel could feel his heartbeat thumping against his shoulder blade. Warm lips brushed his ear.

"Stop kiddin' around, Dash," Porphyrio whispered. "You know you've wanted this as much as I have."

Dashiel was horrified to feel himself responding to the familiarity of the embrace. It would be such a simple thing to relax into it, let the walls drop away, and allow the inevitable to happen.

He wrenched himself out of Porphyrio's arms and spun around to face him again, his face burning with shame and anger. "I wasn't kidding," he snapped. "Don't touch me again."

"You can't stay sore at me forever, darlin'," said Porphyrio. "You love me, and you know it. Sooner or later, you're gonna give in."

CHAPTER 17

D ASHIEL'S BODY ACHED FROM his night on the couch. To say he had slept would be putting it generously—worry and loneliness had gnawed at him throughout the night. Despite his exhaustion, he sat at the little dining table in the kitchenette the next morning with a cup of coffee and a pad of paper in front of him, determined to work.

Porphyrio, lounging in the chair across from him, devoured him with his eyes. "We need to get you a new suit, Dash," he said.

"I just got one," said Dashiel, without looking up from his notes.

"Sure, and it's nice and all. But I meant for the revival. You can't go on stage in that plain old thing. This is your big comeback. You need something truly special. Listen, baby doll, tomorrow I'm gonna take you into the city, and we'll go to Oxxford. Get you a real suit."

Dashiel shrugged. "Whatever you like," he said. Then he paused, tapping his chin with the end of his pencil. "On the subject of clothes, do you still have those beautiful muleskin boots of yours?"

Porphyrio's eyebrows lifted in surprise. "Well, sure I do. Why do you ask?"

"I'd like you to wear them. I always fancied them on you."

"Why, Dash!" said Porphyrio, breaking into a warm grin. "There, you see? You do still care, don't ya? Not that I ever doubted for a minute."

"Don't get too excited. I just appreciate a nice pair of shoes, that's all." Dashiel took a sip of his coffee. It was already getting cold, but he was too tired to care. "Anyway, I think we've got more important matters to attend to. When did you say this thing starts?"

"Four thirty, I think," said Porphyrio. "And the first half-hour or so will probably just be Maude running her mouth. You know how she is."

"Perfect." Dashiel jotted down a note. "We'll go on right after she's done with the opening prayers."

"How come?" asked Porphyrio, frowning. "Why so early?"

"Trust me," said Dashiel, "it'll be better that way."

"If you say so. But she ain't gonna be too happy about us trying to dictate the program to her."

"I'm sure you'll find a way to make it happen. You always do. How about the audience? Any word on who's going to be there?"

"Oh, you know. It'll be a lot of the old familiar faces," said Porphyrio, leaning back and folding his hands behind his head. "Mr. Dearborn. The widow Gunderson. The usual crowd. They'll all follow us down here. Plus whatever local rubberneckers decide to wander in off the streets."

"Good. I'll need you to bring me up to date on the latest developments. Marriages, divorces, deaths, births, illnesses, all of that. Oh, and Maude said she had friends out here the last time I saw her. See what you can learn about the local mediums and their clientele. Ask around, see if any of them are willing to trade information."

Porphyrio smirked. "You still need me to do all this drudgery for you, huh, Dash? And here I thought you said you were the real thing now."

"Oh, I am," said Dashiel with a cold smile. "But that's no excuse for getting lazy. You know nothing impresses like a good evidential message."

"Fine, fine. Don't worry, I'll get you the scoop. Right now, though, I'm more interested in talking about you and me."

"We'll both be there. Doesn't seem to me there's much more to discuss."

"Come on, Dash. You know what I'm talking about." He reached across the table and enclosed Dashiel's hand in a crushing grip. The look in his stormy eyes was equal parts cajoling and menacing. "I want you so bad, darlin'. It ain't right what you're doing to me, giving me the cold shoulder like this. It's wrong and it's cruel."

Dashiel tried to pull his hand away, but Porphyrio held on. "I told you," he said, hoping he sounded calmer than he felt, "I don't want any distractions. There's too much work to do before the big day."

"And after that?" demanded Porphyrio.

"After that . . ." Dashiel paused, weighing his words. A flat-out denial, he decided, could only worsen what already promised to be an agonizing few days. At last, he said, "After that, we'll see."

A flicker of hope passed over Porphyrio's face, only to be replaced with a frustrated scowl. His fingers tightened around Dashiel's. "Damn it, Dash, a man has needs. I don't think I can wait that long."

"You'll have to," Dashiel said. "Because before then, there's nothing doing. I can't afford to waste the time or energy."

"You certainly have become a dull boy in your old age, Ralph," said Porphyrio. He let go of Dashiel's hand and sat back. "But you know what? I don't think this is about the work at all. If you ask me, you're just trying to preserve your virtue for Sweet Papa Short Stuff here."

Reaching into the breast pocket of his robe, he pulled out the photograph Dashiel had taken from Hermann's living room and dangled it tauntingly in front of him.

"Where did you get that?" Dashiel made a grab for the photo but Porphyrio yanked it out of reach.

"Same place you left it, darlin'. In the pocket of your overcoat." He turned the picture over to examine it, then gave a low whistle. "My, he was a fine young thing, wasn't he? You know, if he still looked like this, I could almost understand the fascination."

"Give me that. You have no right to rifle through my things."

"Like you always said, Dash, what's yours is mine," said Porphyrio, flashing a mouthful of pearly white teeth. "But if you really want it back so bad, fine. Go get it." With a lazy flick of his wrist, he tossed the photo to the floor at his feet.

Dashiel got out of his chair and knelt to pick it up. Porphyrio burst into raucous laughter. "Well, at least now I know what it takes to get you on your knees these days, sugar-pie!" He slapped his thigh. "Lordy, Dash, you should see your face. Come on, relax. You gotta learn to take a joke."

"Oh, was some part of that supposed to be funny?" said Dashiel. He tucked the photo into his pocket, then grabbed the edge of the table and hauled himself to his feet. "Well, I wouldn't expect a call from Hal Roach anytime soon if I were you."

"You know what your problem is?" said Porphyrio.

"Yes. You."

"You're wound way too tight, that's what. We gotta do something about that."

"Maybe you're right," said Dashiel. "I'm going to go get some fresh air, see if I can't clear my head." He turned and started to walk out, but Porphyrio grabbed his elbow in a vicelike grip.

"Woah, now hold on just a minute there, string bean," he said. "You ain't going anywhere unless you go with me."

"I'm a prisoner, then."

"I suppose if you want to put it that way, Dash, we both are. Just a couple of prisoners of love." He released Dashiel, who winced and rubbed at his throbbing elbow. "Anyway," Porphyrio went on cheerfully, "I wasn't planning to keep you cooped up in here the whole time. We're drivin' to Chicago this afternoon, remember? In the meantime, if you want fresh air, you can just hustle your cute little caboose out onto the balcony over yonder."

THE BUSY AFTERNOON provided a welcome respite from Porphyrio's badgering. Having driven into the city and placed their order for Dashiel's suit at Oxxford, they lunched at the Coq d'Or. Then they purchased a bolt of bridal silk and a bottle of ammonia and started back to Willowvale.

When they got back to the hotel, Dashiel cut the silk into strips while Porphyrio drank and sulked. Excitement sparked deep inside of him. It had been so long since he'd done this kind of work in earnest.

The respite did not last long. The next morning, Porphyrio greeted Dashiel at the dining table by slamming a glass of whiskey down in front of him.

"What's this?" asked Dashiel.

"Hair of the dog," said Porphyrio. He poured a second glass for himself and gulped it down.

"I don't need that. I wasn't the one drinking all evening."

"Breakfast, then. Come on, down the hatch."

"No, thanks. Coffee and a roll will suit me just fine."

Porphyrio scoffed. "You ain't touched a drop since you got here. Have you become a goddamn teetotaler or something? As if you needed a way to be even more insufferable."

"I'm no teetotaler," said Dashiel. "I've just gotten choosier about my drinking companions, that's all."

"Have a drink with me, Dash," Porphyrio pleaded. It was dizzying, how quickly he could jump tracks from cold contempt to plaintive tenderness. At one time, it might have been enough to throw Dashiel off guard. "Just one drink. Is that really too much to ask?"

"At nine in the morning? Yes, it is."

Dashiel pushed the glass away hard enough that it went sliding across the polished surface of the table. Porphyrio caught it before it tipped over the edge, shrugged, and slugged it down himself. "Fine. But I wish you'd just enjoy yourself a little, darlin'. Life's too short for all this moping around."

"Why don't you find yourself something useful to do?" Dashiel said. "You still haven't brought me a single scrap of information. I can't prepare the damn silks until I have something to put on 'em. And I need to know what kinds of billets to expect."

Porphyrio bared his teeth in a nasty grin. "See, Dash? Put on airs all you like. You still can't do a thing without ol' Porphyrio, can you?" Slowly and unsteadily, he rose from his chair. "Fine. I'll go out and find you some nice, juicy scuttlebutt. But don't you dare wander off while I'm gone, or there'll be hell to pay."

"I'm not going anywhere," muttered Dashiel.

Porphyrio took his sweet time preening himself and getting dressed. It was some thirty minutes before he finally sauntered out the door. The moment he was gone, Dashiel went to the phone and picked it up. The line was dead.

He waited another twenty minutes before heading down to the lobby. If Porphyrio was still lurking there, he'd managed to hide himself well. Dashiel approached the desk, where the young clerk was absorbed in the latest edition of *The Chicagoan*.

"Morning," said Dashiel, tipping his hat.

The clerk guiltily stowed his magazine under the counter. "Good morning, sir. May I be of assistance?"

"Yes. I'm in suite 502. Something seems to be wrong with our telephone."

"Ah," said the clerk, with a knowing look. "I'm sorry, sir. The gentleman who made the reservation was most insistent that we switch off service to that suite for as long as he's out."

Dashiel squeezed his room key until it bit into the flesh of his palm. "Did he, now?"

"Yes, sir. But you're welcome to use one of our lines here in the lobby." The clerk indicated a row of phone booths along the far wall.

"Right," said Dashiel. "Thanks."

He hadn't had breakfast yet, or much of a dinner the night before, and he was shaky with hunger and nerves when he stepped into the booth. He fumbled his nickel twice before managing to get it into the slot. It was his last nickel. His one remaining shot at making contact before the revival. The operator put him through to Hermann's number, but the phone rang and rang, and nobody picked up. Dashiel fought off a wave of despair as he hung up the receiver. He took a fortifying breath, fished the nickel out of the coin return, then picked up the phone again and called Agnes.

"Hello, Agnes," he said when she picked up. "It's Dashiel."

"Mr. Quicke! Gee, it's good to hear your voice. Are you okay? Is that big circus dope giving you a hard time—Prosciutto or whatever his name is?"

Dashiel smiled. "He's doing his best, but I'm managing all right. Is Hermann in?"

"Not yet. He's probably on his way right now. You want me to have him call you when he gets here?"

"No." He swallowed. "He wouldn't be able to reach me. And even if he could, Porphyrio might be listening in. Just tell him to meet me on the Main Street Bridge in St. Charles on Tuesday at three o' clock. And listen, don't let him forget—if he has any problems in the meantime, he can send me a card with a coin taped to it. Heads up if it's trouble from his ghost, tails up if it's from mine."

"You got it, Mr. Quicke."

"How's the shabti behaving?"

"Last I heard, there were three knots left," she said. "Everyone's starting to get real touchy around here again. And it just seems— powerful. You can feel the whole place vibrating the moment you step in the front door, like you're inside a big drum and someone's banging on it."

Dashiel let out a shuddering breath. "All right. Hang in there, Agnes. I'll see you soon and . . . it'll all work out one way or another. I promise. Take care of Hermann for me."

He hung up and rested his forehead against the phone for a long moment, before wearily making his way to the elevator and heading back up to his luxurious prison.

IT WAS LATE in the afternoon when Porphyrio came back, flushed and sweaty and reeking of booze. He slapped a pile of papers onto the gossip bench, brushed past Dashiel, and crawled into the immense bed without undressing or removing his shoes.

Dashiel perused the papers. Porphyrio had always been good at finding useful information, and that hadn't changed. Among the haul were copies of several detailed files from mediums local to St. Charles and Geneva, newspaper clippings containing recent obituaries from the area, and a small bundle of personal papers and letters. Porphyrio would no doubt be able to enlighten him on the significance of all these items, but Dashiel was in no mood to try and interrogate him. He was confident he could glean enough material from them on his own to make do.

Porphyrio continued to sleep off his bender as Dashiel showered, ordered dinner brought up to the room, and began reading the files. When a knock sounded on the door, Porphyrio stirred and grumbled, but didn't get up.

Dashiel opened the door to find a bellhop standing outside with a cart bearing two steaming trays of veal, artichoke hearts, and roast potatoes. "Just leave the cart here," he said. "I'll take it in."

The young man cleared his throat nervously. "Are you Mr. Dashiel Quicke?" he asked in a low voice.

Dashiel's heart did a quick somersault. "Sure am," he said quietly. "What's up?"

The bellhop pulled an envelope from beneath one of the trays and slipped it into Dashiel's hand. "A man stopped by a little while ago and asked me to give this to you, sir," he said, so softly that Dashiel could barely make out the words. "He said it was for your eyes only, and that I wasn't to let the other gentleman see it."

Dashiel thanked him and pocketed the envelope. When he came back into the room, Porphyrio was up, leaning heavily against the back of one of the Morris chairs.

"What were you two whisperin' about?" he demanded.

"The kid was just trying not to wake you," said Dashiel. "You should have some dinner. It'll settle your stomach. Then you can tell me about those papers you brought in."

"Last thing I want right now is a bunch of meat and potatoes," said Porphyrio, who was looking distinctly green about the gills. "The smell alone's just about enough to make me dish my lunch. I'm gonna take a shower. We can talk after that."

"Suit yourself." Dashiel took his tray and the pile of papers to the kitchenette, but he didn't start eating right away. He waited until he heard the hiss of water from the shower, then pulled the little envelope out of his pocket and opened it.

It contained a folded piece of paper with something small but weighty tucked inside of it. Dashiel unfolded the paper and found a gold-toned coin taped to the inside. He realized at once that it must be one of Hermann's old Cascarets advertising tokens. His heart leapt into his throat.

The side facing up depicted a nude cherub sitting on a chamber pot, its little face staring blankly ahead. A legend inscribed around the edge of the token read: *TAILS YOU LOSE ALL GOING OUT—NOTHING COMING IN.*

Dashiel didn't need to look at the other side of the token to know what it signified, but he ripped it off its paper backing and flipped it over anyway. *HEADS I WIN*, it proclaimed. *CASCARETS ALWAYS WIN. BEST FOR THE BOWEL.*

Fury bubbled up inside him so fast that it sent his head spinning. He shoved the paper and the token into his pocket and stormed into the bedroom. Wrenching open the chifforobe, he began hauling Porphyrio's belongings out of the drawers and dumping them onto the floor. It didn't take him long to locate Porphyrio's little revolver, tucked away under a pile of neatly folded silk pocket squares.

With grim satisfaction, Dashiel kicked the debris aside and made his way out onto the balcony. Having opened the cylinder and pocketed the bullets, he threw the gun over the railing. It clattered faintly as it skittered away across the paving stones and disappeared under the hedges in the courtyard below.

Dashiel went back inside and flung the bathroom door open with a bang.

Porphyrio's flushed face emerged from behind the shower curtain. He squinted blearily at Dashiel. Water dripped from his chin and the end of his nose.

"Dash? What are you doin'?" he said. "Mind the noise, will ya? I've got a splitting headache."

"Good," snarled Dashiel. "We need to talk."

"Well, sure," said Porphyrio. He smirked. "Why don't you step in and join me, darlin'?"

"I'll join your goddamn head to your ass," said Dashiel, "assuming I can figure out which one is which."

"Lordy, Dash, you look fit to be tied!" said Porphyrio, chuckling. "What's eating you, anyhow?"

"What did you do to Hermann?"

Porphyrio's eyebrows lifted in surprise. "Hermann!" He snorted. "What in blazes makes you think I did anything to him?"

"I have my ways of finding these things out." Dashiel moved closer, bristling dangerously. "Let's just say I have it on good authority that someone's been giving him shit, and we both know who that is. So you'd better give me some answers right now, Gomer, and they'd better be good."

"I don't know what you're talking about."

Dashiel turned and punched the tiled wall behind the washbasin so hard that his knuckles came away bruised and bleeding. The bar of soap Porphyrio had been clutching slipped out of his hand and fell to the floor of the tub with a hollow thud.

"I have done everything you asked of me, Porphyrio," Dashiel said through gritted teeth. "I finally had a shot at building a new life for myself. A real one, a decent one. And I walked away from all of it—for you. Do you understand that? The one thing I expected in return, the *one* thing, was that you leave Hermann alone. Now, don't make me ask you again. What did you do to him?"

A peculiar expression clouded Porphyrio's face. He glowered at Dashiel for a moment, but then his chin began to tremble. "I'm sorry," he said in a strangled voice. "I didn't hurt him or nothing. I just had a little man to man talk with him, that's all, to make sure he knew where things stood. I didn't think it was gonna be like this between you and me, I really didn't. Having you so close and not being able to reach you, and you—treating me like a stranger, after everything we've been through together?" Tears poured down his cheeks and mingled with the water from the shower. He buried his face in his hands. "It's killing me, Dash, it's just killing me!"

Dashiel blinked at him, still furious, but unmanned. "Too bad. I agreed to help you with this revival, and that's it. I've held up my end of the bargain so far. But if you can't hold up yours—"

To his astonishment, Porphyrio clambered out of the shower and sank to his knees in front of him. He flung his arms around Dashiel's legs and laid his head against his hip. Water streamed off him in rivulets. It puddled on the floor and seeped through Dashiel's clothes, chilling him.

"I love you," he said, his voice muffled against Dashiel's leg. "I want you back so bad I can't stand it. I pretend to be tough, swaggerin' around full of piss and vinegar, trying to fool myself and everyone else into thinking I'm all right on my own. But inside, I'm a damn wreck—every minute of every day since we parted. I'm nothin' without you. And I never meant to hurt nobody, Dashiel, least of all you. I didn't plan to shoot you. I was so sore and heartsick after you left me, I wasn't in my right senses. But there's not a single day goes by that I don't regret what I did. Give me one more chance, darlin', that's all I ask. Even if you can't find it in your heart to forgive me, at least let me hold you one more time."

Dashiel stood unmoving, speechless, staring down at him and feeling an inscrutable snarl of emotions. Instinctively, he laid his hand on Porphyrio's sodden curls. Porphyrio lifted his head and gazed up at him, his eyes filled with hope and yearning. And for one dizzying, breathless instant, Dashiel remembered why he'd loved him.

Was this what it felt like to be a ghost—trapped in the twilight realm between two worlds, a lost soul in both?

He closed his eyes and focused on the soft hiss of the shower, willing the clamor of his thoughts to die away. The turmoil inside him gradually abated, and a grim sense of purpose trickled in to take its place.

"All right," Dashiel said, not ungently. "All right. Christ, Gomer. Pull yourself together. There's work to be done."

⁂

DASHIEL SPENT THE evening crafting spirit messages. He worked slowly and meticulously. From pilfered letters and papers, he assembled messages in the handwriting of departed loved ones. The file on one prominent believer from Elgin contained an old photograph of the man's deceased wife.

He snipped her face out of the photo and pasted it to a sheet of paper, then surrounded it with cryptic allusions to details he had found in the file. *Remember our night on Round Lake*, he wrote above her head, following the soft curve of her Gibson Girl coiffure. And then, underneath, *I am still dancing among the forget-me-nots*.

Through it all, Porphyrio remained uncharacteristically quiet and patient. He answered Dashiel's curt questions without sass or sarcasm.

Even as Dashiel soaked the silk pieces in ammonia and the suite filled with throat-scalding fumes, he didn't complain. By the time Dashiel finished impressing each image onto a piece of silk with a hot iron, it was almost midnight.

"You've outdone yourself again, Dash," said Porphyrio, admiring the silks as Dashiel hung them up to dry over the curtain rod in the shower. "I had my doubts, but I guess I can see now why you were so set on doin' these. They look mighty fine."

Dashiel didn't answer. He went to the sink and washed his hands. The broken skin on his knuckles burned under the soap and scalding water.

"You must be beat after all that work," Porphyrio went on. "Why don't we eat a little something, then turn in?"

"You go ahead," Dashiel said. "I don't have much of an appetite."

"Well, I can't say I blame you, darlin', after breathing in those nasty fumes all evening. My stomach's a bit sour, too." He moved in close behind Dashiel and began caressing his shoulders. "Let's get some sleep."

"Fine. I'll be along in a little while."

The mirror reflected Porphyrio's tender smile. He leaned in and kissed the side of Dashiel's neck, just behind his right ear. "See, Dash?" His warm breath brushed Dashiel's skin. "This is all I've wanted—for us to put our strife behind us and forgive one another. This is how it's supposed to be."

Dashiel took his time cleaning up after Porphyrio left. It was some twenty or thirty minutes before he ambled into the bedroom, still in his trousers and shirtsleeves.

Porphyrio lay sprawled in the four-poster bed with his hands folded behind his head. At the sound of Dashiel's footsteps, he sat up slightly, pushing himself up on his elbows. The coverlet slipped down as he did so, revealing his bare chest. His eyebrows lifted questioningly as Dashiel limped over to stand close to the bed.

"Dash?" he said. "Are you . . ."

Dashiel took a few more shuffling steps forward, gesturing for Porphyrio to scoot over. Porphyrio drew back the covers and patted the mattress beside him, beaming. As Dashiel had suspected, he was nude beneath the silken sheets. He stood for a moment, steeling himself, before climbing into the bed beside him.

"Oh, baby doll," Porphyrio said softly, reaching out to cup his face in one massive hand. "You don't know how much I've wanted to have you beside me like this again."

Dashiel gave him a quick once-over. "I think I have some inkling. Now, lie back." He pushed his hand away.

Porphyrio's eyes widened. "Dash, what—"

"Just do it."

Without another word, Porphyrio complied. A flush crept up his neck and into his cheeks, and his lips parted in a hopeful, questioning smile. Dashiel put his hands on Porphyrio's shoulders and swung a knee over to straddle his hips. Porphyrio gasped with surprise and pleasure.

"Why, Dash, you saucy thing!" he breathed. "Where'd this come from all of a sudden?"

"Shut up," said Dashiel, "and pay attention."

"Pay attention to wh—" Porphyrio began, but he cut himself off with a yelp of dismay. Dashiel had reached behind himself and pulled his revolver from the waistband of his trousers. He held the gun aloft for a minute, regarding Porphyrio with a cool and clinical eye, then eased the hammer back.

"What the hell are you doing, Ralph?" Porphyrio quavered, slithering backward until his shoulders bumped up against the headboard of the bed.

"Trying to decide where to aim this revolver," said Dashiel. He let the muzzle of the gun linger over the space between Porphyrio's wild and frightened gray eyes for a moment, then casually moved it down until it was pointed directly at his groin. "I figured I'd take a leaf out of your book and try hitting you where it'll sting the most."

The color drained from Porphyrio's face. "Jesus Christ, Dash, have you lost your ever-lovin' mind?"

"Maybe I have," said Dashiel. He bared his teeth in a joyless grin. "But what you're about to lose is going to hurt a whole lot worse."

"You—you wouldn't really do it," said Porphyrio, panting with fear. "You wouldn't have the nerve!"

"Wouldn't I?" asked Dashiel. He shifted back and forth on his knees, adjusting his stance. "You've always been a pretty sharp gambler, Porphyrio. How much are you willing to bet on those odds?"

"I don't understand." Porphyrio's voice came out in a piteous croak. "Why are you doin' this?"

"Because," said Dashiel, "you seem to have forgotten who I am and what I'm capable of. Now, you listen to me if you value your manhood. I am not to be trifled with, and neither is Hermann. Do you understand me?"

Porphyrio swallowed and nodded hastily.

"You violated our agreement," he went on. "And no quantity of crocodile tears will erase that, or all the other damage you've done. If I were a sensible man, I'd just walk away right now and let you find a new goddamn partner like you should have done years ago. But God help me, I'm going to see this thing through to the end. And if it has to end with me putting a slug in you, so be it, but I don't think that's the grand finale either one of us would prefer." He slid his index finger over the trigger and moistened his lips with the tip of his tongue. "Now, I want you to think very carefully about what you say next, Gomer. And you're gonna find out the hard way if I don't like it."

Porphyrio drew in his breath and huffed it out a few times before he finally spoke. "Okay," he said. "Okay. You're the boss. From now on, it's strictly business between us."

"And Hermann?"

He squeezed his eyes shut. "I'll leave him alone, Dash, I swear to God."

"Good," said Dashiel. He eased his finger off the trigger but didn't put the gun away. "I'm going to go to bed now. And in the morning, we're both going to get back to work. Sweet dreams, Porphyrio."

He climbed out of the bed and backed out of the room, leaving Porphyrio sitting alone in the middle of the vast mattress, trembling, with his knees pulled up to his chest.

CHAPTER 18

WHEN THE DAY OF the revival rolled around, the trees in St. Charles were clad in vibrant shades of orange, red, and yellow. Dashiel leaned against the railing of the Main Street Bridge, enjoying the scents of autumn on the breeze as he gazed out over the mirror-smooth waters of the Fox River. A chill hung in the air, but he didn't mind. That chill carried a promise of change.

"When's he supposed to get here?" Porphyrio said, pacing the sidewalk like a caged panther a few feet from Dashiel. "We ain't got all day."

"Any minute now," said Dashiel, without looking away from the river. "You don't have to wait up, you know."

"Well, maybe I won't." Porphyrio scowled. "I'm gonna go get a drink. But you'd better not run off on me. As soon as you've finished your business with him, you come find me." The words were as bombastic as always, but his eyes avoided Dashiel's and his tone lacked its usual bite.

Dashiel raised a scornful eyebrow. "Please. You really think I'd leave now, after all the work I've put in? Go have your tipple, Porphyrio. I'll see you inside."

Porphyrio muttered something under his breath and stalked away, leaving Dashiel alone for the first time in days. He heaved a sigh of relief that came up from the soles of his white wing tip shoes. A minute or two later, gentle fingers brushed the back of his hand. He turned to find Hermann standing beside him, dressed in a quiet gray suit. The cool autumn wind had brought a rosy glow to his cheeks, and his eyes shone with an odd mixture of joy and distress. Dashiel's weary heart rose at the sight of him.

"Hermann," Dashiel said softly. He wanted to grab Hermann and kiss him senseless, but he settled for clasping his hand between both of his own. "God, it's good to see you."

"I'm so glad you're alone," Hermann said. "I didn't think I'd get a chance to see you without that paskudnik hanging around."

"He's going to think twice before getting near you again," said Dashiel, with a smile of grim satisfaction. "He's behaving for now, more or less. But it won't last. Have you got it?"

"I do." Hermann's shoulders sagged. "Are you sure you want to go through with this?"

"I am absolutely sure. I don't see any other way." Reflexively, he started to reach for Hermann's face, then stopped himself. "Listen, I don't know if I'll get another chance to say this—"

Hermann winced and shut his eyes tight. "Don't. Please. Not unless it's about the plan. All the things we really want to say and do are going to have to wait until this is all over." He forced a wan smile. "So, I guess you'll just have to come through it all right, won't you?"

Of course I will, Dashiel wanted to say. *You think I'm going to miss my chance to get my arms around you again?* But his fragile composure was already close to breaking, so he opted for a quick nod. "Okay. When it's all over, then."

"I have to go find the others," said Hermann. "I haven't even had a chance to look around the place yet. Watch for a message from Agnes—she'll tell you what you need to know." He looked away and took a shaky breath, then reached into the pocket of his overcoat and pulled out a small object bundled up in a handkerchief. "Here it is. The last knot's still holding. I did what we discussed and wrote him a letter, but . . . I don't know what'll happen once you untie it."

He hesitated a moment before pressing the bundle into Dashiel's hands. A deep, powerful vibration thrummed through him when he touched it. Then, all was still.

"Just—use it in good health," Hermann whispered. "Promise me."

"I will. I promise. See you soon, Hermann."

Hermann nodded, then pulled the brim of his hat down to shadow his eyes and hurried away. Dashiel watched him until he disappeared a block away through the entrance of Hotel Baker.

He wanted to weep. But if all went well, there would be plenty of time for that later. He unwrapped the parcel that Hermann had given him. The shabti's tiny face stared up at him, its expression wide-eyed and deceptively docile. A single length of red thread was wound around its arms just below the shoulders, secured with a distinctive, loop-shaped knot.

"Ninety minutes to curtain, little friend," said Dashiel. "I hope you can behave that long, at least." He tucked the shabti into his sleeve, where it rested snug against his wrist—cool and hard and strangely companionable. Then he meandered toward the hotel.

Just as he reached the entrance, someone clapped him on the shoulder. A jovial female voice said, "Bless my soul, is that who I think it is?"

He plastered on a smile and turned around. "Hello, Maude," he said, with a tip of his hat. "I was wondering when I'd run into you."

The Reverend Fink had traded her usual furs and satin for the more somber attire of the séance room. Like many woman mediums, she preferred to present herself to her parishioners as humble and homely, dressing in dowdy, floral frocks that buttoned up to the throat and left everything to the imagination. It put people at ease, she'd always insisted. Made them feel she was someone they could trust.

The males of the species tended to be more extravagant in their presentation, and Dashiel was no exception. Beneath his overcoat, he was clad in the new suit Porphyrio had bought for him at Oxxford, a white silk number that wouldn't have looked out of place on one of the gaudier dance orchestra frontmen.

"So," Maude said, looking him up and down, "the prodigal son returneth, eh? Well, I'll be damned. I'd heard the rumors, of course, but I guess I had to see it for myself to believe it. You look good, kid. Finally got sick of peddling that sugar water, did you?"

"Oh, you know I couldn't stay away forever. I suppose you can take the man out of the spirit cabinet, but you can't take the spirit cabinet out of the man. Or something to that effect."   .

Maude snorted. "Well, I must say, I'm looking forward to seeing your little demonstration this evening. Porphyrio says you have quite the spectacle planned." She swatted his arm playfully with the back of her gloved hand. "If it's good enough, I might even consider taking you back. I'd have to bring it up with the rest of the board back at Camp Walburton, of course, after the stunt you pulled."

"I can assure you, it'll be good," said Dashiel, flashing her a toothy grin. "But these days, I've got my sights set a little higher than Camp Walburton, I'm afraid."

She narrowed her eyes at him. "Don't tell me you and Porphyrio are still planning that ridiculous church out in Tampa?"

"I'd say my plans are for me to know and you to find out." He glanced at his wristwatch. It was just after three o'clock. "Speaking of Porphyrio, I'd better go find him."

"Oh, I expect he's steeling himself with a little liquid courage at the hotel bar," Maude said with a sniff. "Not that he'd ever admit it, but I think these big public affairs have always made him a little nervous, the poor dear. Just between you and me, that man is all hat and no cattle, especially without his partner by his side. You ought to have seen the state he was in for those first few months after you left us. Pitiful."

Dashiel offered her his arm. "Well, let's go rout him out. If what I have in store for tonight doesn't raise his spirits, I don't know what will."

Maude gave him a dubious look but gamely slipped her hand into the crook of his elbow and let him escort her in.

The hotel was already bustling with activity. The festivities weren't set to begin for another hour and a half, but the lobby was jammed with a motley combination of mediums, the faithful, and curious members of the public. Suspicious and startled eyes followed Dashiel everywhere he looked, which did not surprise him. It hadn't been such a long time since he'd left the fold, and the world of Spiritualism was a small one.

He checked his coat and hat and made his way to the bar, with Maude following close at his heels. Porphyrio was already seated there, huge and resplendent in his midnight-blue suit and yellow muleskin boots, a silk-lined evening cape slung around his shoulders. Several other familiar figures sat or stood clustered around him, heads together, speaking in low voices.

"There you all are," said Maude, her voice booming over the din of the crowd. She grabbed Dashiel's arm and pulled him close. "Look what I found loitering around out on the street."

All eyes turned to Dashiel, who smiled graciously and took a brief bow. "Afternoon, everyone."

"Oh, brother. You weren't joking," said Dorothy Everard-Hopwell, one of the younger mediums in the Camp Walburton set. She'd only recently arrived when Dashiel made his departure, but he must have left an impression. She regarded him like a chicken farmer eyeing an approaching coyote.

"Of course I wasn't joking, sweetheart," said Porphyrio, without taking his eyes off Dashiel. He spoke in his séance room accent, cool and crisp and devoid of any hint of its customary twang. "It's about time you got here, Dashiel. You're the man of the hour—we've all been talking of nothing else but your glorious return."

"I thought I felt my ears burning," said Dashiel.

Porphyrio gestured to the empty stool beside him. "Come join us. Have a drink."

Dashiel nodded and took a seat, letting the murmurs and cold stares of his former associates go unheeded. The other mediums, who had cleared a path for Dashiel when Porphyrio beckoned him over, gathered close again. The elderly Swink sisters elbowed each other and whispered. Arthur Hensley, who went by Swami Balabhadra to his sitters, pointedly turned his back, the feather in his turban twitching with indignation.

"Is he here to cause more trouble?" someone demanded.

"Can't trust him—" piped up another voice.

"Ladies and gentlemen, please," said Maude, holding up her hands. "I'm sure Dashiel wouldn't have dared to set foot in here unless it was out of the purest intentions. Isn't that right, dear?"

"Absolutely, Maude," said Dashiel, with a deferential nod. "Folks, I can assure you that I'm not here to debunk, defame, or defraud. All I ask is that you give me a fair chance to redeem myself tonight. And if I let you down, well—you all have my permission to kick me to the curb."

"And Porphyrio," Maude went on, "I'm sure you wouldn't have brought Dashiel back into the fold unless you were fully confident that he had turned over a new leaf."

"Why, that goes without saying, Reverend," said Porphyrio. He squeezed Dashiel's shoulder and flashed a dazzling grin at the crowd. "Brother Quicke here is a new man. I know you're all going to like what you see tonight."

"Oh, I don't doubt that," said Maude, raising an eyebrow. "Whatever you boys have planned, I expect it'll be fascinating."

Nobody looked particularly mollified, but the crowd of oglers did thin out a little. Porphyrio clapped Dashiel on the back and flagged down the bartender.

"Bring the man a Gin Rickey," said Porphyrio. He turned to Dashiel and tapped his temple with a gloved finger. "See, Dash? Ol' Porphyrio never forgets."

Dashiel didn't turn up his nose at the libation this time. His mouth started watering as soon as the barman set the gleaming glass in front of him.

"Bottoms up," he murmured to nobody in particular, raising the glass to his lips. He closed his eyes and relished the cool tang of the lime juice, the bright tingle of the soda, and the burn of the gin as it slid down his throat.

"My word, just look at you," said Porphyrio, leaning in close. "The way you're savoring that drink, you'd think it was gonna be your last."

Dashiel shrugged. "Maybe it will be."

"What do you mean?" Porphyrio shot him a suspicious frown. "What sort of a way is that to talk?"

"I don't take anything for granted anymore, Porphyrio," said Dashiel. "Not in this business, or in this life. I just follow where the spirits lead."

Porphyrio snorted. "Seems like you're getting into character a little early, Dash."

"Who said anything about getting into character?" He glanced at his watch again. "When did you say we go on?"

"At five, just like you asked," said Porphyrio. "Don't know why you were so insistent on that. Seems to me like we oughta be the final act, not the opener."

"Good." Dashiel smiled as he lifted the glass to his lips for another sip of the glittering elixir. "Perfect."

Porphyrio smirked, but there was a hint of unease in his eyes. It was a look Dashiel had seen a lot over the last couple days, which pleased him. "Well, I sure hope you're ready, darlin'," said Porphyrio. "This is our moment."

"Oh, believe me, Porphyrio," he said, "I've never been readier for anything."

❧

HOTEL BAKER'S RAINBOW Room was just as impressive as Maude had made it sound. The room was a great, glass-tiled oval, with multi-hued lights illuminating each of the tiles. Dining tables draped in white cloth stood between the polished wooden columns that surrounded the central dance floor.

A stage had been set up at the far end of the room, and the dance floor was filled with chairs, many of which were already occupied. An organist sat near the stage at the console of a massive pipe organ, armed with an arsenal of Spiritualist hymnals and broadsheets. Overlooking the floor was a balcony level that wrapped all the way around the room, giving onlookers a clear view of the floor and stage from every angle.

The mediums huddled in the wings behind the red velvet curtains flanking the stage, surveying the growing crowd. Dashiel had missed all this more than he realized—the whispers of anticipation, the jostling of elbows as he and his associates crowded each other, trying to get a glimpse of promising marks in the audience amid the clashing odors of greasepaint and lavish colognes.

"There's Widow Gunderson," whispered Dorothy. "What a shock to see her here. Anyone ever hear what happened with her nephew? Maybe we can use it."

"I've got the dope, all right," said the Swami with a smug little simper, "but you're not going to hear it from me."

"That's enough, children," said Maude. "I won't have any bickering. I had to pull quite a few strings to set up this bash, and we're all going to be keeping the glory of Camp Walburton at the forefront of our minds tonight. We're in this one together. Arthur, if you have useful information, you'll share it. That goes for all of you. Do I make myself clear?"

Arthur glowered but nodded. While he grudgingly shared his pearls of wisdom with Dorothy, Maude brushed past Dashiel and peeked beyond the curtain. She pulled back and turned to him with a disconcerted frown.

"That kooky little professor friend of yours is out there," she said. "Right in the front row. What's he doing here?"

"Who, Hermann Goschalk?" said Dashiel, smiling innocently. "Well, fancy that. I suppose he's probably here to see me."

Maude shivered. "I don't trust that man."

"Why?" asked Porphyrio, giving her a sharp glance. "What do you know about him?"

"He just makes me nervous," she said stiffly. "That's all."

Porphyrio turned his questioning gaze back to Dashiel, who answered with a knowing lift of his eyebrows. "What did I tell you?" Dashiel murmured.

"I think you've both gone half a bubble off plumb," said Porphyrio. He craned his neck to get a look at Hermann, then turned away, scowling. "The fella's a regular Caspar Milquetoast if I ever met one."

"You know, Maude," Dashiel said, "Hermann's taken quite an interest in Spiritualism. Why, we might even have a true believer on our hands, especially after the show I plan to put on tonight. What a shame your little job with him didn't work out."

Porphyrio leered. "Well, I wouldn't take it too personal if I were you, Maude. What that man really wants, you couldn't have provided anyway."

"All right, muzzle it," said Dashiel. "It's about time to start."

As PORPHYRIO HAD predicted, Maude's introductory remarks were not brief. Having led the crowd in an animated rendition of "Hand in Hand with Angels," she launched into an invocation and reading on the Power of Spirits.

By the time she started the responsive readings, Dashiel began to grow restless. As much as he could, he paced in the crowded wings, and frowned at his watch.

"Now concerning spiritual gifts, brethren, I do not want you to be uninformed," Maude recited from her prayer book, her voice tremulous with devotional fervor. She raised her hands in an expansive gesture of invitation.

"Now there are varieties of gifts, but the same Spirit, and there are varieties of service, but the same God," came the mumbled response from the audience.

"For Christ's sake, Dash, take it easy," hissed Porphyrio. "Quit jumping around like a cat on hot bricks. You're making me nervous."

"It's ten after five," said Dashiel. "We were supposed to be on by now."

"You know how Maude is. She'll wrap up when she's good and ready."

"Not good enough."

"To one is given through the Spirit the utterance of wisdom and to another the utterance of knowledge, according to the same Spirit," droned the crowd.

Dashiel fussed with the object in his sleeve. His palms were beginning to sweat. "If she doesn't put a sock in it in the next two minutes, I'm going on whether she's done or not," he said.

Having finished the reading, Maude signaled to the organist to strike up another hymn. Dashiel was about ready to barge out on stage and bodily remove her when she held up her hands. The last few stragglers in the crowd caught up with the final measures of "Lead, Kindly Light" and fell silent.

"Ladies and gentlemen," she said, "our first demonstration of the evening will be a special one. I present two of our most esteemed mediums from the ranks at Camp Walburton, a pair who have been with us and have worked tirelessly to promote the good work of Spiritualism for nearly twenty years. And although one of them has been away for some time, it's my pleasure to welcome him back on this joyful and momentous occasion. I give you: Brother Porphyrio and Brother Quicke."

Without waiting for her to finish speaking, Dashiel strode onto the stage. He didn't bother trying to conceal his limp, as he had routinely done during his demonstrations over the past three years. The end of his cane beat a sharp rhythm on the stage as he walked. His white suit blazed like a beacon under the hot stage lights.

Porphyrio followed close behind, and they flanked Maude on either side. They were greeted by polite applause from the newcomers in the crowd, mingled with disapproving murmurs from the initiated faithful, many of whom were familiar with Dashiel's bitter departure from the world of Spiritualism.

"Break a leg, boys," whispered Maude, embracing them both. "I certainly hope this will be as amusing as I think it's going to be."

She departed. Dashiel gestured for Porphyrio to take a seat in one of the folding chairs that had been set up on the stage. He stepped forward and gripped the edges of the lectern where Maude had stood during her opening remarks, sweeping his gaze over the audience.

There were quite a few faces in the crowd that he recognized, some of them sitters from his own séances past. And there, in the front row, just as Maude had said, sat Hermann. He clutched his hat tightly in his lap and looked up at Dashiel with wide, frightened eyes. As much as Dashiel longed to acknowledge him, he didn't let his gaze linger. He continued to scan the crowd, keeping his expression neutral.

"Ladies and gentlemen," he said at length, speaking from the chest so his voice filled the space and echoed from the rafters, "brothers and sisters in the faith—good evening. I'm sure that many of you already know me. And those of you who do are no doubt surprised to see me here tonight."

He paused for a moment, and there was a brief murmur of agreement from the audience.

"It's no secret," Dashiel went on, "that I went astray. Some years ago, I began to lose my faith, and with it, my powers of mediumship. And so, out of desperation, I resorted to trickery and charlatanism. That's right, my friends—I won't deny it. I practiced fraudulent mediumship for years under Camp Walburton's banner. I was consumed by guilt, and rather than face what I had done, I tried to bring others down with me. I attempted to expose the entire camp as a hotbed of deception and chicanery. For the next three years, I devoted myself to the mission of single-handedly bringing about the downfall of the Spiritualist faith."

Gasps erupted from the crowd. The Widow Gunderson, seated near Hermann in the front row, pressed her hand to her heart and shook her head, rolling her eyes heavenward. Dashiel sensed some uneasy stirring from the other mediums in the wings.

"But today, brothers and sisters," he thundered, "I stand before you a changed man. Humbled—that's the only word for it. I thought I'd find redemption on this new path, but instead, I found myself plunged into a perdition of my own making. I've been brought low, brothers and sisters, lower than I ever thought possible. If it weren't for my dear friend and partner Porphyrio, who knows where I would be tonight? Certainly not standing before you now.

"But, although I lost my faith and everything else I had along with it, Porphyrio never lost his faith in me. It's he who brought me back into the fold, brothers and sisters. He who restored my faith—and with it, my powers of mediumship, which have come back stronger than ever."

He turned to acknowledge Porphyrio with open arms. Porphyrio rose from his chair, beaming, and pulled him into a tight embrace. "Amen, Brother Quicke," he said, slapping Dashiel heartily on the back with both hands. "Hallelujah!"

Porphyrio broke away from Dashiel and gestured for the audience to rise. "Let's hear a hallelujah for Brother Quicke," he cried, grinning in triumphant exultation.

"Hallelujah!" came the answering cry. "Glory be!"

"Yes, ladies and gentlemen," Dashiel said. "Glory be. Let tonight's demonstration stand as a testament to the power of faith and forgiveness. I humbly ask you all to give me a second chance, just as Brother Porphyrio has done." He raised his hands and signaled for the crowd to be seated again.

"Many of you here with us now are already among the faithful," he said. "After what you see here tonight, may your faith be strengthened, just as mine has been. Those of you who have come here as doubters . . . I say now that you will leave this place tonight as believers. On this, I am willing to stake my reputation. On this—" he struck the lectern with the side of his fist "—I stake the integrity of my immortal soul."

He left the lectern and sat in one of the chairs with his hands resting on his knees, the palms open and turned up. It was a gesture he used often during these types of demonstrations, one that invited trust. *Nothing in my hands*, it seemed to say. *Nothing up my sleeves.*

"We'll begin with the reading of billets. Porphyrio, please blindfold me."

He heard some quiet groans of disappointment from the wings. Billet reading was impressive enough to the uninitiated, but it was far from the flashiest gag in the mediumistic arsenal. Porphyrio wrapped a strip of black satin across Dashiel's eyes and tied it firmly behind his head.

"Call up three volunteers," Dashiel whispered as Porphyrio leaned in close, letting his hands linger on Dashiel's shoulders a little too long. "It doesn't matter who."

"Let's all raise our voices in a hymn of praise, to amplify the power of the spirits," said Porphyrio, moving away from Dashiel to stand at the edge of the stage. The sounds of singing rose from the audience, and Porphyrio continued speaking, raising his voice to make himself heard.

"Before we began, each of you should have received a blank card on which to write any question of your choice to the spirits. Will three of you please bring your cards forward—that's right, don't be shy. Brother Quicke will attune himself to the vibrations of the spirit realm and call forth the answers that you seek. Yes, ma'am, step right up here on the stage."

The first billet was nothing out of the ordinary. Porphyrio placed the card in Dashiel's hands, and Dashiel set it on his lap. With the blindfold wrapped tightly around his eyes and his head upright, he appeared to the audience to gaze sightlessly ahead.

But behind the cover of the satin band, Dashiel flicked his eyes downward. It was the crudest of tricks. Through the narrow space between the blindfold and his cheek, he could read what was written on the card as clearly as if his eyes had been completely unhindered.

Whatever else one could say of Porphyrio, he'd more than amply come through with the goods on their former clientele. Dashiel did not have to extemporize or grope for an answer. "Mrs. Gunderson," he said with a warm smile. "It's been so long. The spirits have seen your question, and they've answered. I'm afraid that your nephew has broken his engagement to the young lady. But don't fret. He'll find the one he's meant to be with."

Dashiel heard a ripple of impressed murmuring from the newcomers in the audience, along with a huff of indignation from the wings. Dorothy or the Swami, no doubt, irked at being beaten to the punch. He suppressed a smirk.

Porphyrio took the card and ushered the distraught Widow Gunderson off the stage, and a second card materialized in Dashiel's hands. He was at a disadvantage this time. Porphyrio tapped the card twice as he handed it to Dashiel to indicate that the writer was a man, but the message was written in a hand Dashiel did not recognize:

What horse to bet on next year's Illinois Derby?

"Well, sir," said Dashiel, "I am sorry to disappoint, especially as I sense that you are a newcomer among us. I'm afraid that the spirits don't tend to be very forthcoming about such material concerns. But they are happy to pass your question along to me, nonetheless. As one humble, earth-bound soul to another, I'd keep an eye on Roman Soldier."

He heard a smattering of laughter and applause from the audience, and a surprised and amused "Wow, golly! Well, thanks anyway," from the sitter.

Porphyrio withdrew the card and handed him another, this time with a single, sharp tap. Dashiel could sense his annoyance, and the reason for it became apparent as soon as he glanced down at the card in his hands.

L third row, red silk. Rose garden on your 7:00.

The message from Agnes. He composed his expression into a neutral blank. "L" could only be Lucille. The second part was more cryptic. An alternate exit, perhaps? The audience and mediums alike had all entered the ballroom through the lobby. But he thought he remembered catching a glimpse of another door behind the stage.

Dashiel's face grew solemn, and he swayed in his seat. "Dear child, I'm so sorry," he said. "The person you're asking after is here with me now. She made her passage just earlier today. But she sends you her love and blessing, and wishes you to know that she is not gone, only transformed." It was his stock response to a message from a plant—a pile of nonsense that sounded like an answer to a typical billet question.

"You don't say!" answered Agnes after a brief, uncertain pause. "Oh, gee, but how can that be? I knew she was sick, but I just saw her this morning." She blew her nose noisily. "Oh, this is awful. I think I need some air."

"Do what you must, dear." Dashiel blindly reached out for her. Her hand met his, and he gave it a reassuring squeeze. "Why don't you step out for a minute?"

"Good idea," came the answer, a trifle too loud and enthusiastic. Dashiel tried not to wince. Agnes's hand slipped out of his, and he heard the click of her heels moving away across the stage. "Keep your hands to yourself, you," she hissed at Porphyrio a moment later. "I don't need your help."

Dashiel slumped in his chair as if exhausted from his efforts. "Just what in the hell was that all about?" Porphyrio muttered in his ear. "We agreed that one of your compadres was gonna be here tonight, not a whole posse."

"And here I was just going on about your unwavering faith in me," whispered Dashiel. He patted Porphyrio's arm. "Trust me, Gomer. It'll all make sense soon enough." He subtly positioned his wrist so he could glance at his watch from beneath the blindfold. "Get this blindfold off me. We need to move it along."

Still quietly seething, Porphyrio untied the blindfold. Dashiel made a show of wiping the perspiration from his brow with a trembling hand.

"Ladies and gentlemen," said Dashiel, rising to his feet with Porphyrio's assistance, "I wish I could answer more of your questions, but I will have to leave that for my fellow mediums. I've just sensed a change in the vibrations in the room. I'm receiving an important message."

Porphyrio played his role with aplomb. He clung to Dashiel's arm and gazed at him earnestly. "What is it, Brother Quicke?" he asked.

"It concerns you, Porphyrio," said Dashiel.

"Me!"

"Yes, brother. Please, be seated. I believe your Master Teacher is with us today."

Porphyrio sat with bowed head and clasped hands, the picture of deference and devotion. Dashiel moved to stand behind his chair and laid his hands on his shoulders.

"Brothers and sisters," said Dashiel, "as some of you may know, my dear partner Porphyrio is descended from a very ancient and noble lineage. In fact, he can trace his family line back to ancient Egypt, and it is from that proud civilization that his Master Teacher hails. Is that not so, Brother Porphyrio?"

"It is so, Brother Quicke, yes," said Porphyrio. His hands were still clasped, his eyes squeezed shut in an expression of spiritual ecstasy.

"To have this most exalted of spirits with us tonight is an extraordinary honor, ladies and gentlemen," Dashiel went on. "He has a gift for you, Porphyrio—a reward for your extraordinary devotion to the cause of Spiritualism, and for your efforts in bringing me back to the path of light when I had gone astray."

"Hallelujah!"

"Indeed, hallelujah. Everyone, raise your voices in song. Help me make manifest this gift for our deserving brother. I entreat this wisest and most powerful of spirits to do his divine work through me." He signaled the organist, who struck up "Surely the Curtain Is Lifting." Dashiel raised his arms. "Sing, brothers and sisters, sing! Make yourselves heard! Louder—I feel the power of the spirit moving within me."

Dashiel flung back his head and rolled his eyes heavenward, reveling in the raucous cacophony of organ and song that vibrated through the wooden slats of the stage beneath his feet. He spread his arms wider and swept his hands upward, as if beckoning the power of the hymn up into himself. As he did so, he gave a deft flick of his right wrist, dislodging the shabti from its snug spot in his sleeve. Another quick, deliberate movement sent it tumbling into Porphyrio's waiting hands.

He drooped forward, leaning heavily on the back of Porphyrio's chair, and lifted a hand to signal for the music to stop. Porphyrio triumphantly held the shabti aloft.

"Praise be to the Infinite Intelligence that works through you, Brother Quicke, and glory to my Master Teacher, who has seen fit to bestow this remarkable gift upon me," Porphyrio said, rising to his feet. "Behold, ladies and gentlemen—here we have undeniable, physical proof of the power of the spirit realm. Dashiel, what can you tell me about this apport? Did it come with any message?"

Dashiel lifted his head and smiled. "I know very little about such objects, Porphyrio," he said. "But I'm receiving a strong impression that . . . yes, there's someone here who can tell us all about it." He straightened up and closed his eyes, pressing his fingers to his temples. Loudly, he said, "Is there a Professor Hermann Goschalk among us?"

He opened his eyes and scanned the crowd, pretending to search for an unfamiliar face. In the front row, Hermann rose to his feet, nearly crushing his hat against his chest, and cleared his throat.

"I beg your pardon," he said. "That's my name."

"Ah," said Dashiel. "Good evening, Professor. How fortuitous that you happen to be with us tonight. But of course, there are no coincidences where the spirits are involved. Am I correct in understanding that you are a professor of Ancient Studies, and the curator of a small gallery of Egyptian artifacts at Dupris University in Willowvale?"

"Why, yes," said Hermann, ducking his head bashfully. "That's all perfectly correct. However did you know?"

Off in the wings, Maude let out a quiet snort.

"No detail escapes the notice of the spirits," said Dashiel. "And if there are any living souls in the audience tonight who doubt the professor's bona fides, I'm sure they can easily verify his credentials. Isn't that so?"

"I suppose so," said Hermann, with a nervous laugh. "Yes, absolutely."

"Why don't you step up here for a moment, Professor Goschalk?" Dashiel said, holding out a hand. "I'd like you to examine this object and give us your professional assessment."

Hermann walked to the stage and shook Dashiel's waiting hand, then stepped up to stand beside him.

"Brother Porphyrio, the apport, if you please," said Dashiel. With a cold glint in his eye, Porphyrio handed the shabti to Hermann.

Hermann set his hat down on one of the chairs and took the shabti in both hands.

He turned it over a few times, then fished his spectacles out of the front pocket of his jacket and put them on. Having examined it thoroughly from all angles, he turned to Dashiel in wide-eyed astonishment.

"Why, it appears to be a genuine ancient Egyptian shabti," he said. "Yes, I'm quite positive that it's the real thing! This is only an educated guess, of course, but I would say that it dates to . . . oh, the latter half of the Eighteenth Dynasty."

There were some appreciative oohs and ahhs from the audience.

"Incredible!" said Dashiel. "Then, you're willing to state with absolute certainty that this—shabti, did you call it?—that this shabti is the genuine article and not an imitation?"

Hermann nodded. "Yes, I am. And you're quite correct, I did call it a shabti. A servant for the dead that could act on behalf of its owner, or even serve as a temporary home for the immortal soul." His eyes locked on Dashiel's for an instant, filled with a quiet apprehension.

And then, with a quick, subtle movement of his hand, Hermann tugged loose the last knot. The length of thread drifted to the stage at his feet.

Dashiel felt a gentle, heaving tremor, as if some great beast beneath the stage had stirred in its sleep. But it was over as soon as it began. Aside from some scattered murmurs from the audience and a flicker of uncertainty on Porphyrio's face, it seemed to pass unnoticed.

Hermann turned to Porphyrio and handed the shabti back to him with obvious reluctance. "What a fitting gift for a man of your calling, sir."

Porphyrio gasped and blinked confusedly as the shabti touched his hands again, as if it had given him a hard static shock. But he was quick to recover. He took the shabti and held it up, lifting his gaze heavenward. "I am humbled," he said. "Truly humbled and amazed that my Master Teacher saw fit to bestow such a thing upon me. What a beautiful manifestation of the love our guardian spirits have for us."

"Thank you, Professor," said Dashiel. He patted Hermann's shoulder and gave his hand a firm shake. "You may be seated."

Hermann picked up his hat and started to walk away, then stopped. He turned back to Porphyrio with a frown. "It's the real thing, all right," he said slowly, "but I can't for the life of me figure out how such an object could have ended up in your hands."

"Why, Professor," said Dashiel, drawing himself up. He raised his voice so that his words reverberated across the room. "Don't tell me you still doubt, after what you've just witnessed. You saw it manifest itself with your own eyes."

"No, no, I'm sorry," said Hermann, holding up a hand and shaking his head. "I—I'm a man of science. I can't believe that you just . . . plucked a genuine shabti out of the ether. There must be some other explanation."

The audience was beginning to whisper and murmur, as were the mediums in the wings. Porphyrio stared at Dashiel with bulging eyes, and a mottled purplish-red hue climbed up from beneath his collar and into his cheeks.

"What is this, Dash?" he hissed. "What's this damn fool doing?"

Dashiel smiled. "All right, Professor Goschalk," he said. "Fair enough. It's only natural to have doubts—God knows, I've struggled with them myself. But if you'll indulge us with the gift of just a little more of your time, I do believe we may be able to lay those doubts of yours to rest. Will you stay with us a while longer?"

Hermann took a few steps back. "W-well, I really don't think . . ." he stammered.

Dashiel could feel Porphyrio's eyes boring into him. Unperturbed, he took Hermann's elbow and guided him toward the row of chairs lined up on the stage behind them.

"Please, have a seat, Professor," he said. "I insist. From here, you'll be able to observe everything we do close at hand."

Without a word, Hermann took a seat, looking small and self-conscious under the harsh glare of the stage lights. Dashiel strode back to the lectern.

"Brothers and sisters," he said, "I'm glad that there's at least one doubter among us tonight. A little doubt, once in a while, is healthy. It helps keep us accountable. If Professor Goschalk here had come to one of my demonstrations three years ago, his suspicions would have been perfectly well-founded. Tonight, however, I'm sure will prove to be a different story."

The audience was beginning to sit up and take notice. People jostled each other and craned their necks for a better look at Hermann. A couple of the old regulars in the front row stared at Dashiel with stony disapproval.

"The next phase of mediumship that Brother Porphyrio and I would like to demonstrate is an old favorite of mine: the precipitation of spirit messages on silk. Now, my dear partner Porphyrio has never been very fond of this one." He turned to wink at Porphyrio, who shot back a tight-lipped grin that did not quite reach his eyes.

"It takes a great deal of effort and concentration to do properly," Dashiel went on, as Porphyrio began spreading out several lengths of white bridal silk on the small central table onstage. "It's an area where many mediums who have gone astray, including myself, tend to cut corners. Lord knows I know all the tricks."

His remarks elicited a combination of laughter and uncomfortable muttering from the audience. But he smiled blithely and continued. "That's why I've decided to do things a little differently tonight. Porphyrio, we won't be using those silks."

Porphyrio froze halfway through laying out a piece of silk, then slowly straightened up. "I beg your pardon, Brother Quicke?"

"You heard me," said Dashiel. "Just so that there's no question of any trickery or funny business, I'm not going to use the silks we brought. We wouldn't want anyone to go away thinking we might have prepared some identical pieces in advance with false spirit writings on them."

As Porphyrio blinked incredulously at him, Dashiel turned to the audience.

"I must apologize, ladies and gentlemen," he said. "Both to you and to my partner, whom I seem to have caught unawares. The fact is, I did prepare some false silks for this demonstration, but not for the purposes of misleading or doing harm. No, my only intention is to instruct and illuminate."

Amid gasps and cries of indignation from both the wings and the audience, he reached into his cuff and drew out a little bundle of white silk, which he unfurled like a banner. It was the one with the photograph of the dead woman impressed on it.

"Is there a Mr. Ullemeyer here?" Dashiel asked. "If so, come forward."

A portly, red-faced man with a black derby hat and a silver mustache stood up in the fourth row and made his way to the stage.

"Do you identify the face on this silk?" Dashiel asked him.

Mr. Ullemeyer took the silk from Dashiel and stared at it, wide-eyed. "It's my Myrtle," he said after a moment, mopping his brow with his handkerchief. "The message—it's about the day I asked her to marry me. We went for a picnic on Round Lake."

"I'm sorry, Mr. Ullemeyer," said Dashiel, "but the message is a forgery."

The audience rippled with dismay. "Charlatan!" someone called out from the back of the room. Some of the curious newcomers in the crowd snickered and whistled.

"But—" stammered Mr. Ullemeyer.

"I hold only myself responsible for this deception. I obtained a photograph of your wife, along with personal information that you shared with another party in confidence, and I used them to construct this message. All it takes is a little ammonia and a hot iron. You may be seated."

Dashiel took the silk out of the stunned Mr. Ullemeyer's hands. The man stumbled back to his seat among the whispers and pitying stares of the crowd.

"I have several more of these false messages prepared, but we needn't go over all of them," said Dashiel. He pulled the rest of the silks out of his cuff and tossed them on the stage at his feet. "Suffice it to say, they were all produced in much the same manner."

"Get him off the stage!" someone hissed from the wings.

"Dashiel, what the hell are you playing at?" Porphryio demanded.

Dashiel whirled on him. "Faith, Brother!" he admonished, so fiercely that Porphyrio flinched and took a step back. "I'm not finished. From now on, I renounce this sort of crude imposture. Brothers and sisters, you're about to see the real thing."

At Dashiel's signal, the organist began playing "Message from the Spirit Land." Dashiel sang. His baritone voice was unpolished, but commanding. It seemed to placate the wary faithful in the crowd. He gestured for the audience to join in and they did so, reluctantly at first, but with growing enthusiasm.

"Some morn the spirit friends will rap, and I no more in doubt will be," sang Dashiel as he scanned the crowd with his eyes. "But, O the joy when I shall hear the loving message sent to me . . ." He spotted a flash of scarlet in the third row and made his way to the edge of the stage.

Porphyrio's hand clamped painfully around Dashiel's elbow. "Dash, this ain't what we talked about," he whispered through clenched teeth. "If you've got some kind of a plan here, you need to let me in on it soon, because—"

"Watch," murmured Dashiel, "and learn. You'll get your answers soon enough." He shook his arm loose from Porphyrio's grip and raised his hands in exultation. "A moment of quiet, please," he bellowed over the music. "I'm receiving a powerful impression."

The organ stopped, and silence fell over the room.

"Would the lady in the third row with the beautiful red scarf please stand up?" said Dashiel, beckoning the woman in question to her feet. She pointed to herself with a quizzical expression on her face. "Yes, you, madam. Please be so kind as to join us on the stage."

Lucille stood up and headed down the row, then walked up the aisle to the stage. Dashiel took her gloved hand and helped her up beside him.

"Good evening, ma'am," he said with a bow. "I'm much obliged to you for joining us. Now, correct me if I'm wrong, but your name is Mrs. Lucille Luckett, is it not?"

Her eyes widened. "Yes, it is! How in the world did you know that? All right, don't answer, I know what you're going to say."

There was some light laughter from the audience, and Dashiel smiled. "Mrs. Luckett, you're not a member of the church of Spiritualism, are you?" he asked.

"No, sir. I've been AME all my life. I don't know what moved me to come in here today. Just curiosity, I suppose."

"I believe curiosity is one of the noblest gifts that the Infinite Intelligence ever saw fit to bestow upon mankind," said Dashiel gravely. "And I hope that today, you will leave with yours fully satisfied. Madam, may I ask you about that lovely scarf you're wearing?"

Lucille touched the scarlet silk scarf that was wrapped around her hair. "Oh, this?" she said. "It was a gift from my dearly departed Aunt Phoebe, God rest her soul."

"Ah," said Dashiel, nodding. "Such objects are especially potent as conduits between our plane and the spirit realm—which is why I'd like to ask a great favor of you. If the answer is no, I fully understand. Would you allow me to borrow that scarf for our demonstration?"

"Oh!" said Lucille. Her fingers still lingered on the edge of the scarf. "Well, I don't know. It's one of my favorites."

"I can see why, ma'am. Putting the sentimental value aside, it's a gorgeous piece of fabric."

She eyed him with intense suspicion. "What are you gonna do with it, exactly?"

"Hopefully, with the help of my partner, I can precipitate a genuine message from the spirit world on it," said Dashiel. "A text, or perhaps an image. If it doesn't work, you'll get your scarf back, just as it was. If it does, why, you'll have an inestimably precious document in your hands—a piece of incontrovertible evidence that those who have passed on can still communicate with us from beyond the veil. And since my partner and I have never handled this particular piece of silk before, I'm sure you and the rest of the good people gathered here tonight will agree that there can be no question of deception."

"Well . . . I suppose that's all right, then." Lucille reached up and began to unpin the scarf from her hair, removing a series of bobby pins and dropping them, one by one, into Dashiel's waiting hand. At last, she unwound the scarf and handed it to him, revealing an immaculate marcel wave underneath.

Something pinned to the inside of the scarf caught Dashiel's eye—a second scarf, identical in color, rolled up into a tiny bundle. Unlike the first, this one was marked. Some dark lines were just visible on the tightly wound fabric. He palmed the bundle and slid it up his sleeve.

"I'm much obliged, ma'am." Dashiel went to the table where Porphyrio had laid out the plain white scarves and brushed them aside. For a moment, he held up the red scarf so that the audience could see it clearly, then spread it on the table where the white ones had been. "Let's gather around the table," he said. "Porphyrio, help me move the chairs. If you would stand for a moment, please, Professor."

As Dashiel and Porphyrio moved the chairs to form a semicircle around the little table, Lucille went and stood beside Hermann. They exchanged polite nods, as if they were two strangers meeting for the first time.

"Whatever you're up to, darlin', it better be good," muttered Porphyrio, glancing at Lucille with suspicion.

Dashiel shoved the final chair into place and beamed at him. "Oh, trust me, sweetheart, it will be."

By now it was nearing five-thirty. The curtains were drawn over the windows that surrounded the Rainbow Room, but Dashiel could see the world outside was darkening. He took a seat at the table and instructed Hermann and Lucille to sit on either side of him, while Porphyrio sat across from the three of them.

"Put your apport in the middle of the table, Porphyrio," said Dashiel. "It'll help focus the spirits' energy." Porphyrio glared at him but complied.

Dashiel folded the scarf over lengthwise several times, then again widthwise. Then he rolled it up into a narrow little bolt. Like any medium worth his salt, he'd mastered the art of compressing large pieces of fabric into impossibly small packages. He spoke to the audience as he worked.

"For this portion of the program, ladies and gentlemen, I'll have to ask for your patience. But I can assure you, it will all be worth it. You are about to see a demonstration of spiritual power that you will never forget. I will need you all to pray, to meditate, to focus your energy on helping to manifest the spirit message. Brother Porphyrio? Take the silk."

With a quick flourish, Dashiel palmed the rolled-up scarf and slid it up his sleeve. At the same time, he produced the marked roll of red silk. This he pushed across the table to Porphyrio, who closed his hands around it with a subtle nod. It was a sleight of hand routine they'd performed together countless times.

"Join hands with me," said Dashiel, laying his hands on the table with his palms up. On his left side, he felt Hermann's warm fingers intertwining with his own. Lucille removed her soft kidskin gloves and took hold of his right hand.

Across from them, Porphyrio sat with his head bowed and his eyes closed, giving the appearance of intense concentration. Dashiel closed his eyes, too. "Ladies and gentlemen," he said, "I must ask for silence as we attune ourselves to the spirit realm."

With his mind, he reached out to the shabti. During the nearly two hours that he'd carried the little monster in his sleeve, he'd found himself surprisingly unaffected by it. Its anger had still been palpable, like a glowing ember pressed close against his arm. But it was no longer the wild, amorphous rage that it had been. Even now, with the last of its magical bindings removed, it felt focused. Controlled.

Dashiel ought to have been terrified, but he was strangely euphoric instead. He felt like a kid climbing into a car on the Coney Island Cyclone, too far past the point of no return to be fearful any longer. His face broke into a broad, involuntary grin. The sun was setting now. He couldn't see it, but he sensed it in his bones. His grip on Hermann's hand tightened, and he felt an answering pressure in return.

A prickly sensation crept up Dashiel's neck, and agitation rippled through the crowd. People whispered, cleared their throats, and coughed nervously. Seconds later, Porphyrio began to gag and splutter.

"Sweet Christ almighty, what is that smell?" he gasped.

"Don't lose your focus, brother," said Dashiel. His grin broadened, but he kept his eyes closed. "Keep praying." He settled back in his chair and breathed deeply. The familiar cloying, putrid odor filled his nostrils and coated his tongue. He willed himself to relax.

A new sound mingled with the murmurs of the audience and the buzz of the arc lights overhead—a rhythmic susurration, so subtle that anyone not listening for it would likely have missed it. But Dashiel felt Hermann and Lucille sit up a little straighter on either side of him, and he knew they heard it, too. Someone in the audience cried out in surprise. Dashiel didn't have to open his eyes to know what was happening.

"What is that?" someone in the wings said in a tremulous voice. Probably one of the Swink sisters. "What's he doing?"

"Quiet," retorted Maude in a harsh whisper. "Oh lord, I don't like this one bit."

"Dash," said Porphyrio hoarsely. He kicked Dashiel's ankle under the table with the toe of one of his muleskin boots. "Dash!"

"Brothers and sisters, please remain calm," said Dashiel, without opening his eyes. "What you are seeing, smelling, and hearing is what the esteemed Dr. Hippolyte Baraduc first identified in eighteen ninety-six as the Odic cloud—a genuine physical manifestation of the spirit form."

"The Odic cloud?" Porphyrio whispered, incredulous. "Dashiel, you can't be serious! What is this thing, some kind of smoke bomb? How the hell are you doin' this?"

"It's a spirit, Porphyrio," Dashiel replied in a low voice. "And right now, I'm not doing a thing. But I'm about to. Keep your hands on that silk."

Waves of malice pulsed from the unseen spirit in front of him. People in the audience jostled and snapped at each other. "Let go of my arm!" someone hissed at their neighbor in the front row. "Take off that damn hat, lady," said an angry voice from the back of the room. "How's a fella supposed to see what's going on?"

Cautiously, Dashiel opened the door to his mind. He focused on the spirit with all his senses, allowing the world around him to fade into the background of his consciousness. *Come on, old friend,* he entreated silently. *You know what to do now. We both do. It ought to be much easier than last time.*

This time, the cold presence entered him in a slow trickle instead of a raging torrent. Still, it was a shock. His muscles instantly tightened and spasmed. His back arched convulsively, and supportive arms encircled him from both sides.

As the darkness swallowed Dashiel up from the inside, he heard Porphyrio's voice calling out sharply to him. But he sounded muffled, and so far away—fainter and fainter, until there was nothing at all.

❧

Dashiel was in dark water. Not a turbulent sea this time, but a still and inky marsh, like the one he'd seen in his half-remembered dream on the night the shabti entered Hermann's apartment. He was able to stand in it, although he could feel nothing beneath his feet to support him.

Darkness spread out around him on all sides in an endless expanse. Vague shapes stirred in the shadows, like reeds swaying in a light breeze.

For a moment, he felt and understood nothing but disorientation and terror. But then he remembered to feel and to listen. There were others with him. On his right, unseen fingertips pressed into his wrist, feeling for his pulse. A woman whispered in his ear. *Lucille*, he remembered.

"Stay with us, Mr. Quicke. Keep breathing."

On his left, a man's voice spoke in pleading tones. "Go easy on him this time. He's your friend, remember? Just let him help you."

And there's Hermann. A warm glow of affection surged through him, mingled with confusing emotions not his own. Frustration. Distrust. A hint of hopeful anticipation.

"What's going on?" said a third voice, hoarse with panic and confusion. *Porphyrio.* "What's wrong with him?"

Yes, now he remembered.

Dashiel drew in a trembling breath, then exhaled. He did it again and again, with focused deliberation, until it began to feel easy and natural. The uneven lurching of his heart slowed and settled into a steady rhythm. He knew where he was now, and what he was doing.

You are in the in-between realm, he told himself. *The place Hermann told you about, where the living and the dead meet in trances and dreams. And you are not alone. Don't panic. Look around.*

He scanned the murky horizon until he spotted another figure standing nearby, staring at him.

It was an old man, hunched and wizened. He wore a simple white linen tunic and kilt. Only a few strands of silver hair clung to his scalp, and his dark brown skin was etched with a mosaic of wrinkles. Like Dashiel, he stood up to his hips in the black waters.

"Amunnakht?" said Dashiel.

The old man didn't respond, but his eyes met Dashiel's with a baleful, penetrating gaze.

"Can you understand me?" Dashiel asked.

Still, there was no answer.

"All right," said Dashiel. *Keep breathing,* he reminded himself. "Please, just listen. I'm here to fulfill a promise. But if you want my help, you need to work with me. I won't be any good to you if I'm dead, too. I won't become a powerful spirit like you. You'd be on your own. My friend wrote you a letter explaining all this. Did you read it? Did you understand it?"

If Amunnakht comprehended a single word of what he was saying, he gave no indication of it. Dashiel took a cautious step toward him.

"Listen," he said desperately, "all I need you to do is look at the man sitting in front of us. Just look, that's all. He has a message for you. Just . . . let me open my eyes and talk to him."

Dashiel sensed something shifting within him, as if the spirit were withdrawing a little bit of itself. He flexed his neck and shoulders experimentally and felt his earthly body respond. At the edges of his vision, a faint light encroached on the endless expanse of the black marsh.

The infinite darkness faded away, and the sounds and sensations of the living world flooded in.

⁂

DASHIEL'S HEAD JERKED upright, and he sucked in his breath in a painful, ragged gasp. He willed his eyes to open. This time, they obeyed. Porphyrio sat frozen in front of him, his gray eyes wide and staring. His hands were still clenched around the bundle of silk. A tense hush had fallen over the audience. Hermann and Lucille clung to Dashiel on either side.

"Dash?" said Porphyrio. His voice came out in a whisper that echoed harshly in the stillness of the room.

With great effort, Dashiel pulled his right hand out of Lucille's grasp and raised it, pointing to Porphyrio with a wobbling finger. He felt as if he were moving through molasses. A thin trickle of ectoplasm dribbled from the corner of his mouth.

"Show," he rasped. It was his own voice that emerged from his throat, guttural and hoarse. But it mingled with another voice that was not his—a keening, unearthly whine, like the high-pitched buzz of a thousand insects.

The audience broke out in fearful murmurs and cries of alarm.

Porphyrio shrank back in his seat, then rallied himself. "Brother Quicke?" he said faintly, making a game effort to play along despite his obvious fear and confusion. "Is—is my Master Teacher speaking through you?"

"Show us," said Dashiel again. More ectoplasm oozed from his ears and seeped onto his collar. He rose halfway out of his seat in an unsteady, lurching movement, still pointing. Hermann flung an arm around his waist, preventing him from tumbling forward into the table as the stage rumbled and groaned beneath their feet. In the wings, someone screamed.

"Show . . . the silk," Dashiel said.

Porphyrio leaped to his feet and stumbled backward. "What is this?" His eyes flicked wildly between Dashiel, Hermann, and Lucille.

"I think you'd better show him the silk," Hermann said breathlessly as Dashiel twisted and thrashed in his arms. Shouts of alarm rose from the audience.

"Be ready to grab that snake thing of yours, Hermann," said Lucille. She'd given up on trying to hold Dashiel's hand. Her fingertips pressed into his throat just below the curve of his jaw, searching for his pulse. "His heart must be going nearly two hundred beats a minute."

"Show it," roared Dashiel, in a voice that bore only a passing resemblance to his own.

"All right, all right!" Porphyrio's voice cracked as he fumbled with the silk and almost dropped it. "Here's your damn silk, now stop this nonsense!"

Porphyrio yanked the silk open, then stood staring down at it, his brow wrinkled in bafflement. Dashiel abruptly fell still, then slumped forward. He was losing himself again. Fighting to hold on, he forced himself to draw air in through his rapidly tightening throat. His breath came in high, whistling gasps. The putrid flavor of ectoplasm filled his mouth.

"It's just a bunch of squiggles," said Porphyrio.

"No," said Hermann. "It's not. That's perfectly legible Late Egyptian hieratic."

"Is that so?" demanded Porphyrio. There was an edge of panic in his voice. "Well, why don't you let us in on the joke, Professor? Tell us what it says!"

"You ought to know," said Hermann. "You produced it yourself, didn't you? I saw it with my own eyes. We all did." He dropped his voice to a desperate whisper. "Please look up, Dashiel. He's got to read it."

"Hold his head up," said Lucille. "Oh, lord, this is crazy. I don't know how much longer he can keep this up—"

"Is this still part of the show?" someone quavered from the front row.

"What are they doing to him?" another voice piped up. "Someone call a doctor!"

Dashiel felt hands pulling his head upright. He wrenched his eyes open and tried to look at the markings that covered the scarf, but he couldn't focus on the text. His eyes rolled and jittered, refusing to cooperate with his attempts to scan the lines of writing. He let out a gurgling moan of frustration. Ectoplasm streamed from his nose and mouth in a viscous flood, splattering the stage at his feet. Someone in the audience shrieked in horror.

Porphyrio recoiled, but he raised the silk a little higher, as if he were shielding himself with it. "Good God, what's wrong with him? Is he poisoned or something?"

Someone was wiping Dashiel's streaming eyes with a handkerchief. "Right to left, Dashiel," Hermann whispered. "The text, it goes from right to—"

"Oh, Hermann, we have to end this," cut in Lucille.

Dashiel could feel Hermann shifting beside him, no doubt groping for the snake amulet in his pocket. A spark of anger blossomed deep within him.

The thought of retreating now was too much to bear. With a final burst of energy, he broke free of Hermann's and Lucille's encircling arms and flung himself forward.

He stumbled against the table and toppled it, then rose unsteadily to his feet and staggered around it. Porphyrio stood rooted to the spot, transfixed with terror. Before he could move, Dashiel was upon him, grabbing his wrists in a grip that was clumsy but crushingly strong.

Dashiel pushed himself to the front of his own mind, lifted his head, and steadied his wandering eyes.

"I'm not . . . poisoned," he wheezed between gurgling breaths. That high, whining drone still overlaid his voice. "Don't you know the real thing when you see it, brother?"

Porphyrio opened his mouth to cry out, but all that emerged was a faint whimper. Now the screaming in the audience began in earnest.

"Enough, stop it!" Maude cried out from the wings. "Someone, turn off the lights . . . get them off the stage!" But if anyone was listening, they didn't respond. Dashiel raised Porphyrio's hands, with the scarf stretched between them, until the silk was level with his eyes.

Searing pain ripped through his muscles from the sheer effort of holding himself upright and forcing his eyes to be still. He felt as if a band of iron was tightening around his skull. But he kept staring at the fabric, taking in the elegant, curving lines of the text written on it. Unlike the scrawl Dashiel had produced at his last séance, this one had been meticulously rendered by a steady, confident hand.

Read it. Come on, you old bastard, read it.

Porphyrio squirmed helplessly in his grip. "You're hurting me, Dash," he said in a breathy whisper. "What the hell are you doing?"

Dashiel didn't answer. His eyes were moving under someone else's power, now. They flicked back and forth rapidly across the lines of text, moving not from left to right, but right to left. The meaning of what Hermann had said sank in. With a twinge of horrified amusement, he realized he'd been trying to force his passenger to read the lines backward. He relaxed, giving up control of everything but his own breathing. His knees and ankles began to buckle, but, impossibly, he remained standing, like a marionette on slackened strings.

As his eyes scanned the final line, Dashiel found his gaze pulled downward to focus for a moment on Porphyrio's boots. An inferno of rage not his own exploded within him. His back convulsed again, flinging back his head and shoulders. Porphyrio let out a howl of pain as Dashiel's grip tightened on his wrists.

As if in answer, a banshee-like shriek ripped its way out of Dashiel's throat, mingled with a droning, harmonic hum that seemed spun from the electric buzz of the arc lights and the sympathetic vibrations of the organ's pipes. The hinge of his jaw popped as his mouth opened painfully, impossibly wide. Ectoplasm poured from his throat in a torrent, along with eddying tendrils of ink-black smoke.

Pandemonium broke out around them. Dashiel was vaguely aware of the sounds of screaming and thundering footsteps as audience members, hotel staff, and mediums alike scrambled over each other, pushing toward the lobby exit in a crushing wave. Above him, the stage lights hummed and flared into blinding brightness before exploding one by one in a shower of sparks. The wooden columns supporting the room creaked and groaned, and showers of plaster drifted down from the ceiling, dusting his face and hair. A deep, thrumming vibration passed through the floor beneath his feet.

As the last traces of his spectral guest slithered out of him, Dashiel collapsed to his knees and began toppling backward. Before he could hit the stage, a pair of arms caught him, encircling his chest from behind. He caught a brief glimpse of Porphyrio stumbling back toward the far edge of the stage, engulfed in a whirling cyclone of shadow. His screams were barely audible over the piercing howls that filled the room and echoed from the walls, seeming to come from every direction at once.

While the person behind Dashiel hoisted him by his shoulders, someone else grabbed his legs. The two of them carried his limp body off the stage. As Dashiel's head lolled and bounced against the chest of the rescuer behind him, he watched the lights in the glittering glass floor of the Rainbow Room blow out in an expanding circle around them. His eyes drifted shut just as the room was plunged into almost total darkness. The screams of the people thronging around the lobby exit at the far end of the room intensified.

"Rose garden," Dashiel whispered, remembering Agnes's note. "Behind the stage."

Then he slipped away into oblivion.

CHAPTER 19

W HEN DASHIEL CAME TO, he was lying on his back in the grass, looking up at a blue-gray sky streaked with pale silver clouds. The branches of a rosebush, sprinkled with late autumn blossoms, bobbed overhead. His ears rang in the quiet of the garden. It was cold, even for an October night. He shivered so hard his teeth clattered. Someone had pulled his left arm free of his ruined suit jacket, and his sleeve was rolled up, exposing his skin to the chilly air.

Agnes's worried face appeared in his field of view. "All clear for now," she said, jerking her thumb at the Rainbow Room's exit behind them, "but who knows how long it'll be before someone comes through that door looking for us. Say, his eyes are open! Are you okay, Mr. Quicke? Can you hear me?"

Dashiel wanted to answer, but even nodding his head seemed like an insurmountable effort. He stared silently up at her with unfocused eyes.

"Dashiel?" Hermann was kneeling at his head. His voice was husky with exhaustion, and his face looked ashen. He patted Dashiel's cheek. "Please say something. Lucille, why is he trembling like that?"

"He's still in shock," said Lucille. She sat by Dashiel's side with his legs drawn across her lap. "But his pulse already feels stronger.

The Digifoline must be kicking in. Put your coat over him, Hermann."

Hermann stripped off his coat and laid it over Dashiel's chest and arms while Lucille loosened his tie and collar. "I'm so sorry, Dashiel," he said softly, stroking back the hair that clung to Dashiel's damp and clammy forehead. In the dim glow of the lamps that flanked the garden's entrance, Dashiel could make out tears clinging to his dark eyelashes. "I really hoped it would be gentler this time, after I wrote that letter and all . . ."

"Honey, it was gentler," Lucille assured him. "Otherwise, we would have lost him. But it was in him a lot longer this time, and he was putting up a hell of a fight. You hang in there, Mr. Quicke. I gave you an injection that should have you feeling a whole lot better in about fifteen minutes."

Dashiel wanted to thank her, to say something reassuring to Hermann, but he was still shivering too hard to talk. Instead, he rolled onto his side, coughing and retching, and vomited up great gouts of ectoplasm onto the grass. As agonizing as it was, he felt better now that it was over. The tremors began to subside, his breathing a little slower and easier.

"That's good," said Lucille. She rubbed his back, massaging a bit of warmth back into him. "That's what we want. Just get it all out. There, you see? He's looking better already."

"Saints preserve us," said Agnes. She hastily crossed herself with her right hand and covered her nose and mouth with her left. "He still looks plenty awful to me. No wonder there aren't many real mediums. Here, Professor, take my hanky."

Hermann accepted the handkerchief and cleaned Dashiel's face with it as well as he could. Dashiel swallowed, trying to moisten his burning throat. "Thanks," he whispered.

"There he is," said Lucille. "Mr. Quicke, you're not out of the woods yet, but I believe you're going to pull through just fine. Let's not do this again, though, you hear? I don't think your heart could take the strain. Not to mention mine."

"Never again. Won't have to." Dashiel closed his eyes and pressed his cheek into the cool grass, riding another wave of nausea. Once it passed, he groped for Hermann's hand and squeezed it as firmly as his feeble, trembling fingers would allow. "Checkmate, kiddo," he murmured. "It worked. It's over. Whatever you wrote on that silk must have been hot stuff."

Hermann made a sound that was somewhere between a laugh and a sob of relief. "Oh, Dashiel," he said, "that's the best news I've heard in months."

"You can say that again," said Agnes. "If things had gone on the way they were much longer, I would've had to either quit my job or commit homicide." She glanced around nervously. "We'd better get him out of here before someone finds us. I already pulled your car around, Professor, just like you asked."

"Is it safe to move him?" asked Hermann, with a fretful glance at Lucille.

"I think so," she said. "I can't do much more for him here, anyway. Let's get him back to your place so he can rest up. Come on, help me lift him again."

Agnes led them through the hedges to a side entrance and out into an alley, where they found Hermann's car waiting. Once Dashiel was safely tucked away in the passenger seat, Hermann embraced Lucille and Agnes. "I can't thank the two of you enough. If there's anything I can do to repay you both, anything at all . . ."

"I'll tell you what I'd like, Hermann," said Lucille, giving his cheek a fond pat. "Next Tuesday—if Mr. Quicke is feeling up to it, God willing—I want the four of us to get together and play a nice, boring, ordinary old game of bridge."

"Count me in," said Agnes. "And Professor, bring some of that nice brandy of yours. I think we all need it."

"I cheat," mumbled Dashiel.

"That's all right, Mr. Quicke," Lucille said with a prim nod. "You can't be any worse than Miss Sophie from the maternity ward. Just as long as you don't invite any dead folks, I'll be happy. See you at home, Hermann."

THE WORLD CAME back to Dashiel piecemeal. The first thing he became aware of was morning sunlight heating his face, then the softness of the thick blankets draped over him. The air smelled of jam, toast, and fresh coffee. Something heavy and warm and living rested on his legs—a purring cat.

Dashiel remembered little of the trip home or the night that followed, but he knew where he was. He let out a shuddering sigh of relief.

"Horatio," he croaked, pulling one of his hands from beneath the covers and groping for the cat. A cold, damp nose touched his fingertips, followed by a few licks and a gentle nibble. "All right, don't get excited. I missed you, too. Where's your old man?"

"Right here, Dashiel."

Dashiel opened his gritty eyes and turned toward the familiar voice. Hermann sat perched on the edge of the bed with the morning paper spread across his knees, smiling down at him. Dashiel reached out and stroked the small of his back, half convinced he'd turn out to be a feverish hallucination.

"You're awake!" said Hermann. He took off his reading glasses and set them aside, then reached down and pulled Dashiel into his arms.

"I'm alive," Dashiel answered, pressing his face into Hermann's shoulder and bunching the fabric of his shirt in both fists. "I'm home. I'm free. We're both free. And oh, God . . . Hermann,

I love you. I tried not to, but I do. It was a lost cause the from the moment I first put my arms around you. Christ, I love you so much."

Hermann didn't say anything, but the hitch in his breath and the way his arms tightened around Dashiel were answer enough. They stayed that way for a long time, locked in an embrace so close Dashiel's ribs ached.

"I wanted to tell you before, on the bridge," Dashiel said. "But—"

"I know," whispered Hermann, kissing his temple and stroking his hair. After another lingering moment, he released Dashiel and pulled back to look at him searchingly. Hermann was unshaven, still dressed in the clothes he'd been wearing the day before. He looked bone-weary. Dashiel suspected he hadn't slept much, if at all. "Is it really over? I'm almost afraid to believe it."

Dashiel nodded slowly. "I think so. Amunnakht has what he wants, or at least he thinks he does, which is close enough in my business. He's got someone to pin all that anger on. And my former colleagues won't come near me now, I can guarantee you that. There's nothing that scares a phony medium as much as the real thing—and oh, boy, did we give 'em the real thing."

"And Porphyrio?"

"Porphryio." Dashiel fell silent. Part of him hoped he was dead. Another part, older and deeper, prayed that he wasn't. He'd done what he had to. That was all there was to it. "I don't know," he said at last. "Maybe he ran away. Maybe Amunnakht dragged him off to the realm of the dead. Either way, I don't think he'll bother us again."

Hermann nodded, but he looked troubled.

"Anything interesting in that newspaper?" Dashiel asked.

"I should say so!" Hermann picked up the paper and tapped a headline in the lower left corner. "You made the front page."

"Spiritualist Gathering at St. Charles' Famed Hotel Baker Ends in Pandemonium," read Dashiel. "Well, I'll be damned."

"It says that the two mediums who were on stage when the disturbance broke out are both unaccounted for," said Hermann. "And that Reverend Fink fled the scene before she could be questioned. It wouldn't surprise me if the police come by with some questions for us."

"Let them," said Dashiel, closing his eyes. "What could they possibly charge us with?" A deep shiver ran through him. He broke out in a painful coughing fit. Hermann wrapped his arms around him again and cradled his head against his chest.

Dashiel lay there listening to the gentle beating of Hermann's heart for a long time before he spoke again. "He seemed so much stronger this time," he said. "Amunnakht, I mean. Stronger, but more controlled. It's a damn good thing you softened him up ahead of time, or he would have killed me for sure."

"Ah, yes," said Hermann. He hesitated for a moment. "I nearly worried myself to death over whether it was the right thing to do, but . . . I wanted him to be strong enough to take on Porphyrio, and for him to be sure that we were on his side. So, I fed him."

"You what?"

"When I left the letter for Amunnakht the night before last, I also left him a food offering. I thought maybe you'd have more of a fighting chance if we paid him our proper respects. I wasn't sure if my message would be enough."

Dashiel lifted his head to look at Hermann. "Not another cheese Danish, I hope."

"Oh, no," he said gravely. "I gave him a proper meal this time. Well, the best I could do in a hurry. The offering formulae for the dead always call for beer, bread, and various meats. So, I brought him a bottle of Schlitz . . ."

"You're truly a son of Milwaukee, aren't you, Hermann?"

"Naturally. I also had Agnes get me a frankfurter from that stand in front of the Naper Building."

Dashiel's eyebrows shot up. "You gave the ghost a *hot dog*?"

"Well, the thought came to me rather at the eleventh hour," said Hermann. "So, I needed something quick and easy. Don't give me that look, Dashiel! It covers all the bases. Bread, meat—ostensibly, anyway—and an assortment of vegetables, if you get the right fixings. Not to mention a quantity of salt that would be an untold luxury for a Bronze Age man. I asked for everything, but Agnes told me that, if I made her put ketchup on it, she'd never speak to me again. I suppose she knows best. I never eat the things myself."

Dashiel nodded thoughtfully. "So, you wined and dined him in style, and left a letter explaining that we were about to deliver his enemy right into his greedy little mitts."

"Exactly," said Hermann. "And I also explained that he'd better take it easy on you this time, since you were his one shot at getting his eternal revenge."

"I guess he must have liked it." Dashiel smiled. "I'm still alive."

Hermann rested his cheek on Dashiel's hair. "Thank God. And thank Him again that the old undead shlumpf didn't recognize my handwriting on that silk. I did my best to make it look different."

"Well, it worked. Whatever you wrote, it made the old bastard spitting mad," said Dashiel. "What exactly did you put in that message, anyway?"

"Would you like to hear it?"

Dashiel grinned. "Hell, are you kidding? Of course I would! Come on, lay it on me."

Hermann put his reading glasses back on, then got up and went to his desk. He rummaged among his papers until he found a sheet scribbled over with notes. "Ah, yes. Here we are." He smiled modestly, cleared his throat, and began to read:

"Speech of the beatified spirit Ramose to his neighbor, Amun-nakht: How stupid you must be, that it has taken you three thousand years to find me. Your intellect is less than that of a flea. Look, wretched one, upon the man who brings you this message. He is my descendant. Behold his feet, for upon them he wears the descendant of your beloved ass. If you want what is yours, come and take it from him."

"Perfect," said Dashiel. "Your masterpiece. I'm sorry about the shabti, though. I suppose you'll have to fill out that deaccession form after all."

The exhaustion of Hermann's sleepless night seemed to catch up with him all at once. He lay down next to Dashiel and stretched an arm across his chest. "Good," he muttered, closing his eyes. "I'd happily fill out a million of them."

"Once I feel a little better, we ought to celebrate," Dashiel said, stroking Hermann's arm with a languid hand.

Hermann smiled, but he didn't open his eyes. "What do you want to do? See another picture? Go dancing?"

"Oh, I don't know." Dashiel sighed drowsily. "Why don't we start by growing old together, then figure out the rest from there?"

He let his eyes drift shut. In the square of sunlight streaming through the bedroom window, with Hermann stretched out beside him, and Horatio curled up on his legs, Dashiel slept.

ACKNOWLEDGMENTS

THE WRITING OF *The Shabti* was a labor of love, and not just my own.

A million thanks to my family—to my Mama, who was my main co-conspirator in the creation of this book and supported me with unbridled enthusiasm; to my husband Glenn, who helped me claw my way through some of the most difficult scenes; to my daughter Miranda, who made me feel like a star whenever I started to doubt myself; and to my father Mike and my brother Malachi, whose sincere and loving interest helped keep me afloat through the trials and tribulations of the publication process.

Another million thanks to my beta readers: Jamie Ginsberg, my sweet, supportive friend who has been along on this ride with me from the very start. The indomitable Elisa DeCarlo, who blessed me with her encouragement, pride, and the occasional dose of tough literary love. L. J. Clarke and Adrian Paly, whose thoughtful comments helped steer me in the right direction and assured me that I was off to a solid start.

I'm indebted to every member of the CamCat team for making one of my lifelong dreams a reality. I'm especially grateful to my publisher, Sue Arroyo, who gave me one of the best phone calls of my life; and to my incredible editor, Helga Schier, who granted me both the direction and the confidence I needed to hone my story to its full potential. Elana, Meredith, MC, Bill, and everyone else involved in bringing this book to fruition—thank you all so much for believing in me and in *The Shabti*.

Finally, although I never had a chance to meet him, a word of gratitude to M. Lamar Keene, the real-life phony medium whose memoir, *The Psychic Mafia*, was one of the biggest sources of inspiration for this book. Thank you for being brave enough to tell your story and for telling it so eloquently. I hope you are enjoying a splendid existence beyond the veil.

ABOUT THE AUTHOR

MEGAERA C. LORENZ IS AN Egyptologist and tech writer/ editor who is fascinated with all things odd and uncanny. After earning her Ph.D. from the University of Chicago in 2017, she decided to pursue her lifelong interest in creative writing. She loves to craft stories that tap into her interests and expertise and combine them in strange and surprising ways. She has lived in the Chicagoland area for nearly 20 years. Currently, she resides in St. Charles, IL with her family, which includes two kids, two cats, and a hyperactive Belgian Tervuren.

If you liked Megaera C. Lorenz's

THE SHABTI

you'll enjoy

Audrey Lee's

THE MECHANICS
OF MEMORY

ONE YEAR AGO

NEVER FORGET

"COME WITH ME," Luke said. "Before it all disappears." He leaned across the kitchen counter and pushed at the lid of her laptop.

Hope swiveled in the turquoise kitchen stool, feet hooked in the rungs. Luke moved through the sliding glass door and onto the tiny patch of uneven concrete in the backyard, black Nikon hanging from a worn leather strap off his right shoulder. Hope watched as he pointed the camera at the sunset, then turned to aim the lens into the house, fingers focusing.

"Don't." Hope covered her face with a laugh. "Yuck."

"Then get over here." He waved at her. "It's magnificent."

Hope slid off the stool, grabbing two lowballs and a bottle of single malt from the counter.

The desert sunset was spectacular. Shimmering sheets of fuchsia and amethyst were splashed across the scarlet sky, palm trees and rough mountain peaks silhouetted against it. And above their outline, a moon so luminous it may well have been dipped in gold, hanging lower than seemed possible.

Without meaning to, Hope reached out to touch the moon.

"Didn't I tell you?" he said.

She smiled. "You did."

Luke snapped more photos, from every conceivable angle and with every possible lens attachment. He paced the length of the yard, barefoot, camera case knocking against his hip.

"So antsy," Hope said, depositing glasses on the end table and climbing onto the lounger.

"Stay just like that," he said. He pointed the Nikon at her, shutter clicking, like gunfire.

"You could simply enjoy the sunset, you know," Hope said. "We could enjoy it together."

Luke set the camera on the table and reached for the bottle. The Macallan made a hollow pop of anticipation as it opened.

He handed her a glass and settled in, Hope swinging her legs over his. Her toenails were painted dark blue this week, fresh from a pedicure with Charlotte this morning. Luke didn't care for her weird nail polish choices, especially when she went blue. Corpse toes, he called them.

"Tomorrow you'll be a big TV star. Are you nervous?"

Luke took a sip of his scotch. "Maybe."

"Is it because Natasha Chen is the host?" Hope asked. "What with your thing for Asian ladies?"

"So now I have a thing?" Luke laughed, hand trailing through her long hair. "You were supposed to be meek and submissive. I was grossly misled."

"At least I'm good at math," she said. "I'll try to work on the meek part."

"Good luck," Luke said. "And it's not because of Natasha Chen, it's because I don't want to make a fool of myself in front of tens of viewers."

"Impossible," Hope said. "You're brilliant and amazing. And a published author. It's very sexy."

"Nerdy science books don't count as sexy," he said. "And you forgot devilishly handsome."

"I'll never forget." She closed her eyes, focused on the feel of his fingers. "Don't ask her to say something in Chinese, though. Total turn off."

"Damn, I was going to open with that," Luke said, tracing her earlobe with his thumb. "After the ribbon cutting at the new facility today, Jack hinted this could mean a big promotion."

Hope opened her eyes. "Are you sure that's what you want?"

Luke shrugged. "It's the next logical step."

"I know." Hope sipped slowly. "Just, be careful what you wish for."

Luke pulled her close and Hope breathed him in, fingernails tapping on the glass. It made a tinkling sound, like bells.

"Let's run away instead," she said. "Scrap it all and start a new land. Become rulers of our own destiny."

"Is this before or after we become dealers in Vegas?" Luke's mouth twitched. "Or start an ostrich farm? Or open a kabob restaurant called Shish for Brains?"

"It has to be mutually exclusive?" Hope laughed.

"Where should we start this new land?" Luke took her hand, pressing his lips against her palm. "Also, we're going to need something catchier than New Land."

Hope closed her eyes. "The Bahamas, of course."

"Of course. And how will we pay the bills?"

"We won't need money," Hope insisted, "because we'll be in charge of the New Land. To be renamed later. But if you must, we can open a waffle stand."

"I do make a damn fine waffle," Luke said.

"We'll call it The Waffle Brothel." Hope twined her legs together like a pretzel. She trailed a finger up his arm, just to the elbow, then back again.

"Horrendous," he murmured. "You're making it hard for me to concentrate."

"We could live in a lighthouse." Hope stilled her finger on his wrist. "And have kangaroos."

"You're like a kindergartener on an acid trip sometimes," Luke said. "Kangaroos aren't even native to the Bahamas."

"Kangaroos are evolutionarily perfect," Hope said. "They have built-in pockets. It's genius."

Luke smiled. "Then we'll import them. And build a kangaroo sanctuary on the beach. So we can see them from the lighthouse."

He lay back and Hope matched her gaze with his, to the endless universe spread above. The red had all but disappeared, the moon even brighter now against the darkening sky. A scattering of stars emerged, blinking at them like jewels.

"Given your exhaustive attention to detail, it sounds like a solid Plan B." He placed a hand on her thigh, a lazy, casual gesture Hope felt far beneath the layers of her skin. "I'm in."

"Promise?" Her voice held the barest of a tremor, almost imperceptible. Imperceptible, to anyone but Luke.

He held his face level with hers. Sometimes they shared these glances, moments of razor-edged intimacy. Moments when they were the only souls of consequence, raw and infinite, a singularity. Moments when Hope wanted nothing more than to be swallowed whole, by Luke, and by whatever lay within.

Hope broke the connection, bottom lip in her teeth. Then a grin appeared, and she held her pinky in front of his face. "Promise?" she asked again.

Luke burst out laughing. "A pinky promise? You really are five." But he hooked his pinky into hers, and with his other hand, pulled her on top of him. "I'm sold," he said, into her hair. "Waffles in the Bahamas it is."

Hope closed her eyes as she kissed him. Maybe they could.

ON THE NIGHTSTAND Hope's phone vibrated, rattling the jewelry she'd dropped there a few hours before. She typed a hurried response and activated her phone's flashlight, leaving the bed and padding quietly to the bedroom door. As her hand touched the doorknob, Luke's voice cut across the silence.

"Sucker." He was propped up on one elbow, face sleepy and amused. "You know she only calls because of the French fries."

Hope smiled, moving back to his side of the bed. "I don't mind," she said, placing her palm on his bare chest. "She'll have her license soon. And then college. There isn't much time left."

Luke's face softened. "You want me to go too?" He yawned, mouth open wide like a bear.

"No way," Hope touched his cheek. "You'll ruin girl time."

At the door, Hope paused to tap a small white picture frame mounted above the light switch, twice. For luck.

"She has you wrapped around her finger, you know," Luke called.

"I know." Hope blew him a kiss. "So does her dad."

"SHE DOESN'T GET me at all," Charlotte said, popping a piece of gum in her mouth. "If I tell her anything, she uses it against me. I have no privacy." She let out a long, theatrical sigh, punctuated with maximum adolescent exasperation.

"It's a scary world out there." Hope glanced in the rear-view mirror and changed lanes. "All parents want to protect their kids."

"You don't know my mom. And I don't need protection." Charlie cranked the air conditioning and tapped her blue fingernails on the dash. "Were your parents like that? Nosy?"

"We didn't exactly have open lines of communication." Hope turned down the air. "Remember, I'm first generation. If it wasn't about getting into Harvard or becoming a lawyer, it wasn't discussed."

"So you were a big disappointment," Charlotte said.

"You have no idea." Hope laughed.

"Can you help me with my essay on Hamlet?" Charlotte asked. "It's due Tuesday."

"Of course," Hope said, pulling into the parking lot of the Burger Shack. It was the only place open all night, thus the de facto home to anyone within a twenty-mile radius that was hungry or high, or both. Charlie called it the Stoner Shack, but even so, she couldn't deny their chili cheese fries were transcendental. Years ago it had been a kitschy fifties diner, but today the only remnants of the former Shake, Rattle, and Roll were the defunct jukeboxes welded to the tables.

They stepped from the car, Hope locking it with a beep and a flash of headlights. Charlie led the way across the pavement, walking in a wide circle to avoid a kid throwing up in the bushes.

"I don't know why she can't be chill like you are," Charlotte said, holding the Stoner Shack door open for Hope.

"I'm far from chill," Hope said. "I have the luxury of not being your actual parent. I just get to be your friend."

"Aww," Charlie held her right hand out, fingers and thumb curled into half a heart. Hope matched it with her left.

***

THEIR PLASTIC CUPS were nearly empty, though the silver tumbler on the sticky laminate table was still brimming with Oreo shake. The plate between Hope and Charlotte contained only a few soggy fries, a generous pile of chili and cheese, and a puddle of ketchup.

"Straight out of the fryer," Charlotte said, returning to the booth. She set a fresh basket of fries between them, spots of grease soaking through the paper lining.

"Perfect timing," Hope said. She ran a fry in a zigzag through the chili and ketchup.

"Oh no, now you're doing it too?" Charlotte said.

Hope tilted her head. "Doing what?"

"Making patterns with your food." Charlie made a face. "Is that a two?"

Hope studied the paper plate. "I never realized I did that."

"You guys already share one brain. And the looks..." Charlotte mimed gagging. "You act like you're my age. So cringy."

A gaggle of boys entered, calling loudly to each other and jockeying for position at the counter. One was the kid formerly puking by the entrance, but he looked recovered. Another peeled off from the clump, pausing by Hope and Charlotte on his walk to commandeer a booth.

"Hey Charlie," he said shyly.

Charlotte's cheeks reddened, and she tucked a lock of hair behind her ear. "Hey."

"I thought you'd be at Brody's tonight." He shoved his hands into his pockets. The kids around here usually had two distinct auras—money or no money—but Hope couldn't tell with this kid. He didn't have an air of entitlement, but he didn't seem like a townie either.

Charlie crumpled her napkin into a ball. "I had to study. We can't all be gifted like you."

"I can help you tomorrow." The boy glanced over his shoulder at the crowd filling their sodas. "I mean, if you want. If you're not busy."

Charlie flipped her hair. "I'm not busy."

Hope pulled on her straw noisily.

"I'll hit you up tomorrow." The boy backed away with a wave.

"What happened to Adam?" Hope asked.

Charlie tapped her nails on the table. "He turned out to be a douche."

Hope made a noncommittal noise.

"Don't be all, 'hmmm, that's interesting,'" Charlotte said. "I know you guys hated him."

Hope tried to keep a straight face. Luke wasn't even able to say his name most days, referring to Adam only as "that arrogant little prick."

"But you were both right." Charlie put her chin in her hands. "Did you ever date an asshole?"

Hope made a face. "Almost married one."

Charlie perked up, looking intrigued, but Hope tilted her head toward the boy. "So, is he a prospect?"

"He's smart. He's different than all the idiots around here," she grinned. "But don't tell my dad. He'll go ape shit."

"Look Charlie, you're the most important person in the world to him," Hope said. "Which means no one will ever be good enough for you. But it also makes you lucky to be so loved."

"I know," Charlotte rolled her eyes. Again. "I'm so tired of the Adams of the world."

"Me too," Hope nodded. "But there are good guys out there, too. They just aren't as easy to spot. Trust me, the good ones are worth it."

"And that's my dad? One of the good ones?" Charlie wrinkled her nose, still too cool for feelings, though her eyes looked wistful.

Hope smiled. "I'm certain of it."

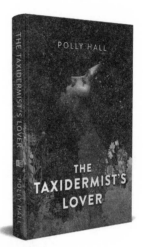
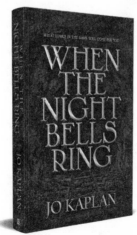

CamCat
Books